D1441977

A CLEAR VIEW
OF THE SOUTHERN SKY

STORY RIVER BOOKS

Pat Conroy, Editor at Large

A clear view of the
southern sky : stories
33305234698516
4ass   04/07/16

A CLEAR VIEW
OF THE
SOUTHERN SKY

Stories

MARY HOOD

Foreword by Pat Conroy

The University of South Carolina Press

© 2015 Mary Hood

Published by the University of South Carolina Press
Columbia, South Carolina 29208

www.sc.edu/uscpress

Manufactured in the United States of America

24 23 22 21 20 19 18 17 16 15   10 9 8 7 6 5 4 3 2 1

Library of Congress Cataloging-in-Publication Data
can be foundat http://catalog.loc.gov/.

ISBN 978-1-61117-500-4 (cloth)
ISBN 978-1-61117-501-1 (ebook)

"The All and Nothing It Had Come To," "Mad Woman in the Attic,"
"Some Stranger's Bed," "A Clear View of the Southern Sky," "Witnessing,"
"Leaving Room" and "Virga" first appeared in *The Georgia Review*.

"The Teacher" first appeared in *descant*.

"Come and Go Blues" first appeared in *Atlanta Magazine*.

"Seam Busters" first appeared as a standalone novella from the
University of South Carolina Press.

This book was printed on recycled paper with
30 percent postconsumer waste content.

Do not say, "Why were the old days better than these?"

Ecclesiastes 7:10

CONTENTS

FOREWORD

Since I first read her fiction, I've wanted to write a hymn of praise for the Georgia writer May Hood. Not only did I find her work significant, I found her voice one of a kind and sensational. She came into the writing world fully formed, nonpareil, and her short stories reminded me of Alice Munro, George Eliot, Margaret Atwood, and her strange immensities made me think about the long ago summer when I applied myself to Balzac and Chekov. The great writers of the world affect me like that and I find myself prisoner and catechist of their superb gifts. She blew into my reading life with hurricane force winds. Early on, I found myself enamored by the breadth and ambitious scope of her writing. I believe she is one of the great writers of our time and I have shouted that out to anyone I know who wants to encounter the best American writing that comes from small towns around our vast country where literature goes to hide.

In the early 1980s I met the legendary Stanley Lindberg, the editor of the *Georgia Review,* as we were both searching for great books at the Old New York Book Shop in Atlanta. Mr. Lindberg was in the process of making the *Georgia Review* one of the best literary magazines ever published in this country. On that first day of our introduction, he told me about the discovery of a great Georgia writer I had never heard of by the name of Mary Hood. I read the first story of Mary's he published and later read her stunning first collection of stories *How Far She Went.* Now we know how far she went. I believe today, and I've believed for a long time, that Mary Hood is one of the three or four best writers ever produced by her complicated, rough-hewn state. On November 10 of last year, it was one of the great honors of my literary life to introduce Mary Hood at her induction into the Georgia Writers Hall of Fame and to see her honored as one of the greatest artists ever to grow up in the sunshine and dark winds of Georgia.

When I read *How Far She Went,* I made a phone call to my young editor at Houghton Mifflin, Jonathan Galassi. At that time, Jonathan thought I was over-excitable and I believed he was not excitable enough. But he passed her book around and a subsidiary of Houghton Mifflin, the highly literary and distinguished Ticknor and Fields, announced they were publishing Mary Hood's second book, the delicious and unforgettable *And Venus is Blue.* I'm not sure my phone call had a single thing to do with the publication of her second book of short stories, but I now know that history works its easy magic in the strangest ways. Terry Kay had just published his first novel with Houghton Mifflin and soon after that I heard from a beautiful young editor that Ticknor and Fields was publishing Olive Ann Burns' splendid novel *Cold Sassy Tree.* The destiny of four Georgia writers began to arrange itself into a constellation of cold stars that would manifest its presence again in Mary's selection to the Georgia Writers Hall of Fame.

In the hardscrabble world of Mary Hood's fiction, none of her characters in their Georgia-haunted lives could ever dream of such a fate as their creator has made for herself. She enslaves the creatures of her story with the whole airborne gamut of human emotions—dignity in the loneliness and agonies of their foreclosed lives—but she never grants them the genius that has brought her to the Hall of Fame. Mary Hood, daughter of Georgia, stood before us that day as one of the state's most honored storytellers. Indigenous, she is as much a part of that red clay soil as Vidalia onions, Stone Mountain, boiled peanuts, the Bulldog football team, or the burning of Atlanta. I believe her writing will live forever.

Here's why. I don't believe that Mary Hood is capable of writing an uninteresting sentence. She can say in three words what I can say in a hundred and sixty. I come across very few southern writers who sound like no one else who has ever written, and Mary Hood is one of them. Each of her short stories is self-contained and self-sufficient, like some Noah-less ark adrift in black storms. In Mary's floods, there are never any destinations —only arrivals at the point where the water grounds you, at the exact spot that Mary Hood has imagined for all her readers. She creates with a jeweler's eye and the patient craft of a watchmaker whose devotion to precision can make the whole world beat to her infallible sense of timing.

I would love to be a garden in her books and hate to be a dog. She writes about wildflowers as though they were citizens of the silent world saddened by the south she makes for her suffering humans. In one early story, Mary makes small havoc out of an abandoned woman who cannot master the secret of growing a plant called "Solomon's Seal." Mary turns it into a moral flaw as some relevant mystery to a life grown hopeless.

Many of the poor dogs in Mary's books run off, get shot at, get poisoned, and one favorite pet gets drowned. It is part of Mary's golden wizardry that the death of this pet is also a selfless act of pure love. Yet even when Mary goes dark on us (and, God, we southern writers love to wax dark) she leaves us enlivened, shrewder, even hopeful about the state of the world she brings out for our inspection.

Last year, I agreed to be the editor for a new series of fiction that would publish Southern Literature. When Jonathan Haupt, the publisher of USC Press, asked me to serve in this capacity, he asked me what writer I'd choose above all others if I could have any wish as an editor come true. I said Mary Hood. My next three choices were Mary Hood, Mary Hood, and Mary Hood again.

Mary's prose style seems moon-driven and airy as fallen snow. It contains the weight of myth and the lightness of a corps de ballet. Her dialogue forms the perfect shape that her characters will take. Like all the truly great writers, Mary Hood has mastered these high wires of brevity, abbreviation, and conciseness. The courage of her writing comes from a careful balance of whisper and fury. She possesses perfect pitch and never sounds a false note. Her deeply imagined characters speak as if they are offering their own true and often forlorn commentary on the book of life itself. A man can utter a toss-away sentence aloud and reveal the entire dimension of his own fate. A woman can answer him and seal her own. Yet she is funny as hell and has made her gift into a priceless treasury of art.

Please note that I've not mentioned that giantess of southern letters who was born in Savannah and grew up in Milledgeville and who makes of any southern writer—man or woman—weak with envy. You know the one I mean—the woman who tied a peacock to the tracks of the Dixie Limited and set a high standard for all the writers in the world. I think that Mary Hood has been compared to her far too often and I believe it has cluttered Mary's own extraordinary achievement. Mary Hood stands alone and no comparison can do justice to the body of literature she herself has created.

In this brilliant new work *A Clear View of the Southern Sky*, Mary Hood is writing at the top of her form. In her title story, she begins with the words, "Sometimes you just can't kill the ones you need to." Again, with swiftness and authority, she leads you into those back roads and small towns of Georgia where people's lives are simple, except when they are not. She has affinity for the rural southern poor where women wear yard shoes and the men carry rifles in their pickups and the pastries are filled with fruit and jellies and vegetables put up for the winter. She can make a blood drive seem like an encounter at the OK Corral. Some of the stories you are about to read will find themselves in the anthologies of our grandchildren. Already, her short stories, in their vessels of fire and stone, are read by college students with discerning teachers all across the land. Three or four of these stories rank among her finest and she has set a high bar for herself. She writes about Georgia, but the whole universe, known and unknown, can be discovered here in the glory that is hers alone.

An acknowledged master of the short story, Mary Hood finished this book with a novella that is the crowning achievement of the collection. *Seam Busters* takes us into a factory that makes camouflage gear for our nation's soldiers. I believe Irene Morgan is the deepest and most singular character ever to grace the work of Mary Hood. The factory where Irene works becomes a fictional world as real as the plantation in Yoknapa-tawpha. The town of Ready, Georgia, comes as alive as Twain's Hannibal and its only treasure to offer is the integrity of its citizens. The novella's ending will break your heart, but do so quietly like the conclusion of a great sermon, something like the one on the Mount.

A Clear View of the Southern Sky. I can come up with no better sum-ming up of this woman's life and work. In your hands, reader, lies a treasury.

Pat Conroy

A Clear View of
the Southern Sky

English as a Second Language:
Two Different Uses of Like

Sometimes you just can't kill the ones you need to. They drink themselves
to death, or OD shooting up or get shot trying, or end up shanked in an
alley or holding cell, or they ramble their hack down the slippery slope
before you can even offer a hand to push. But there's always somebody
else needing shoving. Things tend to stay roiled up. That's the problem
with watching the evening news. *¿No comprende?* Even if you don't *habla*
you can catch hell on Univision, every lurid detail and close up. That's
what got Edayara García into the "Cities of Refuge Ministries" English
as a Second Language class, making a hard choice, taking the straight and
narrow gate right into Allendale State Prison. Don't think she's sorry. She's
here today because when she finally had had enough of legal abrogations
and plea copping, she bought and cleaned a gun. Went up to the National
Forest, where it was legal, the same forest where some jerk several years
ago killed the old couple on the trail, which is not legal, but he got to live
and they didn't, so what does that tell you about legal? She adjusted the
sight, and practiced on the public range. She keeps a journal now; most
of it isn't in English, but she says she may write a book one day, when she
learns. "Life Story," she says she will call it. She wants the title to mean

1

more than one thing, since most things in life do. It will not be dull. Yara is good with plotting. It is one of her strengths.

The man who sold her the gun told her where to take it, what to do, how to get the most lead into her targets. She had used a dictionary to brain out what she wanted to know, before she went shopping. He studied the paper, perplexed. Neatly printed atop the first page, a little uneven, like a child's early schoolwork, she requested that he triage his advice "in ardor of importants." She handed him the composition book in which he jotted it all down for her, so she could look up words later. It fit in her purse, along with the box of cartridges. The gun seller was not charged, because he did not know what was on the other pages. Ready, Aim, Fire! he had written. Then he got serious. His number one counsel under Ready was: Practice. The last advice before Fire! was: Don't hold your breath; exhale; bite your tongue. He showed her what he meant. It made her think of the straining horses on the carousel.

When she got there, early in the morning, there were already a few deer hunters at the range, keen for the coming season, breaking in new camo. One jumpbooted coven at the end of the open-air gallery had Kalashnikovs and coolers full of ammo. Whatever those guys were planning, it wasn't paintball. That posse was going to make a day of it, bless their hearts. They didn't like it much that she was there: a woman. But her pathetic little stubby pawnshop bolt action didn't threaten them, and her matronly silver-gray hair braided thick as a man's wrist, trifocals, faded flannel tunic over knee-sprung sweats, and flatfooted Dollar General sneakers—her own kind of camouflage—didn't interest them at all. She chased her dream, they chased theirs. They kept holding up the rest of the shooters so they could move their targets deeper downrange. A little bit farther, they'd be in coal country. They seemed to be taking the long view. If Georgia had offered that kind of welcome in '63, Sherman would've marched home via Detroit, not Savannah. Yara didn't think of it as trigonometry but she had already brilliantly done the native math in her head, scoping out her shots the day before on a walkthrough; they were not long shots, strictly local. They weren't going far. All she had to do was be consistent and get used to the kick. She practiced hard, she loved firing, and she got used to the kick in a hurry. Time was of the essence, of course, but she somehow felt she had entered a counting-down place where purpose anointed her and she could make no misstep and every moment was golden. They said she could have used that in her defense. She already knew she wasn't going to run or defend. She already knew what and all she *was* going to do—it had come to her in a flash after seeing how, when the perpetrator came out of the preliminary hearing smiling in that bullet proof vest, the deputies had shouldered around him, protecting him like he was El Queso Grande—a movie star or the president or the pope. She had been transfixed past the desolation of that moment by the irrupting and completely evolved vision of her idea: the simplicity and possibility of the event, then the embroideries of perfecting, which means in her heart, murder was already done. She'd remember thinking, "Well, that's it with communion." In Spanish, of course. It isn't that she didn't know God was watching. He'd been watching her a long time. *Que le mire a ésta.* Let Him get a load of this. Grade school guidance and grief counselors, translated badly by someone who worked for the courts, had warned her, had said if she didn't let it out it would break out. So she dropped out. Every time she remembered what they had said, she could only laugh and ask, in all innocence, what? Because she knew herself. She never asked when? If they had been thinking *when,* it was so long ago they had forgotten; decades. Yara had known and had counted on her steady go with the flow self longer than they had doubted, her whole life in fact. That is, she thought she knew herself, right up until she didn't. It was a shock. She has said it. She suddenly recognized herself, recognized her face in the mirror in third person, as she would identify someone in a lineup: There! *She's* the one. Who she had been until that moment ended that night while watching TV. She had always stood her ground two reasonable steps back from the brink, and now, finally, she was stepping up; she was going over the edge after this perfect stranger, who wasn't so perfect at all. You have to hand it to her; she did not bunt. Her first swing-for-the-fences thoughts, when they finally did "break out," were just a thrill of wishing, not a goal.

Nothing but righteous indignation, a comic strip of sanctioned hate. Then the Cutthroat Rapist—as the press had nicknamed him—and the law made that deal. Life, not death, in exchange for his telling all he ever was going to tell about any others he had killed including where he had left their bodies through the years, and especially the recent girl he bragged "almost got away"—trading the death penalty for her head and body so her family could have "closure." You think it ever "closes," all day all night terror like that? Yara knew—and her mental comic book suddenly turned into a documentary in high def, playing non-stop She had three weeks, from the plea deal to the sentencing hearing. She worked at her day job, the first two weeks, and took her vacation days and sick days for the rest. That would have to be enough.

She made sure she wouldn't miss. That's closure. One to his head, that was all *he* needed. But she knew she wanted two shots, needed two. One into that vest o' life first, to knock him flat on his sorry *culo,* so he'd realize, so he'd have time to comprehend what is possible in this great land of ours with liberty and justice for all, and that little sip of chaos, that *momentito* of grace, so he could wonder if he should expect that second shot. She wanted him to wonder. She'd wait as long as she could. He'd be harking. He might even be thinking he was lucky. Fortune's boy. Surrounded by all those vested keepers of the public's even tenor, he wouldn't be wearing a bulletproof helmet, so there you go; she saw it all, in her mind's eye watched it over and over, as she made her plans. No one else would be hurt; she saw that too. Ricochet? No. And other objections? None. She knew knew knew knew knew better. Nothing scared her off. Some instinct had kicked in. She didn't premeditate; she implemented. No matter how his lawman entourage crowded around, she was going to get that second shot. She just knew. The way she knew she'd never regret wiping that smile off his face.

After that, they could have her. She didn't worry about whatever comes next. She didn't script a thing, she would just wait for them. It wouldn't take long; there's always someone around to flip a phone, point a finger. Buildings all around her were higher, and folks were crouching at the windows, watching the show. She knew they'd phone it in, send the swarm. She put the safety on and didn't wipe off prints. She just laid the gun down, and sat down beside it, resting in the shadow of a satellite dish. What did she care about her rights and options? She was not making any deals, or expecting any. She will tell you, she had worked through all this already. She was satisfied with what she'd get for what she gave. She had her driver's license and her insurance card bookmarked into her little white confirmation *Santa Biblia* in her day pack. She had her keys on a clip on the zipper pull. They could find the car, if it turned out she couldn't tell them. Her birth certificate and her registration were in the glove box. Also, her boss's number at the plant, where she stood all day on the line in chicken blood, gutting and hanging the birds by their tied-at-the-heels waxy yellow feet, hitching them on the hooks passing along overhead. Co-workers would miss her, but not at lunch when they hunkered down over their meal, laughing and talking, still wearing their aprons and boots and shower caps, passing a cell phone around, part of the story everybody knew and lived. Yara lived it too, but had no appetite for lunch. She'd take off her apron and hat and let her braid down, and scuff through the chlorine pan and around to the side yard in the sun. Sometimes an angel-white bird escaped the crate as they unloaded the trucks in back, and the men would chase it, its one and only time in the sun; they'd make bets. When there was no escaped bird to run down, they threw knives into the clay bank, and bet on that. Lunch was only half an hour. When she went back in, to put on her apron and cap and gloves and start work, she smelled like sunshine and not that bloody trough. For a few minutes, before she went numb again, she had that.

She liked the smell of sunshine and "clean." She had cleaned out her refrigerator, mopped the kitchen of her furnished rental trailer, put out a fresh towel, made her bed fresh, pulled back the curtains and pinned them with the little paper birds her grandmother had taught her to fold from bright magazine pages. Somebody would have to bring the garbage can back from the road, but somebody would. Her clothes and personal items were packed. If she was allowed to have them, they were ready. If not, whoever got the place next would have the good of them. Yara had no family. Her life was in order. She had nothing to do now but wait there on the sunny roof.

The morning had gone according to plan. There had been a slow elevator that smelled like machine oil; its scent mingled with gun oil, and it made her feel part of larger works somehow, but still she rode tense, knees flexed, and kept the cord of the beach umbrella bag with the rifle in it slung over her shoulder; she held the gun tucked hard under her elbow at her side. She rode alone; no one else dinged for a ride. She expressed herself up past the other floors, then climbed stairs, then crawled up a ladder through the hatch to the roof. Adrenalin got her up there, to it and through it, but now she had shot it all. She didn't dare look down a second time once it was over. She wasn't afraid of being fired at. She was afraid of falling. Sooner or later a head and the strong arm of the law with gun raised would pop up over the top step of that ladder and take control of everything. She just rested and watched the clouds. She's always been afraid of heights.

"I am no like the highs," she chalks on the greenboard, pausing to look around that small bleak room at Allendale, with its scallops of paper acorns and autumn leaves bordering the tack-ravaged cork board, which is empty. No news. Is good news? Her classmates stare back. She turns to the greenboard. "I am like you," she prints, slightly uphill, considers, places the chalk in the tray, and returns to her seat.

Describing a Person

Yara takes a "Style Trial" worksheet and passes the others on. This is something different. The teacher says it might be fun. "You ladies like fashion, right?" They watch him as he paces the width of the room, turns back, and just misses knocking over the wastebasket. He has arrived late, and they are already seated, counted, and counted again, before he plunges in. There is an officer in the hall. There is always an officer, listening, learning. Some are guards, just guards. Others are officers. It is not a matter of rank. It is a matter of respect. The inmates are facing the teacher, wearing their everyday set of tan scrubs. All but one are wearing scuffed athletic trainers of various types and quality. Unless they go to the greenboard to write, he will not read on the back of their shirt the words Prisoner of the State of Georgia, in all caps, cold and bold black letters as large as possible arrayed in three centered lines. There are extra copies of the worksheet. He takes them up and puts them in his messenger bag. Above the clasp are three gold-plated squares with initials, and the leather is supple as a hound's ear. Yara imagines he has cuffliks. He is a monogram man and a cufflink man without sleeves or cuffs. Did he leave the jewelry at home out of fear? Without offering other advice or help, he checks his watch—but it isn't on his wrist, he seems to have left that at home also; undisturbed he consults the clock on the wall and announces, "You have fifteen minutes. Let's see what you can do with this."

Describing a Person: Adding Details

The worksheet has been photocopied off an internet ESL site. It might have been in color, but now it is in black and white. It is a bit light. There are two columns with illustrations small as stamps, and the answers have to be put in a business card-sized space on two dotted lines below each illustration. A question about the picture takes up most of each "card." In the upper right corner of the worksheet are the words Reward Intermediate. Yara takes some of her work time to consider what this might mean. At first Yara misreads it; she thinks it says Reward Immediate. And she thinks that means something worth thinking about. She likes Skittles. Their other teacher used to pass the bag of Skittles around, hand to hand, and let them reach in, or pour! Just now and then, and sometimes on a harried day the bag was not very large, but was machine-vended, one serving size, yet even a few Skittles, even a one Skittle reward, has a zing to it. Very tasty. Then she notices what that word really is, on the worksheet. Not *immediate*. Reward, yes, but not immediate; intermediate. She knows the word. Is it about the reward? or about the lesson? Yara sighs. It is a natural mistake; it is printed in very small type. It does not seem to be instructions for the worksheet. Perhaps it is a remark intended for the instructor, who is a substitute, and nervous, and sweats profusely in his brand new olive green "Cities of Refuge" T-shirt. He has already taken off his corduroy jacket and hung it on the back of his desk chair. The corduroy jacket is not the same color as his corduroy pants, though it may once have been. Or perhaps he has new pants. The jacket does not look new. Yara has already noticed there is a button missing. Mr. Lanigan, he writes on the board with practically no slant in a round hand. He slashes an underline below it—a wide flat Zorro "z." He holds the piece of chalk between his thumb and index finger, straight out, as though he were going to feed it to something. He is not like Zorro. He has sparkly blond peach fuzz for hair, a one week old buzz growing out. He does not groom facial hair or flaunt tattoos. He has on no jewelry. He does not wear glasses. He does not smell like cigarettes, and he does not smell like after shave. Perhaps he has asthma? Sometimes that inhaler stuff can make you tremble. He uses a fountain pen. When he tries to put the cap back on his pen, after calling the roll, he is trembling so hard he has to lay the pen on the desk, and with the cap in his left hand and pen in his right, he edges them across the desk toward each other, and then, victory! Mr. Lanigan is not married, Yara decides. She brings her mind back to the page.

Style Trial—Clothes

1. What kind of clothes do you like? Yara cannot understand the illustration. It appears to be a sock-footed clown trying to choose something from a wardrobe of bunny costumes, or perhaps it is armor. So what is that thing that looks like a tail in front? What does this have to do with going to trial? She did not have a trial. Or trial clothes. She pled guilty. There was a hearing and sentencing, though. But she wore the orange jumpsuit. It was clean.

2. What do you wear to work/school/college? Yara looks around. The others seem to be farther along than she is. She is not sure how many minutes have passed. If they have fifteen minutes and twelve questions, she cannot take so much time to work things out. The illustration appears to be a cowboy looking at a computer. She is tired, maybe a little annoyed.

She decides to tell what she knows, and forget about the cowboy and the *computadora*. For Yara, English is personal; the struggle to win each word is personal. She locks onto its meaning and takes it down. "Same" she writes, in the space on the first line. That's the concept, that's it. On Sunday she makes sure she is wearing fresh-laundered and ironed scrubs. Just like today's scrubs, only ironed. That's what they do. That's what makes it Sunday. Some never have visitors. She is not the only one. She is not unhappy about it; this is not a matter of blame. Or shame. But in case she seems negative or grumbling somehow, about the scrubs, she corrects that, on the second line, with "Yes." She underlines it.

She skips questions 3 and 5. Maybe if there is time. Question *4: What clothes do you wear to dress up?* has already been considered, hasn't it? She simply puts a check mark, and moves to the next column. She cannot make out what the illustration is. There appear to be two hats. Is it a cowboy wearing one? And the other? Is there something in the middle? A horse? Or is it a woman in a flowered dress? Looking in a mirror? She examines the question. The question itself does not clarify the matter. There are no hidden clues that she can discover.

7. What clothes do you find most attractive on a man? Yara notices the Korean cutting her eyes around at her, fanning herself with the five purple-polished fingertips of the left and the thumb's up on the right. She always has a little money for toiletries; she is not indigent, a word which Yara thought was "indignant" when she first heard it, and it worked just as well that way, too. Is Kiko on that same question? She is good at characterization and mimicry, she can make them laugh—as now—with just a hot-stuff gesture, although when she reads, she raises the page higher and higher and slides lower and lower in her chair, until all they can see are Kiko's eyes, peeking over. She always thinks of funny things to tell. No one has ever seen her cry. She is small but tough. She is a member of the all female fire department, and is one of the few longtimers who still wears boots. The others get out of them and into athletic trainers as soon as possible, because their feet hurt. Maybe Kiko's boots fit. She has small feet and wears two pairs of socks. She is going home to Atlanta in two more years with a GED and firefighting skills and bright—maybe even career—prospects. She'll have to take the bus to the fires; her license has been lifted for five years. While she is at Allendale, she is not wasting her chance. She can already comprehend English, and read it and write it, but when she talks it, nobody can understand. And she doesn't speak Spanish at all. No help there. Yara goes back to the page. She cannot imagine what this question has to do with any ideas she has on style and her trial. She will tell the truth. "No thing," she starts. She scans the worksheet for verbs that might help, ready-made. She is going to disclaim, "No thing I clothes is for attract on a man at trial." But then she breaks off, after the first two words, startled so badly that she drops her pen. She never picks it up. Mr. Lanigan has blown a whistle! It is a plastic whistle; that is how it got through the detectors at the front gate. He thinks he is telling them that time is up. But that is not what a whistle means. All of them react in the same way. All of them rise without a word and zombie from the center of the room toward the edge, array themselves blank-eyed, with their back to the faded inspirational posters, shoulder to shoulder, hands in plain view, and wait, in absolute silence, for Lockdown. It is a process, and not to be taken lightly. While they are moving, before they turn their backs to the wall, Mr. Lanigan, in his in clueless dismay at what he has accidentally accomplished, has plenty of time to read what is written on their shirts.

Have To and Don't Have To

Mr. Lanigan does not come back.

Ice Breaker

The new instructor says to call her Miss Haidee. It doesn't sound like it is spelled. "It rhymes with Friday," she tells them. They whisper it, practicing: Miss Eye Day. She looks windblown. She is Hungarian, with sparkling black eyes, and long dark hair which has been burned with black dye. She has a ratty teased topknot. They have no way of knowing, but she has arrived topknotless with her hair in a sleek twist, held in place by rhinestoned chopsticks which she has to surrender at the front gate, along with her driver's license and car keys. The gate officers confiscate the chopsticks, and make her take off her shoes, and they hand scan her when the walk-through detector goes off. She explains. She does not want to go home now. She explains and explains. They wand her again, and pat her down. They hand her back her shoes. She is wearing a bronze crucifix on a cord under her turtleneck, but it is the steel in her hip, from a bad break, which alarms the scanner. She arrives in class put back together in many unseen ways, and her hair—as she thinks of it—"a ruin." She does not complain. She does not have time to resent. She speaks with a French accent. She is very tall. She likes scarves. There is a soft white boa surpliced around her neck, tracking angora onto her black cashmered shoulders. There is a bright brave square of flowered silk tied to the handle of her tatty briefcase. A great fringed square—a piano shawl—of olive and cocoa and deep rose lies draped across her trench coat on its chair. She is wearing a simple square dark stone in old gold on her left hand. The ring looks heirloom, like it has a history of many revolutions. She has no polish on her short but unbitten nails. There is a Band-Aid, the stretchy kind, around the tip of her right index finger, very dark against her pale skin.

They cannot judge her age; she is not old, but she does not seem young. Her brows are waxed to perfection. She wants everyone to get to know each other, even though they already do. "Enough about me," she says; "tell us about yourself," and goes down the roll. Everyone gets a question. They may respond with a word or phrase or they may "complete a sentence." When she says "complete a sentence" she breaks off, embarrassed. "*Dommage!*" She strikes her forehead with her hand. She seems really sorry about her tactlessness. She says so. "What was I thinking? I wasn't." She says, "You're on the right track, but I am off in the daisy field!" She is flushed, and takes a moment, draws a deep breath, recovers, and moves right on down the obviously unrehearsed lesson page; she has the only copy. They are having to listen carefully, to use their ears and phrase their answers orally. Wondering what their question will be, they peer at the paper she is reading from; they can see through it in that room's harsh bouncing afternoon light. It looks like a chart, or an application. Is she reading them an old job application? A medical record? "I'm not going to ask your weight," she says, with a sparkle. They can see she is not afraid of them; she trusts them. She is a little afraid of herself. This is endearing and yet an agony. She keeps looking at the clock, not the door. She has come prepared to use every minute. They try to help. They answer promptly and as best they can when she asks: What is your name? How old are you? Then she asks Malena her current address. "Oh!" she says, "Double *dommage!*" and something else, maybe in Hungarian, and looks up and wildly around, and her topknot bounces loose and an earring slings off, and when everyone laughs, she laughs a heartfelt ha-ha kind of head-tossing laugh like Meryl Streep and they give her back her earring and she hooks it on again and forgets about her hair and they all press on to *Hobbies and Favorite Meals.* She wants everyone to describe a favorite food. She likes to call on them in alphabetical order, so they brace themselves for their turns. She is temporary. They get used to her. She is filling the gap. In her real life she is a poet. She would be doing that right now, "If not for you," she says, and hands out a "conditionals" worksheet. "I Googled," she says. They have never seen such a worksheet, they—as she—never having heard of modals or conditionals until this lesson. She tells them she comes to English as a speaker of other language; that is her only credential. They do not groan or sneer. They do not entirely understand. They trust her; in time it will all make sense. They lukewarmly wait, their ice broken.

"If Not for You":
Modals Practice in Hypothetical Conditionals

The worksheet says the second aim of the lesson is to create a love (or hate) poem. "Obviously you know how to do this," she says. What she means is, "I believe you can love and hate." Or perhaps, "I know you have feelings." Yara believes that there are some things and feelings not worth knowing or having. She already knows there are some things not worth believing. She click-click-clicks her pen. Three quick clicks. It is a typical gesture; she is pumping herself up. Lunch and her medications are at optimum right this moment. Across her page she writes the topic in her own hand, ready to make a list, not a poem. "If not for you," she subjuncts. Nothing she is preparing to list is hypothetical.

Unreal Conditionals: Rules for Present and Past

When Miss Haidee leaves, under her desk there is a single page which has fallen from her portfolio: *Praise Phrases: "Good on You!"* The corrections officer picks it up, while straightening the tables and chairs. She pauses to read the instructions at the top of the page. "A little praise goes a long way. However, there are many ways to praise. You need to offer something more than the same few phrases repeated over and over again. Your little friends in class and our clerks and public servants need to hear more than the traditional 'Good' or 'Very Good' or 'Fine' or 'OK.' Get huggy not shruggy with your word choice. Our world needs soul-deep encouragement. Seek and use warm and simple personal verbal ways to celebrate their achievements. Wisdom suggests you otherwise do not touch them." The rest of the page has dozens of comments posted from "good on you" to "magic." In her own hand, in green ink, Miss Haidee has written: "Walk the walk: keep adding to this list!"

Miss Haidee has gone for the day, begun the long walk out, escorted from pen to pen by another officer, between the razor wired chutes and alleys. Like a ship in the Panama Canal, she is moved forward from lock to lock, the pens slowly filling with those also leaving, being counted, being recounted, and being passed forward into the next pen. The classroom officer is not tasked or cleared to go after her; this is not an emergency warranting a call to stop her at the gate, or somewhere midway. After consideration, she decides that Miss Haidee knows that marked-up page by heart. She folds the sheet of Ways to Praise and pockets it. She turns off the classroom lights. As she starts down the dim corridor she thinks of Jonathan and his men worn out with battle, dipping their spears into the honey, brightening their eyes.

Hours to go. She is not even halfway home yet. She turns and prowls down the hall, checking doors. Her boots squeak on the old tiles. The autumn shifts end near dusk now, before her day is over. The nights may be getting longer, but the days aren't getting any shorter. Neither is the road home. By the time she walks all the way out, cranks her truck and drives back the way she came, and turns down the last lane home, beyond watchtowers and xenon floods by about thirty miles, she is looking for a light in a window.

"That's nice," she tells her only grandchild Gilda, when she gets finally there and the golden bug light on the porch is on. It's just the two of them now; they're the family. Gilda's father is upstate, at Hays, finishing the last seven years of a life sentence before any possible parole. They don't want him back. Gilda has a few years to go, but she is talking about teaching school some day. She's raked a path through the leaves to the damp grave-earth of their old dog, Sassafras, who died without much trouble to anybody, during a summer nap. Gilda has moved the porch pumpkin to the grave. She's carved 4 + EVR into the pumpkin. Gilda's only dog, a remnant of her short life with her mother, whose own life was gone in a flash. Gilda's had counseling. She's been loved. No one can love her into forgetting. She's not going to forget. She is the kind who brings things on along, uses them right, passes them down. She has a fresh pot of coffee brewing. Before the officer even unlaces her boots, she onesteps up on the stool and locks away her gun in the high cabinet. Piece by piece she disarms and stands down, putting things where they belong, so tomorrow morning will be a walk-through and out the door. She takes off her socks and slaps through the rooms barefooted in her housecoat to seek refuge in the den. She pauses on the edge of the seat, staring at her toes. Newly surprised, always surprised by what Gilda's pedicure last month on her birthday accomplished; the endless kick just knowing the polish is strawberry-scented. She settles deep in the recliner, gropes for the lever and gearshifts herself back. For a moment, she's all the way flat out. Laid out. Eyes shut, she doesn't even seem to be breathing. She is in between, molting. Her legendary hardcore hall-growl welcome for the newbies says it all. "At home I'm a mama but at work I ain' nobody's mama; I'm a mutha." She doesn't have to prove it that often, but she always has to be

14

willing, ready and able. She is. That furrowed and hard-knobbed ebony war mask begins to slide, and her dark aura brightens. Deep breath, and she blows the day away, like fifty years on a homemade candle-dripped cake.

"Mama G, you a'right?"

The guard nods, and uptilts herself in the chair halfway, into dining mode. "Heaven on earth," she says, smiling at the tray. "You outdone yourself this time." She sips the coffee and eats her supper and watches satellite news. She leans forward for a closer look. "Be seeing some them soon," she says, pointing. She will never get seated on a jury; she has seen it all and knows too much. She shakes her head, like she can't get over that white gal in big old sunglasses. "'Barbie Bandit,'" she marvels, quoting the reporter. "What she up to now?" She puts her hand out, waggles the fingers, and Gilda comes close enough for a side hug. "You my smart one. What you learn today?" She looks up, holding the girl's hand, and really sees her, fills up looking. She flicks away the tears. She's home. She's ready to listen now. She's ready to phrase some praise.

Wishes and Regrets in the Past, Present and Future

Miss Haidee does not come back. She does not get to hear them read their "If not for you" homework list-poems. One is romantic, two are religious, one is a kiss-off, Malene decides to kiss *up* and honor teachers everywhere, Kiko astounds them by writing about her mother in her vegetable garden, with straight lines of onions and no laughs and no weeds but Kiko. Five students choose not to share. When it is Yara's turn, she moves toward the lectern, where the new teacher, Mist' Steve, is standing. No one else has stood to read, but the instructor, pleased, steps aside, starts for a chair on the front row, out in the classroom with the students. Yara turns, when he does, and follows him. "You read," she requires. She presents him with her page. It is hard won, he can see that at a glance. All across the top and around the edges she has written vocabulary words, curt definitions and translations back into Spanish, and notes to herself, also in Spanish. She has not taken the time to rewrite it, to make a clean and final version. This is semi-official. She doesn't want it to count. He sees that. He also sees how much it does count. It counts against, as much as for. He is careful with his face and takes his time; he's a poker player on Friday nights. Yara's actual response, beneath the "If Not for You" topic title, is a bewildering worm-tangle of revisions. "Read what in red," she tells him. "Not in loud." For a moment, because he has taken an audible breath—and thinking he is going to "share"—she reaches for the page, but he does not let it go. He has seen a mistake in all the promise; it has leaped into his eye from the tangle. There are others. He studies her, his mind very busy, his eyes very still. For a moment, she is reminded of someone . . . yes . . . the gun dealer, just before he told her Ready, Aim, Fire!

He rises and starts back to his desk. He looks at all of them, waits to speak until Yara has taken her seat again. He jots something on her paper. "See me," he tells Yara. Yara spears up her arm. "Give back?" she says.

"You bet," he says. "But not yet, kiddo." He is a seasoned classroom teacher, with formal training but no formality. He wears suits. He leaves a necktie hanging on his rearview mirror, if the need arises. It seldom comes to that, one of the advantages of being retired. He takes off his jacket and rolls up his sleeves. He wears expensive M-frames on a cord around his neck yet aims his marksman's stare over cheap drugstore readers. You have to get close, almost too close, to breathe in his cologne. Seventeen years since he lit a cigarette, and yet he still inhales when someone else does. The only bad habit he's ever kicked. Not tobacco, not leather, but there is something else, as well, some attar purely alpha male. He's it. They know it. No ice breaking this time. No games. He is not afraid, not trembly with good intentions or weary with doubt. Not needy or displaced. He can afford to do this, and even if he couldn't they suspect he would, though they do not know why. He is unpaid. He will be able to deduct his mileage. He has signed on for at least a year. He will be back. He will be a little early. He's been a public defender, but not in the usual sense. His wife's a caseworker. His grandparents—both sets—came from Sinaloa, a long time ago; California was his first state, English is his first language, but not his only language. Mist' Steve served in the Marines. He has some keloid scars, and from time to time, wishes for more, or at least the manic clarity of issues during a fire fight. He has taught in middle and high school. He has coached hockey. He has a pretty high threshold for chaos and pain. He and his wife have raised five children, a boy, a girl and a mixed gender set of triplets. That was five different campaigns against drift and undiscipline. His wife has told him more than once that every baby is born a barbarian, and every competent writer was born a baby. He rereads for pleasure. He loves slang. He is willing to cut some slack, trade some traditions for the salt of the street's wisecracks. However, he has no intention of sitting through this kind of capital—and lower case—punishment week after week without fighting back. And fiercely. Just a matter of breaking it to them gently now. Or whatever it takes. He wishes them to understand more than English. They are being cheated in this room. They have been babysat. They have not been learning; they have been playing, and they don't even know the rules! He rests his forehead against his right palm, for only a moment, and then he tells them, head up, hands flat on the desk, ready to push, "You or I may regret my saying this, but I hope not." He stands to deliver his soul.

Group Dream: An Old Exercise (p. 75, HLT magazine)

The students lie (or sit) with eyes closed, in silence. Anybody may initiate a dream (which may be the beginning of a real dream they have had, or simply an image that has come to their mind). Others may join in at any time to add details or to move the action along. Gradually, a composite dream emerges.

By the end of the session the greenboard is covered with many new ideas. All of their handwriting is up there. They have pages of notes, and sentences to practice. They have homework: to begin a journal, which can be in any language they choose, including pictures, but when they read it to him, they have to translate. They have to tell him their story in as perfect English sentences as they can make. Before he turns to go, to begin the long transit back out through the razor-wire scrolled arteries of hard time and across the scabby upheaved slabs of the yard with the cracked planter of faded polyester flowers, back along the bleak breezeways, past the windows where heads will lift and watch him because he is male, and not a guard or officer, he pulls on his jacket. He picks up his portfolio, and says, briskly, "See you next time," and they know, then, what they have not known before, that it is up to them. Yara looks at the paper he has handed back, the first thing she has received with correction on it, and she wants to know what she feels so she can write it in her journal. But there is no word for it in English. Not yet.

The Teacher

Once, when she had been to the garden center, Cheryl lost her keys. A handful of keys, and she never saw any of them again after driving home and opening the front door with them. Car and door keys—and all the others—were on the same ring. They simply vanished. She had driven home with them; she had opened the door with them. She went over and over it. She looked everywhere. She slept badly, and had bad dreams.

She had another set of car keys. She had duplicates on other rings to all the keys except the bank box. She did not want to go back to the bank and tell them that she had lost both keys within an hour of signing for them on those voucher cards. It was going to be expensive to drill out those locks, and it would be embarrassing also because the box was empty. She had planned to store genealogy papers, savings bonds, a few silver dollars—childhood gifts from Uncle John, her great-grandmother's tiny wedding band, a small rock wrapped in a piece of paper that explained, simply, Mary Mine, a christening gown and cap, a few precious letters from the Civil War, her great great great grandfather's pocket Bible sent back from Camp Chase a week after Appomattox. Her mother had been dead six years before her father remarried and moved to Florida. She wanted a safe place for the few things her stepmother neither wanted nor honored. Cheryl had chosen a medium size lockbox, and within an hour had lost both keys! She considered not telling the bank, just paying box rent on the empty box for years and years, forever maybe, or at least until enough time had passed that misplacing both keys would only seem a hazard of long life and many adventures, and not some early clue that she was a "loser." That she was going to be an old maid. Not even the tidy kind whose windows and good deeds shine, and whose shoulder pads fit, whose sleeve cuffs are tailored to length, not turned up, lining showing, causing Mrs. Brown at church to ask, "Can't you sew?" An unstructured loser whose house smells of burnt toast and cats and the kitchen drawer is cluttered with tea balls and wadded recipes and rusty coffee strainers. What if Dan found out? She had just met Dan. She wouldn't tell him, that's all. A woman would be a fool to tell a man everything anyway.

She asked Dan's friend with a metal detector to come help her find "an earring." He found a screen door spring, a bottle cap and a penny from 1976. Within two weeks she had decided to tell the bank, pay for the drill-out and re-keying, and just get on with it. That would be the healthy thing to do, just get on with it. She did.

Years later, after she and Dan were married, she dreamed she saw the lost keys lying on top of a toy cotton bale in Sears. "Back-to-school," the sign announced. And there were her keys, part of the vignette for fall, the little tractor tire fob and its red hub unfaded by time and misadventure. Cheryl felt such joy and relief in the dream, something unlatching in her. Her heart tried to knock her awake, but it didn't. She slept on. In the dream her mother found her, and they stood side by side.

"May I help you?" her mother asked, as though she worked there.

"Just looking," Cheryl said. In the dream she didn't reach for the keys, or her mother.

She felt that her mother understood how she had suffered; had wondered —in the heat of the crisis—if she were losing her mind, and if so, were the keys the cause or the symptom? After the dream in which her mother told her, "There's gone and there's lost," Cheryl noticed that the emotional stress had passed. The missing keys still mattered, but were now only on her conscience, not her agenda.

The stranger in the personal care home in Cleveland was not like the missing keys. In the first place, she had never met him, she had only heard of him. Or, better said, she had only overheard of him while she was sitting at the recovery and refreshments table at the Red Cross blood drive.

She had donated as often as she was allowed once she found out she was Blood Type O negative, and also came up negative for human cytomegalovirus. This meant, they had told her, her blood was ideal for premature and distressed newborns. She had a special "Hero" sticker on her card and they always moved her to the front of the line. She still had to fill out the forms, answer the same questions as anyone else. "Have you ever been pregnant?" was the hardest one for her. The number changed over time, but "live births" remained zero. She and Dan did not have any children. *Yet*, she'd say at first. But now she was forty-something if asked how many children she'd answer twenty-three or whatever number were in her class that year. She invested herself in them, in teaching and caring and preparing them not only for first grade but also for life. Dan sometimes said he was spending the best years of his life in kindergarten. They had planned on the day of the blood drive to meet at the church—it was their anniversary—and donate side by side, her idea, but he was a fireman and got called out. He beeped her to let her know.

That was the first thing that went wrong. Then they missed the vein in her left arm, the needle went in wrong somehow, and in just a few minutes the blood ceased to flow into the bag. The blood already collected into the bag had to be discarded; they couldn't just switch arms with the needle. All she had given had to go to waste. They would have to start over with a whole new collection kit. They were apologetic, but she was determined. "I've got more blood, I've got two arms and two legs," she said. "I'm here to give, darn it. Do what you have to, except cut down." She liked sounding brave and perky, but she meant it too. She imagined a jaundiced prune of a baby plumping and plumming up, drip by drip, from the pulse of her heart. "There's all kinds of ways of giving life," Dan had told her more than once. He had brought a German Shepherd back to life with CPR. For Cheryl giving blood was not sublimation or a substitute for anything. It was, simply, what and all she could do, so she did.

They found a good vein in her other arm and the bags and tubes filled. Soon she was sitting at the recovery table. It was late in the day. Cookies were strewn and decimated from their first orderly ranks on the plastic tray and the trash can was nearly full of paper napkins and other debris.

End of shift, less than an hour to go. They gave her latex gloves with ice in them to hold on her puncture sites. Both arms were bruised, but not badly.

"Just stay here fifteen minutes," the supervisor said, taping the ice packs into place. Cheryl had to hold still. She leaned forward on her elbows and drank through a straw. She felt fine. This was nothing. This was sort of how it always went—good blood but it ran deep. She wasn't allowed to lift her pocketbook, or bags of groceries, or anything like that. That's why they made her wait, because she had said she was going shopping after she left. She still meant to, but she would stay and drink two cups of juice and eat a few cookies.

Some other firemen, a paramedic and a county deputy came to the table after donating, rested a bit, then went on back to work. Everybody knew her and Dan. They reported Dan's call was out in the woods, a brush fire, and it was good she hadn't waited on him. The crews were winning but it was taking time.

Behind her, at the welcome table, two women were signing in to donate. "I've donated before," one of them answered, "in Ohio."

The other one hadn't, and said so in a bright midwestern accent that carried and bounced off the bare walls of the fellowship hall. "That makes me a virgin, right?"

"Try 'rookie'," her friend said. They shrieked with laughter. They were the only ones.

Cheryl winced. 'Indoor voice' was not a concept they had ever grasped. She imagined they had not attended kindergarten—some people didn't, they just pushed and shoved right into first grade—and that was why they did not know how to behave now. The two chatted with each other like jays in different trees, filling out their health, sexual and travel histories on clipboards. "Gosh," Rookie said, "Who knew?" Then, "Oh." Gradually silence fell. But not for long.

During the next step in the check-in process—sitting privately in the curtained-off cubicle and answering questions orally, having blood pressure checked and a finger stuck to test for anemia—Rookie fell out. There was a clatter of something being pulled down and crashing, and a thud.

"We're OK, no harm done," the nurse called, and in a minute or so an orderly helped the dazed woman into a chair at the recovery and refreshment table.

"Gimme grape juice," she said, just like that. She ate the last five Nutter Butters as fast as she could, scattering crumbs while chatting on, a running monologue. Just one of those crazy-makers who comment and command, Cheryl thought, and can turn a whole classroom into a sideshow to their own personal circus. Cheryl knew the type, dealt with them—in miniature version—daily. For Cheryl, giving blood was always a quiet time, almost like communion.

To the fireman, in uniform, Rookie announced, "I'm a groomer. What do you do?"

"Not much," he said, finishing his drink and standing. "And a whole lot less now I'm married. But I always leave 'em laughing." He left them laughing. The supervisor came over, checking around. She looked at Cheryl's bruises under those icebag gloves.

"What happened to *her?*" Rookie asked. "Why do you get those? No, don't tell me, I don't wanta know. I never fainted before but now I know I can."

"Five more minutes," the nurse decided, looking, then putting Cheryl's ice back on.

"I'm the one who fainted," Rookie said again. "I need some more juice. Ya got any cranberry? I always get a bladder infection when I stress."

Two more donors joined them. Again she announced she had fainted and was waiting on her friend who was also a dog groomer. One of the gray-haired newcomers needed ice on her arm. Then a soldier did too. The attendant fixed them up, handing out "Be nice to me" stickers, glancing past the curtains and saying, "What's going on back there? This is my purple heart table today . . ." She ejected the last sleeve of Fig Newtons onto the platter.

Rookie's pal, the other groomer joined them at the table. "It wasn't bad," she said. "You anemic?"

"We will never know," Rookie said, and that got their merrymaking going again.

The gray-haired woman in bank uniform—khaki trousers, oxford cloth shirt and badge—asked, "Did you say you groom poodles?"

"She does. I'd rather not. But I can. You got one?" Rookie tipped her cup back, emptied it, giving it a little tap to get the last bit of ice.

"No no," the teller said. "I was just wondering why they have to look like that."

Others at the table laughed, but not the groomers.

"It's about show style and breed standards," Groomer said. "They don't have to look like that."

"Those round things on their—"

"I know," said Rookie. "Dontcha hate 'em? And their weepy little eyes like suffering old folks." There was a pause. "Notch you-all," she clarified, glancing up at the attendant. "Ya got plenty on the ball, plenty left in the attic, you know? Besides which, gray poodles don't *go* gray; they *are*. So there's that," she said.

"Ya just maken it worst," Groomer told her, rolling her eyes at the rest of them. Another pause.

"Ya know what I mean," Rookie said. "Come on! That old guy in my mother—I mean *our* ex-mother-in-law's personal care home in Cleveland . . ."

"We're serial sister-in-laws? Wife-in-laws? Both of us divorced her son?" the other one explained. She sighed. "Me first."

"Age before beauty," Rookie said.

"Then there's still hope for both of us." Elbow in ribs time. Then a high five for a good one, and back to business at hand.

"He had the same squinty little brown eyes and frizzy hair. Like a poodle?" Rookie said.

"The gimp, not our ex—," the other one explained.

"Poodles are supposed to be real smart," someone said.

Rookie gave a jay-like turn of head, bright eyes unblinking. Continued. "Up every morning, tied his handkerchief into knots at the corners and stuffed his Brillo hair up into it. Like a shower cap. And wrapped himself in a sheet instead of putting on his robe and beat his head on the wall."

"Not the poodle, the man?" the groomer who had donated said, right merrily.

"He mumbled. You couldn't get a word in. Or look him in those damn little eyes. Not weeping. Seeping. Ya know? Like a poodle, only you can get bleach and fix a poodle up, hide those stains."

"He didn't let anyone near him, not even with food?" Rookie's pal explained.

"Boiled egg and a packet of plain instant oatmeal."

"Every day?" The bank teller pushed back her chair, started to go, paused.

Rookie considered it. "Every meal, yeah. When I was there. Like I said, he was—well, I don't know what." She glanced around, over her shoulder, risked it. "Coot doesn't cover it. He was on some kinda trip—his way or no way."

The donor-groomer said, "There was a sign on his door: 'Knock first? push rolling tray in? leave? Do not touch client while he is sleeping? Do not wake client by touching but by voice?' And of course no fixing windows or God forbid touching his stuff?"

"Not that he had any. Just pajamas and handkerchiefs."

"Can you think? Handkerchiefs? When's the last time you laundered one of those?"

"Long sleeve pajamas," Rookie said.

"And no stripes?"

In unison they repeated, "No stripes." And laughed.

There it all was, a cranky old black man who didn't want to be reminded of chain gang stereotypes. Ohio was where the slaves thought heaven was—across the river was freedom. "They called the Ohio 'River Jordan,'" Cheryl said, surprised she spoke. She did not want to encourage their roadshow. But there it was. Tact and fact—tenets of her teaching—could open eyes and hearts. It was never too early or too late.

Cheryl kept it simple. "Some African Americans cover their hair to work. Habit of a lifetime. They knot the corners of their bandanna to make a hat and call it a 'do rag.'" Should she mention the chain gang stripes? She mentioned.

The groomers looked at her, then at each other, then flexed their brows. Laughed. Played their trump card. "He wasn't black, he was a Swede!" Almost in unison. The donor added, "Or Swiss. Or something. Spanish? I don't know: jabber jabber jabber?" She scowled, pushed her drink cup away from her, shook her head, letting them in on something. "Don't try to figure him out. He was where he needed to be, next stop a padded room."

"He coulda been a lot easier on all of us," Rookie said. "He *required*," she said with a particular emphasis. "Laundry done separately or he'd have a sulk'n fit. He had this thing about cooties."

"And we had to wear gloves to bring it in to him, anything . . . laundry, food? He wasn't sick, it wasn't like we could catch anything? It was all about him! He was—"

"Crazy."

"One Fourth of July I was making shorts for summer, no A/C, it was an old dump, y'know? fans and breezes, nature's own remedy. And shorts. Everybody wanted them, just cut off the pajama legs, and the bottoms of the long gowns and hem, y'know. Straight stitch'n. I did his too. He threw 'em at me. Called me something and then he threw 'em away. He wouldn't wear them. I sewed the sleeves and legs back on and threw 'em back at him. He wore the pants. Never would wear the shirt because the sleeves didn't cover his arms." She made wild gestures as he must have, trying to explain what he wanted, what he would not allow. "Jabber jabber jabber," she said again. Her mockery got a few weak laughs.

Cheryl's ice bags were off now, and she was ready to go. She picked up her purse, to see if she could, and nothing inside her arms snapped or began to bleed, so she thought she must be okay. She unrolled her sleeves down over the Band-Aids. She didn't want to go out in the world with needle tracks like some junkie. "Maybe he had scars," Cheryl said, drawing on her coat.

"Yeah, burned and sensitive about the scars," someone suggested. "My brother—"

"Ya think?" Rookie agreed. "But that wasn't it. It was his tattoo."

What kind of shameful tattoo would an old Swede have invested in? In
some foreign language no one could read anyway? Back at the beginning
of the century before this one. Tallship? Coal-stoking steamer? Had he
been a sailor? Or maybe it was some tacky pinup doll requiring no translation. Cheryl absolutely hadn't intended to encourage them at all, but she
found herself asking.

"Nothing," Rookie said.

"Just numbers," the other one added.

Perhaps because she had given a bit more blood than usual Cheryl
took longer to figure it out. As she left the hall, she considered. She was
envisioning a crest of numbers, something like that. Like a wine label.
Or—a cattle brand . . . She was across the highway, already parked at
Big Lots when it hit her, and knocked her to her knees. Her purse strap
slipped from her shoulder and landed hard. Nothing spilled. She gathered
it idly, tranced, working it all out as she walked to the store. The more she
comprehended the slower she moved. She came to a stop, started back to
her car, thought better of it, then changed her mind and turned back. She
had to. She had turned too suddenly. A little dizzy, she could feel her heart
beating in her ears. Her long bones felt hollow. She seemed to be wearing
lead boots. Despite her excitement, she forced herself to walk deliberately,
so she would not fall. Even so, it hadn't been but a few minutes yet both
groomers were gone. She didn't seen or hear them in the parking lot—and
wouldn't she? They must have parked on the other side of the church near
the street. They must have left right after she did.

The attendant at the welcome table wouldn't let her pass. She tried to
explain quickly. "I just gave blood and I need to speak to someone."

"Is this a medical problem?" The greeter stood, rolling her chair back
with a little wiggle of her haunches.

"No."

Then the trouble began. Cheryl had to explain why she wanted to
speak to someone, why she wanted the names of those two Ohio women.
The Red Cross—she was told again and again—had a policy.

"We do not reveal the names of donors."

"One didn't donate. Give me her name?"

"No. No, ma'am."

"Would you give her *my* name?"

The clerk stepped back. "I'll go ask." When she returned, she said, "No. Supervisor says no."

"Then let me speak with your supervisor."

"My immediate superior or the director of this unit?"

"Anyone who cares more than you," Cheryl said, beginning to tremble.

When the supervisor appeared, Cheryl got the same results.

"Well, could you please give them my name and have them call me? This is urgent."

The supervisor stonewalled. "Our records are absolutely—"

"It really is urgent. It may be life or death."

The supervisor went to her desk and made a note on a business card, brought it to her. "Call the Atlanta center on Monroe Drive. Here's the direct line."

"May I use your phone?"

"No. I'm sorry. Besides, she won't be in until Monday."

By then, Cheryl had called every listed veterinary clinic and groomer, breeder, housesitter and dog-walker in the Atlanta directory. The Metro Yellow Pages yielded to the suburban ones. Another week. The Red Cross, meanwhile, simply said no, again and again. It was absolute and it was final, even when she explained.

Cheryl called the synagogues and the Temple. She called the Atlanta Holocaust Museum. She called the Holocaust Museum in Washington. She phoned directory assistance in Cleveland and called every synagogue, congregation, and personal care home in their Yellow Pages. Directory assistance did all they could. She spoke with some good folks, all along the way. She called nursing homes. She spoke with Ohio rabbis: ortho-dox, reformed, and conservative, messianic. Everyone seemed interested in her story, but no one could help. When Cheryl woke in the morning she imagined the lost man was waking yet one more day, tying the knots in his kerchief, donning it as kippah, and beginning to thank God.

The blood drive had been in March. When the school year ended, Cheryl spent whole days commuting across the state to the university library, searching in archives, phone books, and online resources.

"Without their names, or his name, what can we do?" they'd all tell her, after trying.

She prayed about it. In various locations. When the summer break had passed and school began again in August, Dan thought she would ease up, but the quest continued. In October she got a return call from one of the veterinarians in the suburban metro area.

"Did you ever find him?" he asked. Just that. So she knew he wasn't calling with good news. He said, "After we spoke, I couldn't stop thinking about it. I've joined a synagogue and I take my son with me. We observed Yom Kippur."

"Oh," she said.

"I just wanted to tell you," he said. "If you find him, let me know."

Near Thanksgiving she was on her way along the sidewalk at the strip mall to pick up dry cleaning when she stopped to browse a table of old books. She liked to buy the old ones with gold lettering and edges, but a paperback caught her eye, something Dan would get a kick out of—a US Army field manual from the Vietnam era: *Survival, Evasion & Escape*. Five dollars. She picked it up. That was when she noticed the large weathered green frame—a card table top—in the front window of the vintage shop. Sandwiched between the table and its glass top was an embroidered silk shawl. The label said, "Fortune teller's table, New Orleans, 1950s." Cheryl stood there and stared. The embroidery was in Hebrew. The fringes were blue and white, sun faded, yellowed, but obviously once blue and white. As she was paying for the book, Cheryl told the clerk, "That's not a Gypsy anything; that's a Jewish prayer shawl."

"No," the clerk said, checking an index card in the tabletop file. "No."

This was not her store; it belonged to her aunt who was in France. The writing on the card was plain. She showed it to Cheryl. "Gypsy fortune teller, New Orleans. Table top only; legs in poor condition free if they want them on shelf in back room price firm."

"If it was used by a fortune-teller," Cheryl told her, "it is no good now." The framed shawl made her cry. Like something dead in a trap. For the first time in all her looking for the Holocaust survivor in the personal care home in Cleveland, she thought, "Maybe he is dead by now." He, like the shawl, mis-labeled and profaned due to ignorance, stupidity, and the carnage of waged peace. "I ought to buy it and burn it," Cheryl added. Then thought better. "No. No profit given or taken. God forbid. Not buy it. You shouldn't sell it. Not a penny for it. Don't touch a cent from it," she warned her, getting warmed up. The shop girl shrugged, stared. Mute.

Cheryl left. But she had to come back. She had to make sure the girl understood. "Do you understand? You've been told. Not that ignorance is any excuse."

The clerk's fingers ascended the five hoops in her left ear, turning them with the perfect purpled nails on her left hand, each finger with its ring, even the thumb, then she looked out the window, past the fortune teller's tabletop. Then glanced back at Cheryl, then past. She sighed, heavily bored. "Why do you hate Jews? That's so . . . World War II."

A messianic rabbi, early on, had told Cheryl not to worry. She had phoned him and spoken to him briefly. He had invited her and Dan to services. Dan had had to work; she went alone. Her first time in synagogue was for Simchas Torah. The men danced in the aisles, and from that first evening, she had understood why, yearning on the far and final side of the hall while joy made its way among the worshipers, fringes touching lips and Law and lips again, as the bearer and the Scroll threaded through the dancers.

"Now," the Rabbi said, the next week, when he phoned. "Let's talk." He was a good listener. Cheryl had been doing more research.

"They'll find him?" Cheryl had hoped, when she finished explaining, imagining nine Jews descending on the care home bringing *tallith* and *siddhur* and a real *kippah*, and gathering up the survivor—no longer lost in translation—into *minyan*, into the garners of the book of life, his name written, his survival in the gentile wilderness of postwar bureaucracy—Medicare assignment—and loopy Christian rehab over at last. Rabbi Allen had smiled, but wouldn't say. "You'll figure it out," he told her.

He told her again, when she visited him in the hospital that next summer. She wasn't sure how ill he was—she had heard it was serious—or if he would remember her. Or if she would be allowed to speak with him. His door was wide open, and he called her by name.

"I'm still looking," she said.

"For what?"

"I can't stand it," she said. "He's still missing."

"He's not missing a thing," Rabbi Allen told her.

She had to say something about that. "Nobody he matters to knows where he is." An accusation and the thorn, the very thorn, in her heart made her confess, "I'm learning everything I need to know too late."

"Not everything," he said. Which could cut either way. She tried to think.

"Which one of you is still waiting in the dark?" he said.

So many things ran through her mind. Not a word came out of her mouth.

"Take a chance," he said. But she didn't.

"You'll figure it out," he said, shaking his head. Smiling. High beam. His blessing.

If the rabbi knew a better answer, he took it with him. After Thanksgiving, she received a parcel from his widow. "He wanted you to have this," she wrote. It was a menorah. She took it to school and set it up for show and tell one day in December. The two K-5 classes joined sections for the morning. Mrs. Brown's students formed an inner circle—on the carpet were Deshaun, Tyler, Kylie, Mary Grace, Emily, Jesús, the two Justins, Jimmy, Timmy, and Shameka. Rose was absent with chicken pox, Tyrone and Luís had half-days, one getting his eyes examined and the other his hearing, so they sat near the door to leave when called for. Cheryl's crew—David, Cal, Angela, Jevard, Omar, Starr, Archer, LaQuacia, Leonardo, Dwayne, Tasha and Rocky—formed the outer circle in their little chairs. Everyone could see the table. They had been learning all week.

She had been reading them the Chanukah story about the light in the window. They were good listeners. Each of them had a plastic dreidel, and knew about the game, about the chocolate coins. That would come later, during snacks. The menorah had only one candle now. "They add a candle every night," Cheryl said. "But they light it from this one each time. Every candle takes its light from this one." She pointed to the taller one, already lit. "Does anyone know what it's called?"

Leonardo knelt up in his chair to get taller, and waved his arm.

"My turn," Tasha blurted, "*My*—" but Leonardo got picked since he raised his hand.

"Where does that candle get its light?" he said.

Witnessing

Geneva Burnet had one of her dreams that summer morning. They always came just before getting up. They were bad dreams, and they shook her awake. What else to do but get up? Perhaps her restless rest had brought her to the place where the things she hated waited. She no longer tried to understand. Maybe, as the doctor suggested, it was low blood sugar. This time she made the best of her early start: showered and dressed, smoothed the bed, microwaved some oatmeal and drank a cup of coffee sitting in the dark on the screened porch. Day came on, one bird at a time. The redbird, first. Then the wren.

Geneva tied on her yard shoes and let the hens out into their lot, gathered eggs, and made that first walk through the garden. Her eyes felt parched and her hands trembled as she worked the latch. She could have used some more sleep, but what use lingering in bed and having another nightmare? The dream wasn't anything really. Just Earl, on the deck in the sun, the pecan trees behind him, and the way he—there were no words for it. No. She always came to the end of words. Even if she had words, why would they convey? Sometimes she let her mind creep up to the images, steal a second glance. If she could just describe it, nail it and him down, but how could she? It was so real, and he was back, he was coming in, about to jerk open the door straight-armed the way he always did so he could swing it, fling it past him, not step aside. In the dreams it was locked, and if he tried it, tried to open the door and it was locked, would his masklike face change, would it show astonishment, would his expressionless gray eyes seek hers, actually see her if she called his name? She couldn't speak. Each time, from nothing she had done or said, he'd begin to diminish. Not palely dwindle, no. Not be demolished. Simply, he would unsustain, unbillow, and gentle as a sun-dried sheet settling into the laundry basket, flatten in his earth-toned work suit onto the acorn-stained planks and—no other word for it—be hauled—by some force unseen and incalculable—backward by the heels backward, down and flimsy and pliant and faster and faster, snatched away, under the puppy-chewed banquette then down, rasping bonelessly backward over the edge of the porch, his arms extended toward her like Superman in flight, his hands the last to go, palms down but inert and the fingertips dragging lightly along brailling the boards—he still wore his ring—and then, finally . . . gone. Withdrawn. Vanished. Disposed. Yes. That was all the horror. Not so much, really. In her dream she was always as surprised to see him coming toward her as she was to see him go. Her heart would knock her awake. She'd lie there panting. The worst of it was the "by the heels" part. She hated that worse than any other bad news her eyes and heart might ever again take in, all his strength and certainty and intention and spark hollowed, emptied like a leaking grain sack and dragged away.

It hadn't been like that, not at all; he'd died at work, clean and in his right mind, sitting at a desk, something sudden, instant, with his heart, and gone. He didn't even fall from the chair. And she had never locked a door between them in their life. For a while after he died, nerves and counsel and vigilance required she tie a turkey bell onto the inner knob of the doors, so she wouldn't sleep through a home invasion. She got a lot of advice, and took some of it, but not about moving in to town or keeping any of the guns. She rested a lot better after Earl, Jr. cleared them away. Months would pass, and she'd not dream of him, but when she did, she'd wear the mood all day, like a wet shawl.

Today she just squalled and got it over with. Harsh, rib-bruising bark-ing sobs that left her throat raw and caused her to wonder if she'd started something she couldn't stop. When she'd had enough of that, she washed her face, combed her silvershot hair and clipped it into a perky topknot, put on her new sandals, and drove to town for a French pedicure. That was something different. It tickled her to see her toes looking like old-time nurses lined up in their white caps. She let Beatrice grill her an egg salad sandwich at the drug store, and afterward stopped by Sidney's, to see if they had any more Mexican zinnia plants; so far the deer and the gold-finches were sparing hers.

When she got home, she drove around to the back lane so she could set the flats of seedlings in the shade and water them. No automatic gates. She had to park, get out, and open them, lifting and shoving the right-hand one off into the honeysuckle because things were so overgrown. When she did, a brown thrasher flew out. Geneva drove through, parked, and walked down to shut the gates. While her back was turned, a silver Mercedes pulled in, came right on up. Geneva could feel the breath of the engine on her bare calves. She looked around.

A handsomely dressed woman emerged from the driver's side, apprais-ing the yard and house. Good gold jewelry, professional haircut, and linen over silk. Did she want directions? Was she lost? She was speaking into a cellphone. She ended the call and thumb-flipped the phone shut, pock-eted it. She had a dark leather portfolio with the seam unzipped, ready, clamped under her arm. No one came out this way unless they meant to buy or sell. Diesel fumes and quality cosmetics clouded the air. Geneva closed the right-hand gate, brought the other one up, and waited in the gap. The brown thrasher flew down from the apple tree and slipped into the vines again, working her way undercover along the fence with little shivers of vegetation, vanishing onto her nest. A single leaf fell.

"If I can help you," Geneva said.

The handsome woman turned to the car, signaled. Index finger, straight up. From the passenger side, a pale and very pregnant young woman in a denim jumper and red turtleneck T-shirt unfolded herself. She did not look at Geneva. The one in linen and silk did. "We are visiting in your neighborhood today and we thought we'd stop by and see if you have any questions for us."

For a moment Geneva did not have any questions, and then, silently, *Tax assessor? Avon? Census?* Ah . . . "Are you Jehovah's Witnesses?" She stood quite still. She did not waver even slightly from nervousness or annoyance. She had the home field advantage, which cheered her, but she also had regrets. *A minute sooner, and I'd have been through out here and back in the house.* She let herself regret using the back drive with its clunky old gates, and more poignantly regret the sixteen ounces of sweet tea at lunch. She needed to go to the bathroom. Soon. She braced herself to be civil, wily as a serpent and gentle as a dove. And brief, brief, brief.

Most of the time, when Geneva saw strangers coming to her door in pairs, she did not answer the bell. She just wasn't ready for this, today, wasn't up to it. She drew in a careful and steadying breath, and tried to think of an "opener." Geneva had not tried to testify about anything or to change anyone's mind in years, and besides, so far as she knew, no one had ever changed the mind of a Witness. The pregnant girl looked tired and rumpled, like it had been a long day. She was not a stately ship of the line like the driver.

"You're my neighbor," Geneva said to the girl, recognizing her. No more purple bangs. Sometimes they walked, the girl and her dog. Up the hill, down the hill, up the hill, down the hill. Along the old logging road. Sometimes straight through the woods. They'd vanish into the shadows.

"In the A frame," the girl said.

The driver said, "This is Amy, and I am Mrs. Burke. Iona. Burke."

You don't own her, Geneva thought. She looked at the apprentice again, the dark circles under her eyes, her swollen ankles, her sheaf of shining hair held back by a schoolgirl headband.

Last summer Geneva's church had offered a class in Witnessing to Witnesses. Geneva had picked up the brochure in the narthex, intending to memorize the practice questions and scripture references, but found she couldn't memorize them, and then decided not to attend. *Genesis? Something about Genesis?* She didn't remember the first thing. *If she just asked them to leave right now, would they? What if she shut the gate and sprinted to the house?*

"Do you oppose evolution?" Mrs. Burke asked.

"Yes!" Amy didn't hesitate.

Mrs. Burke—there was no other word for it—glared at the girl, then settled her hand onto the Amy's arm.

Geneva glanced at Mrs. Burke's hand and then at Mrs. Burke and then at Amy and then away. In the lengthening silence, "She means you," Amy whispered.

"I'm the one who found your dog's tags and collar," Geneva told Amy. "I'm the one who left it in your mailbox."

"A message," Amy said. She sounded like a little girl. "That was you? I got your message . . . I just didn't call back. Well, you know that." She brushed her hand across her forehead. "My husband works at night; he sleeps during the day."

"You might be interested in some options," Mrs. Burke said. She was looking through papers in the portfolio. Amy helped her steady it.

"He's the one on the motorcycle," Amy whispered over her shoulder to Geneva. She looked pleased.

Geneva noticed the wedding ring and sensible little diamond on the girl's finger. Her hands were puffy, and reminded Geneva of going to the mall a few months after Earl died, and asking at Macy's if they had something to help the gold band slide over her arthritic knuckles. She had never planned to remove the ring, but the swollen finger had turned a dull rose color, and throbbed. The jeweler had to cut the ring, but first had asked if it were inscribed, and when she said yes, required her to sign a paper that she consented no matter what destruction of the inscription ensued, and then in a moment it was done, the gold cut through and the ring lying on the glass countertop. Forty-six years. It looked so small. The cut was clean.

The jeweler studied his work through his eyepiece and said, "What was the inscription?" She told him. It was simple, basic, all they could think of and afford at the time: her initials and Earl's.

"Well," he told her, "this is your lucky day. And I may buy a lottery ticket on the way home myself . . ." The jeweler's blind and random cut had fallen exactly between the two monograms; they were intact. He could repair the gap, resize the ring, and she let him. But she did not wear it again.

"You have a tall husband. Maybe you will have a tall baby," Geneva told Amy. "I did."

Mrs. Burke made her best offer, several tracts, a business card, a website and free Bible lessons in the privacy of one's own home. Geneva waved her off. "No, ma'am," she said, "no sale. Final answer."

Amy looked worried. "You realize," she said, patting herself above her heart, "Some of us will reign, and some will serve." She broke from pledge-pose, and moved her hand with its bitten nails palm up across the air between herself and Geneva, offering nothing but the warning. Mrs. Burke said, "Only 144,000 will reign in Heaven. Do you know how many billions of people will live and die on this earth?"

Geneva thought about it. She stepped back inside her boundaries and closed the gate. "All of them," she said, dropping the latch.

Amy got in the Mercedes and shut the door. Mrs. Burke said, "If you change your mind, let us know." She tucked a tract into the fence, wove it into the chain link. They were gone, backed out and heading down the hill, before Geneva got to the house.

That fall, Amy stopped by on a walk. She had the baby in a stroller, and the dog was trotting along with them. Amy hesitated. "I know your chickens are fenced. You don't have a cat do you?" She gave a hand signal and the dog bellied down, alert. "He'll chase 'em. He loves to run. He about climbs the tree after a squirrel." She uncovered the baby's face, held the blanket away so Geneva could see. "Spitting image," she said. "Baby Jeff."

"Junior?" Geneva had never seen the man without his motorcycle helmet, so she was not in any position to compare.

"Well, see, Jeff's the junior. So Baby Jeff is Three." They were sitting on the benches in the yard, by the birdbath. "Me and Jeff and the baby is three," Amy said, "but what I mean is the baby is Three in Roman numerals. They're on his birth certificate."

Amy wouldn't come in the house, and she wouldn't take refreshment. "If you don't mind, we'll just sit here a little, then walk on. My husband works nights," she said. "He sleeps in the day, but he's a light sleeper, and we just clear out so he can. The baby's teething." She glanced at the sky. "They say it's gonna to rain tonight. Jeff'll take the car."

Remembering her early marriage, tenant to her own in-laws, Geneva said, "It's complicated."

"No," Amy said. "I'm stocked up, just in case."

"If you ever need anything—" Geneva began, but Amy said, "We're fine. We're perfect."

The dog launched after something in the woods, barking, leaping into sight and struggling under deadfalls, rustling and rummaging. He came sashaying back with a stick in his mouth. He lay in the sun, chewing it to pieces. He had a caramel colored chest, round silky hound ears and straight black legs. One ear was temporarily inside out. The girl flipped it back into place, and the dog looked up at her, gazed long, then returned to his stick. "He's a good dog," Amy said.

"Good company when you're there alone at night."

"He's not allowed in anymore," Amy said. "When we get our bonus, we're going to add on a run to the pen." She plugged the baby with his pacifier and lightly tented his face with the blanket. "Sometimes he barks." She giggled. "Rolly, not little Jeff." The sun was warm and mild but there was a breeze. A blue jay flew to the birdbath, looked at himself in the water, then flew off.

Geneva just couldn't let it drop. "I could call, on my way to the store, if you need anything."

"Don't!" Amy said. She popped up, scanning around, looking down the hill. She sat again. "I thought I heard him. What time is it?"

Geneva wasn't wearing a watch. She held her arm up toward the sun, and counted handwidths down to the horizon. "About 2:30, give or take five minutes."

Amy stared.

"Farmer trick," Geneva said. "It works, but you have to keep up with the almanac, when sundown is, if it's the afternoon, and sunup, for reading the signs before noon. Doesn't matter the length of your arm. An hour for each handwidth. Just subtract the number—" Was the girl even listening? She'd popped to her feet again.

"Here he comes," Amy said. She rolled the stroller down the concrete drive, and stood at the mailbox waiting for him, the dog at her heel, head lowered but level, tail at midmast, short bristling hackles rising along the stubborn streak on his spine. Amy worked her fingers under the collar and held him back. Jeff didn't stop at the corner, just geared down into second, and rounded up onto the main road. The sedan drove right by. For a moment it seemed he had not seen them, then he braked hard, jammed into reverse, raced backward and squealed to a stop. His window was already down, but he opened the door, leaned out, spat, shut the door. "Y'all get on home," he said. That was all. He roared off. Burned rubber hung in the air. The dog launched himself into the road and chased, barking; Jeff outran him.

"I wish he wouldn't do that," Amy said.

Rolly trotted back, flecks of foam on his dark grin. Geneva and Amy lingered. Geneva had found a few fallen persimmons and was showing Amy how to peel them. "It's ok," Geneva told her. "There's been frost."

Jeff was long gone one way, and Rolly another, off on a squirrel quest, when Amy said, "I thank you, Miss Geneva. But don't call. Ever. Please. When I'm Witnessing, I ride with Mrs. Burke, and the baby too, she don't—doesn't mind. I told you, we're perfect." Amy threw her persimmon seeds away instead of saving them to cut in half and find out if the little plant leaf inside looked like a knife—bad winter—or a spoon— good. Geneva mentioned it. Amy said, "We've got cable."

Geneva tried to think of something clever. Amy made her feel old. Maybe she was getting there, but she was no granny. There wasn't a rocker or an antimacassar on the whole place. Her own tireless grandmother had had such kind hands and ready ways. A granny would be clever with needles and would have been knitting something, sitting on her porch and accomplishing something granny-useful when Amy stopped by. Something for the baby or a nice soft scarf to lay—right this minute—around Amy's neck and cover that tattoo of barbed wire.

"I'm glad I know baby Jeff now," Geneva said. "Thank you."

Amy was pretty when she wasn't worrying. In that whispery confidential way she husked, "I wish you'd change your mind."

Geneva was baffled. She whispered too. "About what?"

"God," Amy said. She handed Geneva a crumpled tract from her sweater pocket. "*Is There Heaven on Earth?*" It had a rainbow on it, and tigers and butterflies. Amy pushed the stroller out onto the tar and gravel and started home. The dog was barking somewhere on the half-mile shortcut through the woods. Amy went slowly, tilting the stroller up off the front wheels, easing it over the rough spots. She looked back once, but she didn't wave.

Before Christmas Geneva saw the girl's car stop right in front of the house. Amy got out, tilted the seat forward, and let the dog in. He clambered up on the seat next to the baby. They drove on. About two weeks later Amy knocked at the front door. The holly wreath was still up, and the swags on the banisters. Amy was leaning against the storm door, staring through the holly circle, watching Geneva come on. Geneva had the wood door open, so that blue ribbon cactus of hers could get some light.

"Have you seen Rolly?" She spoke through the glass, using her hands as a megaphone. She didn't even wait till the door was unlatched. When it was, she wouldn't come in. "Rolly, my dog," she said. "Has he been by here?

"Rolly." She shook her head. "Not today. And I haven't heard him."

"Yesterday?" Amy shifted the baby on her hip. He was snowsuited in blue with a red-white-and-blue toboggan cap and swaddled in a blanket, but still his diaper was foul. "I gotta go," she said.

"Not yesterday, either," Geneva said.

Amy turned back. "When Mrs. Burke dropped me off, Jeff was already gone. So was Rolly." She sniffed. She turned away. "He's never stayed away all night."

"Has Rolly had his shots . . . and all that?"

"You mean cut? Yeah—yes, ma'am, he's clipped and chipped, all his shots and boosters. Well, mostly. I didn't have the money for rabies this year, but they say it lasts. . . . I was going to go to the clinic, but it rained." She chewed a chip off her thumbnail. "Rolly was dorm mascot. I went to college for a year. That's where I met Jeff. He chases squirrels and cats and cars, that's all. I mean Rolly." The baby was big now, and when he struggled, she had to wrestle back. He was patting at her hair with a red-mittened paw. "I'm so upset I don't know what I mean," she said. "I don't know what to do." She started back to the road.

"Do you want me to call you?"

"No."

"I could call Mrs. Burke?"

Amy sighed. "No. She don't—doesn't like him either." She settled the baby back in the stroller and they went toward home.

Geneva thought of something. She ran after the girl. "Do you want to ride around with me now and just look for him? We could."

Amy stepped back, drawing the stroller out of reach. She looked at Geneva sideways. "All I was wanting was to know if you've seen him. I wasn't longing for a ride. I got work to do."

For heaven's sake. "Good luck then." Geneva stayed busy herself, cleaning the oven, and afterward, deciding to clear out all the fancy leftovers from the refrigerator, smarten things up, and get ready for the new year. She washed collards and put the peas on to soak. It was toward evening when she thought, "I ought to pray about that dog." She had made a cup of Lady Grey and was sitting listening to the radio, but she turned the swap meet down. She did not know why it soothed her to hear folks trying to trade screen door springs and old commodes and dried up nanny goats and percolator knobs and canning funnels. The show was about over and Geneva had got as far as, "Now, God—" when the timer went off for her pound cake. She had to go see, and afterward, it was one thing and another. She let the cake cool, then cut it in half, and drove down the hill to the A frame. The sedan was gone and the motorcycle too, and the dog, and no lights on. They weren't home, so she slid the foil wrapped package into the mailbox and tied the silvery Happy New Year balloon to the flag. She took the other half of the cake over to Beatrice's. Her sister was down from Charlotte, and they played Hand and Foot and Mexican Train until two in the morning, stoking along on chicken salad, captain's crackers, cocktail peanuts and ginger ale with a splash of cranberry juice in it.

In the spring, when wild cherries and pears had bloomed, the apples were about to, and all the leaves were out, tender and bright green, and golden-dusted air so thick the light had a stormy look, here came someone stomping up onto Geneva's porch, tracking through the pollen. He didn't ring the bell. She was in the back of the house ironing when he raised his fist to the door.

It was Motorcycle Man, as Geneva thought of Jeff. She had never seen him without his leathers on. He didn't look so tall or lean. He was worked up over something. She hesitated a moment before she clicked the thumb latch off. He didn't wait for her. He opened the door himself.

"You know my wife," he accused. "I'm Jeff."

"What is it?"

"The dog," he said. He turned and looked toward the road.

"Please just tell me," Geneva said. "Please just tell me what I can do to help."

"Not a goddamn thing," he said. "Just keep in the house. I'm about to use a gun and you need to stay off of me and out of my way and you do not need to call the law. I'm just telling you. You understand? You will not call the law."

"You have a gun?" Geneva didn't see one.

"I'm going back home to get it. The dog has been in the hospital for seventeen days, and a month of rehab—did you know there is dog rehab and massage? And transfusions? Witnesses don't do transfusions, y'know. She didn't call Mrs. Burke, and she didn't call me. Didn't ask me. Just signed the dog in at the desk with me as owner, because I'm not a Witness. She okayed all of it in my name. She knew better than to ask me; already knew I'd vote like a true believer . . . Cat scans and x-rays and IV fluids? Fractured pelvis and an eye patch and a drain in his shoulder and a concussion? And he has just been home three freaking days and has done it again. Chewed through a ski rope and chased me up the hill just now and got his lights knocked out by a car coming the other way. I know two legs are broken, and maybe his hip again. I just got the last one paid off."

"Rolly?" Geneva tried to see. "Just now?"

"He's out there," Jeff said. "He's not going anywhere." He laughed. "Trust me." He had his left arm up, propping the storm door open. "I dragged him over to your mailbox. I tied him there. His jaw's broke; he won't be chewing."

Geneva could see, looking under the buttress of his arm, something dark on her side of the road.

"I want you to stay in this house," he told her. He wiggled his right foot, balancing on its heel. He was wearing boots with zippers. "I want you to stay off the phone," he added. "Just leave this to me."

"Amy," she said.

"No," he said. "No."

"She'll ask me," Geneva said, from a place of agony. "She'll be looking. Never ever tell her? She'll go on looking, listening, hoping."

"She's pregnant again," he said; "for the first time I'm thinking that might be good news. Maybe a girl."

"Oh," Geneva said. "A girl."

"It's ok," he said. "We've got a boy." He didn't give her time to think. He stepped back from the door. Before he pushed it shut, he said, "Close your main door and stay away from the windows. I'm not asking, I'm telling. It's my business. I don't want you running out, or reporting it, adding to our troubles." He was gone. Just like that. He pulled into her drive, then backed out into the road and zoomed toward home. She stood in front of the main windows till she saw him come back through the same dust he had just raised. He didn't park in the drive. He pulled off on the far shoulder. He tipped the front seat forward, and got a sack—geranium pink—from the back floorboard. Pillowcase, she was thinking. She had seen those sheets on their line; it made Geneva proud of her, though she had never mentioned it. Nothing smells better than sheets dried in fresh air and sun.

The gun was in the pillowcase. Jeff loaded it while he was standing there. He laid the pillowcase on the road, and dragged the dog toward the edge of the ditch. It struggled a little, but not for long. He leaned from the waist, and straight-armed, put the gun— . . . at which point Geneva stepped back, stood behind her closed and locked front door, her hands over her ears, her eyes winked shut. One shot. She crouched against the wall, trying not to think about what could possibly be next. Nothing. She waited a little longer. The silence fooled her; it wasn't over. When she stepped across to look from the front window, he was untying the ski rope from her mailbox post, dragging the body on the pillowcase headfirst across the road, down the bank into the woods. That was bad enough. Worse, he brought the pillowcase and rope back, stood a moment by his car door, studying the fabric in the bright light, smelling of it, then gave it a shake, a smart snap, and put the gun back in it, pocketed the shells, and laid the swaddled gun on the floor of the car. He stowed the section of ski rope on top. Again, he used Geneva's driveway for his turnaround, but this time he backed in. She didn't think he looked her way. He rolled silently down the hill with the clutch in. A quarter of an hour later he roared by on the motorcycle, helmeted and in his leathers, on his way to work again, dressed for speed now, making up time.

Geneva went over and over it. For hours. *Nothing that happened here today is a crime,* she told herself. She knew without having to see it that the dog was unburied; Jeff had simply dragged him out of sight and dumped him. She knew the heat would not be her friend, and that it would take buckets and wheelbarrow loads—loads and loads—of ditch dirt and yard dirt and woods dirt—to make a good enough barrow over the corpse to keep Amy, as she pushed the stroller and walked along—never giving up her faith, hope, or love—from sniffing out the truth. Geneva imagined how tired she would be from all that digging and hauling, and how work sweat and fear sweat would reek around her and dog stink and green flies as she shoveled while he slept the daylight away, drapes drawn in his air conditioned house. He'd sleep when he slept and wake when he woke. Geneva would be ever and always uneasily harking as Amy herself harked, for oncoming bike or sedan.

She decided to wait until morning to start digging. It would be cool, and he would not be roaming. She would have to keep an eye out for Amy, that's all. She was bound to stop by. "What do you think happened to him?" she'd ask the girl. And then she'd say, "What do you think is the best possible thing that could be happening to Rolly?" and let Amy think of that, and then she'd tell the girl, "Well, that's my prayer," and maybe that would be all there was to say. When Geneva worked all that out, she was able to sleep. Sometime in the night she jumped awake, remembering the way he had brought the pillowcase out of the woods into the light, studied it, smelled of it, and then put it back in his car. For his pillow, or Amy's? She thought about how they would lie in that house, and no way to tell the truth.

She thought about how she had climbed the garret stairs five years ago, up to where Earl had his little workshop, his "home away from home" as he had called it. She never had bothered him up there. She hoped she never had bothered him anywhere. She hoped he had felt respected, cherished, honored, and obeyed. She was going up to bring down the suit coat Earl was to be buried in, and found the opened carton of cigarettes camouflaged along a rafter and the half-empty bottle of Wild Turkey not even hidden in the wall insulation, and the condoms in the pocket of his deacon's suit. He had died in November, just before Thanksgiving. It was terribly cold for a burying. The cold set in. That was the year some folks joked that hell froze over. That was the year she found out that frostbite, like burns, heals from the edges, snow that lasts on the ground three days will soon be snowed on again, and no matter how long a spell lasts, something breaks it, and even the hardest winter is right before spring if you hold on to love long enough.

Mad Woman in the Attic

The first week of July a tropical depression stalled out upstate and it rained and rained. RoyBoy's almost fiancée, Connie, was getting her tattoos laser-removed instead of going to the beach. Connie was between jobs, so she was using up her tax refund and severance pay for a slight cash discount and financing the rest on two credit cards. These dermatologic deletions were to be a surprise for RoyBoy. Since Connie's tattoos did not have any green or yellow ink, the consultant told her it might not take but one long session front and back especially on the older ones, but he warned it would be seriously unpleasant to get them all ablated in one afternoon. Even though Q-switch laser zapping did not take but a few minutes per square inch compared to getting inked, it was more than ten times as expensive to erase one, with a follow up of three weeks of healing and the prospect later of more zapping if needed and then three weeks of getting over that. "Bloodless, low risk, minimal side effects" the ruby and alexandrite laser ads in the *Tri-County Trader* said. Treatments would kill all of Connie's summer, just about. No tanning. All covered up, maybe itchy. Maybe scabbed. Connie had purchased two containers of medical makeup that blocked out port wine birthmarks, but she couldn't hope to use it again to even things out until after the laser scabs fell off. She was probably going to have to sleep on her side for almost two months and no more soaking baths for the duration.

RoyBoy was worth it.

Connie had caught RoyBoy on the rebound, caught him on the first bounce; a sense of urgency—anything to keep him from bouncing again—made her willing to suffer. He was worth catching, as good as a prince, thinking locally not globally, which was pretty much how Connie thought. Since this was a surprise for him she didn't answer her cell phone or he'd have been right there at the clinic out of sympathy because he had heard it wasn't easy to get tattoos removed and also because it could be somewhat tricky, depending on where the tattoos were.

RoyBoy knew where they were.

RoyBoy was not her first almost fiancée.

When RoyBoy had arrived with Connie at his mother's house in mid-May to have dinner and get acquainted, Eleanor, taking one look at Connie's visible and public illustrations said, "Forget working in a bank," as though that was every girl's American dream.

Actually, RoyBoy's un-inked and recently ex-girlfriend Sandy had worked in the bank and still worked in the bank, which is why RoyBoy had joined the county employees credit union after they broke up. He didn't even want to risk drive-through window encounters although there had been a time when he lived for them, mapping the detours into his day. After Sandy and he broke up like a cheap mirror he switched to the night watch, changed laundromats, changed grocery stores, reset his auto-tune in the truck, and fell off the wagon. Some thought he slipped; others thought he threw himself. Connie, a bit off course herself, recognized signs of despair, followed him out to his truck near midnight at Short's Steaks, got him into her car instead of his truck and drove him back to her own place, listened, learned interesting tidbits about Sandy—"She keeps a vanilla bean in her sugar bowl!" "She's never had a moving violation." "She likes to iron!"—and heard about RoyBoy's plans to move on up into plain-clothes. While he slept, Connie washed and dried his uniform, ironed sharp creases back in, French-pressed some coffee, made him breakfast, left him alone to shave and dress, and drove him back to Short's to his truck when he was ready to go. Before he did, she borrowed his pen and wrote something on the back of one his business cards, the official ones with the county seal and the sheriff's address; she reached through the window and slipped it into his shirt pocket and buttoned it safe. He could look or not, later. Of course he looked. When he did, he was surprised to see not a telephone number or name, just letters and digits—her license plate. He could detect her if he cared to. Unlike Sandy, she'd had some wants and warrants, mostly parking in the wrong place or going too fast. It was the first interesting thing that had happened to him in months. The next was finding that Connie was better than he remembered, when he did look her up. Maybe better than Sandy. His cauliflower heart had taken quite a beating over the years, but it was still beating. Love, it seemed, was not going to ruin him. "She's good for me," he told Eleanor. For the first time, Eleanor felt a kind of dread about this one and not just annoyance.

In June—because he asked her—Connie went with him to close out his bank account; nothing in it for her except the chance to be seen in public with him, doing something official. It felt like taking a next step. Connie saw it all as steps; each one, however small, was important. Connie had bought a new pair of shoes for the trip to the bank because, even though they were "just stepping inside for a moment" as RoyBoy put it, to Connie that moment felt momentous. Connie wanted more than a moment, and she watched her step. They both cased the bank like robbers. No Sandy in sight. Inside, Connie inquired, making it sound like she wanted to see Sandy. No, it was Sandy's day off; no, she wasn't in the vault.

Truly, the day was going well. Connie sat on a bench in the lobby, hands in her lap, knees together, ankles together, tanned legs on a clean diagonal, apparently effortlessly poised, back straight, a Miss America candidate waiting to be questioned about global warming and breed-specific dog bans. RoyBoy returned from the vault, extended his hand, and she took it lightly and stood. He held the door for her, and Connie walked out as though she had a crown on her head. It was a relief, but also a letdown when they drove away. They both sighed at exactly the same instant. That cued a simultaneous laugh. She kicked her shoes off at once and hooked them by their high heels to his gun rack.

"Next," she said.

When they parked at the credit union, she pulled on her short red cowgirl boots, jumped from the cab and landed flatfooted, settled herself, unclipped her twisted-up spiral curled perm and shook it into a froth, clipping only one side back up, leaving the rest to blow free. She used her reflection in the storefront window to judge how far to roll her skirt up at the waistband to show a bit more leg. This time she held the door for him, and inside, she introduced him around. She knew a lot of the clerks and customers. So did he. It was Connie who had suggested the credit union; before her job got furloughed, she worked in the county tag and tax office. She had already applied for a job in the clerk of court's office, and also in probate, but hadn't heard yet. Those clerks dressed up a bit, sometimes they testified in court, and it was another reason she knew she had to move on past her tattoos. Mainly, though, she had to admit, it was because of Eleanor. RoyBoy's mother had some kind of power over him, even though he couldn't be in the same room with her for an hour without getting so mad he'd slam the door when he left.

In May on that Sunday at dinner Connie and RoyBoy both felt it when Eleanor implied bank, not credit union, as the American dream. That let RoyBoy feel he had come down in the world. Wasn't the credit union lobby busy and noisy, a storefront on a side street with a drive-through at a kiosk in the back parking lot? The credit union lobby was practical and working-class, not shabby, not even secondhand, but charmless, with chrome-legged plastic chairs in kindergarten colors, eerie flickering fluorescent lighting in bars across the low ceiling, and off-centered runners of indoor-outdoor carpet on the linoleum, no posh rugs laid atop carpets, no wing chairs and upholstery in cathedral colors, no oil paintings of local merchants and board members, no red velvet roping on brass standards channeling traffic to the tellers, no little crystal bowls of mints on the counter, no dark vast mirrors reflecting back the chandeliers, no urns of silk flowers and churchlike whispers and gentle tones, no holy hush as in the bank where Eleanor sat on the needlepoint seat of a polished chair at a polished table with a cool marble top clipping coupons. Farmers and

Merchants had been there from the beginning; its façade was quarried local stone and the bank's name and dates were carved deep. Curbside, there was an upping block, where ladies and gents had stepped from carriages, or mounted to horseback. As a child, RoyBoy had asked if that was where they had the slave auctions. Eleanor hadn't missed a step. "This is where white folks get bought and sold," she said.

Sitting there at Eleanor's table on Sunday, Connie struggled against feeling that no matter what she might dream, or how high she might rise, or even how well the laser tattoo treatments went, she would never "qualify"—not even—she thought ruefully—for a job in the credit union. And certainly not as an in-law to Eleanor. Eleanor was lucky like that about inflicting collateral damage. She had once taken down three clay pigeons with a skeet gun and only one cartridge, but that was in her prime and with practice. A trick shot. Still, loaded with rock salt not pellets, she could tell she had stung her son and his girl as well. The sweethearts reached for each other's hand across the heavy heirloom linen tablecloth, but the gap was wider than they could close. Eleanor had seated them to each side of her throne. They made a perfect triangle. Once, last year, in early days when Eleanor had picked on Sandy, RoyBoy had got up, politely said, "Excuse me," and moved his plate and silver and sweet tea in its Waterford goblet across the table, and settled himself hip and haunch beside his girl, a chess move challenging the queen that had only made things worse and left Sandy a hostage pawn between them. Eleanor never took hostages, though. She never took any sweethearts seriously either; she just watched and waited. Eleanor's genius strategy was to withhold. She besieged with indifference and never, ever gave ground. She had no idea what had blasted Sandy from RoyBoy's orbit, but she could truthfully say, "It was nothing I've done."

RoyBoy's losing Sandy was not Eleanor's fault, but she triumphed nevertheless at RoyBoy's devastation when the sudden abyss between her son and what Eleanor called "that born again cheerleader" widened. RoyBoy had said he couldn't and wouldn't tell her what had gone wrong or how his dream had been betrayed. All he would say was "It's over," a simple decree, and he was so calm, so sure, Eleanor shivered, thinking how like his father that was. Perhaps one day Eleanor would learn the details, but what—when all is said and done—is true love? One more relic for the attic wrapped in a tissue of lies.

RoyBoy was the marrying kind, but he had always said, brutally frank considering his own parents' story, "I'll be true, and I'll marry only once, and it'll be for love." As though it were all up to him!

At thirty he was still single. He had come along late in Eleanor's marriage, almost too late, when Eleanor, at forty, had tried everything else to get and keep King's attention. Eleanor had outlasted them all, all of King's flutters—the school teacher, the lady golfer, the dental hygienist, the choir director, the women's tennis champion, the floral delivery gal, the veterinary assistants—there had been two of those flashing through like meteors, six weeks apart, the year of their divorce. The list was well-known, contemptibly familiar and unchallenging, like a paddock with easy practice hurdles. Only one jump on the circuit made her pause. Every time, Eleanor faltered her only falter, a momentary balk and then she rose like a champion and took her fence—the fence that divided her marriage into before and after: King had gone fishing in South America and come back with, more or less, plans for a trophy wife slightly older than their son. Eleanor had landed hard, but she had kept her seat. In fact, she had kept everything, including the furniture, house, and photo albums.

Eleanor thought RoyBoy, in instincts and susceptibilities, was very like his old man. In college, RoyBoy had even swained a lady vet, but it wasn't fate or destiny, it was like many romances, circumstantial: at the time, RoyBoy had had an accident-prone puppy. He had been no more than a big-footed accident-prone puppy himself. The dog grew out of it. The lady veterinarian married someone her own age, another vet specializing in large animals, with an established practice.

RoyBoy was wearing his uniform. How Eleanor hated that uniform. She had hated it long before she ever saw it, from the day when she and King had asked what their son wanted to do with his life, and he'd said, law. What he meant was law and order, preserve and protect, maybe make detective one day, that kind of law, not, as his parents had hoped, hang a shingle and build a show house and a make seemly slow rise to a judge's bench and maybe politics later on. Here he sat, nine years after college and still a deputy, no nearer plainclothes or a concealed weapon. Imagine wearing a gun to Sunday dinner! He and Connie had plans, he told Eleanor when she phoned to invite them to come by after church if they weren't too busy. She knew they wouldn't be in church, but she did not mind playing the game. They would, he promised, "work her in" but they couldn't stay. And, had warned, he was on duty that evening. Eleanor tried not to think of how, after Connie dropped him off in time for his shift—they came to dinner in her car—he would buckle himself into that earth-toned patrol car and prowl the county in the dark all night looking for someone else's trouble. Back in the woods as she was, she could still hear from time to time the sirens, the helicopters, wind-born beastly howls.

Above all, Eleanor hated it that RoyBoy had got sober, and she hadn't. She knew because of the blow up with Sandy he had lost sobriety for a few weeks, and she was pretty sure Connie had helped him back.

Eleanor had made RoyBoy move out, the first wild year he came back after college, after he finished special forensics coursework at Glynco and earned his credentials and badge. She didn't want to listen for him to come in. She already had broken herself of that habit, with King.

RoyBoy used to stop by for a drink after work. Sometimes King did too. Family time. Eleanor acted like she and King were still married. King flirted, like he and Eleanor had never been married. RoyBoy didn't act at all; the mask that came off when he was drinking revealed the same Roy-Boy he'd always been, a child whose parents had used each other up and divorced, whom their son could not divorce.

Eleanor said, "It used to be harder, getting rid of tattoos. Had to cut." At that moment they were watching Lou Fisher, Eleanor's Sunday help, carve the rare prime rib.

"Count on Mothah to go all out," RoyBoy said.

"What if I told y'all I knew firsthand?" Eleanor took a spoonful of horseradish and let it gently roll onto her plate without touching the spoon to her food, then passed the little dish by its silver bail on to Connie.

"Now you may have heard I'm headstrong," Eleanor said to Connie, picking up her knife. Connie started to nod then didn't. RoyBoy leaned across, took the silver and crystal condiment server from Connie.

"What if I said I got a tattoo—and remember: no lasers and do-overs back then—before my wedding day?"

Astonished, RoyBoy put down the horseradish with a little thump.

"What if I told you, impulsively, passionately I borrowed my brother's car and dashed up to Phenix City and I had King's 'X' tattooed on my spine—King's brand," Eleanor explained to Connie, "positioned exactly to show above my wedding dress, low cut, long train, Valenciennes lace, double tier veil of illusion, wafting tuberoses and orange blossoms, everything proper, revealing just enough of that mark so every soul in the First Baptist Church could see it and know that I was the property of Roy Albert, that I was the King's own."

"Really?" Connie said, reviving like a wilted hydrangea after a drenching.

Eleanor sliced through her meat, stacking it on the back of her overturned fork in the English fashion, charm school lessons never failing.

"Well, hell *no*, chickie," Eleanor said reasonably, her fork poised. "Do you think I am out of my mind?"

During the first week of July the tropical depression, Alberto, had dumped about two feet of rain on saturated ground as it moved slowly northward over the state. By the sixth of July, the runoff from the northern watershed was gathering force with the high waters farther south. Brooks and streams and rivers rose, widened beyond banks, and swept on toward the gulf. What seemed to be the flood of the century was beginning to swell into a five hundred year event. RoyBoy turned his wipers on their highest speed, eased his cruiser to the crown of the road, and kept moving along the centerline. He left another message on Connie's phone. The Laser Clinic wasn't anywhere near the river and Connie's apartment was above the dam, so all he told her was to stay put. "Sweetie," he said the first call, for hello. "Baby?" he pled the second time, signing off. The next call was at 3 A.M., when he got the word that Sumter County deputies were going house to house, knocking on doors, telling folks to grab their kids, dogs, life jackets if they had any. Connie was miles east of there, but also miles south. Where the hell was she at 3 a.m.?

"Jesus goddammit, Connie" was all RoyBoy prayed that time. Within minutes, power and the phones began to fail. When Connie, who had been deep far gone in medicated sleep because of the tattoo treatments, finally picked up messages, she listened to all but kept that last one, punching 9 to save it for fourteen days, replaying it again and again in the shelter just to hear how he said it, no kidding around, all man, and especially the sound of her name, the way his stress made him sound so close, close enough to kiss. She hated being high and dry, and him being on duty, out there in it.

Before midnight, while they still thought the dam would hold, Roy-Boy rang his mother, told her she needed to keep the radio on and pay attention, and make sure her cell phone was charged. She'd lived on the river for more than forty years. "I've got an axe in the attic," she told him. "And I've got batteries for the lantern and radio and shells for the gun." Her help had gone, but Eleanor didn't need any help. It was inconceivable that she would ever be anywhere but above it all. The same with King, on the other side of the river, high and dry. Maybe that's why she and RoyBoy didn't worry about him, didn't feel they needed to warn him. It could not be imagined or forecast how the river would swell, and not only with water. The surge from the breached dam would shove along scouring debris and natural chaos, but there would be other havoc besides limbs and whole oaks and sycamores—the surge gathered in trailer homes, ski boats, semi-trucks, roiling mounds of fire ants bobbing along like basketballs, reptiles, rare birds, King's lions, the zoo's buffalo, lawn chairs, caskets, emus and ostriches, zebras, deer, crocodiles, domestic and exotic livestock of all sorts, as well as fieldworkers, trapped motorists, household pets and pests. Not all were lost. But some were never found, hide nor hair.

After a time, there would be no more surging, just the slow rise. It would go on for days. Bridges and roads would be gone. Some detours would take months. Or helicopters.

The *New York Times* reported one hundred dams, mostly recreational lakes, farm ponds, golf courses, and landscape features had given way in the record rainfall. "They were never built for flood control," the newspaper reported. Only two of those dams stood under state or federal regulation and the unregulated dams were considered no threat. When inspectors discovered that the Warwick Dam on Lake Blackshear near the southwest Georgia town of Cordele had been submerged, the water level was approximately the same on both sides of the earthen dam. All floodgates had been opened and the dam was reported as holding against a surge of 1.5 million gallons of water a second. RoyBoy, among many other emergency workers, had plenty to do, calls to make, and warnings to deliver. The last house call turned out to be his first rescue. RoyBoy had his hands full; he was glad he had finally gotten through to his mother. Now he would just do what he had to do, all he could, for anyone crossing his path, and hope that it was enough.

The water was eight inches over the road, and running fast to the southwest. RoyBoy backed around, careful to be sure he kept all four wheels on solid ground; he had the driver door open and he was looking back. The rearview and side mirrors were no good in the storm and dark. Suddenly the woman he was bringing out pretty much against her will and—as she put it in ignorance of her better judgment and full faculties—unsnapped her seatbelt, jumped from the patrol car and scampered back to her house. What was her name? What—"Mrs. Pitts!"

"I have to," she hollered, splashing off toward the dark house. "Wait for me." She had his LED torch. She left him holding the decrepit, dim-eyed sweet-breathed Chihuahua. In less than a minute she splashed back with a rumpled Christmas-themed shopping bag. "Got her," she said. She was in and settled before he could refuse livestock cargo. He could only see a towel covering whatever it was. Something shifted. Then something hissed and pecked the sack and shook its head up into the gap and he caught the warning spark in the broody hen's eye.

"Whoa," he said, thinking about the shelter rules. Before he could say "No," she had the towel tucked in all over, like a top crust on a chicken pie.

"She was on the back porch, on the shelf. She's got maybe another week before they hatch. If the yard's not dry, or I'm not back by then, what'll she do? "

He didn't know anything much about chickens. Too bad they weren't ducks. Before he could say so, she added, "she's not just a hen. She's family." They were almost to the shelter when she thought of the jar of peanut butter and heart medicine, both for the dog.

When they got to the armory, he helped her out, even gave her slickered back brisk little pats, flat-handed, farewell farewell; no hugs: rain and a hug weren't going to do that shopping bag much good, not to mention the little dog. RoyBoy almost got away then, but Mrs. Pitts followed him out again, knuckled on the shotgun window until he powered it down. She leaned back in, insisting they go back for the medicine.

Back? Couldn't she hear? He tapped on the radio. "*Lissen*," he said.

That road was already closed, the bridge under twelve inches of rising and turbulent water. Mrs. Pitts was no quitter.

"A matter of life and death," she said. The little dog's pop eyes gazed out at him from the cave of her raincoat; warm, curled against her chest, he yawned. Pink tongue and gums, gleaming fangs. "*You* lissen," she said.

"You need to tell that to somebody else, ma'am. Somebody in that building." He pointed. He could hear the National Guard generators keeping some of the lights on, powering the pumps. "There'll be somebody," he said. Anything to loose her grip on the car, to step her back, back, to let him get away to give someone else their chance. But now she had reached in, grabbing up the flashlight off the seat, shining it in his eyes. He took it back, gentle, extinguished it, then yelled, "Go!" so loud she swayed as though shoved, and he won. He raised the window, checked in and cleared via radio, hunkering down like a silverback over the wheel. He had his orders, and for him they were holy. RoyBoy hauled, mingling his strobes with the fluorescent lightning flickering on and on and the rumble of what must have been thunder. It was and it would be for God only knew how long raining straight down like Christmas tinsel.

Eleanor didn't give a damn about meteorologists, public safety, or the Corps of Engineers. She didn't panic or even rouse until the lights went out and she couldn't find the cell phone charger. Too late anyway. Probably it was in the car. Couldn't she just quick charge it off the car battery? She was wearing her keys around her neck. She had her little cold stocking stuffer magnesium flashlight on its cord around her wrist, and she headed for the garage. She wasn't the pioneer type, and she wasn't amused. In the blackout, she had lit candles; before she left the house, she checked to be sure they were safe: unattended, one harmlessly flaming in the shelter of a saucepan on the kitchen stove, three hurricanes in the hall on the bench on a metal tray well away from anything flammable or ruinable by wax, and a pair of votives in deep jars on the mantle. The house was still and quiet, oddly festive, even cozy. When she opened the door to the garage she stepped down to the concrete floor, and was surprised by the chill of water. It wasn't much, perhaps an inch. Even so, her peeptoe slippers were swamped. She kept them on, slogged to the car, and opened the door. Pleased, when the ceiling light came on, she clicked on the map lights as she slid in, connected the cell phone to its charger, and wondered if she ought to crank the car. But she couldn't, because she couldn't open the garage door. And she didn't want to die of fumes. What if she just backed the car, fast, through the garage door? Smashing her way out? And swung around and kept on going; there must be somewhere to go.

She couldn't remember what RoyBoy had said about the roads. No, not the roads. He had said, "shelter in place," in an official tone that had annoyed her. It was clear to her now that she was going have to do what he said, simply because she couldn't do anything else.

She did not know how long it would take to charge the phone. Was it charged yet? She tried to make a call. Nothing.

Would she run the car battery down by listening to the radio? Save it for later? Three minutes later was late enough. Of course, the radio was working, but did she want any more news? She charged the phone while a CD played. She amped up the volume a little, wished she had brought what was left of her drink with her. Mostly ice. That's what she always said. "Mostly ice and a little icebreaker."

When the CD looped back to track one, Eleanor turned off the ignition and settled the key lanyard around her neck. The cell was fully charged. When she stepped from the car she had a thrill—the water was now licking her ankles. Was, in fact, already above her ankles. For a moment she aimed the flash light at the floor, not believing it. Wasn't there a drain? Did she need to open it? She peered under the car, waved the light back and forth, Water coming in? Through the drain? Maybe it would go out, if she could get the garage door open. If she could get the door up, the garage would drain out and down the driveway . . . Wouldn't it? But how to lift the door without electricity. She had no clue.

As she watched, she realized the water *was* coming in around the door, and also coming up from the floor drain.

It took some time for her to comprehend.

Water coming in through the floor drain was not rain but river water. King had engineered the storm drains, diverting some rain to cisterns and the rest directed through tunnels bored at some expense out through the bluff and into the river, lined tunnels through limestone and grated against detritus and padlocked against trespass. The water she was standing in was the river. The drain was an open invitation to the flood of the century.

King had graded the land and sited the house with its two storeys deep in the rock. He himself had graded and blasted and engineered the drive, planning the garage and first floor to be underground to improve the heating and cooling, with a southern exposure along the back. The second floor, therefore, was really at ground level. He had not worked recklessly. He had built to be above and to withstand the hundred year floods. If water was coming in then the river was already above century flood marks. When Eleanor had got this far in her considerations, consternation and anger washed over her like fire. She had trusted him with her house, home, and heart. Who was he to be trusted like that?

She thought about it, counting old losses, imagining new. For the first time she realized the storm was not going to pass her by. What was downstairs? Downstairs was the archive of their marriage; even his mother's china was there, stored, displayed in the breakfront. He had left it to her.

Now she faced it, acknowledged it. How their stuff—his stuff—didn't fit in with the new life, all modern and earth-toned and organic, glass, steel, and stone. Was there anything here she ought to or cared to move to higher ground? Without exertion, without raising a hand she could, she saw, inflict serious damages. Oh but hadn't she always played fair?

Something inside her said, *Maybe not*. She looked around.

Stunned, she set the flashlight atop the car and tried the phone, the only number she not only knew by heart but also by touch; King's. He didn't answer, but his machine picked up. She left no message, just dead air, because before she could think what to ask, to say, to claim or to blame, she realized that the other side of the river might as well have been on the other side of the moon.

"Houston, we have a problem," she murmured, folding the phone shut.

Her feet and legs were cold, heavy. Where they were wet and now drying, they felt like she was wearing boots without socks. She got the flashlight and went back in to the house. Even when she saw the water on the lip of the garage step, she believed it would stop. Of course it would stop.

She took off her ruined shoes, tossed them out into the dark garage, closed and bolted the service door like the flood could be turned with a key. Or awaited permission. She imagined it out there, patient and slack and humble as a stray dog. She had no intention of letting it in.

She lay on the couch, dozing, and when her little dog in its crate in the kitchen woke her, yipping and whining and scratching, Eleanor roused. When she put her feet on her mother-in-law's Persian carpet, they squelched three inches of water. By the time she got to the kitchen, it was more like five inches. Something awful was happening, and fast, and Eleanor was more than annoyed. Time to take this whole mess seriously.

She found candles, her cigarettes and lighter, made several trips, and got the dog and the crate and some pet supplies relocated upstairs. She brought up the rest of the ice from the freezer, using her club trophy from the golf tournament for a bucket. She pocketed some crackers and some white cheddar, sacked a fresh bottle of lemon vodka, and half a bottle of brandy. She remembered to go back down, find another set of replacement batteries for the flashlight. The main floor bath made gurgling noises as the drain began to backflow. She fled.

Eleanor sat on the stairs, moving higher step by step, as the waters continued to rise. She could hear the slap of waves against the house, too, so the underground swell was being joined by some exuberant overland wash. King had built with bunker concrete and steel. Eleanor did not fear the house would wobble and unsocket itself like a baby tooth. Nor did she imagine she would—but she did—have to wade through water to get to the mantle and lift down her .410 cutdown single-shot gun. Handful of shells into her pocket. This time when she started higher on the stairs, she turned at the landing to look. Water was welling higher than the candles on the coffee table, and she watched them wink out. The smoke drowned too. The hurricanes in the hall were next. And the kitchen, suddenly, was dark.

She sat on the landing, at the turn. Nothing so organized or verbal as thoughts filled her mind, teeming in neutral. Freewheeling discoveries. A few regrets. The darkness and silence seemed to stimulate flashes of insight, images long forgotten, moments. If she could call anyone, or write a letter, was this when? Sobering. More sobering: Who? A very short list. And she couldn't imagine wasting time apologizing to anyone. "Ridiculous," she said. Blank, she pulled herself to her feet, turned, and climbed the rest of the way. She was seventy-one years old, and for the first time she realized—this was the exact moment—she was done with middle age. A ripeness, not a decadence. She claimed; she chose. She laid that burden down. Like those ruined slippers she had shied into the murky waters of the garage.

She was fit, had kept trim and moisturized. Had a coach and a trainer to keep her golf game strong. It had been a while since she had needed to rearrange her trophy cabinet to make room for a new one, though. She didn't like the idea of a handicap. Or of age as a handicap. She still looked like herself in the yellowing photos. Her favorite image of herself was a painting from a Polaroid taken in a club, when she was singing. She sat on the piano, and the artist had captured the folds of the midnight blue velvet, the luster of the pearls. The painting was her brand. It had been moved to her dressing room. She liked to be reminded. She paused before it as she collected clean dry clothes. It had hung downstairs until King left. The girl he left behind him, that was how she thought of it. It never occurred to her she might need to move it to the attic.

She settled the things she had brought up, and got the dog into his crate.

"Now," she said. Taking—and leaving—stock. She had climbed to get this far; she would keep on climbing; she would not go back down. There had to be another way, and she would find it.

Shivering, she washed up with the vodka, scrubbed herself dry and changed to sober clothes, survival gear. Not vogueing, just layering on. She stayed chilled even though the house was humid and mild. Socks this time, and her New Balance walkers. For some moments she pondered the jewelry in its velvet-lined chest. Nothing costume; all pawnable. She shook her head, considering any use; bribes? What if the ATMS were swept away? Who cares? She had A-1 credit.

Instead of putting on, she removed rings. Bracelets. The watch. Her earrings. Anything that might snag or tear from her or make her vulnerable to electrical shock—or restless refugees in a public shelter. Would it come to that? It might.

When she next checked the water it was over the landing; she went to her closet and pulled out her windbreaker. There was a pair of gloves in the pocket. She might need them.

There was no possible way her mind could comprehend what was happening beyond her walls. She let her mind go only once toward a second storey waterline, then actually laughed. The candle reflections in the bathroom mirror brightened her spirits. The dog perked up his ears, tensed his legs out through the bars of his crate, reaching for her, stretching, then relaxing back again, watching.

She hadn't smoked indoors for years. Hadn't smoked since noon. Now she made up for lost time.

The dog sneezed. She did not bless him.

"What the hell," she asked the dog not unreasonably, "am I going to do with you?" The dog had a pedigree and a mile-long name which she had boiled down to "My Hero." He scrabbled to his feet, wagged his stub.

An hour later, she was zipping the dog into a canvas LL Bean tote. He could breathe, but he couldn't get out unless she let him. It wasn't time, but she wanted to have a plan. This was rehearsal. When would it be time? The answerless question gave her some concern, considering how things were going. Adrenalin surged, along with the nicotine. Heart quivered, steadied up again.

What if she had to use the ax through the roof and climb out onto the shingles? At least they were rough, not slick. The gloves would come in handy. The boat bag's handles were long enough to fit over her shoulder; if she held her elbow to her side, she could keep My Hero from slipping away. Once on the roof, she could hang the handles around a vent pipe or something. There'd be something. How long could he live zipped tight like that? A toy terrier for godsake; a hyperactive purse dog! What had she been thinking.

She decided to let him run, now. All over the upstairs he went barking and marking and playing and seeking, seeking, seeking, in and under every familiar place, running back, touching her foot with his paw, then dashing off again. She tossed him his ball. He carried it his mouth, running to the steps to drop it, to chase it down, an old and favorite game, but when he saw the ball hit the water, he barked, barked, and inched backward from the brink, trembling. She had to leash him, walk him back and forth, back and forth. They both needed the exercise. They patrolled the hall pursuing their own thoughts. He helped her focus. Too late. She couldn't find the extra batteries for the flashlight. Maybe she had left them downstairs. Were they in her pockets, from before? She checked her discarded clothing. No.

When the torch faded, that was it. In its last waning glow she jumped, jumped, batting at the clothesline cord and plastic pull for the attic; she dragged the folding stairs down by main force. The attic's breath was warm, stale and strange with cardboard-crated befores and afters. She set the gun up there, but waited until water broke over the short first step of the attic ladder before she zipped the dog back in his tote and gathered the comforts she had left, vodka, crackers, cigarettes, lighter, and 3 junk-drawer casserole candles with a ludicrous burning time. Eleanor despised them; whoever needed a casserole to stay warm for just 27 minutes?

When she tried to estimate what time it was, how long until dawn, her mind slipped, counting down hope instead of hours. Her whole life had been about arriving here, this very moment, and clock time had no more meaning than a road that had washed away. Now dawn had to be just three candles away. Or else.

The attic was only a crawl space—Eleanor could hunker but could not stand up—with itchy fiberglass batts between rafters and loose plywood scraps laid for a path between stored items. Eleanor knew what was in the cartons, secondhand Mayflower moving boxes labeled in King's own hand: WEST, WEST, WEST. Things that mattered, but not enough to make the trip to King's new castle on the morning side of the river. The new ax was fitted between studs right at the opening by the stairs, cradled in place, never used. She got it loose and practiced her swing, chip shots at first then drives. Hard to swing from a crouch. Sidelong was easier. Overhead was impossible. She swung wildly, hit something, felt the card-board cave with the blow; next shot she used the blade of the ax, felt it cut through. Something jingled as it fractured. So—Christmas past? Too dark to see; she gave it a nudge with her foot. Settling of contents and old scores. She practiced on a few more boxes. Game got old.

Cardboard cartons were easy. But the ax seemed mere, almost a hatchet with a smooth ash handle. The edge was sharp but the head was no larger than her fist. It seemed impossible that she could break through the roof with it. The thing was, if she needed to, she would have to. Or die try-ing. One thing Eleanor had always believed about herself: she had what it took, or she could get it.

She took a deep breath, gusted it out. Came a pause.

There was an intermittent trembling and groaning in the wood of the house, a response to something going on down beneath Eleanor in the dark. Slow topplings and subsidences and flotations and crockery and

Revereware clatters and collisions. She tried to steady her mind by figuring it out, like a puzzle, but rude thoughts leaped up at her, frightening her with second thoughts and hindsights. What point now in wondering if she should she have found the circuit breakers and flipped the main switch? Was there something she should have done in the garage about the gas water heater and dryer? What if she had used tape over the sink drains in the kitchen? The one in the bath tub? The one in the shower? Why hadn't she drawn out fresh water into some plastic container and brought it up here earlier?

While she was thinking these things, a picture came to her. It was as clear as if she was watching it on TV. The garage, slowly filling with turbid water, and the car—her pearl white Caddy!—slowly rising too, floating. So well built it rose on the flood, and finally was buoyantly rubbing its roof against the metal rails of the garage door ramps, scraping itself and groaning against the boxed remote control motor housing. Bumping, slowly, blindly into the workbench where Jackie folded laundry. Slightly turning, with the drain turbulence, the pearly Deville tapping its bumper on the empty spring water demijohns, bowling them over. Being nudged and greeted by bobbing cans of spray paint, florist's foam, an orphaned kayak paddle, wasp spray . . . and inexorable, muddy water slowly filling, seeping in, slowly coating outside and inside with river sludge and gumbo until the car gained weight and sank, bubbling down under the trespassing river.

"Steady, gal," Eleanor said.

She wasn't drinking. She had left it off, afraid she would not be able to work or think quickly enough. Also, she might need it more, later. And she was offering it up. Rationalizing. Negotiating. Playing "If, then" with the Big If. Wasn't much time to reform in, and very little to offer to exchange for life. She sat on the framing of the attic hatch opening and swung her legs. Every raw, unlovely wooden surface was hard, every builder grade jack edge splintery and sharp. She tried not to think about the roofing nails that in some places had missed the rafters and come through the decking. She must not forget: if she stood, she stood to tear her scalp or pierce her skull. Also, if the attic should fill—but that was preposterous—and she should drown, she would float like the Cadillac, scraping and bumping against the raw wood. She did not believe that could or would happen in daylight. Nothing could stop the world from turning. Eleanor did not intend to die in the dark.

She still had those last three little candles. She had decided to light only one at a time. And not yet. She had carefully gathered the loose scraps of plywood used as flooring and laid a straight path directly to the back wall. When her knees were bruised to mush, she sat on her bottom and scooted, shoving the ply squares along with both feet. Finally, she finished the run. She could see the flashes of blue lightning through the shuttered gable end vent, like an old-time TV left flickering when the station had signed off for the night. She decided then, but it wasn't a decision, really, it was a knowing, "like this" it seemed to tell her. An idea presented itself. She trusted it. She did what the knowledge suggested. She scooted back from the stair hole, then crawled on hands and knees, inching slowly and carefully to keep on the plywood path, taking along with her the ax and the tote with the dog. There was no need for the gun yet, the knowing seemed to be telling her, and no need at all to hack through the roof, exterior grade thick plywood decking, tarred felt underlayment and two layers of shingles, no. All she needed to do was to hack at the shutters, just slice them midway, stroke on stroke, each stroke cleaving through the screen-wire also, and in a few minutes, she would be able to smooth the edges with the back of the axhead, then the handle. There would soon be a wide open window, big enough, free air and sky. She began the work.

How dark would it be when morning came? Would she even notice when morning came?

Morning would come.

The river kept coming.

Eleanor knew if she used the vent for escape, there was not going to be any time or energy for hacking the roof, for climbing out. No Plan B. She knew what there would not be, but Eleanor did not know what there would be. She worked in the dark like she was killing snakes.

It seemed to her, as she worked with the ax, chopping against the frame and down through the slats and screening, that the rain was not as heavy, but the wind—or was it water—was still loud and rushing. She wanted to hear a helicopter; that would be like Noah sending out the birds.

Not the end but the beginning of the end. She thought her work would do. She rested.

Free-floating thoughts and shards of memory rose up in the murky air. She rested near the opening she had hacked. It would have been good to sleep, a brief respite. But she couldn't let go. Her mind's eye never closed. Unconnected musings, and yet somehow cogent, compelling, and in no way a pleasure, drifted through her consciousness. Slowly she accepted the possibility, then the certainty, that she had kept RoyBoy a boy—hence the nickname. Was that why? She tried to think of a defense. At first the nickname had created a distinction between the father RoyAl and the son RoyAl, junior, long after RoyAl, senior had become "King" and his son was no longer a boy. RoyBoy had corrected her again and again, and—now she thought about it—he'd finally stopped trying. His business card simply stated his name and rank.

She had not meant to belittle him. No. She was sure of that. She called him the world's oldest bachelor, but she was always relieved when the romances cooled. Connie wasn't cooling, though. Something about Connie, maybe the way RoyBoy's dignity this time, his steadiness, his confidence, and his—she faced it—his joy had riled her, made her more willing than ever to keep on putting him in his place with the "boy" word. She admitted it: she wanted to topple them both and the pedestals they had installed each other on.

Connie would say, "Oh, man!" not "Oh, boy!" when RoyBoy did something she thought was wonderful. Some ordinary thing. She was always currying him like that. Eleanor ignored it, but at times she wanted to throw something. And of course, RoyBoy repaid in kind.

Eleanor thought again about a note or message. What could she possibly say? Where and how would she say it? Carve it in the roof? One big God bless us every one scratched into the shingles or daubed with mud and blood on the wall? Well, hell hell hell! Eleanor was trying, but she just couldn't fake being sorry. She acquitted herself of any evil intent. She'd had no intention of—well, what intentions had she had? She resisted answering. Why dig into all this now? Right from the beginning she had been sure it was all a matter of time and passive aggression and Connie would be gone, like all the others. It hadn't been "true love" yet. That was all she had to say about that. But this whole summer—and Eleanor did not like to think about this but it was floating along in the stream of debris—when Connie's confidence and certainty grew, and when they seemed to have bonded as a couple and were serious in a way none had been before, Eleanor had begun to gin and tweak things. Lay some mines. She was almost contrite about that. It seemed irrelevant now, so she didn't dwell on it.

Most provoking of all, when Eleanor had stepped up her game, Connie had responded with kindness and warmth. Connie had been gently —in deeds not words—showing Eleanor a thing or two about how to love a man. Or how to simply be nice. Eleanor didn't trust love and she hated "nice." That had cooked it. Especially Connie's speaking boldly, in RoyBoy's presence. Not rebuking Eleanor but standing her ground. What would RoyBoy call it? "No duty to retreat?"

That meal on Mother's Day—Connie had brought a loaf of bread-machine white bread. As though Eleanor didn't have any bread? Eleanor had excused herself, vanished into the kitchen, got out her blue bowl and had made biscuits—the kind her Uncle Dan had always made, with two ingredients—self-rising White Lily and whipping cream. While they baked, Eleanor took her seat at the table and let the Sunday helper bring the meal in, and of course the heirloom biscuits were perfect, hot, and worthy. RoyBoy said so.

"Of course," Eleanor had said. "But save your praise for Connie's . . . loaf? I'm sure I'll enjoy some toast next week."

Connie had sat there, figuring, then put her hand out, toward Eleanor's arm, but did not touch her. "I wasn't tryin'"—it sounded like "trine"— "for praise. I was tryin' to save you some—"

"What?" Eleanor said. "Steps? Time? Money? Bless your heart."

"Trouble," Connie said. Her face pinked up like she'd been slapped on both cheeks.

68

Still, the gal wouldn't back down. Connie shook things off. Another lesson.

Before they drove away, Connie had asked Roy to stop, then dashed back to the house, tapped on the front door, and getting no answer, just opened it and ran in. She passed through rooms still smelling of drifting candlesmoke and found Eleanor on the terrace out back. She was looking away, downriver, not that the water could be seen. It was all trees and hayfields. No traffic noise; peace, another world.

Connie's footsteps and shadow approached, and when Eleanor noticed, she held up her left hand to halt her and said without turning at all, "What?" She let an audible breath out, with fresh-lit cigarette smoke from both nostrils.

"We're okay?" Connie said.

"We?" Eleanor's head swung left to right and center, but again, she did not turn.

"You and me," Connie explained. "I want us to be okay."

"You and I?" Eleanor said. She had had just about enough of the girl's Piedmont accent, that Alabama Check-R-Mix mill-village twang that called salad "sellid", and daddy "deddy" and pain "pehn," her "Hell was full so I come back" bumper sticker, and her tattoos, especially that blue plate one, with the drooping willows and the flying swallows kissing for good luck. "You and I are not a 'we.' What about you and RoyBoy? Not much of a future there either. A wee we."

A redbird chip-chipped deep in a shrub. Far off, across the field in the briers, a quail called. Another redbird answered the first one. Nothing answered the quail. Nothing. Nothing. And then one did. One clear true syllable querying, *White?* Connie had been holding her breath and now she exhaled in a dry sob.

"Roy and I are okay. More than okay. Very okay. Totally okay." She sniffed. She did not come forward, take a chair or kneel. Eleanor thanked God for small favors.

Finally Eleanor turned toward the source of the shadow. "You and I will never be okay," she told Connie. "We're about as okay as—well, as far as that goes—about as far as I could throw you."

The sun-burnished soft grasses in the turnrow sizzled with insect song and dragonflies zigged and zagged in the air over the field. There was the scent of warm roses.

"As far as you kin throw me." Connie laughed. "Oh, Miss Ma'am, I betcha would!" She touched her lightly on the shoulder and was gone, her corksoled wedgies powering her across the bluestone terrace and around the side of the house. She didn't go back through. Somewhere in the house the little dog was barking at the window, watching her go.

Eleanor thought about that, how Connie had run, but had not fled.

Eleanor thought about RoyBoy too.

Her thoughts eroded slowly into truths. Not one big truth but a confetti of verities. The solid foundation remained sunk and submerged under a lifetime of debris. Was it to keep him young so she'd stay young? How stupid. That couldn't be it. She denied it completely, after a moment's reckoning. But then what? Was it something worse?

Had Eleanor stopped the clock, so to speak, when King drifted away? When he left her—and the clock? And everything else. It was true she had never sprung forward or fallen back in all those years. The glass domed clock kept its own seasons. No adjustments or maintenance. Was it even ticking any more? Chiming? She had not noticed. When she went back downstairs, it had been high and dry on the mantle, but no longer. Would the water extinguish it, like the candles?

Her gun had hung sovereign above it on the dark wall. She had long ago stopped noticing the anniversary clock's blank face. It had nothing to tell her she wanted to hear.

So—Eleanor realized—she had become a person who would ignore and begrudge a clock. The housekeeper had the duty of it, used the key and wound it once a week when she dusted. Actually, in years, Eleanor never had to look at it at all. It had been a treasure. And now, it was gone. One good thing: she would never again have to ignore it.

Eleanor had rested long enough. She considered what came next in a strictly practical way.

She retrieved the shotgun, the handful of shells. She had no need of light; her hands could break that gun down and put it back together again in pitch dark. She used to sit at a window like this, when she was twenty, waiting in the dark. One of her college beaus had a car; he'd come and get her, gather her along with her pals, and they'd dump classes, go quail hunting before breakfast, AWOL from campus they'd ramble, bring down enough birds for the whole gang. Cook a campfire breakfast, fried quail and gravy and stolen leftover biscuits and a little bourbon in their coffee to warm them up again.

No use thinking about the bourbon or the coffee, either one.

She loaded a shell, swung around to face the window and fired toward the trees. Just because. Just to feel that power in her hands again, smell the smoke. She could not bear to think of her mother's gun submerged, just one more cherished thing in the before of her life, washing away. Nothing but birdshot, not buck. And a ladylike single-shot .410, cut-down walnut stock smooth as satin. Not enough power to blow a hole in the roof. Still, she ought not to have wasted one shell like that. Plus, she woke the dog. She unzipped the tote, tried to console him, offered him the last cracker. He licked the salt off it. He wriggled and vocalized. It sounded like garbled shortwave, from faraway. You you you. Needy.

"My Hero," she said, rubbing his throat, keeping him off her. She despised clinginess.

She snapped his leash on and let him walk a bit. He wasn't keen; he slumped against her and trembled in the dark. His desolation was infectious.

Eleanor shook him off, decided it was time; she lit one of the candles and set it at the end of the board, right at the edge of the hole in the wall. That way, when she looked, when the dog looked, they'd see light. Dawn would be half an hour closer. She was burning up dark, not daylight. Just rocking back on her heels, appreciating the flame, she thought she heard something. In fact, she was sure enough to ease her head out the opening and hark. Thunder, she decided, not whacka-whacka-whacka. Hard rain seemed to be over; sometimes none at all. Sometimes wispy, half-hearted drizzle, moving northeast. What her grandfather called "fairing off show-ers." Eleanor hoped.

What was she hoping for? Death experts would call this the negotiat-ing stage. She hadn't taken a drink since she had come up the last step into the attic. Eleanor was nerving through this night as she used to cross long bridges; endurance and momentum. Sooner or later, keeping in her lane and keeping on, she'd reach the other side. The attic had brought her to her knees. She vowed she would be dry—in more ways than one—when she got out of there. She was anxious, shaky; she had faith, and yet her mind was not willing to imagine or rehearse helicopter adventures, even if she longed for rescue, especially in the dark. Swinging above the water and trees in a basket hanging by a thread? Maybe in the dark it would be better. Would they let her bring along the dog? Her gun? But no, what she thought she had heard did not come again. No helicopter. She was actu-ally relieved. She had thought she was ready. She wasn't.

The rain had definitely stopped. Things were dripping, but the pelting downpour had stopped. What now?

She held the little candle on the palm of her hand, stretched it out, waved it around; leaning out, she took a moment to survey. That scrap of flame, as little as that, filled her vision, blinded her; her eyes watered; she couldn't see past, it made the dark darker, but her heart clanged as something floating thumped and drummed and scratched its way along the wall below her and was gone. Was it an animal, trying to find a way in? Her gun lay just behind her, broken open, unloaded. She drew back inside, set the candle on the edge; now it was lit she did not want to blow it out even though it was useless as a lantern. She had sensed rather than seen the water and its motion. Instinct warned her how the world beyond her walls was chaos. Primeval darkness. Unpeopled. A word from Genesis haunted her: *void*.

A gust of wind blew out the candle; its smoke trailed invisibly in toward her and then was drawn out into the night. This time the total dark destroyed her; helpless, she couldn't find the matches. Jerky, she knocked the gun into the insulation-filled bay next to her plywood path. Was it wrecked? Had fiberglass got into the breech? So many mistakes were happening all at once she began to curse, like she didn't care, because she did. New stage? Same old anger, bitter dregs. She groped in the rummage her bashing had left strewn. Something to throw, hard. Away. Hands found something: cool, lumpy, her fingers remembered—a green-glazed pottery rhino RoyBoy, age nine, had given King for Father's Day. Shaped by his boyish hands. Left behind. Packed away. Never missed. Somehow she dropped it. Horrified, she heard it bounce, hard; it vanished into the fiberglass. She knew it had, because it made no sound. Still, it broke. Her fingers brailled it out—the snout was gone, and the horn, so now it felt like a stubby snubby pig. There was no seeking the missing parts now.

She told herself it really did not matter. At. This. Moment. But she kept crawling around, groping, sobbing. She actually found the horn, wrapped it in paper with the main piece, stuffed it back in one of the cartons she had not smashed. Why did that have to happen? Why did the one thing in this attic have to—she admitted it—touch her when she touched it? Or was it not the only forgotten thing with that kind of power over her? That was an unnerving thought. When would the night be over? When would it end? Would she keep on having these thoughts? Hindsights? Thus ended Eleanor's negotiation phase. Back to anger, this time pure as flame. She couldn't lay hands on the ax. Just as well.

Eleanor was done with pretending she didn't mind. With playing nice. With keeping her cool. With asking. Now she was telling. "Leave me alone!" she screamed. She wasn't going to die like this! The dog whimpered. Enraged, she amended it, what else could she do? Calmly as she could, she explained, "We are not going to die like this" Eyes bugging out, hearts raddled with adrenaline, deafened by whispers in the wind. She wept. Furiously. Seriously. A fifty-year flood of tears. She had time. When it was over, she lay back on the plywood and felt a little silly, aghast, amazed, and purged.

"Not better than sex," she said. Keeping it real. She sat up. Finger-combed her hair. Rolling her shoulders and stretching. She reached for her cigarettes, patting around, brushing the boards carefully, seeking. She touched the stock of the gun. Oh.

She got herself and the gun back together, chambered a shell. Swung and fired out the hole in her house at non-hurricane Alberto, not even, not ever more than a storm and now nothing but a killing depression. That for you, Alberto. The dog squealed. At first she thought she had wounded him with bounced-back shot. No. He was safe; it was the noise. Eleanor liked the noise. If she could holler that loud, she wouldn't need a gun. She crabbed nearer the opening and fired again. Straight up, right at God. That was prayer. One shell, one prayer left.

"Can you hear me?" she hollered. No echo. No reply. But who was she to ask? What right did she have? And who was listening? On the other hand—no, not quite to acceptance yet, but rounding the curve, resignation in the rearview, Eleanor sobbed, "What the hell else do you think I can do?"

In the resounding silence, the caboose of the storm rattling on off into the distance, an odd thing happened. Eleanor's mind delivered up an irrelevancy, a memory of her own voice—a clear complete memory of the curse she had offered King's third wife when they finally met, blessing her with a handful of fresh-cut Etoile de Hollande roses and a riddle in pleasant and more than civil tones: "Remember this joy."

The second odd thing was also audible—but this time hearing not her own voice but her own name, not inside her head, but from beyond the house, her own name, "Eleanor!" not a question, imperative, and a puttering, trolling sound, and then "Eleanor?" shouted just below the gable opening.

She crawled, knees on fire, dragging the dog in its pouch, dragging the gun still loaded with its last shell. She eased up as far as she could and leaned out. Friend or foe? Below her, but in safe falling distance, King rocked in a johnboat. "You rang?"

"Damn you," she said, to get that off her chest once and for all.

"Dam's gone," he said. "Here comes the lake. Need a lift?"

"Water's up to the medicine chest in your bath," she said. Decades of used razor blades rusting in the wall. Did he still use double-edge? Maybe an electric. From the look of him, none lately. Patchy grizzled beard. It was never going to be pretty.

"Come on."

"Need my gun?" she wondered.

"God, I hope not," he said. "But it's been, all told, a helluva night."

She set the tote on the edge. He signaled her to drop it, but it was too far. Not a chance. "Fragile," she explained

"Brandy?" Hopeful.

"Piss and vinegar," she said.

"Any port in a storm," he said, still holding out hope.

She broke it to him gently. "The most worthless dog in the world."

"Dead?"

"What do you think?" She pulled on the gloves, fitted the straps of the dog pouch over her shoulder, and eased herself onto knees and elbows, then wagged backward till her right leg swung free to find the ladder; she had to pretend there was a ladder, a ladder right there, waiting. One wasn't. Only King.

"Time's rolling," he said.

She managed to risk the other foot, then scraped her knee, too close to the house. Her own weight stretched her; the grip of the driving gloves helped her so well she almost decided not to let go.

For that long moment she had been born; she hung by her own strength and grip. He let her. Here it was. It had come to this, her journey, alone, helpless, a damsel, no a dame, no a damn fool in distress. Crazy peace comforted her. She wasn't alone, this wasn't the end, and it was one more jest of God that My Hero and she were about to drop into King's hands, the very hands that had set her aside.

"I didn't bring your mother's Irish spoons," she said.

"Insured," he said. "Come on."

She had a dim view and time for doubt about this boat ride.

"Don't push against the wall or grab either," he warned, "or we'll both get dunked." Could she let herself go? "Point your toes, point your toes," he ordered, "in case I drop you." Advice from his skydiving days. She dared not do more than glance at him. "Don't look down!" he barked. In the murk, more than sleep-deprived, he looked older; he was older; he had been, no doubt, through more fresh hell than she—but his gnarled hands—*now! she stood on tiptoe on nothing but air and dropped*—when he finally took hold—were strong.

She slid down the front of King and landed safe into the center of the boat. They wobbled, and Eleanor sat hard. He immediately stepped around her to the tiller. "This may not be what you had in mind," he added. She put her gloved hand over her mouth and stifled.

No conversation, just facts. Odd updates. He had news of RoyBoy: fine, busy. Working the other side of the river, bridges were out or under, major damages to infrastructure.

Eleanor knew all she needed to for now about major damages to infrastructure. "When did you see him?"

"Phoned," King said. "Wanted to come by and help me get the animals evacuated. Couldn't." All local, county, state and guard, emergency, fire, police, and first responders on twenty-four hour duty. "Didn't need him," King said. That brought Eleanor's head up, sharp, but wordless. Hadn't she played the same game?

"So they're safe?"

He knew what she meant. "They're on different sides of the river, but he'll build a bridge if he has to. You know Roy."

Finally, she said, "So the horses are safe, the burros, the mules. Cats, dogs, ostriches, emus, et cetera . . ."

"And the African Gray and the barn macaw." Eleanor didn't give a rip about the macaw; it had been a nuisance, and all she learned about it was summed up in the phrase *never again*. She had cursed that bird—and vice versa—when it was young. When she was young. God, how long did they live? She unzipped the boat bag and My Hero poked his muzzle out, sniffing. She turned the bag so the wind wouldn't scoop into his ears.

"Where are we headed?" she wondered.

"Somebody's roof," he said, "if we can't get to dry ground, which there isn't any."

"Your roof?"

"Gone," he said.

"Wife number three?" she wondered.

"Gone," he said. "But not with the roof. Separate vacations." He turned and saluted vaguely northward. "*Adios, muchacha.*"

They hit something, and he tipped the trolling rig up out of the water just in time; they were up and over an arm-sized poplar snag, smooth trunk, easy over but a brutal slap back down into the flow; they swept on. It seemed as though the sky were a softer gray, dawn-lightened. She could see thickness in the clouds now, lighter and darker swirls, wisps, fringes, layers.

"Keep ya'self in the boat," he warned. "If you should exit, head for a tree; I'll catch up. If fire ants or rats or snakes get on you, just ease under the water, you know? They'll slide off or crawl past, nobody's hunting, just fleeing. Even the fleas." He tilted the motor out of the water; in the wider stream there was serious deadfall. He had to constantly correct the boat, shoving away from tangles, snags, flotsam with his cypress oar, but the best he could do was seek clearings and go with the flow; the current was in charge.

Sometimes that's enough.

They were bucking along now in one of those clear places.

"I am done with middle age," she announced.

"What?" he barked. Irritated, he leaned forward, pulling the foam plugs from his ears. He hated rain in his ears. He hated jokes he didn't get, puzzles he couldn't solve. And rain in his ears. Rain had resumed, and the gloomy dark. She repeated herself. "I am done with middle age."

"What does that mean?" he said, furiously bare-handing the rain off his face, clearing his fogged up glasses with a wet rag.

She laughed. She had to laugh. "I don't know."

Virga

"Red River Valley" was the song the old woman was humming in Clark's back room when Ada Yazzie knelt before her to wash her feet. The man wouldn't wait on them till she finished. "Nothing personal," Clark said again. "Store policy. Old folks can get a little"—he searched for the word—"rusty, yeah. No offense."

The old woman knew enough English but didn't bother with his, never lifted her gaze past his suede and snakeskin boots, mainly kept her eyes shut, and went on humming. She was ancient. If the sun and dry winds had withered her, they had also preserved her. She had survived by turning her back, not by entreating.

Ada had seldom touched the old woman. They both jumped from the cold hard water, the latherless soap, the sulfurous brown paper towels. She worked lightly, no scrubbing. Ada ignored the man. She had to slip past him to the lavatory sink. Her hands and her heart hurried; she had liked the leathery way the store smelled when they first walked in, but now she was holding her breath against the man's cologne and that camphor smell from the toilet. The basin and the bowl had years of rust stains, the porcelain dulled by harsh and useless scouring. Ada wanted to turn the taps on full, and let the water rush out and swirl, to fill her hands, and drink from them, and sling them dry afterward, but she didn't. She was as careful as though she were home, and the water had come miles to her in a drum on Albert's truck, and she were accountable for each drop.

The old woman seemed asleep, except for the humming. They had walked for two hours after Albert Yazzie's half-ton blew a gasket near Sunrise. It got towed south to Winslow, but they walked and hitched.

"She was clean when she set out," Ada said.

"Jesus! When was that? Kit Carson's last ride?"

There was no one around to enjoy it, no other customer to dilute Clark's attentions. He settled his shoulder against the doorframe, a shoebox under one crooked arm. He stared down.

As soon as Ada patted the soles of the old woman's feet dry, and stood, the man pulled up the bench and sat. When he measured the old woman's foot he had to use the children's Brannock device, her little hoof was that hard to fit. She wasn't hard to please.

"Like these?" He dangled a kid-size pair of deerskin oxfords from two fingers. Red. That was what she had said, the only word she had spoken. She watched him tie them on her feet and then she stood, turning her back, fishing a trucker's wallet up from under her velveteen shirt. Clark was watching her in the mirror, spying, a little smile for how easy it was. All he was stealing was a look, but he knew better; not looking away was Anglo, knowing he wouldn't answer for any insult. Ada caught him. Watched him in the mirror he was watching the old woman in, until he realized he'd been caught. Ada knew what those mirrors were for; Maxine had caught Ada just like that, in the camp store mirror, had caught Ada's reflection stealing Tampax when she was twelve years old and still talking to her doll and getting answers . . .

Then, Ada's brothers had been in the video game room blasting away with the money they'd found in a pay phone coin return. Ada and the old woman were on the bench out front watching the day drain off behind the San Francisco Peaks, waiting for Albert's truck to come from the grocery store and pick them up. Henry and Bernard kept on playing, faking the games and sound effects when their money ran out, setting Douglas on watch at the side door to catch Eddie's signals, all he was good for so far, too short to even see the screen in the booth, and unable to concentrate on pleasure the way he could focus on dread. Plus when he shrieked, he could strip varnish. It was better than a whistle or a horn. And all he'd yell would be, "Albert!"

Albert Yazzie was a hard man, careful and practical. They didn't call him father. They called him sir. He took his responsibilities seriously, and he didn't want any help when he laid in supplies. Once a month he shelled out for generic cans by the caseload, lard by the bucket, flour and meal like a Mormon, and he didn't want any of what he called their bubblegum suggestions wrecking what little he had left for a beer budget.

He did most of his drinking at home or on the way; in town he bought it one can at a pop and took his time. He paid for it with scrabbled-up coins or single wadded bills, to fool anyone who might be hoping for a piece of his Park Service check cashed that morning and stashed in his left boot.

He took care of his family, but he was no Ranger Rick; he had a reputation: no one had to throw cactus at him to make him buck. His right boot was the one with the knife, not to get into trouble but to get him out of it. "While I'm breathing, I'm toting," he said.

When he stopped at any of the little lunch spots to bean up, always alone, he'd order the cheapest fare, and spoon it down in a blur hurry, drain that one beer then head for the door. He never stayed long, never stood for a round. When owlheads at the bar asked, "What are you saving it for?" he'd hardly pause to think. "Generator and satellite dish" was no answer, it was a Santa Claus dream, so he'd glance out the door at wall to wall Arizona and say instead, going for the laugh, "Rainy day." It could have been his nickname, but he didn't have one, not even in the Army, not even with his kids. No one called him anything but Albert.

He liked to drop the kids off before he shopped, and the old woman too—his grandmother's sister from Two Grey Hills. Since he had discovered the dinky campground store and playground west of Dry Lake, he dropped them there. It was miles off the main drag and away from the strip malls. If they stayed in town what they did, the old woman too, was look at things and decide they needed them. One time it was refrigerator magnets. The youngest one, Eddie, had the kind of tantrum over them that no threat or distraction can cure; there was heartbreak in it, and grief, like being stripped of love and hope and left raw and exposed on a bleak rock brow for the vultures. He didn't cry like that—none of them had—when their mother died. This was craziness, all these tears for plastic butterflies. "We don't have a refrigerator," Albert kept trying to explain, louder and louder over Eddie's riot. The store manager came, and a deputy, so Albert bought the magnets.

All the way home Eddie had sat bunched on a lambskin in the corner of the cab snubbing and snuffling and chewing on the corner of the package. He lost interest before he lost the magnets later but for a while he stuck them to the sides of this steel drum or that, or the fender of the truck, or the washtub, eye-high to a three year old, proving whatever it was that needed proving.

Albert made sure after that episode the kids didn't tag along with him. He'd charge the older ones to watch out for the younger, and all of them to stay out of the manager's hair. Maybe he'd give them money, enough for one arcade game each, or candy or popcorn to share. He expected them out front—their chip bags empty and the last salt licked from their lips—when he drove in, and no trash, literal or figurative, in their wake. He wanted to keep things smooth between him and the campground.

When he came to pick them up, he'd top off the truck's tank at the diesel pump and brim the jerry can with unleaded for the lanterns. Before the store had changed hands, he and the night clerk—sometimes a geezer, other times a local kid just past the birthday which made it legal—would knock back a couple of cans of Albert's beer still sweating from the grocer's cooler. Meanwhile in fair exchange, the kids would be around back at the hose tap, filling rinsed-out gallon milk jugs with city water. It made better coffee than the alkali stuff windmilled into the tank at the tribal reservoir.

Albert hadn't pushed his luck about the tap water lately. He didn't know the new owner, Maxine. She wasn't the clerk type; she was the boss type, and her own steady hand had painted the warning over the old Bardahl sign: New Management . . .

Maxine came out of the store, leaving the door wide open, propped with a chunk of lava. *"Ya ta hey!"* she said to Ada and the old woman on the bench. Ada didn't answer. The old woman nodded, inviting her to sit beside her. From a pocket in her red-flannel underskirt, she drew a weaver's comb, offering to sell it for tobacco. When Ada saw it, she stood up. She walked around. Albert didn't want them trading, but Ada didn't have a say, about the old woman. The old woman had not been a weaver for many years, and she kept her wallet from dying of starvation with these plundered little handfuls. There was always someone who'd pay.

Maxine examined the comb; she was interested in the old ways and means. Didn't her cash register stand on an antique wood and glass show-case filled with local rocks and fossils and bits of bowls and tools? Every-thing labeled, even the old thumb-buster pistol and part of a fire-scarred trapdoor Springfield she had sifted out of the debris in the canyon where trash had been cairning up for years over the bones of a Navajo vengeance against bride-stealers. Maxine stressed that she did not collect bones, even if she could have told sheep from horse, man from maiden, Apache from Dine'. She had other rules too.

"I can't take this," Maxine said, handling the comb. The old woman looked at her, signaled Ada to come translate. "Museum quality," Maxine said. It was handcarved and smooth with decades of lanolin from the wool. "I can't afford it. No way."

"No way," Ada said.

The old woman stood abruptly. She was spry. "*Ya ta hey,*" she said with an angered shrug. She moved off across the gravelled lot, beyond the fenced-off LP tank to sulk by the road, her back turned.

Maxine hustled after her.

Ada didn't follow. Maxine's English was good enough if the old woman wasn't so stubborn. "Too good, too much. No trade," Maxine was saying. "Worth too much." She glanced Ada's way, appealing for help. She tried Spanish when Ada held back.

The old woman let her rave, then bottom-lined, in English. "No trade. Cash dolla."

They were silhouettes: Maxine taller and sturdy in her Levi's, her broad hands heavy with their seven turquoise rings gesturing across the gap between her and the desiccated little weaver bundled in skirts and velveteen. Maxine lit a cigarette for each of them.

Silence while the old one smoked and Maxine considered. Ada sat on the bench alone, and waited. She could hear her brothers in the game room. None of them had ever so much as even touched a ten dollar bill that was their very own. They had nothing yet that was their very own except their blood, nothing worth pawning or selling or trading away. Ada touched her silver barrette, her mother's, a bride gift. That was out of the question, of course. She watched the two women smoking. They might have been landforms, dark against the last light in the world. They were a mile high. There was nothing between them and the first clear stars but those sheer mouthfuls of smoke. They were laughing! They had forgotten all about Ada. Maxine was pointing with her whole arm across the desert, northwest toward the Vermilion Cliffs where heat lightning shimmered. Underfoot, through the marrowless cooling bones of the earth they could feel the tremor of the westbound Santa Fe, mile long, miles off. The old woman was shaking her head. The wind had dropped, but sounds of traffic on the highway were still blown away like the smoke around their words.

The campground was empty. Under repairs. Only the store was open. The sole customers were Ada's brothers still horsing around in the game room, out of coins now, but rapt and rowdy at doubles table tennis, their sneakers squealing on Maxine's fresh wax job, their shouts pingponging with each swaggering score or missed shot, nothing to Ada but background noise; she was used to them. She knew them by heart. The boys were making their points and the old woman and Maxine were out in the dark dealing for dollars and Albert was Billy Hell knew where. Not there, that was the main thing. Ada slipped from the bench then and went into the store. The door was still wide open. She really thought that all she was going to do was look at the shackled bird.

Maxine had a sage-green parrot with a tiny silver anklecuff and chain tethering it to its beak-stripped perch. It could move back and forth and even fly over to the counter and step along on its crippled-looking feet. From time to time it croaked caustic Spanish in a shrill, tired way, as though it had learned from someone old and bitter. Something in Ada hoped the chain would break, but she was afraid too of what the bird might do with freedom. She picked a grape from the bunch in the feed-bowl and rolled it along the counter. The bird nabbed it and slowly palpated it with its dark and leathery tongue that was like a tiny gloved finger. When it had swallowed, the parrot ruffled itself all over, flew to its perch, spread its wings and flogged the air. The noise was like the sound in Ada's dream that past winter, the final dream she had had as a White Shell Girl, before she changed into a woman.

In her dream a tree fell, a tree larger than any she had ever seen alive. As large as the trunks in the petrified forest. There were no leaves on the tree, for it was winter, and there was snow. The land was white. When the tree had begun to fall, Ada saw that she could not stop it, and she did not try. She simply watched. The tree slowly tipped toward the earth and when it finally struck, the snow hushed the sound. The tree split like a pod along its lightning-hollowed length. From the opening flew birds, east, south, west and north, dozens of birds like bats from a cave, or swifts spiraling upward in skeins, all kinds of birds, all sizes, all colors—jays, larks, thrashers, wrens, doves, hawks, sparrows, desert birds, mountain birds, waterhole birds, cave birds, fetish birds and real birds, birds brown as owls and birds bright as coral and turquoise. They flapped free and flew with a card-shuffle sound higher and higher in the clear sky and were lost in the sun, leaving no trace, no track, not even a feather. Ada's heart beat like a pot drum as she stepped up to the hollow trunk, bent, and looked in.

Among the dry splinters and limed walls of the tree's heart there was one brown knot. It looked like wood, but a slight wind turned the soft feathers and called Ada to put out her hands to it: a bird! She deeply pitied its sudden ruinous exposure, its deathly stillness.

When she lifted the bird to her, it was warm. She knew then this sleep wasn't death but life waiting for its season. Since there was nowhere else to shelter it, she put it inside her shirt. She felt its tiny cold feet uncurl and grip to her as it resettled itself in its sleep, in hers.

Ada had slept all the rest of the night on her back, her hands lightly doming over her heart to protect the little bird dreaming in her dream. When she woke, the sun was already well up and Albert was outside shaking the frost off the blanket on his truck hood, hoping for one more crank from that old battery. It was a schoolday. Ada stood quickly and in her sleepy confusion as she felt the first lunar trickle down her thigh she thought she had—despite her care—crushed the little bird, and this was its warm blood leaking, not her own. Then she understood the movie at school that gave all the science but not the magic. Ada decided she would tell no one about this Changing Woman business. The old woman was her only female kin close enough for confidences and yet not open to these, holding it against her because Ada had been born to a Zuni mother, not Navajo.

"Let *them* teach you," she had answered when Ada asked her if there would be a singing ceremony and a blessing cake.

But how could they teach her, when she had never seen any of them again after her mother died and they cast the death sand and cloth into the river? Albert had vanished for four days while his wife's spirit traveled to the underworld, and when he came back, purified and safe from haunting, they had moved away from Zuni, where the roads were paved and the broken bottles sparkled under streetlights, and family and neighbors lived nearby.

Ada's mother's mother had had a washing machine and water in the kitchen from a tap and a flush toilet and bathtub. They had used bar soap that smelled like clover. For almost a year Ada had been taught by the nuns. Ada's school uniform had been starched, with a smell of wintergreen and lemon, and ironed smooth, and the meals cooked with electricity. Only the ceremonial bread had been baked outdoors.

Albert had moved them back to his own people, a winterhouse on dry land, and another place, near stream water for summer grazing for the horse and sheep. The stream was ankle deep, never even wading depth, and nowhere along its length a hole where a person could float or bathe. Ada learned other ways. Ada watched the old woman and learned how to be private in the bushes, in the summer place. At the winter lodge there was an outhouse. And a wooden crate up in the pinyon tree for icebox. She got used to drinking powdered milk and washing in cold water and wasting nothing. Chores toughened her hands, but her skin was too thin to do what the boys and Albert did, taking up a live coal in their fingertips to use as a match.

No matter how nice the clothes smelled when she folded them into the black bags to bring home from the laundry, everything—winter and summer —stank of firesmoke and frybread, even, despite Ada's best efforts, her own long hair. Once Ada got a free sample of shampoo at school from a girl who sold Avon. The shampoo had the scent of berries and vanilla, and when Albert smelled it, he reacted as though it were contraband, perhaps shoplifted (how else?) candy, or more impossible, perfume. He ducked inside and lit the lantern. His shadow reached to the wall. It dodged and trailed as he searched. He sniffed his way through the *hogan* till he located it. He pulled Ada out of his own shadow. "On you? That's you? Where is it?"

She thought he meant the shampoo. She said, "It was a sample, it's all gone."

"No, it's not," he said. "I could smell you out by the corral. He leaned closer. "Did you roll in it? Bring it here."

Ada found the empty packet, no bigger than one of those single por-tion sugar servings. He read it, read the list of ingredients, pronouncing them all, proving something. "'No animal testing?'" he read, and threw it in the stove. His hands were tough enough he didn't even hurry touching the handle.

"Your hair," he said.

"It was free."

"Plenty to do in the barn," Albert warned his sons.

The boys got out, then, even Eddie, who ran after them up the slope in boots not quite all the way on, lurching as he tried to zip his jacket, crying, as always, over the gap between himself and his heart's desire. Now Ada was alone. The old woman was already gone, somewhere in the hills since noon, looking for a dark lamb she had dreamed about losing.

"Nothing's ever free," Albert told her. Just what he said about the gov-ernment "commodities" and school lunch. He was like the coyote who sniffs the bait and trots on. Ada thought of the way the boys checked every pay phone for returned coins, and how she never left a penny on a sidewalk, even face down. Things worse than bad luck.

"You hear?"

"Yes, sir."

He flipped the hair on her shoulder with the back of his hand. "You get that stink off of you by dark or I'm cutting it off." He picked up the horse's bucket where he'd thrown it on the way in, and dipped it full of water from the blue barrel. She thought at first he was going to wash her hair himself, or maybe dunk her head in something he used on the stock, but he went on past her as though she weren't even there. He whistled; the mare trotted up to the fence and he put his hand on her neck, talking low. The boys gathered to him also, like doves around a puddle. Eddie said something and they all laughed. That was when the girl's face burned like fever.

They didn't use shampoo. The boys and Albert used bar soap, or soap-weed when they were camping, and all Ada was was trouble. She'd learned early if she wanted to soothe her chapped hands, she'd better use lard, nothing Albert had to buy special. That's what it was, this time, about the shampoo. He hadn't begun that other crazy stuff yet, about her being fast, about her "looking for trouble." She had gone past the White Shell stage by two years or so when he started that. He had never noticed her changing, and then one day he did. He seemed to be angry all the time, full of blame for crimes she hadn't even thought of.

Albert knew how to make soap and tea and medicines from the desert plants, and if she had asked him, he could have helped her find and brew snakebroom to ease her stomachaches, but she was ashamed to ask. Ada made do; she wore clumsy rags to school and got monthly supplies from the nurse, but when school was out for summer she had to think of something else.

She did not intend to steal from Maxine. It all happened gradually. First the open door and the way the parrot flapped its wings and reminded her of her dream. Then the coin-sized little fossil like a crushed bug labeled

"400,000,000 years old" in Maxine's showcase. Eight zeroes. Ada counted them twice. "If that was dollars, I could own the world," Ada told the parrot. The bird made her uneasy, watching. She was glad when it turned its back and went to sleep, hunched, indifferent; it reminded Ada of the old woman, the way she could pull the blanket on its wire and shut out the whole world. Even though Ada was inside it with her, in the same sleeping space, she knew she had been left alone.

Suppose I could buy anything in this store, Ada asked herself. She walked up and down the aisles looking but not touching. She stood in front of the sunglass kiosk. She lingered at the magazine rack. She leaned against the freezer unit and studied the ice cream novelties. She glanced at the candy counter, the kitchen utensils on their hooks, the detergents and mousetraps and insect repellents for hikers and rockhounds. She stepped over the metal detector. In the end, she touched only what she took, and she stole only what she needed. She did not pretend it was someone else's hand; she did not pretend it wasn't happening. She did not think at all. She had the single box concealed in back between her skin and waistband; plenty of room in her brother's hand-me-down jeans. They were boy-cut; she wasn't. She had her oversize T-shirt pulled loosely down in back and was about to go outside again and sit on the bench when Maxine came in to get the dollars for the old woman's deal on the weaving comb.

Maxine put the comb in the locked showcase. She made a label too. She was writing it as Ada was halfway out the door. "What's her name, anyway?" Maxine asked. "She says she won't tell me."

Ada turned around. "She won't."

The mirror was behind Ada, a circle mirror like a hubcap, high up on the wall. Maxine swiveled on her desk stool, adjusted her glasses, and gave another look. "X-A-P-M . . ." she spelled, then said, "Well, well now, how do you spell Tampax backwards?" She could read it plain as that, through Ada's old T-shirt. Could see the blue package where Ada had stuck it. Ada didn't cry. They just looked at each other.

"My father was *un hombre de campo*," Maxine said. She made a fist and shook it. "Like rock." She gestured toward Old Mexico. "Country on four sides. My mother—" She studied Ada, made a shot in the dark. "How long has your mother been dead?"

Ada didn't say anything. She took the box from its hiding place and laid it on the counter.

Maxine did not act as though this were in any way extraordinary. "Glad to," she said. She rang No Sale on the cash register and bagged the supplies and handed them back. Transaction complete. Maxine asked, "Is that all you need?" Ada just stood there. Finally Maxine put the package in Ada's hand. When the girl turned to leave, Maxine said, "Welcome to the club."

That was how their friendship began.

Albert ended it three years later, the Saturday his engine blew and the old woman bought the red shoes. The truck had been towed to Simpson's All-Nite All-Rite Garage. When Ada and the old woman left Clark's shoestore, they headed that way, walking till the sidewalk ran out. Traffic was heavy for a Monday because of Memorial Day weekend, and tourists cruised slowly along the street, rubbernecking the jewelry and "native" crafts spread on camp tables and blankets and pickup tailgates. On the outskirts, a winter's worth of hammered silver and skyblue stone strewn in the sunshine. Business was brisk. The old woman knew many of the sellers, and she zigzagged across four lanes to visit. The crepe soles on her new shoes had thawed ten hard years from her stiff gait. Ada dodged after her.

The late spring sun had charmed her denim jacket off; she tied its sleeves around her waist. A fuzzy-armed fellow with a freckled hand reached to Ada's ear and touched the ring. "Is that—"

"No, sir," Ada said, and moved past him. The crowd blocked her way. She lost sight of the old woman, but she could hear her talking to someone at Jenny Tsotsee's booth. The man who had touched her earring caught up. "How do you know what I—"

Ada sideslipped into the throng, and left him behind. She threaded past the tables and trucks and up the graveled grade to the rails. She made a visor of her hands and stared hard through the shimmer. She could see

Albert's crew cab on the pocked asphalt apron where the tow had dropped it off its hook. It wasn't even in the workbay yet. When they pushed it in, it would still be hours, maybe all night. A long night, dozing on plastic chairs somewhere public with fluorescent lights buzzing, or maybe Albert would herd them all to the truck stop, and they'd prop each other up in a booth, nursing cold milky coffee and making their ketchup on crackers last, trying to look like customers not vagrants, the way they got through it when Eddie had pneumonia and the clinic kept him three days.

Albert had told them to gather at Simpson's for lunch. By the sun, they were near noon, but they had missed Albert by twenty minutes, no more. He and the parts man were already on their way to Holbrook, the nearest place open, for a headgasket. Albert left them a message, to be there at four o'clock, or—"And I quote," the mechanic said—"'Ya ass is grass.'" Albert had left them two bucks each and makings for a do-it-yourself lunch—bologna and loaf bread, a bag of corn chips. If they wanted Pepsi, they could throw their money away on it. He wouldn't.

They set to, even the old woman. Ada and the younger boys ate in the truck, doors wide open. The old woman sat in there too, but Henry, the oldest, had hopes, maybe even plans, and kept pacing back and forth on the shady side watching the road for Frank Luo who had already circled by twice, inviting him—"You seventeen, what permission?"—and Ada too, if she wanted, "Just to ride around." He backed around, kicking up sand. They had to turn away to keep the grit out of their food and eyes. "I'll be back," Frank warned.

Ada started not to go. But it was hot and Eddie was a dead weight in her lap where he had fallen over, and the old woman and Douglas and Bernard were already conked out, catching up on sleep lost in their early start. Ada wasn't tired, but if she had been, where would she stretch out? On the three bags of dirty laundry in the back?

Ada checked the time. Almost two o'clock. She didn't really want to go, but Henry meant to. He was bouncing up and down, stiff-legged, on the balls of his feet, raring. Frank looked excited too, but in that glazed and jittery way he always looked, like the boys at school kiting on White Out and Magic Markers.

"Going as far as Dry Lake?" Henry wouldn't ask flat out, just hint, and hope.

"What's out there?" Frank glanced at his fuel gage, then his watch.

Before Ada could say laundry, Henry made arcade noises and rumbled, "Mortal Kombat, Whirlwind, ThunderJaws," in a robot voice.

He tapped himself on the chest. "Looking at Whirlwind all time high."

Frank said, instantly, "Ya not."

"One-oh-eight-one-two, two twenty," he said.

Ada knew Frank didn't have a clue. "Ten million, eight hundred and twelve thousand—"

"ArchRivals," Henry said, like she wasn't even speaking.

Frank's face lit up. "BasketBrawl?"

"Hell yeah," Henry agreed.

And just like that they slapped palms. They got in the front seats, and Ada risked their temper by how long it took to stuff the three bags of dirty clothes in the back seat and then wedge herself into the Civic on top. It was a quarter a load cheaper at the campground to wash, and only a penny a minute to dry. Ada figured if the garage didn't get the truck repaired by dark, they'd be spending the night in town anyway. At least this way, it wouldn't be in a laundromat, lugging clothes up and down the road at all hours like a string of ants hauling off whole raisins. She squirmed herself upright and balanced the bleach bottle on her sneakers. The detergent was her armrest. As they bounced along, she counted time. If she planned everything just right, she'd more than make it, have the clothes clean in the bags, her own self clean in her clean clothes, and her hair dried under the hand-dryer on the wall in the restroom with plenty of time to spare for Frank to get them back to the garage by four.

Even so, she hurried. Frank went on through the store to the game room. At least Henry carried one of the bags in. He dropped it at the door of the laundry, and vanished. Maxine helped Ada get the other two in. Ada, overfilled the machines, because she had only the two dollars. Albert hadn't given her the money for the wash yet. She had some change in her pocket, and she had enough. As soon as the machines were churning, Maxine stopped back by. She had Ada's shampoo kit, which the girl left there each time. Shampoo and a comb, towel, one of Albert's shirts big enough for a coverup. Ada ran to the LADIES and stripped, put on Albert's shirt, and ran back to the laundry with her clothes, stuffed them in the wash, and fled to the showers. She wore the towel around her shoulders, like a shawl, as though she were just coming from the pool. Maxine had no pool. Ada liked to look that way, even though she was dry.

Soon enough she was wet. She always went to the farthest stall, pulled the canvas curtain, and spun the handles all the way to hot, so it would be warming up as she laid out her things on the bench: shampoo, creme rinse, shower gel, luffa mitt, and pumice stone, for her heels, knees, and elbows. She even had a tiny jar of cream for them, after. "Skin polish," it was called, as though she were furniture, or shoes. All of these things she had afforded over time, and at great sacrifice. She had learned how to look for "sensitive" on the labels; that meant there was no fragrance, or very little, any of which she could attribute to the laundry detergent, if Albert mentioned it on the way home. She had first kept her things in a grocery bag, but Maxine had presented her with a large plastic foosdsaver with a snap-on lid. Ada kept it and the towel in a nylon backpack which Maxine hung on a hook in her storeroom. Sometimes Ada woke at night and thought about it hanging there, safe, secret. For a long time Ada did not have her name on it, and then she did. The first night she had left it there, labeled, it felt as though she had given herself away. She felt she had done something wrong. Like the old woman said she felt when the tourists wanted to take her picture and then just drive off with her in their camera, forever.

Even though she loved the toiletries and the ritual, what Ada loved most was the water. She gathered her hair up in a coil and pinned it with the barrette, to keep it off her shoulders while she bathed. She stood adjusting the shower to its fullest hottest blast, till her skin smoked in the cool air, then she turned off the hot and let the cold humble her. She dialed up moderate steam, she reached to the showerhead and aimed it low, she stood on one leg and sanded her heels smooth as riverstones. She had a razor and she used it. Albert would never know, how would he know? She wore jeans and tees and jackets, she wore socks and ugly shoes.

She scrubbed her skin with the luffa mitt and foaming gel, and rinsed and rinsed till suds swirled around her ankles. She always did all this before she unclipped the barrette and let her hair fall.

She had lathered twice and conditioned and was letting the water comb her long hair into obsidian sheets, had turned her back on the spray and then swung around, water streaming over her crown and shoulders, then her upturned face, as she reached for the handles to turn them off when Albert kicked the door open, splashed through the water draining into the center of the dressing room floor, and found her. He didn't call her name, but Maxine did. Maxine ran behind him saying, "Ada!" and then "Mr. Yazzie, no!" and then "You can't," and "Ada!" again. But by that point he had ripped the canvas curtain to one side of the stall and gone right into the shower, catching Ada by the hair.

He dragged her naked from privacy into the dressing room by the lavatories and mirrors. "Look at yourself," he said. "Look at what you are."

Maxine said, "*You.*" Maxine said, "*You* look at what *you* are. I'm calling the law and I'm bringing my gun back when I come"—here she had the shirt the girl had been using for a robe and was trying to get it onto her wet arms, Ada trembling, Maxine shaking, and Albert so steady—"and I won't be late." Maxine got the shirt onto Ada's other arm, and began to button it. "Let go!" she said, fiercely. And he did, only to take hold of the girl's hair.

Ada had her eyes shut. Ada was inside, behind her eyes. Ada was somewhere between times, like that backpack hanging on its hook.

Maxine ran. But what difference did it make by then? Albert had already kicked the bench out of his way, and all her little kit, comb, razor, barrette, and polishes had gone flying. Some of the bottles broke. The shower was still running. Ada listened to that. That was what Ada heard. When Albert opened his knife, she didn't know what it was. She didn't brace or flinch till he cut; he cut just once. Right above his fist wrapped in her hair, he freed himself with one fierce swift downward slice. His hand was trapped but nothing would stop him. He was in control; he cut the hair, only the hair. Not himself, not Ada. He cut the middle of her hair off right at the back of her skull, one rich fistful. He left a gap on the right and a hank over her other ear. That was all he left, and that was all he cut. No fixing it, no hiding it, she'd have to lop the rest with her own hands and the sheep shears. It would be shorter than Eddie's, after they shamed him home from school with lice.

Albert let her go then, and walked out. At the door he threw the hair down, so when Maxine came back, with a pair of clean jeans, she stepped on it and screamed. Albert and the boys were in the laundry, even Frank Luo was helping stuff the dryer-hot clothes into the same old bags, not folding. Nobody said a thing. Ada dressed and got her feet into her shoes, no socks. She wasn't crying. She went to the hotair hand-dryer and started to groom her hair, and when the air went over the blank place, she reached up and felt it, slowly, and still she didn't cry. She didn't look in the mirror or at the floor. She just waited.

"Honey?" Maxine said.

"He'll be back," Ada explained. Waiting.

"Let's go," Albert said at the door; this time he didn't barge in. One of the campers had come, and was watching. Several were gathered in the parking lot, looking and then looking away. The boys had the laundry out to Frank's car by then, but Albert had come in a wangled Park Service pickup, and after a moment, Frank and Henry slamdunked it into the back. One of the bags split. The sky looked bad, really bad, and they could hear thunder. "Nah," Henry said. Like he knew.

Maxine, with her little pistol, followed Albert out. "Listen to me," she said. But he didn't even slow down.

"You be glad this thing's not loaded," she said.

That made the boys laugh.

"Aw-right," she said, "Listen to me."

Ada pushed past her and got into the truck.

"Not up here," Albert said, like he could smell something.

Ada got out and stepped up on the bumper and over into the bed. Henry rode in front.

"Don't go," Maxine told Ada.

But Ada was only fifteen.

"Citizen's arrest," Maxine told Albert. Frank Yuo had his Honda cranked and revved, and was out of there. Nobody even waved. "What do I tell the police when they get here?" Maxine said to Albert. At least he had rolled down his window.

"Tell them they missed me," Albert said, and drove off.

He picked up the others at the garage. The truck wouldn't be ready for three days. The old woman rode up front, with Henry and Eddie. The rest—"Shake and bake time," Bernard said—jostled along in back. The wind dried Ada to the bone in only a few miles. Her hair—the barrette was gone—flew and whipped. The sky was dark and promising, clouds heavy with water already beginning to fringe at the bottom so that she drew her breath, to catch rainscent on the land. She rode with her back braced against the side of the truck, facing north; she could see all the sky from east to west. The clouds ran ahead of them, and behind them. Plummy rich clouds with the rain falling in long gray and silver streaks. Virga rain, rain that falls but never hits the ground. A desert kind of rain. Maybe a bird besides the thunderbird could fly through it, go up where it was raining, like the nuns' kingfisher flying through the rainbow. But there was lightning, sometimes hail, and other dangers. The thunderbird could catch the lightning in its claws; his hurled bolts hit the ground, but the rain did not. In a land so dry, it was enough to hope that the sky itself would somehow have the good of the storm, though it never refreshed the earth. She could imagine that, how that could be, but she could not imagine why.

Some Stranger's Bed

It was in an oystering month when Shally woke—sober after how long?—
opening her good eye and attention to watch the seasoned bateau slip
down the creek along the edge of her left periphery, a small wooden
boat high on the low tide, gray in the mist, and already so far out in the
Beausauvais River the sea breeze didn't blow the motor noise her way at
all—unless she was deaf, now, too? She turned her head, heard her burned
hair rasp against the pillow, smelled sulfur and lye soap and the rusty iron
bedstead like blood, and the metallic medicinal scent of iodine scorched
dry on a cotton rag.

There came another knock. That's what had woken her, a rapping. Not
evil. Not righteous. Then another. She scrabbled up a fistful of lank sheet
under her hip—too weak to raise her arm?—and hollered, "Door!" As
though she were accustomed. And accompanied.

Not opportunity, she decided, after the second knock.

"Somebody?" Her own voice was all.

There was no one. She felt it then—abandonment. She slept again.
When she opened her eye the next time she was as far along as before, but
no farther, in solving the mystery of herself. She took it all with determined
cheer, the way she always did, till she could remember. Soon enough she'd
remember. This time was different though, for she woke hollow, well past
the usual wretchedness and heavy weather of a long night with a bottle.
And she woke clean, in a clean bed, and she woke alone.

Morning, she reckoned. The bateau had been empty of cargo—no piled oysters freighting it low in the water. She was so sure about the oysters! But where else would the boat be going? Outward bound, toward a day's work on the flats.

She had to start somewhere surveying the world, had to apply a label or flag and start somewhere, starting over; something in her knew about tonging oysters and heading outward to do so, to the flats where the boat was headed—which meant she was what? A water woman? Bound to some water man? Waiting on some man? Waiting on some oysters? How could that be? *Who* could that be? She reckoned this boat did not carry a luckless man, some man giving up early, heading back. No. He was a man on his way. Some freshness, some clue from the air itself, a hint she could not name persuaded her he was headed out. It was morning. Her best opinion.

She considered her opinion of luck. A low opinion. She'd given up on it—it wasn't worth a penny wish. Years and years gone now, any resident hope she had ever had for luck.

Years and years? Was she so old? So unlucky? She closed her good eye and considered some more.

It was interesting to furnish her mind like this, one bit of salvage at a time, randomly dragging in this prejudice or that, propping it up like a mirror shard, catching a little glimpse of herself. Hope was next. Hope: *yea* or *nay?* Her policy on hope—how did it differ from her policy on luck? Something stirred: deep, central. Anger? Nausea? Not nausea, she decided, but dread.

She knew what to do about dread. She slept again, dove back into oblivion, into the dark below fact and fear, and she hid behind one sealed bum right eye taped shut beneath a patch of gauze. The other lid lowered like a blind, healthy, quivering as she watched her dreams.

Eventually she peeled that good eye open again from its nap and dragged it around the walls, twice around the room, higher and higher each time until she found the sky in the window. The screenless casement was open. This was a shack on the marsh, the open shutter a clue that mattered in the mystery, in the solving. Her heart gave a thump. What was it she knew, in her heart, but hadn't yet remembered in her mind? The storm shutter tapped flat against the wall in a stir of breeze, swung back halfway. So that was the knocking, solved. Now what?

Oystering months have an *r*. Yes!

She liked solving whatever it was this way, slowly, easing up on it. It was a game, it was like outwitting someone other than herself. May, June, July, and August ruled out. That left only eight. Any month on the Beausauvais can have good weather, open window weather. A window can stand open on any good day or night—or never close at all. But this must close, sometimes, since the shutter moved easily on its hinges, slammed but didn't creak. What if that wasn't the Beausauvais out there? Had to be, since it was the only name she could come up with. That's how her mind was working; she could hardly trust it, but she did.

"All right, all right," she said. "I need more clues." She sulked. She believed someone must be near. Not hope, but deduction. Things had been done to her, for her, but by whom? Surely not that up-at-dawn stranger in the boat.

"Your turn," she said. Louder, she said, "Now. You." Ceding what she thought was her turn. Playing fair. With whom? Might as well be talking to God, since she'd already given him notice and was done with that. Things inside her wavered; things outside shimmered. She slept again.

Woke angry. She lay thinking, too weak yet to thrash or fan around. Yelled, hurling her voice like a stone, a dry pebble—"You!"—but without expectation now. She noticed that. Noticed how she didn't let her self care, just in case. So that was her whitepaper on hope: *behave against*, not *believe in*. She felt old.

Was she so old? Head too heavy to lift and look. Hands way off at the ends of watery arms, and tangled. Missing! No . . . bandaged. No . . . what?

Sleeves. Sleeves! She had forgotten sleeves—as an idea, as an item. The concept opened a whole new wardrobe door in her mind. She peered in.

She marveled. She began to suspect she had been very ill, very far gone. Maybe this was not "the morning after." Who knew how many mornings this was after? All of them, of course. She felt like she had fallen from heaven and landed on a soft place. Which is exactly what had happened. She had thrown herself away, thrown her life away, cursed God and died. Or thought she had. And He had thrown her back.

"It's not over," she realized, when she lay considering it, knowing she was alive on earth, and she was *she,* female woman, in some stranger's— some giant's—boiled and starched (she smelled it) Sunday shirt. Was he giant? Or was she small? Was she grateful?

She thought of herself, what she recalled of herself, easing up on her bodily self fact by fact: *how* she was, not just who. Didn't have to face *who* right now. She took stock of her extents, inventoried the whole and here and now of herself in tiny flexions, surges, and ebbs of muscle and nerve.

The view from the window hadn't changed all day. Had it been all day? If it were a window and not a painting, it could have been all day. If it were a painting, there would be no change, no clue, and there would go her only hint: oystering. But she had the boat in her mind. Hadn't she seen the boat? Heard the boat? Or had she dreamed the boat? She rolled her bruised cheek deeper into the pillow to aim her good eye on recon out the window. This took heroic moments. She tried to remember. Same day, had to be the same day, maybe the same hour or two. A very still time.

There was no boat, but she was certain there had been a boat. She was sure the framed scene was window and real sky, not a painting. Why would anyone hang a picture of what was already there?

Yet not a bird trespassed that sky by wing or cry. She ruled out spring. No marsh creatures calling, no peepers.

"November fog coming in," she decided, but almost immediately changed her mind. Not fog but a whiff of steam, of stink, from the pulp mill. As soon as the wind shifted on the turn of the tide, she'd get more than one lungful of reality. She recognized it, that stillness, that pause, as the moment before the turn. There it came, and the breath from the mill; she breathed it in. It got real, then. Everything she was thinking up about this place got real. She quickened, she believed—she *knew*—she was somewhere real. These mill stinks were part of her life from birth, the first air she had breathed in her life, so she knew where she was, more or less. She had made it back that far on the broken circle.

For the moment, she placed herself between now and then, right in the heartless heart of time. If she'd thought to, she could have called herself by name, now, but she was so busy remembering things the sulfurous smog brought to memory that it never crossed her mind to know her own name. She just was. She was so busy *being,* in a cold morning forty years ago, watching the train lurching toward the Hercules Powder Company with a heavy load of pine stumps to be rendered into household cleaners and terps [yes, turps][turps?] and gunpowder and rayon underwear. This is what her cousins told her went on behind those gates, the barbed-wire atop the fences and around the guard house keeping people out, keeping people in. Like prison. She grew up imagining it, believing it, every bit of it—especially about the gunpowder that put the POW! in her uncle's squirrel gun and her auntie's pink ribbon-striped Sears Catalog rayon step-ins, which Shally assumed were a by-product of gunpowder itself, not merely of pine stumps.

One day, when she called Hercules a prison, her aunt corrected her. Explained a lot of the mystery away, how it wasn't prisoners in there behind those tall fences with the barbed wire on top, it was folks doing chemistry. The very word thrilled her, and later, when she heard of chemistry between courting couples, she brought the early memories all to bear, including the barb wire and the high gate and the gunpowder and the underwear. The danger signs and warnings against trespass. So what if it wasn't a prisoner doing 'chemistry'? It was still thrilling. It was still dangerous. High explosives were what she thought of as the reason why her aunt hung underwear on the line between two towels—to keep the heat of the sun from kindling them. Shally thought that's what her cousins meant when they spoke of "hot pants." Shally's mama had had them, and everybody said so, but when Shally asked about it, her auntie laughed and said, "Child, that is *ignorant.* What you don't know you ought not be studying." Laughed again and shook out some white lady's nightgown and pegged it on the line folded over so it didn't look like anything but a square of blue cloth. When Shally pinned socks and stockings—yes, some white ladies were too fine to even wash out their own nylons—her momma's sister came along and covered them with a towel too. Anything underwear stayed under. Shally stood on a milk crate to reach the lines. The whole back yard was strung with lines. They started at the very back, and worked toward the house. When she had been little, she had loved to run between the lines of cool damp sheets, a strip of sky above her. Now she was old enough to help, and she did, an apron lumpy with clothes-pins tied around her waist. She hung washcloths and towels on one line, like things together, and sizes matching and colors, so it was easy to sort them—just unpin and drop them into the baskets later. Shally and her Aunt Lillian worked together out in the sunny lot all morning; in the afternoon they plucked things down into the baskets and hauled them in, and after supper they ironed. At first Shally was allowed to iron only the flat things, sitting at the mangle, driving sheets and coveralls through the rollers, but after she found her skill and patience, when she could be trusted not to break or melt a button, she did collars and cuffs and ruffles and pockets by hand, setting things up for her aunt's perfecting finish.

Tuesday evenings, they used Uncle Sampson's Chevrolet, and delivered. White folks home at night, all of them; during the day some ladies wouldn't answer the door, or would make excuses, like the mister took all the money with him when he went to work. If you went after suppertime on Wednesday, they'd some of them hide in the house with the lights off, pretending they were at prayer meeting at church. Sometimes you could hear the TV! Note on the door saying, "Lillie—Leave the things on the porch glider," but if you did, they—not all of them, though—would complain things were messed up and smeared and dew-spoiled, and want a discount. But the way Sampson saw it, "Nobody get a second chance," and he'd take the things home, and on the note that said leave them, he'd write, "Come and get."

Her Aunt [Lillian] separated the lady things into one parcel, the man clothes into another. Boy things from girls. Even in baby sizes. The lesson was the same, every time. "Whole world don't have to know what you naturally got, or who you mixing it with," her aunt said. "Remember that, and forget the rest." Even when Shally hadn't been thinking about her momma, there it was, that task of forgetting "the natural." She associated "nature" with the smell of pine. The washing always smelled like pine. Fresh and sunshine sweet and subtly piney, those clean things airing on the line, but in the house, nose-burning pine reek in the mop bucket and in the commode. For a long time Shally thought it was just their house, but after she got to school, and visiting friends after, and stopping off at the bus station when her cousin Tobe got the job as janitor, there it was again, that piney wonk. And in the alley behind the market, where they threw the water and dried the mops, and she had to step carefully around cloudy puddles to get to Mr. Otto's ice house, she realized that the pine cleaner, so amber in the bottle, yet magically white in the bucket, was for everyone. It didn't matter what the signs said, when it came to dirt: WHITE or COLORED needed the same remedy.

The muley trains ran night and day, Seaboard and Southern, hoggers hauling in the uprooted pitchy stumps in open gondolas. There were lots of wild berries along the rail cuts, and the easy path to them was there on the tracks. Shally ran with the gang. Not on the rails, too hot for bare feet, but sparrow-hopping tie to tie. Everything was a game. You could feel the rumble of the trains underfoot before you could hear them. She always stepped off, well away, and watched. Sometimes the men running the engine hollered or waved back. A new picture came into her mind, whole other calendar and day.

"Lord God! I got to get this uniform clean," she realized, jumping forward almost twenty years. "Can't go to work like this!" Remembering a pot of coffee flung in a quarrel about whether it was hot enough. The grounds flinging out, too. As usual her temper accomplishing nothing but more work for herself.

She raised her hand, or tried to, to brush the grounds away, woke herself to the here and now grunting from how hard it was to try to lift her arm. She figured it out, this time. Realized it was loose sleeves and she was caught on them by her own weight. That was the problem.

She was lying there in some stranger's bed, clean and square as a laid-out corpse. Buttoned up and tucked in neat. She gathered herself, her strength and wits, and wind-milled herself free of restraints, kicking the top sheet back, ripping a shoulder seam open in the shirt. Free, she lay there panting like something newborn. Before she could backslide into sleep, she railed and flailed some more and rolled over. Sat up.

Exhilarated, she touched her soles to the bare boards and teased herself with three tries. On the fourth she was up, standing flatfooted, and walking. Upright. Unpropped.

"Yes'm," she said, turning all around, slowly. She looked the place over, but she remembered nothing about it. From this vantage, she could see a line of trees through the open window, a dark smudge of headland way off.

Her hands touched the bandage on her eye, trying to figure it out. She fingered the bruise on her skull, pressing it a little, but no pain instructed her memory. She was healing. She wanted a looking glass. She desired it, yearned to see for herself. She wasn't afraid of what she'd see: herself, of course—who else? She moved through the two rooms of the little shack, came to the tacked-on water closet built onto the back porch, a mere booth, with cold water only. She figured right when she reasoned that a soul who'd fit the shirt she was wearing was man enough to shave. He had a small mirror, brass frame dark with weather and salt, its glass mottled. Must be a tall man for sure. Solitary, no comforts in sight for a woman. She tilted the mirror her way, but still she had to stand on tiptoe, lean up on the lavatory, and peer sidelong.

"All right," she said quietly, after looking.

What she saw was a henna-burned, dark-skinned, bright-eyed (the one she could see at any rate), knob-cheeked, used-but-not-used-up, dried-out alky who wasn't about to blink. Or die. She said again, "All right," as though she were agreeing to something. Life, maybe. Life, certainly. Out there in the marsh she had made a deal with her maker, had torn up all contracts and covenants heretofore acknowledged and thrown them in his face. She'd done her best to extinguish that last spark of life, and the breath of God's merciless mercy had blown her back into the world. She had added it all up out there, moving from disgrace to disgrace, and she decided going beat staying, no matter where she wound up. She sure hadn't planned to wake up this side of hell.

For a long time she had figured her disgrace was because of her baptizing. She had finally done it, finally agreed to it, the year before she met Cyrus, the year she was practicing solos every Sunday and thought she had to belong. The choir director had made it plain enough, "Visitors and drop ins don't solo." That year she had thought maybe a person learned how to be right after committing to it, and not the other way around, still believing perfect was possible, and freedom too. She was sixteen. She thought the folks singing around her meant it, were living the life they sang about in their songs. And their "devil under cover" preacher was young and fiery and single and came to them from Atlanta, and had toured with the Morehouse singers. Came in full of bold ideas and challenges. Claimed it was time for the redeemed of the Lord to say so. Taught them songs about freedom. Just the way he said freedom out loud, not holy-like, like the older men. And in all that stir and singing, Shally had stepped forward. She could sing. But it was more than that.

She had thought that was faith. She had signed up for full immersion. And now it was her turn for baptism, so out into the wide bend of the creek water she had gone, her sleeves floating upward like wings and the weight of her long white robes dragging her down as she waded out, her head wrapped in white, the deacon and Reverend Akins each with a hand on her arms. One would lay her back, handkerchief over her nose, the other would raise her up again, in the name of the Name. And just then, when she was already dunked under to death and about to rise filled with light, here came some wild white boy from the country club rounding that bend in a ski boat, losing control on the turn, and just full throttle wallowing across toward the beach, scattering everyone like chickens— even the preacher and the deacon. They abandoned her. It was every man for himself. The barefoot skier lost the rope and found it again when the driver swung back and caught him on the move—no idling—and they got past without cutting up anyone in the churn and wake. They were gone around the bend before Shally fell back under again, and rose up on her own out there, saving herself, and scrambling toward the bank. She'd been scrambling ever since. The truth was as plain as the rooster tail behind that Johnson outboard, which just kept on going: Of course. It was up to her.

That was the end of that. She had trusted these church people with her life, and with her soul. And they had left a gap and her drowning in it. She had dragged herself up out of the water along the bank farther downstream from the rest of them, and made her way home.

"We can do this again!" one of them called after her, and she had turned, looking, taking it all in: the huddled group with their black umbrellas raised against the sun, the choir still swaying and stamping.

After that, she had found another church. Right in town, other side of the river. She still liked to sing, and sometimes she soloed. And she always liked to dress up. Most of all, she liked the way some of the younger members talked about how things ought to be—and could be. Like there was something to do about freedom, and to think about, and to live for, not just sing about. She'd been trying to fit in for a long time. Maybe if she couldn't fit in she could stand out. High school got more interesting after that, and she started thinking about college.

She pointed at her reflection in the stranger's shaving glass and her reflection pointed back. They'd know each other anywhere: Shally Jenkins, born Jones. Named for her daddy's grandmother, raised by her mama's daddy, on the other side of the river. The very shapes of her fingers and thumbs—she looked at her hands, at the drumsticks of those thumbs—were her grandmother's own. She smiled at herself with her grandmother's wily smile. She thought of something; checked the mirror, open-mouthed. She still had her teeth, even the gold one.

"They'd have had to pull it to pawn it," she said.

No earrings. She'd pawned them herself. Also the finger rings. She didn't know where the POW bracelet was with Cyrus's name on it, or her graduation watch. Maybe with personal effects, in lockup. That hurt, remembering how she couldn't go back for anything or they'd lock her up again. Make it harder, too, this time, since she had walked off.

They should have known she would. "Or die trying," as Cyrus would have said. Maybe *he* did die trying. Or maybe he was dead before he hit the ground. Or dead swinging in a tree, his chute strings tangled in the jungle, on the other side of that river in between the two Vietnams. No one knew. All they knew was that his chute had opened. That was hope enough for Shally; it had to be. Government hadn't done one thing—or the Air Force either—to bring him or his dog tags home. Shally said MIA isn't KIA, and until someone proved it, she'd just keep on waiting for him, praying for him, and daring God to prove up. And she had stood it somehow, almost twenty years, for her boy Jacob's sake, and then Jacob died, and she just—Well, what *had* she done? She didn't even remember a lot of it. But the part she would have loved to forget was always waiting for her in the morning, like a stray dog on her doorstep. It was waiting here now. She felt the anger flame up like fire, or try to. But there was nothing left; she was a desolation, a burned-out match.

She'd given up faith in God for spit-in-His-eye spite in the year since their son had died. She'd gotten lost—all the way lost—on the way home from work a week after her son's funeral. Once Shally started drinking, she didn't want to be found, didn't want Cyrus to come marching home now, asking her about what had happened, what she had let happen, the hell on their homefront she had never seen coming while he was gone to war. Her grandmother had had a cherry tree, and the birds got every one of them the year Shally was seven, the first summer after she moved from the coast, and had sworn with a stamp of her foot she was old enough to keep watch. Now Shally felt like that tree—picked clean. Her grandmother had said, "There'll be another spring." Maybe so, that time. But not this time, not for Shally. And there wasn't anybody left to say it, anyway, even if it were a lie.

Months passed. Things she would never remember happened while she was trying to forget. Now Shally stood in the stranger's house on the marsh, alive on earth when what she had expected was . . . she couldn't think what. Whatever it is that "alive on earth" isn't. She had wound up here by the salt sea, had followed the highway east, walking away from the county work detail, only thing that would've stopped her was a bullet, and that would only have been a shortcut, a favor, saving her a few blisters from cheap shoes and no socks. Oh. she had been so sure of where she was headed, she couldn't fail to get there.

This wasn't it. Waking alive wasn't it.

Chapter by chapter, she had walked through and out of the story of her life in her campaign against God and man, losing every battle. She had left behind her whole broken family, scattered living and dead along that U.S. highway like Styrofoam cups and burger wrappers eddying in the breeze of passing trucks. That one road, she now saw, was not just a line on a map; it scarred and directed the pilgrimage of her entire life.

"Highway 82," she said. And that was her answer, it always had been, to who she was and also to what came next.

She was going back. There was nowhere else. She'd—oh, she remembered it now!—carried a bottle in her hand and waded out into the marsh. And sat. Low tide. She'd sat down in the bottom of the gully where the tips of reeds and spartina caught the polleny gold sunlight above her head. She was hidden like Moses in the rushes, without a boat, or God.

"God," she said. She had thought. Had thought about it. Anything else to say about it, something else to decide? Time for the creed or a prayer here. She had cleared her throat and spat. Then sat deeper, untucking her legs and stretching them out in front of her. Drank, drunk. Considered. She was through. She was through resisting arrest and life and death and anything else. She was done. Done with struggle and wriggle and accusing and blame. Done with waiting. She wished—she had tried—to throw it away, not just give up. If there was a wish, a last wish, that was it and all of it. Something to show her contempt, a big strong toss-off, not just some dying weepy gesture. She wished to go out shouting, making a scene. Something loud and unpleasant.

Dying, what was that? Nothing to God—hadn't she noticed?—but part of the plan. No, not plan. Doings, that's all it was. Makings and unmakings. She *had* noticed. "Lord, you gonna win," she said, "but ain't gon' be pretty." He'd have to defeat her; she wouldn't just let him win.

She had tried to get up but she was too far gone. She tumbled back into the mire. One foot was bare, the shoe sucked right off it into the black muck. The little crabs came up to her, tested her toes. Fiddled with her shoelaces. They got used to her. They got bold. She didn't even brush them away after a while. They were everywhere. Eyes like little stalked pearls, gray as mud. They rustled around, sideways, one claw up to fend, to fight. She thought they were funny at first, but they kept on. Oh, the way they kept on. She began to talk to them. Something like them had been at her all her life, scuttling, nipping. Not the biting; it was the nipping that focused her fury and despair.

"All adds up," she told them. Tribute. She raised the bottle, a toast to attrition. They paused, vigilant, waiting. If she clapped her hands, they'd vanish? She tried it, and they rushed off. But they came back; she noticed them again, and she slapped her hand against the bottle. They side-scuttled and waited. "Not yet," she told them.

Soon enough.

One had got up on her hat.

She wasn't wearing a hat.

Confused, she swung at herself, her fist around the neck of the bottle. Some little last spirit rose up in her and she was fighting again, fighting it out, hand to hand. Brawling with herself. That's what had happened to her eye, as the tide turned. She had clobbered her own lights out.

She'd been waiting on that silvery creeping water her whole afternoon but she didn't even notice it when it came. It found her slumped, her fist still clenched, her brain halloing down the poisoned well of alcoholic insult as she tumbled into the dark, headed for the black bottom. No stars. Wasn't any sky in hell. Hell was like an open wound. She fell and fell.

And she'd wound up here. On clean dry floorboards above the marsh, clean and dry herself, and backtracking, grappling up memories and anything else she needed, all she cared to haul away. Yes, away. Sure as hell wasn't going to stay.

She wondered if she could see from that patched eye. She peeled the tape and looked in the mirror: tears and blood seeping out from under the swollen, drooping lid. She considered. She sighed. Rubbed the tape gently back down. She could travel. Even with a patched eye, she could travel.

One eye was enough. If she just had some coffee, something to eat, she was on her way.

Part of Shally wanted to stay. One more night, that's all. Just to thank— courtesy and curiosity, not real gratitude—whoever it was who had found her, had dragged her out of the creek and brought her here and cleaned her up and smoothed on the butterfly strips and laid on the adhesive tape, nipping it with his teeth, taping her back together. Whose place this was. Whose place *was* this? Nothing worth stealing. Nothing new except the blades for his razor.

It was crazy, his leaving the blades like that. Like she wouldn't reach for the razor. She did. She had to. She knew it when she saw it, knew it was the next thing to do.

She had to get on with it. Her orange prison suit wasn't anywhere in sight, so unless he had taken it out and buried it, what had he done with it? She considered that he might have taken it to town to show someone who cared. From the look of her eye, and the worst cut already sealed and scabbed and puckering, and the color of the bruises, it had been several days, maybe almost a week. If he had been going to turn her in, he already would have, and saved himself some trouble and wash water. But since she couldn't be sure, she got on with it, soon as the water was hot. No stove, just a propane burner. She brought tap water to a simmer and took her time. She believed, she had to believe, she'd have time.

She used bar soap. She took off what clothes she had—nothing on under the man's long-tailed white shirt almost down to her knees—and stood with the door open for more light but needed still more, so she brought the mirror out and balanced it on the rail, and stood on the back porch working in broad day. Anyone passing by on the creek would have seen every bit of her, but no one did. She'd have waved.

She shaved her head first.

She lathered up with his worn-down hand soap and worked by feel. She slung the razor clean, rinsed, and cut another swath, easy, easy. The wind blew the scrapings away. She wasn't worried about anybody doing any conjuring with her skint-off hair; she never glanced at it again. Let a bird have it for a nest lining next spring, some flycatcher maybe, mix it all up with a snakeskin and raise babies like she had been raised, on cast-offs and hand-me-downs.

She'd sworn she'd do better by her own, and she had. Everything had got better when she left the coast, got herself delivered to the only family who'd have her, way inland, where she was headed back, now, soon as she could go. They were gone, but she wanted to talk to their graves. Or maybe she wouldn't. Maybe there wasn't any point. Some things just couldn't be explained. Or forgiven.

Shally's arms got tired.

She set her bare self down on those sun-hot boards and rested, watching the late-season butterflies pattering south through the bright air.

When she could, she shaved on. Finished with her skull. Did her brows. Had to work around the bandage. She rinsed carefully, let the tepid water pour down over her arms and legs, rinsed her back. Shook herself like a duck. She changed blades again—the next to last one—and shaved all over, and when she was done, she flipped the blade, and used the last edge of it to smooth down the rough places. She heated more water and rinsed again. Scalded the razor. Dried it. Then she put the last new blade in the razor and set it on the shelf. She put the mirror back.

She had nicked herself in a couple of places, but nothing serious. She poured a little Wesson oil on her hands and rubbed it on, from skull to footsoles. She was bald as a statue. Eyelashes were all that was left. The breeze on her skin felt like silk.

She used the stranger's oyster knife to pry the fake nails from her fingers, scraped the glue off and everything else till she made the quick skin below the nails burn rose pink. De-taloned, shorn, clean, she dried in the sun, then poured herself a cup of coffee from a fresh pot. Coffee was all she had to drink, the strongest thing she could find. She drew her own conclusions about that: one pillow on the bed, one mug, one spoon. No dresser, no woman things, just a nail for his clothes and a cardboard box. He was flying low, and solo, and definitely not first class. In the whole place not a whiff of alcohol, not even after-shave or witch hazel. No glittering empty bottles littering the low tide, no malt cans glinting from the midden of crab and oyster shells.

She drank another cup of coffee and ate ate the rest of his stale bread the dried out ends last, torn into tough handfuls. She could have used an egg. Some beans. Sardines. She finished the bread and it made her hungrier to know it was all gone. She imagined a panful of fish, crisp little ones just turned up at head and tail to fit the skillet. She imagined grits. Buttermilk. Sausage. Her grandmother's fresh plum juice. Anything.

She crouched and looked, felt in and atop and under and along every shelf. When she found the box of canned goods, she yanked it forward and stared, chose a can of pears and a jar, already half gone, of peanuts. She ate and ate them. Drank more coffee, punched a hole in the can of pears and drank off the juice, then finished the peanuts. She used his knife to hack open the pears, and with her bare hands slipped the pieces onto her tongue and swallowed them whole, like oysters. Nothing had ever tasted so good.

She was still naked.

She washed her face and hands, shook them dry. Standing on the edge of the porch she rubbed her gums and teeth with a finger dipped in salt. She rinsed and spat, rinsed and spat.

Lunch, or something, was making the pulse drum fast in the hollow of her throat. Maybe the coffee, maybe the sugar, maybe the salt, maybe feeling how the sun was moving on toward late, toward fate, and she needed to make up her mind, get this show on the road. She sat in the sun, reconsidering her options: stay one more night—just to see who he was—or go on now while the going was good. Sleep was a trap. She didn't need any more sleep. Or traps. She needed action, to get moving and keep on moving, that was how she felt, and what she decided. The bed didn't tempt her, with or without him. She pulled herself to her feet and found and shook the shirt she had waked up in, washed it with the bar of soap, hung it in the sun. She wouldn't be around to bring it in dry, or press it smooth. It filled like a sail. She buttoned it around the railing, so it wouldn't fly away. If she stayed an extra hour, an extra night, it was as good as dropping anchor.

Better to go. No apology, or explanation, nothing to extricate herself from later by guile or by God.

"If his heart breaks, it'll mend," she muttered, not really believing serious damage was in store. She prowled idly around the room, finding what she could use of the man's clothing. Nothing fancy or fitting, but better than jailhouse scrubs, for sure. She'd been in for vagrancy? Public drunk? Mayhem? Disorderly conduct? Resisting an officer? She didn't quite remember the charges. She figured she was still wanted, though. She wasn't running when she left the work detail, she just saw her chance and stepped off, and she did not look back. Free as she'd ever be, she simply walked away. That first night she had expected to hear dogs, or gunshots, or helicopters, but she hadn't.

She imagined the oysterman taking her orange jail clothes and finding a way to weigh them down and drown them in a land where there are no rocks. It made her laugh—the first time she had laughed this side of the line she had drawn across her life. A scornful, tough, realist's laugh that bet neither on hope nor luck. Nor kindness.

"Time to move on along," she said.

Shoes, now. She couldn't find her own. Not under the bed. Not on the porch, or fallen to the ground. No way would her feet fit his. Wouldn't do to take them anyway—they looked like churchgoing shoes. Real and righteous shoes. Polished and set aside, stuffed with newspapers. Ready for the streets of gold.

She'd do without, till she could do better. Had to be careful so long as there were sandspurs around, and the road pavement burning hot and the shoulders wreaking agony with broken oyster shells. She rolled up his khaki work britches four times, to just above her ankles. The waist and hips were loose on her but not impossible. She used a spare shoelace and snaked it through the belt loops and tied it in front, pleating the pants safe and close. She wore his work shirt untucked. No unders; she'd never borrow anything like that. Just slid her clean self into the khaki and buttoned his brown shirt with its monogrammed patch like a service station attendant's. Shook her head, thinking how old-time that sounded now everybody pumped their own. Meter reader, she decided. "Adams" the patch said. All she knew of him, all she knew of his name, if that was his shirt.

She didn't leave him a slice of bread, or peanuts. She left things tidy though. And was making a note, in her head, but couldn't find paper or pen. This wasn't a writing and reading stand. She did note a couple of King Jameses and a palm-size New Testament, over by the door on a shelf. Was he in the business of giving them out—or taking them home, maybe from hospital stays? Her granny had got one like that, her last trip. Shally shook an interesting tin box, rusted shut: the sound was not pencil and pen, but it was papery and lightly thuddy and sifty. She shook it again, set it down, then picked it up and pried it open.

"Ah," she said, when she saw. Surprised. Another laugh at her own foolishness: it wasn't home-rolled smokes, but pepper and salt packets and a couple of those towelettes from some barbeque stand.

She gave up, reached for his shoe polish and daubed it on the white porcelain kitchen tabletop:

Thanks
Hwy 82
Star Route
S Jenkins

Would he think that was a mailing address? He didn't know her name, did he? No more did she know his. She didn't think they had talked. No. So maybe he'd think she was from South Jenkins. Maybe in Alabama. Or Mississippi. Bound to be one somewhere. Road went on forever, and she would, too. No use laying a trail.

"I'll pay you back when I get some," she said. Out loud to make it a promise, not a lie of good intentions in her heart. Still, who knew how that would go? It could happen, and if it didn't, who heard it but Shally? She gripped the soap bar, pressed upward with both thumbs, bent and broke it, left him the smaller bit, pocketed hers.

What else? What was left?

She knew what was left: nothing. Nothing except her gold tooth, those sundown-shimmering witch-water lanes of asphalt waiting for her, beckoning west, and the rest of her natural life.

Shally Jenkins stepped off toward home.

Leaving Room

Achsa was planting bulbs, a little late, but frost came late, and she was working in cold soil, barehanded, in the going afternoon. Around her she could hear the scuffling and rustling of towhees in the fallen leaves, the quick flick of titmice and chickadees winging to the hollow in the poplar where rainwater welled. Doves began whistling in, dropping to the ground under the feeder for a last gathering of easy seeds. Somewhere in the woods the first whitethroat called, that thin and icy cancellation of mellow autumn, silver as a pin. The whitethroats didn't come to the feeding ground by flight, but by sifting low, sure-gripping along limb by limb through the brush. Hoping, but not counting on. At home in the tangles.

Achsa scattered bone meal into the bottom of the hole she had dug, the bone of *what* she did not know. She did not think of herself as squeamish, yet for a time she had not taken her tea or coffee from bone china, when she had read about the Napoleonic wars and the dead horses and their battlefield skeletons being used to make porcelain, cups so fine you could see the light through them. In fact, Achsa had not gone into her parlor at all, but had taken her coffee on the porch or in the kitchen, sitting on a wobbly chair, sipping from a common yard-sale mug, and had worked to *not* appreciate the finer things. This season of austerity had hurt her and bewildered her, because the finer things—old and cherished and lovely remnants she had rescued from the wreck—were the very things she had chosen to hold on to, to protect her fallen life from vulgarity and meanness as she paid off Rome's gambling debts. It took years, because she couldn't find him to serve papers—not that she had wanted to, and not that she ever did. And it took years because during that time he kept on gambling.

Oh, how intriguing those legal ads were, before they applied to her own situation: notices in local newspapers from faraway lawyers, staking or relinquishing spousal claims and giving first or second or final notice. She wasn't going to send him any news like that, and she had doubted he'd send her any. They had parted company—it seemed to her quite suddenly—and for a long time that was how it had stood. "He's not back yet," was all she explained. After a time, people who loved her quit asking.

When they'd gotten married, she had thought she would be a school-teacher, had a year to go, but had sewed britches for Empire Textiles instead. Through a decade, she had moved up, into payroll, and become the mill's head bookkeeper. She had thought she knew Jerome well enough, but she discovered better. She raised his boy Chip—her only mothering, no babies of her own—and if he turned out to be her hope, he was also her despair. "Chip off the old block," everyone said, especially the boys-will-be-boys indulgers. How cute is that the hundredth time? She only had to raise him—or more to the point rescue him—for a dozen years, then he and his dad both vanished, same day, same road, different directions. Chip joined the Marines. His daddy had gone to hell all the way, no more commuting. He might have come back, but not to her. She never saw him again.

She loved the feel of the tulips, solid in their papery jackets. She set them carefully in the hole, the larger ones on the perimeter, the smaller in the center, each with its spark of life. She had written a quote in her new Bible, years ago, when she changed from King James to New International Version: "translation it is that openeth the kernel"? What had she written? Not scripture, but it was good enough to go in her Bible. She didn't even remember who said it. Odd that she would think of it right then. A kernel is a seed, a bulb isn't, but sounds chewier, like a tulip would be. She was irritated that she would remember only a part, and yet need to know, and feel so restless about it she would consider—as she knelt there—whether she should go look it up. She wasn't sure if she was unsettled because she couldn't remember, or if it might be the rest of the quote held some God message she'd really rather not know. Above all, she didn't like leaving a job in the middle; she was a follower-through. She didn't like forgetting things, either. She was beginning to be old enough to worry about that, but still young enough that if she mentioned it, it looked like she was fishing for a compliment.

Sometimes the promptings of God were subtle and sometimes not, Achsa thought. A sermon in chapel, in college, had stayed fresh her whole life. A visiting exhorter of young females had warned them to open their minds "wide as God, but no wider." She hoped she did not have a narrow mind, but she never had been sure if that was what he meant. What could be wider than God? At any rate, Achsa was a practical thinker, and she preferred concrete suggestions to hints. She felt God knew this about her, and did what and all He could, but God—as Achsa saw it—is a hinter. She had come to believe, for example, that when she was having trouble with the sewing machine tension, or some other frustration with the mechanism of the machine that prevented forward progress, it was God's way of telling her to check her work, make sure she was on track. She would save time and seam-ripping, very often, when she did stop and check her pattern again.

Achsa decided to go in. She left things just as they were, but rolled the bone meal bag secured a rubberband doubled around and sealed tight in case a dog or other bone-loving animal decided to come calling.

She hadn't been thinking about Rome, although sometimes she did. As far as she was concerned, he was as dead as those Napoleonic horses. But here came that memory of their burying the good old shepherd dog they had called Bear, who'd presented himself at their back door dotted with ticks and cockleburs and adopted them at first sniff, living out his twilight years in their young marriage. When Bear had died, they had dug and dug. He would have helped them, if he could, he was a grand digger, and that just made it worse. Finally they had settled the earth back onto the grave and Chip had shouted, "Wait! Wait!" and run into the house and brought the can of pepper from the pantry. His own idea. He shook it all over the grave and around. "So things don't dig him up." Solemn as an owl. Neither he nor Rome could stand to show their feelings. She had always thought that was why Rome had shaken the last bit of powder from the pepper can, rubbed it on his hands and across Chip's face and eyes, so he'd sneeze, sneeze, sneeze, eyes dripping the only tears he'd shed. She had been outraged. But now, looking back, she wondered if it had been not meanness but an instinctive act of love on Rome's part, to help the boy's congested heart let go? She also thought that might be why Rome drank; to keep the lid on and the edge off.

The death of Chip's mama, Pearlie, had blindsided the boy and Rome so hard both their hearts were knocked unconscious. Achsa got what was left, two lanky cool characters with impulses toward wildness, as though she had taken into her heart and home migrant cranes needing rehab and fostering. She had never caged them. They came to rest with her and she let them. It had seemed an honor—perhaps even a vocation—especially when there had been rosy hope. The roses faded toward the end there after Rome—cornered—said, "My legal tender ain't tender!" Really facing facts, and not just the gutted mess at the bank—overdrawn checking, the gone savings and IRS unpaid. She pretty much began to see that there wasn't anything else for love to do but entrust what has already flown to the mercy of heaven. Wild animals do not betray. This Achsa believed, about animals. But she did not know what kind of animal a wild man is. Achsa had learned this about herself, as she worked through the lessons of those years: she would not have chosen differently, had she known. So, in the realm of keeping the mind wide open, was that success or failure?

Halfway to the house Achsa admitted why she was going in. She wasn't going to look up some quote. In her Bible, between the Old and New Testaments, lay the Christmas newsletter from Chip, letting her know that Rome was dead. He had been dead more than a year when she finally got the word. The news hadn't changed things as much as she might have thought.

It was the oddest thing. Apparently Chip was overseas, well along in his career in the service of his country. This was the first message from him in all those years. The two pages he sent were photocopied, for a mass mailing. Impersonal. "Dear friends" and almost two pages before he mentioned Jerome at all. Two pages of what the country was like where he was, a country at war, a life behind the lines and between the lines. How hard it was, on the people, the stress fractures of factions and intolerance. Her eyes had raced down the pages seeking news and relief. Or at least some clue. Why? Why now? Dread and mystery grew. "Bitter end of broken promises," Chip had written. And told how that had come about. Hopes for stability, how "All young men look forward to the day when they can marry and provide for their families in peace." But some things are not easy. Many things are "patched and repaired beyond recognition." Chip made her wait. He made her wait for it. And then two thirds of the way down the second page, there it was: "When daddy died last year . . ." Her whole life swung to a stop right there, just poised and hung on a bit of world history she could have covered with her thumb and never read at all.

She was still living in town then, in the little apartment she had called home since she had lost the house. She had walked to her window and turned the letter so the winter light hit it hard, in case she was missing something. Chip had not written to her, in particular; this was what anybody got. Then she sat down and read it all again, and only when she had done with Chip's did she open the little envelope addressed to herself in Rome's own hand. She wondered what he had found to say. What else he had found to say. Her name, written by him, at the end. "See she gets it," he had written underneath, underlined.

"This is not about rejection," he had said, the day he left.

All that was in the envelope was a photograph. No note, no date. Just a photograph and scribbled on the back, *Well, whattya know? Together again. All roads lead to Rome.*

A photograph of Rome and Chip. Rome long after she had known him, so this was her first glimpse of him older, almost old, and still cutting high jinks. This was the face—the man entire—he had taken away from her all those years ago. It had nothing to do with her now, and she didn't like to look on it, as though by sending it now he was controlling her, somehow triumphing. But he wasn't. He was already dead. Dead a year before Chip came back, sifted through things, saved the letter to be enclosed with this year's Christmas report. She looked; she had to look. Chip was just Chip, pretty much himself in desert camo, a little grizzled and hungry. Silver bars. They'd made a man of him, or at least an officer.

"All right," she said. Achsa was surprised that it didn't hurt. She could just look and look and feel nothing. Look and look at what she had thought was hers, but had belonged to him, always.

There it was, that same wild glint, still twinkling in the photo. In life, it was snuffed—not even a little spark like an ember in a wick smoking slowly out with a flourish of adieu in the dark. She had promised him, as long as she lived she would pray the Lord's Prayer for him every day. As long as she lived, not as long as he lived. A sudden rush of heat had swept up and over her, pure indignation at such a foolish wide-open promise, at all the foolish wide-open promises she kept on keeping. And she would. For some time the "our" in "Our Father" had covered it. She did not name names or get personal. The day Chip's letter came she had gotten personal, had thrown the letter and the photograph in the trash. Thrown them. Hard. But they had not landed hard; they had scattered, fluttered. She had had to stoop, bend to pick up pages, move a chair to retrieve the photo. She had never been a person to make scenes, although she imagined how good it would feel and sound to tear photographic paper. She sat and let her breathing and hands steady. She drew her mind back from the brink. She finally and simply put everything back in its envelope and laid it aside. Then moved it to a bookshelf. Then got it back, and put it in a drawer instead. Took it out again, feeling *that* looked too much like cherishing.

She didn't much care either way, to keep or fling it. But she didn't want what she did to be trivial or vengeful. That was the thing. How would making a scene help? She had never understood vengeance, how hurting someone helped you heal. The Bible said leave room for the wrath of God. Oh, she wished Chip's letter had never come! Not knowing would have been fine. Never knowing. Now she became a little agitated, fiddling. She wished she could hide the letter somewhere forever, and forget it and be healed. Like hiding a dishrag and losing your warts. But she wasn't sure if it was the hiding or the forgetting that healed. And how would she ever forget such a letter?

But she did. Within a year she had moved back to her childhood home, to live with her widowed sister-in-law, and after she had her things settled and pleasant around her, she forgot all about that letter. Every time she remembered it, it surprised her. Now it lay in her Bible between what she thought of as the Wrath of God and the Mercy, the intertestamental no-man's-land where the promise has been made but not yet kept.

Walking back to the house, she admitted she was going to get the letter, now, and bury it once and for all. The odd thing was, she wished Rome well, now he was dead. That made her laugh, then sniffle a little. If she were Catholic, she could marry again. And take communion with the saints. That was no help, since she wasn't Catholic, or a saint. Well, she thought, I am the real thing now, anyway, not a grass widow, but a sod widow. Burying the letter seemed the right thing to do. Her heart felt light, lighter than it had in a long time. She wondered if she could be healed just like that. Was it over? Or was this some interlude of grief? Some stage? She didn't remember the stages, but she was ready for the next one.

She needed a few minutes. The house was quiet and dim. She could hear the various clocks in the different rooms ticking their own version of now. She didn't turn a light on. The Bible was in its place. She found it easily, pulled the pages out of the envelope to reread one last time.

The photo wasn't there. She couldn't believe it. Then she saw it on the floor, where it had slipped out. There it lay, both of them grinning up at her. She scooped and slid it into her pocket. She felt the need to hurry while she still had the whole place to herself, and a little momentum going.

When she got back to the garden, she knelt and dug out the hole, one by one removing the tulip bulbs and setting them in the basket. She got busy with the shovel. She dug wider, deeper. Making room. Leaving room. When she was satisfied, she bent and laid the letter in the bottom of the hole, dragging cool soil back onto it, scattering bone meal, and resettling the tulips. When she had pulled the rest of the earth into the hole and tamped it lightly with her gardening shoe, she had a good feeling. Steam was rising up under her fleece shirt, curling the hair on her nape.

Was there something else? She made no speech. She couldn't think of a thing more to do, except mulch. She winnowed a few handfuls of pine straw. Something crinkled as she bent over: the photograph in her pocket.

"All right," she said, clawing it out. She didn't even wipe her hands. "All right."

Della was due back any time now from her foot doctor, her toenails and calluses honed, red Easy Spirits brisking along. She'd have to see. To catch up. To decide. To know better. This had been her garden all these years.

Achsa knelt again, and worked the photograph into the loam, sawing it upright back and forth, using it, as her grandfather had used the seed packets as labels to mark the garden rows to remind him of what went where and what to expect. In one season they'd fade in the sun and weather away, rain on rain, the very rain that would bring new life out of the dark, as these tulips—which had begun their smolder, somehow, when the world began—would torch up like glory in the new century.

Achsa could almost hear Della saying, "They won't come back." Holding the empty bag, peering at the label, fretting about zone hardiness. Della didn't believe in tulips. Not when Achsa had planted them in her windowboxes at the apartment; not when Achsa had brought them home from the grocery store after Valentine's—marked down in foil-wrapped plastic pots, their blooms already shattered, the green pencil stems bare—to give them a comeback chance in this very yard. Once Achsa had even stopped at the entrance to the golf community and retrieved a trunkload of spent bulbs ripped up by the corporate landscapers who had the same opinion of them as Della.

Here she came. *Tulips are a lost cause, this far south,* Della started to say it, was bound to say it—she said it every year, she couldn't help herself. Achsa heard her draw a breath, then nothing. Della just stood there noticing the photo, the two men buried heart-deep, grinning westward at the last gold light tipping the bare poplars. Wordless, Della unpocketed her hands, picked up the shovel and took custody of the basket of tools. For a moment Achsa held on to nothing, not even a grudge.

The All and Nothing
It Had Come To

Viviana heard the gunshots through the woods, and the scream of the cat. What could it be but tragedy? A call to arms. This was snake country. She set off running toward the Devil's Footbath, the strange pool like a vent from hell with its inexplicable magnetism and sulphurous healing power. She left her stadium seat, blanket, sketchbook, watercolors, and her day-pack without one glance back. She knew where to find King, but even so, she was stunned stock still when she discovered her disarmed husband looking just fine. He had their two chairs set up, the cushions in them, the cooler on the ground between them. The cougar was down and out of the crate on the truck and on a leash. A leash, Viviana thought. Still standing where she had paused to catch her breath, to take in the ski rope, with King calm at one end and the cougar calm at the other. Since she did not trust her eyes, she translated her visions into words, reporting to her brain in small sentences, basic talk, trying to get it right. She was resisting the sense and evidence. A leash of bright yellow ski rope jerry-rigged. King and the drenched cat walking back to the truck as calm and ordinary as any man with a mannerly dog on a leash in a city park. The tailgate was down. The crate hatch was open. The cat was soaked, diminished from soaking, rib-gaunt and hip-slinky. Her cat eyes were clear, indifferent, the pupils contracted. She glanced at Viviana, then away. At a gentle word from King, the cat jumped back up into the truck-bed and slouched willingly into the cage, curled around, stretched straight legs out in front, and lay down. The cat's belly rose and fell as she panted. Her teeth were old ivory, her tongue deep rose. King shut and locked the hatch. This cage was strong enough for two lions. So was King. There was no problem with the crate or King. He was whistling when he shut the tailgate, turned his back on her, put his hands and arms under the battered steel, and hurled the tailgate upward into place, latched it. King wasn't a man who loved his truck so it had to look new. He'd drive it into the woods, first thing, and run it between trees and through cat-briars to break it in, grit it up a little, get over new paint nerves. There was gumbo coating it he'd collected all over the south.

Viviana's heart was still thudding from her run to see what the gunshot had been about. She was panting hard, like the cat, had not found her voice yet. She tipped forward straight-legged, bracing her arms above her knees, but kept her head up, still looking, looking. Adrenaline and pride kept her from toppling. She was almost out of adrenaline. What she saw unblinking was that she belonged to King, but he did not belong to her. Happy birthday to me, she was thinking. This day and her new sketch-book had been his belated gifts.

From somewhere in front of the truck a young woman arose. She was wearing white shorts, quite white and quite short, and what seemed to be a black bra. Her sunglasses were askew in her topknot. She had on flip-flops and an ankle bracelet. Toe rings. She reached up, felt for her glasses, and settled them down onto her nose. She was laughing. "That one dropped me on my butt!" she hollered at King. She had the gun in its holster slung over her right shoulder like a purse. She was point-ing with her left arm. Not at Viviana. They hadn't noticed her yet. The girl was pointing at the edge of the woods, at a paper target held onto a plum limb by bits of twig. It had two holes in it and was split down the middle. Then the young woman saw Viviana. She said something to King but Viviana couldn't hear it. King took the gun from the young woman, who shrugged slightly to deliver it off her shoulder and into his hands. She said something else, and he tilted his head, inclined so he could hear. He laughed. He dealt with the gun first, took some time with it, before he swung around and glanced up, and looked at Viviana standing where she had finished her race. She straightened, started to put her hands on her hips, but had the presence of mind not to assume a ridiculous pose. He walked to the truck and put the gun away. Then he looked toward her again. Thunder rumbled way off, on the other side of the river. The dark clouds were passing them by. So much for the tropical depression.

"Where's your chair?" he called. That was his greeting. The young woman had already sat down, had reached into the cooler, delving in the ice, pulling up items, deciding against, and trying again. She chose one of King's beers and held it out for him to open. Dared him, a little slurred, to ask for ID, dared him to guess where she kept it. She was quite a giggler. She had obviously been into the cooler already. The opener was on a string on the handle, but she folded her grin shut like a debutante's fan, and said, "Do it with your hands."

He did, handing the bottle back and without a second's thought he laid those ice chilled hands on the young woman's bare shoulders. She didn't even jump.

"You need to cool down," he said, and to Viviana, gesturing, "Come on."
Come on? He indicated she could have his chair.

Viviana thought, What is *this?* Was this *it?* Was it over, the great calamity she had been braced for, or was it going to be worse than this? She had been seeing a holistic healer who had asked her a lot of questions, was still waiting for most of the answers, but had got Viviana asking questions herself. She had tested Viviana by machine and the machine had warned of some oncoming karmic dustup. Viviana had paid in cash for this news, always paying cash for every session, had given a fake name and had parked out of sight of the clinic, her license plate backed into a hedge so no one, not even King, especially not King, would ever find out where the money had gone.

Some kernel of self-possession moved her gracefully across the dry scurf of nut-grass and sandspurs, not limping. She stepped up onto the truck's running board, swung in, and took off one sandal, picked the sand spurs, tossed them out, re-shod. The seat was hot, but she eased her back into it, feeling some of the tension go.

You come on, she was thinking. She shut the door. She did not slam it.

The young woman looked around. Waved, a little one handed toodle-ooo of a fingerwave. "I'm Jennifer. You know. At the vet's." She stood, but didn't walk over, just held out her hand, miming a handshake. "I get Wednesday afternoons off. I always come here."

She tipped her head back to finish the beer. Like the brew, she had a long neck. Hers wasn't green. It was lightly tanned, and round, and there was a little gold heart on a hair-fine chain in the hollow. Viviana did not like heart-shaped jewelry. She liked rough cuts and cabochons, she liked natural finishes, and she did not like cute, fake, artificial, or highlights. Neither did King. Did he? Viviana's brain kept kaleidoscoping nevers and alwayses. The tiniest tremor changed everything. She grasped at basic truth. She did not know this person. Either of them, apparently.

Viviana never went to the vet's. The vet came to them. She did not say so.

"I know, I know, there's always a Jennifer," the young woman chattered on. "It's the number one name for my year. If we age gracefully, there'll be nursing homes full of us. Course I don't plan on aging gracefully." She winked. She actually winked.

"Have you finished?" Viviana asked King. It startled all of them to hear her voice.

"That's one hot cat," Jennifer said, and burst out laughing. A skinny red pickup truck turned in, and drove down the two track. She set the empty bottle on the ground, then un-bound, shook, then re-clipped her baby blond hair, gathering up brazen-rooted stray wisps. "Brandon," she hooted. Every word she spoke was brass. "Guess what?" She pointed to the target. "I like firing a gun!" The young man looked at her, extended his hand toward the side of her face. Not to slap. To pull something from her ear. No trick. Half a lavender rubber fishing worm. Other half in the other ear. She obviously had not realized worms were hanging out of her ears. She screamed with laughter. "So that's what King tore in half to keep me from going deaf," she said, looking at the worms. She wouldn't touch them. "I can't believe you put fishbait in my ears!" She ran to the nearest mirror, the one on King's driver's side, and bent to look. Then glanced in at Viviana.

"Isn't this place insane? There's always somebody here," she explained, in a more normal tone, "but there's never a crowd. Even on weekends. It's totally wonderful. Better than the pool, beach, or river. And there aren't any rules. Afterward, your skin is so smooth and tingly, every bit of it." She adjusted her shorts as she walked off. She touched King when she went by, but didn't speak. She and the young man went down to the spring, took off their shoes, stood looking in. She punched him on the arm, and they both jumped in. Then hauled themselves out again, up the slick bank, readying for recycle. The young man said something into Jennifer's ear.

Jennifer hollered, "Yes!" and didn't bother to trot back to ask King, just yelled: "Can we have your ski rope?" They were pointing at a low limb, signaling their plans for some Tarzan stunt. The young man even beat on his chest.

"Sorry," King called back. He muttered, "Monkeyshines," and began breaking camp. He left them each a can of soda, some for their friends, lined them along the chrome running board of the young man's truck. Then he folded up the chairs, tossed them and the cushions in the back by the cat. He wedged the cooler behind his seat, got in, cranked, and eased the king-cab between the other truck and the girl's little car. Two more vehicles were coming down the lane, headed for the hole. They hollered and waved; King wagged his pointing finger. Not a word to Viviana as he turned down the two-track to retrieve the other chair and table. Not a word as he parked, out of gear, idling, emergency brake stamped down and his door open while he closed the pipe gate, locked it and got back in. Not a word for the first five miles at least as they rode back. She had nothing to say, either. She stared out her window, watching what was ahead, and watching it go past, belittled by the objects appear farther than they really are side mirror. He was driving faster, now, maybe to make more of a breeze. She wondered if that was good for the damp cougar. The hot wind and the day were enervating. She glanced over her shoulder. The cat looked limp as a wet and thrown down sandy beach towel.

The truck slipped and wallowed in the deep sand if King drifted out of his lane. They pretty much had to stay in the ruts, or they could actually founder, even with four-wheel drive. But if they met another vehicle, someone would have to yield. She had a feeling it wouldn't be King. She knew his silences. This one was ominous. Patient. Ophidian. Drowsy but on task.

She understood about the gunshots. Explanations weren't necessary. She knew the game. She had played it. King—the great memory-maker—had made sure their times were memorable. Hadn't he let her fire his magnum—that very gun!—at the beginning? As she recalled, the plastic worms he had put in her ears had been green. With white spots. He had moved to stand behind her, with his arms around her, after the first shot had knocked her to the ground, and left her deafened. He had put the mutes in her ears, and had steadied her, and the second time she had blown the top off a sapling. Three more tries. She had never hit the target. She had not liked firing guns. He had taken the gun back from her, fired a round into the bulls-eye, and reloaded. He didn't give her another try, and he didn't need one. They hadn't talked much that afternoon on the way home. She had disappointed him before, but that day was the first time she had felt his contempt. Fortunately, there were other things she was good at.

She sighed.

It was the scream of the cat that she did not understand. "What happened back there?" she asked. In the quietness remaining after the fear and adrenal rush were gone, she found awe—and a sort of letdown—from having stood in that moment of crisis, and withstood, having run toward catastrophe and there being nothing so dangerous after all, just terrible.

She longed for peace for just a few miles longer. Had she spoken aloud? Had he heard her? They rode along. Just as well. She needed this recess between life lessons. From time to time she glanced back at the cougar trembling in the cage. And she felt it in herself. As though that cat was shaking the whole truck, the whole world. She couldn't help herself; she asked again, "What happened back there?"

"What?" He grabbed at a receipt which the swirling wind in the cab had lifted in a vortex. He caught it from the air, fisted it in front of her eyes as it neared her window, stuffed it safe above his visor. He might have chosen any place in the story to start, but, typically, he had figured exactly what she meant. "I had to shove her in. She wasn't happy about it. I jumped with her, of course, when I gave her the shove, so we landed in a big splash, but she screamed. It's shock. Cats run hot, but it scared her." He grudged every word, but at least he was speaking. She couldn't. So she didn't.

At least the cat got one free and forgiven scream. Viviana envied her that. Most of all she envied Jennifer, all the Jennifers mindlessly interchangeably coming on, like a heavenly host of hostesses, pawns in the game, streaming toward her and King, and there wasn't an herbal remedy or a mantra in the whole universe that could deflect them. King could help himself. They couldn't help themselves. They were the feast, the refreshments. And King needed refreshment. She knew how it would be, or could be—or had been this or something like it. All along? She understood now what Eleanor had meant when she advised not to take it personally, because he was who he was not because she was who she was. Or who she wasn't. But how could she be like Eleanor? She wasn't Eleanor, his second wife. And she did take it personally. What is a third wife's legacy? Viviana did not want wisdom to share with the fourth wife. Viviana had to live with the question, work on the answer, wait for the healing, and meanwhile sip not unpleasant and mostly affordable root/leaf/vine and flowery supports. The bitter ones—like field weeds with an eye to their main chance before mowing—seemed to work faster. Because her healer was fighting fire with fire, Viviana's sips were often bitter.

Viviana had her first taste of herbal remedies when she went—several weeks in to King's unexplained absence—to pick up his mail at the pack and ship store. There had been a single postcard delivered to her at home by regular post saying King and his fishing pals were down to Islamorada for the bonefish, but when she called the marina trying to locate him because there was a tax matter he and his accountants needed to clear up, the marina owner said King hadn't been there since the new year and his boat was still in the shed. She asked him to go check, even though he said he knew it for sure. When he came back, he reported it was dry in its cradle, nobody had used it. King's plane, however, was at the airstrip in Homestead.

"There's other boats," the marina guy told her. She hung up as he was saying, "A man like King—"

She'd been worrying about him but that when she began to wonder as well. She did not handle King's business. He had people for all that. She had simply stepped into his life as a new wife and all she had had to do was learn names and phone numbers. Some she was not to call, others she obviously didn't even know about. It was a few more days before she remembered how the accountant had mentioned a mailbox at the shipping store. Another day went by before she found the key to the box.

When she got to the pack and ship, she discovered that the franchise had gone out of business. The storefront corner where the mailboxes had been was now being used for a display of vitamins and little yellow-boxed bottles of Bach flower essences.

"No forward address," the store's owner said. They'd been open only a week. They were still unpacking. "Maybe if you call the shopping center's manager? Or the franchise, even better. They're online. Everybody's online . . . We're online!" She handed Viviana a card. All the new owner knew was the lease was up. "Things must've got a little slow after the holidays," she said. "Time ran out." Viviana did not hear the next thing.

Viviana had fainted.

Dropped like an anchor.

When she opened her eyes, there was the ceiling and slow-turning metal fan paddles turning the dusty air around. She was being offered Rescue Remedy. She did not know what it was. She heard the glass dropper tink! against the lip of the amber bottle. She batted it away before it touched her lips. It wasn't aimed at her lips. The manager was dripping a few drops on her wrist and smoothing them around before Viviana drew her hand back. Both hands. She sat up.

The clerk brought a bottle of spring water, opened it, and the store owner squeezed more drops. Her lips moved silently as she counted them.

They vanished into the water without a trace. "Just sip," the woman told her.

The clerk said, "You don't have to believe it, or even know. It works. Works on dogs cats puppies guppies horses dogwood trees sunstruck ferns frostbitten petunias you name it . . ."

The manager handed Viviana the bottle, and the clerk handed her another business card, one for the holistic healer who was using their back office until her own practice got off the ground and her offices uptown got remodeled. She worked afternoons and evenings. "The office is being abated," the clerk told her. Before Viviana could ask *from what?* the clerk handed her a certificate for one free consult with the healer. Grand Opening Special it said.

"She's wonderful," the clerk told her.

The manager handed Viviana the little bottle of remedy. Viviana had purchased it, of course. How could she not since they had opened its seal just for her?

"Change is hard," the manager told her. Making a face like someone trying to pass a kidney stone." But all you have be is willing. Maybe not even go that far. Maybe just be willing to be willing."

"Are you?" asked the clerk. Now she and the manager were shoulder to shoulder. Before Viviana could think of a reply, the little clerk settled her glasses higher on her nose and said, "She's really nice. Kinda serious. Motherly, I mean, I mean if your mother is nice. She's not a wi-witch," she added. The manager stepped back.

The clerk added, "We're not either, no matter what they say."

Viviana just wanted out of there. She did not imagine she would ever be back, but she accepted the gift certificate and folded it in half and slid it into the flat little paper sack they had put her remedy in.

"The price is right," she said.

The women from the store exchanged a glance and when they looked back, before they could say one more thing, Viviana had turned away, pushing on the door.

The remedy did not cure her insomnia. Viviana used the dark hours to do some research on the plants compounded and distilled into the bottle; it was almost empty now. One night she sketched the ingredients, painted them when she couldn't sleep. They were familiar plants, known to human healing for centuries. They seemed pretty entry-level and backyardish to someone who had slogged through tropical marshes and swung from ropes along rock cliffs on five continents reaching for, tracking down new plants. She had even collected and painted portraits of some whose medical story was not yet proven. Curiosity and science kept her company and took her deeper into research on these common— well, weeds, really, weren't they?—and finally, Viviana began reading the books about dosage and indications; she realized she was willing to be willing to be taught, if not yet willing to be healed, by this holistic way of looking at things. Viviana was finally willing to be willing, or at least willing to be willing to be willing. Maybe just that. But it got her there, to every appointment, week after week. The calm listening and questions from the healer were like a smooth stone dropped into Viviana's life pool and the ripples widened and widened.

She had registered as a client under an assumed name and always paid in cash. She wondered if that deception would hinder her progress. She wondered if the healer already knew she was lying. About more than her name. Still, she did not want to leave any tracks and she didn't want to say or do a thing to betray King. There was enough to work on, around him. All along, inside her, in the congestion and obsessions of her thoughts, she felt things beginning to move, rearrange, and that was change, wasn't it? The inventory itself was brave, and maybe healing. Viviana had not realized how much of her was left, when King went away. Even if he came back, even if he never returned.

The healer had machines to test the levels of Viviana's body's—and mind's —toxicity. Non-invasive, wackily satisfying vintage and steam-punky, a baton of brass in one hand, the healer's ball-pointed probe grounding the circuit at the base of a fingernail on the other hand, Viviana's body answered the probings. She never said a word. She wore street clothes, sat in a regular office chair, wood, no metal. She kept on her shoes. She had to take off her jewelry and her wristwatch. She had to take off her wedding ring. She never felt a thing. She wondered if the machine could read her skepticism as a kind of toxin. One of the little bottles the healer flicked out of the ranks in the arrayof substances they tested her against was labeled in ancient looking script: Cobra Venom. When her body electric mad a match with any of the substances in the little bottles, the machine made what Viviana thought of as a moosey downward groan, a giant aaaaww-wwww of deep disappointment. Every time, the healer would move that sample to the towel with the others, never letting the bottles touch. It took time. There were so many.

Viviana sighed. The healer said, "They can do all of this with a computer now, and print you out in colors."

It was a question, Viviana realized. She glanced at the stack of boxes still to go, filled with the little vials. She clenched her fist around the baton with its cable out the top connecting her to the machine's meters; it was like holding a stick of gold dynamite. The old ink markings on the old labels had been written by a pen—maybe a quill—dipped in earths and gums and gall ink from the other side of the world.

"No," she decided. On they went.

In time, real healing began, as it will. The herbal stuff was for homework, a page if instructions as to how much, what hour, and if food before or none and at what interval pure spring water. In the shop's back room, they tested, they talked. In time, when the healer's uptown offices were ready, she moved on. Vivian went along.

Some weeks into their program the natural healer's tests had warned once again of something awful headed Viviana's way. Something she— the healer told her when Viviana seemed mystified—Viviana should certainly have noticed by now? Some apprehension? Some anxiety? Viviana thought not. Viviana denied.

Some abysmal truth warning her from below? Like a cold current underwater, chilling her ankles, sending adrenal thrills and shakes all over her body? Warning her to get out!

No matter what Viviana said, the healer's machine scanned her through the electrodes and estimated her resistance, making its moaning, droopy outcry for chestnut and rockrose and aspen.

Viviana's confidence in cure wavered. It was no reassurance to be told, ahead of time, some nameless unswerveable horror was oncoming. The way the healer said it, staring into space as though she could see it like a train coming on, reporting, brisk, "Right at you!" and went to her supply shelf to gather tinctures to support body and soul against terror and cowardice. Viviana feared what she did not know. Again, she bought the compounds to help her find strength to withstand, and to have courage. For what? Startled, suspicious, resisting, Viviana had scoffed. But, also, she had ruled out nothing, yet with one last whiff of hope she denied any fear and the fear she denied and the denial she refused to put into words. But her heart knew. What if King didn't come back at all?

If King did not come back, WHY had become almost an irrelevancy. Viviana bought the supports and taped their schedule to the bathroom wall and left the light on, and on waking, if she slept, and at mealtimes and at bedtimes, she did what the healer had told her to do: avoid horror films, bake bread in clay pots, garden barefooted at night, and speak what the healer had said to speak and remember what the healer had said as true: "Good is coming at me stronger than anything that can harm me." Viviana wasn't worried about herself, if that were true, but it was no relief. If it was true, the one who needed her help was King. Wasn't it?

"The crisis is coming," the healer said. "Be ready."

And then King came home! And Viviana let her guard down, peeled off the taped up schedule and hid away the little bottles and sublingual pastilles.

Viviana had feared what she did not know or would not admit and that had the power over her. What plant extract could match the bitterness of that? Of knowing it is about love? About the price of love, that is grief. What Viviana had needed wasn't to do, at all. She had not needed lift a train off a man, or to hold a child above a stampede. Or to climb up an icy cliff barehanded in the dark. Or to leap into the Nile or Amazon to snatch a severed arm back to be reattached. Or to buddy breathe for someone in a dark cave that has suddenly filled with moiling sharks. Or to fly the plane with King slumped unconscious, pale, bleeding, and Viviana guiding them safely to a one hop landing on a patch of rough ground lit only by a gappy circle of lanterns. No.

What did she know? That she had much to learn. What had she learned? This day, she had learned that she was not, no, one more trifler on King's life list. Maybe he had thought so, but she was not. She was just one more? No! Maybe she had acted like one of them, but she was not. She pictured them now, unreeled the whole silent movie of them through the years, as though he had had dozens of disappointed women get the picture and the pink slip at a picnic—jerkily and stereotypically responding with hot quarreling and thick, congested insults and dragon smoke and handfuls of anything torn like turf from the pleasant remembered scenes; she imagined decades of whole lovely glades and picnic grounds of Paradise comically and rinky-dink swing-bladed with sharp female tongue lashings down to pale turf grubs and musty mole-runs. Of trying to win when you have already lost, then the trembling and temporary truce. Then the adrenal kiss and mercy rut. Not a matter of human being but animal behaving. Whatever else she would do or be, not that. And not be Eleanor either, not that way, driven to earth, numbed, entombed, loyal curator of the dream, singing her heart out, alone. And knocking back mimosas for breakfast.

How did Viviana know all this? She blamed the full moon. Sunspots. The holistic healer, the "clarity" they had been working toward, all those breath-prayers to be willing to be willing to change. She blamed, too, that damned naturopathological machine with the electrodes of truth or consequences and its dying moose call. Healing? This was demolition. Garnished with affirmations of "good" oncoming and bracing sips of the healer's vegetable hope and alcoholic attars.

Maybe it is karma, she thought. She didn't want justice, she wanted mercy. If it was mercy, if it was God who knew all this and sent her this knowing, then why? What mercy in knowing it if it could not be changed or repaired? Suddenly, King's being gone so long and coming back so strong hurt in a new way. Not just her heart, but her pride. They had automatically resumed their married life. She had been so relieved, so glad to see him. As though his return were enough for her. Was it? Would he offer sufficient explanation? Would she ask for one? If she loved him and trusted him would she need one? Did she have a choice, a real choice? Was trusting him *because she had to* the same as his being trustworthy? No, it was idiotic, that's what it was. She conceded it. Right. Right. She waited. She waited for him to speak as she had waited for him to come back. Some days were easier than others. But nevertheless, here she was, grateful as a dog to be let back in, when he was the dog! What did the housekeeper think? The barn men? The small loyal army of his employees? Now she had publically joined the losers. King's good-hearted frail club. It was official. Now she was paying for that day in church, that first Sunday back after the honeymoon, when the usher had asked them to wait in the narthex, and two of the deacons of the church had stepped forward, crouched beside Eleanor in her accustomed front pew, and had explained. They had helped Eleanor gather her things and had escorted her and her son to a pew at the back, and after that, escorted King and his bride to the front. It was more than Viviana could bear, remembering now how Eleanor had held the Bible with her left hand slightly above her waist, as though she had a broken wrist and it had healed exactly in the angle to carry the book that was shielding her heart. And how Eleanor had held the young man's arm with the other. Eleanor had kept her head up, but the young man—King's son!—had looked at the carpet, had looked blind, and it had seemed that Eleanor was leading him. Viviana had had no earthly idea who they were. King had pulled the doors shut. An usher waited with them. Silent.

She was stunned now to realize what had been happening inside the church with just that wood of the doors between her ignorance and Eleanor's overthrow. Viviana's own ignorance—and it was not innocence, she could see that now—was sin. Why had she not known, or cared to know? This, though, was the most terrible realization of all—King had known.

Viviana tried to remember what King had said or done in that hour, in that moment what he had looked like. All she could remember was that he had stepped in front of her, reached back with his hand and pulled the narthex's swinging sanctuary doors shut, so all she could see after that was King. On her side.

Viviana had invested in the idea of their love outliving them. Simple as that. She had thought she would possibly die for King, or with him. The holistic healer had worked for weeks to prepare Viviana for crisis, for resolve, for the hair on her ovaries she'd need. Some day. Perhaps this very day. This past hour, running to save his life or share his death. She would have done what it took. She would have! And now—oh how strange—she wouldn't. She felt that she wouldn't. How could that be? What kind of love was that? King had bragged how strong Eleanor was, when her moment came. How steady she had been. King had wanted Viviana to know that it was all right. They were all right, and the boy too, all of them, and it wasn't anyone's fault and certainly not Eleanor's fault and not Viviana's fault. In a long life—he guided Viviana to see—things rearranged. Things lasted, but they rearranged.

Eleanor's love had outlasted the day King had joked, "Don't worry, I'm not marrying anyone named Madge," when Eleanor confronted him. "Just the bottom line," she had said. King had liked that. He'd told Viviana when she had seemed a bit uneasy that first winter, because the trees were bare now, and Eleanor's roof—King's old palace—was visible on the other side of the river. Eleanor had got her own realm; the plats had been revised, the fence and the river making whatever was hers unimpeachable. King had give it to her, her reward for signing the papers, behaving well, and laughing when he told her the joke about Madge's name. He hated the sound of the word—"Madge"—and was having it legally changed to Viviana and then he was marrying her. And then explained to her, one of his jokes, how he was having Madge's name changed to Viviana, and *then* he was marrying her. After his and Eleanor's divorce went through, of course. Because Viviana had never wanted to be "Madge" she was glad enough to sign some papers. Sometimes King told Eleanor things Viviana said or did. Sometimes he didn't tell anyone anything. Sometimes he turned his back, pulled the door shut, and waited till the way cleared and then walked on. Like the day he had had Eleanor listen to that, in her own bedroom. Their bedroom. Had survived that. Had forgiven that. Had signed papers. Had moved to a seat at the back of the church, and because she had been asked to, and everything had been explained clearly, she—being unmarried from King—had walked back down the aisle on their son Roy-Boy's arm.

Viviana did not want that sort of story to include her, but it did. But she was certain of this much—no one was ever going to have to kneel beside her and whisper an invitation to clear out to make room for anyone else. As Viviana began to connect the parts of her past she had glided through, she wondered if there would ever be time and bitter weeds enough to—as her mind now put it—"live it down."

Eleanor's love had outlasted late-breaking news. Viviana did not think her own would. It felt as though the two gunshots—at the hot springs—had put her love down like a mad dog, torn her heart in two like that paper target. Viviana groaned. The truck swerved, then King eased it back in the ruts. He glanced at her, but didn't ask What?

She wanted out—out of the bad movie, out of the broken dream, out of the truck, right now, not one more mile on that road with him, or any road. She was ready enough to jump, to let her actions speak, to step to the rear, escorted or not. Ready to start making things right. She glanced over her shoulder toward her day pack in the back of the truck.

There was an eerie way he had—he had it now—of knowing exactly what she was thinking or feeling. He knew her moods. Some instinct tracked her on his radar, kept watch. She tried to calm her mind, keep her brain shielded. In her imagination, she wrapped that bright and shining sash of the healer's warrior light around her head, like a turban, as silly as that was to imagine any such toy armor or how comical it would look. She remembered how he hated her in fussy hats, had bought her a good panama, said she could pin a real rose on it but swore if she wore a veil to her wedding he would tear it off and use it to wash the white side-walls on the car. Could he really read her mind, or see—if he tried—her imaginary turban of light? She knew it was ridiculous, and yet she hast-ily and mentally wrapped and tied her shield of light anyway to seclude her mind, then brushed herself off—brushed her invisible aura with her real hands, not looking at him, not thinking of the times when—no, no, just imagining blue, empty blue skies, nothing but blue skies . . . At this exact moment being on the same wavelength was not part of his drawing charm. She tried to keep her mind empty, her breathing steady and even, as she figured out what next without his already having figured it and the shortcuts, and so be there when she arrived.

Would he do what she asked, if she asked right? If she chose to go now? She should not have to deceive him to leave him. She should be free to go or stay. She was not considering assets or settlements. She had signed a pre-nup, the treaty before the war, not after. She was thinking about dignity and worth and contrition and—frankly—gossip. She did not want to simply "flounce out." But oh how she wanted out. For her, it was over. What he had been doing in those unexplained weeks away had not brought her to this moment; rather it had been what *she* had been thinking, while he was away. So why blame him? He had loved the woman he left, but not the woman he came back to. She did not want to discuss it. What was there to discuss? Why couldn't it just be civil, if not easy? He couldn't want to look like a loser either. But no matter what she thought, she did not think it would be easy.

He could be distracted by desire, swerved from destruction by appeal to humane instincts, but could never be cured of shrewdness in any deal-ing at all. It would have to be his idea, his way, or no way. She did not want to rile his prey drive. It was all about winning. Some men like to win, some men need to win, some men have to win. King was all of those. Whatever it took. He could stalk, track, or still hunt awake or asleep; he harked in his dreams. He had told her of his hunting dreams where prey creatures were dreaming of him, hunkered and armored against him, resting between rounds. He'd wake, pull on his boots and go right to where he had dreamed them, find them hidden where the dream had showed him to look. He did not always kill them. He wanted them to know he had been able to find them; that was his trophy. He could find them on this continent or any other. He'd come after her and to her the same way. He knew the wiles of prey as though he were the prey itself. He could not be surprised—except by the fact that he loved her. He had said that more than once. She was the prize in surprise. But—what are the odds for a chicken who's a coyote's house pet?

She knew he might do what she asked, now, but not what she wanted. Never. That's because—she suddenly saw—being asked is about being in control. Doing what she wants would be about letting her have control, have sovereignty, however slight. Immediately she realized that she couldn't, wouldn't ask. She had not "covered" this in her healing work. She had not uncovered it. She did not know where it came from. She knew he had never seen it before, the crazy wild spirit of her; she had always been the tamed and trained jessed and belled little falcon on his wrist. So—never mind the bells, the whistles—what would she be without that wrist? She didn't know, but she was going to find out even though she had not wanted to. It was truth enough to make her dizzy. It broke her heart. She broke her own heart and it made her grunt. When he heard that, he drove faster, fishtailing in the sand.

"What?" he demanded.

"I—I saw something back there. Something I never saw before." No lie.

He was already slowing, not braking, just letting the gears and sand do the hauling down. Trying to figure her, scent her change of mood. Test it. He scented a lie. Not understanding. Knowing she was withholding herself made him furious, and more keen. He was laser-ice when he got like this. She had never egged him on, either. Not that she was suddenly willing to. The idea of it horrified her. Broke her ideas of love. To play him, to toy with him. But so be it. Some of what it cost her he would have to pay. That's love. They had not argued often, because it was so terrible. She dared not play to win, and he did not intend to lose.

"You want to go back, say so."

"I don't want to go back," she said. God's truth!

Of course he wouldn't turn around, anyway; he couldn't. Would he back up? His offer wasn't real. She felt that. The truck had stopped now, even though she had said, no. Stopped, they were instantly baking in the still air. So was the cougar in the cage. It was up to Viviana to make everything go again. Speak war now or forever hold your peace time. What peace! How had he done that? Made this heat and this day her fault; just like that it became her fault, like she had thrown a bomb under the truck. *She* had stopped the truck. This was his bullying majesty. In complete silence, she felt it. She felt it. He was daring her to say a word, a real and true word. Just get it out in the air. He knew she wouldn't. His Viviana wouldn't. He knew how to pick 'em.

What if she said, quietly, "Yes, let's just stop here, just for a month or two, till we die and burst and the green flies take us away in sips." They were already stopped, after all. What if she opened the door and got out. Would he leave her there? Drive on? He might. Would he wait? To please himself, only, not to apologize, nothing to damage his idea of himself, not to court her. Never to reform. Even in extremity and crisis, he lived up to his idea of a man who would go to some trouble, who was willing to be put to some trouble to let a woman think she was being pleased and courted. He liked witnesses for that. Sometimes she was sufficient witness. Not today. She didn't have anything else to say. In her silence, he cranked the truck and drove them on.

Time happened. Time passed. A mile, another mile. Mental postcards of the day developed like Polaroids. A lyrical afternoon of sketching flesh-eating plants on the breezy edge of a cliff. A dream of an afternoon, sketching on her own, picnicking on her own, daydreaming and wakening from it by gunshots and the scream of a cat. Now here they were, safe, including the cat. Going where? Here, now, is the all and nothing it had come to—their chance meeting at the headwaters of the Amazon, the honeymoon in Africa, last year in Bali for her birthday, the telescope for his (and the star she had paid to have named for him). The times in between were some of the best of all, on the river, looking up, or in the sky, looking down at the blue and green of earth. It was over? There was no next page? There was nothing to say or to do? As long as they did not say or do anything now, offered no final fatal word, could it hold? Would it last? Pictures fade in time, but even a lightning-struck tree didn't die overnight.

Illumination's bright flash and impact had struck her. It had not shattered her. It seared, though. Took her breath. Its meteoric advent had burned a landmark through her heartwood. Ensuing dust had brought on an ice age. She put her hands to her temples and held on. Shouldn't she discuss this with him? She had been warned; the naturopath's moose-groaning machine had warned her: trouble ahead, big doings. How to warn someone, *If you do that, I won't love you anymore?* when what you really mean is, *I am the sort who cuts her losses.* Viviana knew now why the symbol for truth is a sword. Something like steel eased itself into her mind, dividing—before from after, not just today from yesterday but like birth, some essential umbilical severance of herself from what *had* been into what is and must be from now on the real and only possible thing, the true life journey from the lovely detour. The wrong roads had got her here? She refused to be ungrateful. The only roads. This was not the middle of nowhere; it was the beginning of everything that remained. And she hadn't missed it. These are birthday thoughts, she realized. He had forgotten her birthday or ignored it, and in offering back to her this mixed blessing of a day had given the Trojan gift of comprehension.

She felt something turn in her heart, from anger toward gratitude. Whatever day he had intended today, it had not been this. Or, if so, the gold, not the brass. Something in her softened, as she thought of the gifts he had given her—for her work—and the peace to work alone; of how he had intended good. So many of his gifts had opened her to possibility. How much time was there, that any could be wasted? They still had some left. A few miles.

"Look there!" She pointed across the cab to the ditch on his side. He slowed again, glancing at her, sensing, then seeing that softening, this time braking because of it, judging it real. In the beginning they had done this many times: riding back roads, looking for botanical wonders for her to collect and draw. He'd stop, get out, stretch, wander into the woods to relieve himself, or look for deer sign, or take his tackle and stroll up a stream to rollcast under the overhanging trees for creekfish. He didn't cut the engine this time. He geared into neutral. They were in good shade. She glanced at him. There was no animosity now, no fever. It had always been like that with them, between them. Quick, refreshing squalls. They had chosen each other, and whatever their illusions were, they had always somehow chosen to preserve them. He believed that was what was happening now. She believed it too. If both partners move by the same rules and discipline, a waltz is possible. A beautiful waltz. Even if it is the last dance. Without hammering it out, they had arrived at a civil, even cordial truce. In this hour at the end of their journey—and in respectful comradeship—he could trust her and she could trust him: to behave well because of what had been and what might have been. They were going to behave well, both of them, and that made them both grateful and a little formal. They had been, this day, this hour, to Hell and back.

"Much obliged," she said. She got out, leaning in to pick up her pack and the little folding shovel she used. Business as usual. She always had bags to put the plants in, if she dug. She never took endangered, only rare. She had her compass too, for determining exactly which way the plant had grown thus far, with respect to the sun. She would note it, and set it back in new earth in the same relationship to the universe, so it would not stress or torque or suffer. She walked to the edge of the woods, crouched by a dried pool under a sparkleberry. She probed, estimated, counted leaves. She glanced over her shoulder.

He was smoking a cigarillo, watching her. "Afraid I'm leaving you?"

She studied him. He was twice her age. He looked thin, but she didn't think thin, she thought *trim.* He seemed diminished, but she knew his sinew, his will, and she thought *wiry.*

Wordless, she turned back to her work. She was marveling, amazed to realize what had happened: she was *already gone.* She had gotten free, in plain sight; that was the step she had taken, getting strong while he was away. Now she had to keep on stepping.

He eased his seat back, napping like a tiger. She thought once—without loss of courage and calm—of his gun. It wouldn't cross his mind. Not that she'd run off, or try, or that he'd kill her for trying. This wasn't that kind of battle. Earlier, she had thought she might just head for the woods, but she understood that she couldn't leave like that, couldn't get away, not really. Her mind had achieved orbit, but the rest of her would have to wait for suitable launch conditions. It was not going to happen today. He'd saw the truck around, head back, or duck into the woods himself. He'd 'rescue' her. He'd have to. She wasn't prepared for the woods, their slash and longleaf pine and brush and palmetto scrub and chaney briar brambles and gopher holes—and snakes. And night coming in a few hours. He might have to let the cat out, let the cougar out of its cage. He would too. He could hunt them both down before good dark. He liked a game, liked tracking; it might even interest him keenly. Extra innings. No sudden death. He'd bring both of them back alive. Trophies.

She balanced and set her foot on the shovel, heel-hammered it down into the sand, pried it back, and brought up two plants, their roots inter-twined. She'd separate them later—just splash a little water in now, bag them, and get back in the truck. If she tore them apart, they'd both wither. She back-covered the roots of the plants she left in the ground, so they'd not suffer from the baking heat. The sky was clear again.

"Maybe it rained at home," he said.

"Somewhere," she said. They drove on.

He tuned the radio and they listened to the Braves play late, tie the game, then extra innings for a few miles, then lose on a loud out. Then he skim-tuned past two barking preachers and found some music they both could tolerate. All this time in therapy she had thought she was going to have to risk her life to save his! And she would have. She would have! Saving his life would have been the same as saving her own. But now? How could this be? How could this have happened? He was just someone else staggering around on the back roads of earth. And so was she. They weren't together. They were just riding in the same truck.

They had finally come back to tar and gravel, county maintained. He took the vehicle up onto this civil improvement slowly, gently. Not one ice cube rattled or resettled.

She looked back at the crate. The big cat had roused at the transition, and as they accelerated north toward home, she seemed to be sniffing the air, quickening. She wasn't trembling now. She looked . . . better.

"Do you ever wish you could just let her go?" Viviana had unfastened her seat belt, turned, was kneeling on the seat, reaching through the window and just barely touching the tip of the cat's right ear. The cat was pushing her face and cheeks against the crate, petting herself against its steel, purring like a mud motor not quite cranking on a weak pull.

"That's what she was afraid of, why she's been pouting," he said. "She thought I had thrown her away." He cleared his throat. "That's why I had her on a leash. So she'd know she belonged." Viviana settled back in her seat, belted herself in. He knew it; he always knew when he had won. In another mile he said, "Feel that." He was inviting her to rub her fingertips lightly along his brimstone-baptized forearm. He tried it himself, with his whole palm. "Like silk," he marveled, pleased. Driving right-handed, he leaned across her, his left arm brushing across her chest, ran his southpaw along her right arm, from the bare shoulder down to her wrist. She was sticky with bug spray and sunblock. They had drifted a little, but there was no traffic. He eased the truck over, correcting course, driving with his left hand now, laying his right arm along the seatback, tangling his fingers in the hair at the nape of her neck, one of her known and infallible thrill spots. "Should've thrown you in, too." Just his fingernails raking her scalp. He yawned. "I've known that hellhole to work miracles."

Come and Go Blues

"When I do, it's you," she said every time he asked her if she had "romantic thoughts" on the road. That was now. Neither one of them talked about before, not even in their dreams. Little Martha—four fingers old in the Easter portrait Velcroed to the rider side headliner, and a decade older, now—may as well have been ordered from a catalog and delivered UPS. To her grandmother's house, at that.

Martha's daddy was out of the picture. Literally. Pruned out. All the snapshots without him edited by the same shears, and same precision Jean used now, to trim Gene's beard.

Jokes about Jean and Gene flashed truckstop to truckstop transcontinental, channel 19, landlines, cell, and once Krylonned on a bridge overpass, when word got around. He wasn't used to it. Wasn't used to anything yet. He had known her for a year, but it was still sudden to him, and now he had ten days, three without pay, for a wedding and honeymoon. They were actually going to do it, get hitched on this fill-up. They'd stopped on the border, south of Chattanooga, and got the blood tests and paperwork, as much as they could do. He thought then they'd be running back by there, on the flipflop; it was a marrying town, and why not, name like Ringgold?

"Don't sweat it," she said, when he kept glancing over at the gages. "I've got two tanks, and I know how to coast." They were headed for Florida, and didn't need a map.

"After Atlanta, it's all downhill," he said.

"But the road goes on forever," she said.

That's when he knew, long before she edged left out of the 475 bypass lanes, they were headed for Macon. She was marrying him in Allman country which he thought, somehow, would have been more country than it was. Macon wasn't a town but a city, and his hackles would have bristled if she had simply driven them right to the place, sure of her way. But she stopped at a public phone second time around a long block, looked in the book, the Marmon idling behind them as their fingers walked. "We could have been married in Gatlinburg, no blood test, no wait," he said, pointing down the page to a 1–800 number.

She glanced at him. "You ever been to Gatlinburg?"

"Is this about mileage?" He'd never been married.

"To where?" she said, rattled for the first time. They considered each other.

"Everybody's been to Gatlinburg," he said.

"I didn't see you there," she said. "Ramblin' man."

"Off season," he said. She folded her blueblockers and pocketed them, frowning at the tattered phone book.

Before the silence got any wider she said, "Oh well. Hanging out in public, bound to be some pages missing."

They'd been down that lane before.

"Where were we?" he said.

"Right here."

Floral, floral, limousine service. He muttered down the column, marveling at the complications and accessories for social matrimony.

"Guest books!" she read.

"Tented terraces," he added.

"Horse drawn carriages."

"Ballroom."

"Garden and fountain."

"Seated 150. Standing 500."

"I could kiss you till Tuesday," she said.

He let her try. Who wouldn't let her try?

"Turn of the century charm and elegance," she resumed, but the first elation was fading, the exuberance, the freedom of being on earth again, away from the thrum of the road. It was a warm day, just past winter, just into the noon rush. Things were blooming, he wasn't sure what, but the petals were blowing around like snow. He pulled the tethered Yellow Pages his way, tall enough to read over her shoulder.

"Seven acres of grassy lawn," he read. Somehow that did it. That did it. Were they farming the rice or throwing it?

"Look," he said, but she was already flipping back, closing the book on what she had called—when she told him what she didn't want— "a production number."

They'd already ruled out Judge and Justice. "Been there, done that," was all she'd say. So they checked *Ministers,* and the book *said See Clergy.* But they were still in the *M*'s.

Marriage, of course. "Yep," she said, holding the page against a puff of wind. More confetti from the wasting trees. "I'm feeling lucky," she said. But phonebook "Marriage" was about what went wrong, counseling and "unkinking and shrinking" as she called it.

"Wait now, wait now," he said, brushing off the therapists. There it was: one little entry: *Marriages—civil.*

She tore the page out and stuffed it in her back pocket. "Might need it again," she said. But when she saw his face, she pulled it out, ironed it high on his thigh with her gear hand. "For my files, ok?" She hated sentiment in herself or anyone. Hated froufrou and ruffles and Barbie pink and didn't own—"not one"—a dress or skirt of any kind.

"Neither do I."

"And don't expect me to cry."

"Ditto," he'd agreed.

The Yellow Pages map led them right to the door of O. Kestrel Kirby's time-sueded board and batten home. They never had got as far as *Clergy* in their research, so they didn't know he had the same ad there. *Civil* he might have advertised, but he was Reverend also. "Either way," he said,

"God presides. Just call me a marrying man." He pronounced it mer-rying. And he did have a twinkle. A tall, thin, spry dark brown-skinned man with a frosty halo of hair. He was dressed for his work, pulling his suit coat on over his white nylon shirt. "We can do it in the pahlor or on the poach," he said, stepping out. "Pahlor's got RCA Victor hi-fi music, you wanta stand round and lissen. Y'all? Some like that . . . No finger pop-ping." He looked older unveiled by the screendoor, but sharp-eyed, crisp as bacon, and interested. "We'll need a witness or witnesses," he said, look-ing around. The Marmon rumbled at the curb, it and the trailer eclipsing town. Glancing down at it from the steps, Jean realized, "This was fun up until right about now."

The minister fanned himself with his book. "They come and they go," he said. "Mostly at night. Things look different in the day. Am I what you had in mind?"

"Are we?" Jean said.

"How much are witnesses?" Gene wondered.

"I genly flag one down for free," he said. "Maybe refreshments after."

"Not here," Jean said, getting her second wind. And she explained what she had in mind

The marrying man let them park the rig in his churchyard, and gave Gene the keys to his Riviera. "I don't have no trouble with the driving," he said. "Just the stopping." They all three rode up front. Along the way Rev. Kirby pointed things out. He didn't know that much about Rose Hill. He was going to stop at the gate for directions, but Jean knew where; she'd been to the cemetery before. At the last moment everything felt right. They were the only ones except for a total stranger jogging along the low road who agreed to be their witness. There was a little breeze off the river and more of those short bent trees shook petals down on them as they walked.

Gene slapped at some going by. "What is it?" He'd heard of kudzu. Everybody knew about kudzu. "Peach?"

"Cherries," the preacher said. They were there, now, single filing down the hill. It was shady, dim. The marrying man pulled his glasses a little away from his face, to focus better, shaking his head at the dates carved in stone, doing the terrible math: "Twenty five," he said, "twenty-four." The gravesite was fenced, roped off with what looked like clothesline, a frail, ordinary cancellation, marking off Duane Allman and Berry Oakley; the wedding party stood to the side, but at the last moment, Jean took off her shoes, and backed up, so her heels were over the line. The witness checked his carotid pulse, did some quad stretches, stepped in place, and cleared his throat.

"Now then, chillen," the marrying man said, calling them to order. "It don't take long, and it's only words unless you mean it." When it came Jean's turn to answer, she marveled, after an agonizing thirty-second pause, "You know? I do. I really do." Like it had just occurred to her. Maybe a joke, who could ever know, with her? She'd rolled in one time in press-on tattoos and those fake navel and eyebrow rings, her lips blackened, her hair spiked. Something about Gene's steadiness incited her to riot.

"No rings," she said, at that point in the ceremony when rings are what is next. She drew instead two chains from his jeans jacket, claddagh charms on Italian 18kt snake. Gene's charm was larger; Jean's might have been cut from the center of his. When they had seen that, had seen the way they fit, they knew. Whatever it was that had to happen, had. These things were simply the signs and miracles. She clasped Gene's chain around his neck without looking; he bowed as though she were knighting him. He laid hers on her hair, then gentled it over her head unopened, afraid to fumble. His hands—which could hold nine large eggs and "work the grill like a Ginzu salesman on black beauties" as Jean told her mom—trembled now, relinquishing the chain. Gravity did the rest. She shivered when the gold settled, raised the charm to her lips and looked at him.

What did it matter what happened, and who said what, today in Macon Damn Georgia? "License to thrill," she called the certificate. "All it is," she said, "is the footprint of the beast, it aint the beast." They were zoned now, Gene's eyes as usual squinting a little, to see clearer, to harbor doubt, to make sure and be sure, and hers wide open, like her life, like her mind, but her tenderness deep way back deep behind the sparkle, so far he could fall for years and would never get to the bottom of her fierce hot heart. No telling how long they had been standing there like that, eye-locked. The witness laughed. The minister said, finally, "Lessen you pay for moah, that's all you get for a sawbuck and all you need fore God and man."

"Sir?" Gene said absently, not half hearing it. "I'm not waiting for change . . ."

The jogger laughed. "Me neither." He and the preacher high fived it.

"Mr. and Mrs.," the marrying man told them, merry, shaking their hands two-fisted between his cool trembling palms. "Good," he said. "Good." Jean hugged everybody, then she bent so they could use her smooth hard shoulder for the desk, and preacher and the witness signed documents, gave them theirs. The jogger wouldn't take a thing, just ran along, pumped them a highball wave without looking back. A Norfolk Southern freight came on, and they watched the train rocking along below them northbound beside the southbound river. They noticed the sound of traffic now, and there was a jet outrunning its contrail in an unclouded sky. "My foist wedding here," the marrying man said, stepping carefully up the hill. He didn't count the twenties Gene folded into his hand; they shook on it again. "Pearl of great price worth more to some than others," was all the marrying man said, smiling. He waited in the car for them.

Jean, folding their certificate into fourths and sliding it into her trucker's wallet on its chain to her belt, didn't even try not to grin. "Road legal," was her first married remark.

They stood and looked at the graves one last time.

"I'm glad I didn't die in 1971," Rev. Kirby said. "You folkses borned yet?"

"Yes," said Jean.

"No," said Gene, "but I'm catching up."

"It takes what it takes," Jean said, laying her arm along the seat back, rubbing Gene's neck, thumbing the exact place on his left shoulder. "We haven't wasted a second."

"We won't," he promised.

Rev. Kirby directed them by the H&H for a little wedding supper. Mama Louise came to the front to meet them, pulled a chair around and sat through "Little Martha" on the jukebox. "Y'all dance," she urged, but nobody did. She held Jean's hand in hers, as though she were reading the palm, brailling her calluses. "Ironing!" she guessed.

"He's the cook," Jean said, pointing. "I jam gears."

Mama Louise gave them both a hug. "All I knows I been reading bad news my entire life, and I never yet see where a man get himself kill while washing dishes."

They honeymooned in the sleeper, boogieing south a few hours at a time. Whoever had owned the truck before her had stuck Bob Hataway's Trans America warning up under some kind of sealing tape they couldn't pick off or melt away with a hair dryer or shave with a Gem blade or scrape with a Widget without wrecking the fiberglass hull. Gene read it, with various inflections and lousy accents, sometimes interrupting other conversation or music as with a public service announcement, sometimes in hypnotic cadences, sometimes seatbelted in, sometimes stretched out in the sleeper behind her as she drove. "There comes a time when your body takes control without informing your mind of the change of command," he'd begin, coolly, saving the heat. "Your mind seems to go to sleep even though your eyes remain open." He'd give her time to fight it, lose, and blink. "Your mind fights the change of command and you will be alerted of the conflict by inadvertent body movements." She'd always laugh. She was a sucker for inadvertent body movements. He gave her time for that, too, then deep, deep, slow and low, "Be aware of your body needs . . ."

"God bless America," she said, being aware, aware, the third time midway across Sarasota Bay, no possible parking. He was used to hearing her voice in the dark. She couldn't get over the effect of his. "I'm glad I couldn't peel it," she said, blowing Hataway's warning a kiss after that fifth stop, seeing things in a new light. She could have driven fifteen hours, but they averaged eight.

They did everything except count down the days. Nothing dwindled.

When they got to Homestead, she dropped off the trailer and they ran the Marmon bobtail down the Keys, to Pennecamp, and snorkeled. The next day Jean's mother and Little Martha met them there, and afterward, they made a convoy back to the mainland. Along the way Gene noticed houses for sale, listed higher than ones he'd noticed all the way south in the newspapers he'd bought every time they fueled. He wondered about apartments, maybe. Jean's mother said, "Why?" with her and Little Martha rattling around in that big old place at the end of a sand road. Dogs didn't even need a fence. Jean's mother had given this some thought. It made total sense for him to relocate, as far as she could see, which wasn't, she had to admit, any farther than Coral Gables. She and Little Martha had gone north with Jean at Christmas, to meet his brother and aunts in Harlan. She never had seen anything like those coal hollers, steeps and seeps, icicles hanging off rock cliffs and roads graded onto what seemed to be thin air. She rode along with her eyes shut, Jean saying, "Look, Mama. Oh, you missed it!" They'd gotten lucky, a skiffering of snow on Christmas Eve, six inches on Christmas Day, Little Martha's first chance to play in it. The power was out for a while. Jean's mother—who had a bikini figure, thousands of dollars invested in electrolysis, Jazzercise three days a week, canasta club on Tuesdays, a harbormaster boyfriend and lots of salt-water tackle—did not appreciate how firewood warms you twice and said so and considered anything north of Atlanta to be the arctic and said so. "You don't have to shovel rain," she told Gene.

The newspapers had want-ads too. But how did he know where to want what he wanted? Just somewhere along the interstate, somewhere she could find him, somewhere she could park awhile. That's what got him, on the trip north, the long leg of their honeymoon, how differently they looked at things. He was adopting Little Martha; they'd already seen a lawyer about it. He liked the idea of more—"a house full"—and Jean hadn't said no. He'd been saving for years and a home of their own wasn't going to be impossible, even with her weekly truck payments of $290. She kept a clean logbook and used a laptop to stay in touch with fuel prices, tolls, and regs. She'd been trucking for seventeen years, in her own rig for three, and as she told him, "I don't need advice, just a place to park."

For her, the cab was home. She had all those photographs on the headliner and bulkhead, a quilt of her grandmother's on the bunk, and over the visor a chipped and cracked old brownie snapshot of her daddy's greatgrandfather's brother at the wheel of a vintage Marmon, as though that explained everything. Her daddy hadn't made it past thirty, but that was hurricane Andrew and nothing at all to do with driving a truck. "Gone is gone," her mama said, picking up the pieces. It was Jean who renamed their little boat "Moving Target." Speed was one thing, but Jean wanted power, too. They lived near the highway, not the railroad, or she might have found a different way out. It was almost a relief when she left high school one May day after graduation practice and someone reported seeing her swing up into the cab of a Kenworth idling at the end of a grove.

The next news came from California: they were married and she was riding shotgun on a north-south drybox run. Then it was Utah for a few months while she studied for her CDL, and a trip home to Florida to have the baby and leave it with her mom, "just until," and then long hauls from Arkansas to Pennsylvania, and finally divorced, signing on as newbie on a north south route in a company rig, saving every penny she could for the down on the rebuilt Marmon. For all her baby knew, Jean and that red truck with "Little Martha" painted on the hood were her own personal circus coming to town. Now and then a ruckus, lots of laughs and a few tears, after which the even tenor resumed, the sandy yard empty except for Mama Gail's Bronco and jonboat.

Jean would've laid her life down, waded through blood neck deep, and or been dropped from a height on to nails and fire for that child. But she didn't know how to do any of that except by running. Not away, just on and on. She'd learned out west how they have to cut the rug from the loom, whether they finish weaving it or not. To leave off now would be to waste all her work. Patience is what fills the loom. Every mile whittled her debt and chinked a few more coins into the piggy bank for their future. Besides which, she had discovered what she was glad at, not just good at. She had—in one impulse—found the way to find her way. The running was instinctive, purposeful; it tamed her, she knew it, recognized it in herself, that first ride, the day she left school forever. She could laugh about it now. It was the truck, more than the man, she'd fallen for. But thank God for the man who'd opened the door.

She had plenty of time to figure things out. When she ran across Gene that night, when he turned from the grill and faced his future, she didn't plan on tenure. If he lasted, he'd be just one more landmark along the route. For all she knew, he saw it the same. Who could imagine it worth more? Or lasting longer? The biggest surprise of both their lives his handing her that note.

"Here is what I want you to know," he had said. His sermon was written on the back of a check carbon. Funny paper, like the inside of a Band-Aid wrapper, gave her the same feeling, like there was a wound being tended, nothing too major, nothing past healing. That was the thing about flesh wounds.

She read it then, with him watching, just let him watch. She wasn't a speed reader and he wrote it small as book print. She read like it was a trick, or a test. Or the Bible. She read it again, to be sure she got it all; she had an orderly mind that way. Then she folded it, and nodded—not a yes nod, not a no nod, just an all right I'll consider this nod—and left. Filed it in her logbook. He was working on the southbound side, and she didn't see him for the rest of that trip, and then all the way north, and then the turnaround from Columbus and slingshot out of Cincy over the Ohio, too road-busy to get more than a glimpse of the water, and back down into Kentucky. She didn't call or write, even though the check carbon had his address on it, and her mudflaps had the truckstop phone number. But what would she have said? He'd blindsided her. A few miles she let anger keep her from admitting the answer. "He's crazy," she said. That was all. She couldn't even remember his face or his voice, except for the one line, over and over and over, "Here is what I want you to know," as he handed it to her, with her change. The furtive sly look of the counterman, at the office door, a set up job, so Gene could be the one to wait on her. But not laughing at her, laughing at him. That flew all over her, too.

"I come from coal," he wrote. "We dig in. Live & die by are own—" the ballpoint balked against the waxy paper and he switched to pencil— "light. My daddy walked seventeeen miles in a day & a night to hear my mama sing in a church qwartet. He claimed her on a handshake, walked home again with nothing but her smile for supper in breakfast too. Coal & tobacco, and having to & meaning to, killed my daddy & my mama both. Something better going to hapen to what of thems alive in me. & mine." In felt tip, this PS: "I dreamed threads showing on that front right driving tire, it scard me. You want a new one I can help."

She didn't think she did, hadn't thought she would, ever, but there she stood, telling him less than a week later, yes: "I want a new one," and she didn't mean a retread.

They courted to the rhythm of the road, at the mercy of the dispatchers. They marveled how their paths had ever crossed. They ate at the Chinese All-U-Can buffet and discovered from their placemats they were water horse and fire dog, a match made in heaven. "Marry early," it advised, and she frowned, but he said, "Maybe they mean a.m. not p.m. It's upside down in China."

"We don't have to marry," she said.

He agreed. "*Have to* sucks. Let me know when you *want to*."

That was how he asked.

This was Jean's new route. She had had this dedicated run since October, a reefer out of Homestead, all the way north to Cincinnati on 75, then a turnaround in Columbus and back again. Before this she had worked open fleet, three weeks on, hauling anybody's anything anywhere, gone twenty-one days before coming in for time off. He'd hated that. The sound of it as much as the schedule. "Coming in" was what she'd say, on the cell phone talking herself down to sleep, her LadySmith pistol under her pillow, her rig queued up at some argon-lit receiver's dock, waiting for the lumpers to unload her in the morning.

"Coming in"—like a radio signal. Like her voice passing through the air, invisible, finding its way, ricocheting off towers, bouncing over mountains and dark waters, flung dish to dish by satellites winking like stars. He wondered how she found him, how she ever found him. He had loved her from the first like this, with a heart's harking, when she was just cracking wise, tough-talking but not profane, when the counterman that rainy night vanished to the can to smoke, and Gene had turned from the grill to ring out a customer, tired—nobody on the graveyard shift dreams enough—and her eyes fresh, fresh, taking him in, not tired, never going to be that tired, not looking for a fight or a friend, just looking.

Even later, when she was headed straight for him, she still said it: "coming in" not "coming home."

"Come on," she'd say across the miles, for hello. And "Gone," for gone. Weeks and weeks of gone.

She wanted to tell him—when her route finally turned, and "Little Martha" began adding up the miles and counting down the days—how she felt, how she was arriving at herself, where her life fit her soul like a wetsuit, and her heart sang as she speed dialed the news of her nearing into the pager on his belt, how if she weren't so eager, so urgent, she would haul to a stop right on the side of the highway, wade out into the wind-riffled weeds and slush, kneel in thanks, cry up to what had always been sky to her but now was heaven, and praise something, bless back—like the woman the troopers found wandering on the median out west, arms wideflung, thrumming, blinded from staring at the sun—staggered not by choice but by possibility, "coming in," coming in to her own.

Seam Busters

1

One of the new micro-mini bumblebee-size spy cameras caught Vicki Malachy pocketing—if you could call it that—a generous scrap of the new Crye multicam fabric into her bra. Juki, her mama, who was nick-named for the bar tacker she ran on the other end of the mezzanine, didn't even get to see her go. King and JaNice simply appeared right after lunch and asked Vicki to step downstairs to Mrs. Champion's office, "Right now." This is called "being walked out." They tag team, and nobody around looks or speaks up; coworkers and friends swallow hard and just keep on pretending to be sewing. King went with Vicki, guiding her in case shock and swooning set in or she got some wild hair to flee or run amok. Or she found a way to retrieve the scrap and toss it away. It didn't matter. They have her on tape, and multicam isn't scheduled to be fielded in Afghanistan until summer 2010, so it is more or less a controlled substance, so new you can find it online as multisham looking somewhat like the real deal but without the fine-tunings or the flameproof high-tech magic features the new digital camouflage has. It can also be sold as genuine, which it isn't. Okay for hunters—deer don't use infrared detection—but bad for the troops. The fake stuff won't wash, but the dyes do, right down the drain; a few launderings and you're naked to eyes as well as infrared. It isn't about national security and troop safety only; it is also a copyright issue. All the knock-off artists need is someone using a color copier and posting it online a patch at a time. Sooner or later they'll have it mapped out and duped and our troops—and everyone else's—could be buying and fielding knockoffs on eBay from Chinese "tailors." Is that what Vicki was up to? It wouldn't have mattered if she was planning to make a G-string for herself or a blanket for Jesus in the manger. She was out of there. And even if they didn't have her on film, which they did, Frazier is an "at-will" employer. They have Vicki's signature on a document—everyone signs it to be hired—accepting that the company doesn't need a good reason, or any at all. Silent as they stepped up onto the bridge to cross the cutting floor toward the inner offices, King kept Vicki moving. Although she was usually chatting or crying about something— she was their drama queen in boy belts and hoop earrings and a pink mohawk—she was not crying or chatting now. It was shock. King kept his hand on the outside of her elbow in a very official way, as though he professionally minded if she fell down the stairs, but otherwise was personally uninvolved. No one ever remembers the walk down the stairs. There is a kind of blessed morphine the mind pours into the moment of job amputation; it generally gets you through severance and to your car, maybe as far as Halfway Home, the drive-thru package store that used to be Pure, just behind the Laundromatic. Meanwhile, JaNice pulled a plastic Food Lion grocery sack out of her back pocket, snapped it open, and began clearing anything personal from Vicki's work station, including the glamour shot of her and the snake, her donut cushion, a small magnetized flashlight, a gold lamé purse, and a sequined hoodie with half a vending machine bag of Cheetos in the kangaroo pocket. Food is absolutely forbidden on the floor; you can eat outdoors on the patio or in the break or conference room, that's it. And don't leave any food in the refrigerator in the break room over the weekend. "Attention: These permisisses spayed for bugs ever Friday," the night cleaner, Miss Cora, has posted. She's the same one who posts the "If you sprinkle when you tinkle" signs in the restrooms. There are a lot of things that aren't allowed, including sandals, to spare toes from being broken in accidents. The company doesn't allow hovering—they call it "standing on the seats"—in the bathroom stalls instead of taking the time to lay down one of those fiddly tissue covers, which are supplied and often dispense by the handful or in pieces, which may be a motivation but no excuse. Sometimes Cora just scrawls on a scrap of tractor-feed printer paper from the recycle bin, "What the matter with you all?" Once she wrote, "God is watching." Some heathen wrote a pungent response, and the sign vanished in an hour. Also verboten: smoking anywhere indoors or within fifty yards of the entrance and wearing inappropriate and revealing attire, especially if what that attire is revealing is tattoos or piercings between navel and thigh top. Also prohibited—these are firing offenses, with no warnings; consider the handout sheet you read when hired as your one and sufficient warning—are using "fighting words" and foul language; catfighting, even in the parking lot; bitch-slapping; wig pulling, which happened once, back when "hussy" and "harlot" were still harsh talk and not just lamely funny; and clocking in more than three tardies in one pay period. They don't allow you to do your own packing either when they walk you out. Before NAFTA, before Frazier Fabrics—when this was still part of the Meadowlark Mills corporate empire and when "human resources" was just "personnel"—they had nailed down the walk-out protocols because Sue Rollins, chronically tardy, had seen it coming and had time to get revved up, got way past buzzed and into ugly mean on vodka from her Thermos, tore the audio plug from her ear, and threw her transistor radio at the supervisor who had come to can her. Sue hurled it so hard it boomeranged on its neck strap and gave Sue a shiner. She threw it so hard in fact that when it boomeranged it slung out its 9-volt battery, causing collateral damages to a coworker's eye some distance away, damages which were—after a long and convoluted forensics process—covered by workmen's comp. As it turned out, it wasn't even Sue's radio, but she took it home. That was way before King's and JaNice's time, but King and JaNice have had a lot of practice even so. They are smooth. Just seeing them walking together toward you along the aisles on the sewing floor—especially if JaNice has laid down her clipboard and has both hands free—creates anxiety and reform in the ranks. Rebels and rule benders reach into their pockets and furtively shut down their cell phones. Cell use on the floor, or in the pod toilets arrayed on the catwalk along the walls, can get you walked out too, whether talking or texting. Somebody downstairs can "read" signals, invisible waves. At least that's what got around. It's worth believing it, even if it is a rumor and started by management. Better be safe than sorry. The women who sew know that even if King and JaNice are harmless as thunder, they're hornets for the god of lightning in the house. JaNice's nickname is "No Way" because she says it, pretending she is listening but is actually thinking of how to bust chops. "Burning daylight," she'll say, right in the middle of some new hire's answer to her brisk "How's it going?" She just walks off. The phone on her hip seldom rings more than once before she claws it up and slaps it to her ear. She works while she talks. She works while she walks. She's always picking at something, a crooked cuff or unequal allowances—trying to salvage bad work. She loves the company. She's married, but he knows he's just a man. She used to sew. Seventeen years ago she walked in the front door and signed on, her first job after high school. She has worked nights and weekends and strange shifts and almost every job. She has moved up. Not far, but she will never forget how long it took; she will not backslide. She cannot afford friends. She hates wasted time and bad work. Habitual offenders make her short list, wind up on the daily report on the supervisor's desk. It's a fine line, though. She wants things perfect. She takes a lot of antacids. She wants to look good, but if she traps out too many rats, it smells bad and so does she. She is not unkind, but she is merciless. She presents a moving target. You never know where she is. She wears trendy trainers that tip her forward, halfway into a run the moment she moves. She pisses on little fires all day. Sometimes she holds the clipboard up to her face, her hand at the top, fingers gripping it white-knuckled alongside her ear as a privacy shield against lip-readers, so she can whisper about the workers with King. They pause on their rounds, stand shoulder to shoulder, facing different directions; their eyes are always roving the floor. JaNice has everybody's number from day one. This day Vicki's number was up.

2

There is never an ad in the paper for a Frazier job opening. The company lobby is open weekdays for applicants, even if they have to leave their applications on file and wait months for an interview. They are numbered on a list, like the organ-needy. There's that list, and there's also kinship, friendship, and basic word of mouth; sooner or later there is always a chair needing filling and someone to fill it. War in Afghanistan has been good for Frazier Fabrics: "Quality Product, Innovative Method, American Pride, S.E.A.M.S. since 1987."

Irene Morgan was the one hired to take Vicki's chair. The first four hours of Irene's day one were all downstairs, mostly in Conference Room #2. No one knows where Conference Room #1 is, or if there ever was one. Conference Room #2 sounds more like a kingdom, folks conferring, interpreters, international connections, big doings. Or maybe #1 got annexed into something else and the sign on this door wasn't worth replacing. Conference Room #2 has no windows, no phones, but a good strong table, always polished. One of the two fluorescent tubes flickered and buzzed, Irene remembered, the last time she worked here. Irene thought it was the same flicker now. Tradition is important to Frazier Fabrics.

Mr. Frazier's father began the tradition in the 1970s and 80s, and since they went "divisional" and his son Scott took the lead, he himself has been photographed with all the presidents since Ford; the walls are filling with handshakes. There is one strictly local photograph—a panorama—from the ceremonies at the setting of the new flagpole. Irene moved closer to see her own face in the crowd, but she couldn't. Just her elbow, as if she had her hand up to keep the sun out of her eyes. Or were they saying the pledge? But that would be hand over heart, wouldn't it? For Irene it would. Everybody looked so young!

She stood there remembering so many things she had forgotten in the years since she left to take the job at Happy Time Clocks. Only eight dollars a workday more at first, but over seventeen years, disallowing the occasional twenty-five cents an hour raise and incentives she might have earned at Frazier as well, it had made more than a fifty-thousand-dollar difference, more than three thousand dollars a year, a little which had made a lot, had made all the difference. She had known it would; she had done the figures before she even talked to Deke about it and sold him on the long view. That was the good of his being a farmer—a man who plants crops and trees; he knew how to wait on the turning season, the accumulation and averaging of the years. She knew it was worth it. It was harder work in some ways, on her feet more, but all she had to do was stand—and stand it—for as long as she could. She knew how to stand. She knew how to stand it.

From her first paycheck she had bought some industrial-strength surgical hose and started out, as her mama would have said, the way she meant to wind up, with trim ankles and no varicose veins. Her daughter Jenny had a piano very soon that first year, paid off paycheck by paycheck, her own piano, not a rental, and lessons. Sometimes she still played for church, evening services and revivals mostly. All three of the kids had needed braces and got them, and with the Hope Scholarship, Davy had finished two years of college before he joined the army after 9/11. He'd made a career. 101st Airborne. A staff sergeant, he was "over there" now. His wife, Sherry, and their two children lived in Kentucky; their second baby was three months old. Davy would be home from Iraq for the baby's first birthday in December, if all went by plan, then back on another tour—Afghanistan in February. Jenny had gone on through college on the Hope, loved school, and was teaching eighth grade social studies in the county she grew up in, commuting to classes in Camden for her master's in summers and at night. Easy enough when you are young and able; it is only looking back that it seems impossible what you can accomplish bone tired. Jenny and Kev, her husband, were both teachers, but Kev was studying for his Ph.D.; he wanted to be a principal. Tonya, the baby of Irene and Deke's almost empty nest, didn't want anything but freckled Brad Barnes and freckled babies of her own, and he wanted her and most of the same things and still did. They were leasing to own a quarter section across the creek from Deke and Irene's hundred acres—big help for Deke since Lucky and Brenda, their longtime tenants, had retired and moved back to South Carolina. No man should have to work that hard alone, but when two who believe in it and are hoping for a profit work together turning hay or spraying fire ants and thistles or tagging cows or sweating and swearing the privet and kudzu out of the fence lines, it doesn't seem so much like stupidity or exile to be a farmer.

This time Irene wasn't applying for a sewing job at Frazier Fabrics because of the children. Irene was there for Deke. He had a cough. Some sun spots on his hands and those Popeye arms of his and places on his face needed looking at. And he was beginning to lean toward the ankle that didn't get set right two years ago. He had the VA, but there were other things besides insurance. She wanted to buy him a Gator, so he could motor around on chores instead of walking or riding the tractor. Sometimes in the evenings they would share the pedal boat on the pond, feeding the carp, listening to the martins, watching the clouds, churning themselves along on the sky reflected in the water and dreaming dreams like rank beginners. He'd farmed chicken and beef his whole civilian life, since his war ended. He was so glad to be home, under clear sky and out of the jungle, he wasn't worried about rain. Didn't need to, for years and years. Weather patterns had been changing, though. The drought years had been hard on the fields and wells; the couple had drilled deeper and been buying hay, even had to lay some out in the summer. And this day, while she was at Frazier, filling out employment information and waiting on her hiring interview, the hauler was there loading up the spring calves for sell off—all of them, not just the steers. Someone else could pay to fatten them. She and Deke didn't need more heifers. Irene didn't mind missing the roundup; she'd hated to hear the cows, though, all night long the night before bawling in the lot, with the fence and grove between them and their babies. They got as close as they could and wouldn't give up until they dried up. Every year when the truck drove out and away, the calves were bawling too. They could hear each other; they knew each other. It never helped to turn up the radio or TV; you heard them with your heart.

Irene used to help Deke with roundup, with anything at all to do with the farm. They still laugh about one early anniversary when she had some bruised ribs from a barn incident and Deke gave her a headgate because she was not strong-armed enough to dose the cows. Cows don't run at you; they just lean, and hard enough that she was crushed against the gatepost. That was the last time he shopped for her at the feed and seed store, though.

She even took care of the broiler house at first. No more. No more starting each day easing into the crowded chicken "factory," with its autofeeder, power windows, and twenty-four-hour daylight, carrying a five-gallon bucket to gather up dead chicks, many of them pecked to death. She now has a flock; she loves her own special chickens, green-legged free rangers, bantam golden Sebrights. Irene swears that no chicken on earth is smarter: "They just have sense." They take care of the Japanese beetles, and, Irene believes, they'd run off the snakes too. She believes they know their names. They fly to her, hurtling along with bowed wings, and she feeds them shredded cheese. Deke can't see smart and dumb the same way—would they come to her if there were no cheese?—but it is okay with him if she keeps them for their company even if they are ugly, which they aren't. They are beautiful. They all have beautiful names, except the one with the funny comb like Frankenstein's bride. Still, she's "Bridie."

Whatever delights Irene delights Deke. He nailed up a peach crate to the front porch wall for the one hen, Mercy, who likes to sleep high but close. Way high, so nothing can jump up to her. Each evening Irene sets up a little pole ladder Deke invented, notched to lean against the crate, and Mercy hops right up it, rung by rung, and settles down. If Irene forgets to set it up for her, Mercy paces back and forth on the porch railing, waiting, antsy, murmuring, readying like a basketball player about to make a free throw. One night when Irene forgot the ladder, they found Mercy on the ceiling fan blade bunched down next to the motor housing. So that's something else to remember: porch light and fan *off.* Sometimes another of the hens will come and share the same dorm, but usually it's just Mercy, alone. Irene's like a kid at Easter gathering the tan eggs. Most of the time the chickens lay their eggs in their nests in the car house, but once in a while Mercy will deliver one on the porch, right on the welcome mat. When Deke finds a bronze feather with its black lace, he'll pick it up for Irene's collection. She has a vaseful. When her hens die, she takes it hard, buries them with honors and prays them back to God. Deke loves that about her, but in so many ways she remains a mystery. They still study each other, still matter. That well has not dried up.

Irene has always canned and frozen and put up from the garden and orchard and berry thickets, and she used to sew for the girls and now makes clothes for the grandies, and she has always kept a good house, with a fresh pitcher of sweet Luzianne waiting for Deke in the refrigerator summer or winter. Pretty old-fashioned life, with a lot of laughs, even if buzzards are always circling somewhere, high in the sky, waiting. That's just life on the land. Marketing the animals makes her sad, but she's no vegetarian. "Just don't name the pig," her granddaddy used to say. That's pretty much her policy on it too.

Irene's search for a "town job" in the late 1980s wasn't a comment on Deke's providings, Reaganomics, or farm life in general. Deke and she weren't conspicuous consumers. They always had enough cash for new and nice things for Sunday and school, and plenty to share any day or hour. They had the old cluck-cluck tractor that Deke restored—and which he still trusts like a friend even though he's got a Kubota now too and a decent truck with a ball hitch—and bicycles for the kids. After the kids were all settled in school, though, she began thinking about wage pay and insurance. All the wives were doing the same thing, or selling Tupperware or Avon. She first worked at the Frazier plant sewing, and then when she heard that Happy Time had dental benefits, she went there. After Irene got the job at Happy Time in Camden, she and Deke bought a second-hand car for her to get back and forth. After a few years, when Davy got his license, she found three other women on the same shift and pooled. It had all worked out just right. Carpooling freed up the wheels for Davy to drive to school. That got him, and his sisters too, off the bus. Things like that made a difference at their age. She knew that from her own country childhood and town schooling.

When Happy Time closed and was outsourced to Mexico, all that changed, almost overnight. Irene and the other shift workers showed up one Monday and the Happy Time gate was chained. No management showed up. There was yellow caution tape along the fence, and a notice was posted, all the notice they got. Time, someone said—the only laugh of the day—had run out. Even the machines had been crated and carted south. Her whole rainbow, steady-even-floating life popped like a bubble and headed for the drain; there hadn't been a whisper or rumor about it. Now a lot of places had closed or were bottom-lining, offering part-time work so they didn't have to bankroll benefits. Irene had been looking for months, since before Thanksgiving. Her unemployment and COBRA benefits were about up. Irene had said she'd never show her face back at Frazier or in any other sewing plant, but she had changed her mind. She had thought she was well done with sewing, with being dragged forward all day with the cloth as it went under the needle, doing her part but never finishing anything, just shoving her piece on and picking up the next one. Now she was thanking God for the second chance.

This time she had hardly read the paperwork Frazier's human resources had handed out, the hefty spiral-bound of rules, addresses, weather info for snow or flood times, whom they are to notify if Irene can't or won't, whom she is to notify if and when and before, just scanning the pages to find where to put her signature. She was that sure, that ready: this was it because what else was there? She'd looked. She turned back to the stack of papers before her, trying to pay attention, choosing options. There weren't so many options: beneficiaries, numbers, avowals, permission to be "surveilled," next-of-kin disclaimers. One page she had set aside, one question to come back to.

Irene looked to see if Mrs. Champion was still out of the room. She even looked around the ceiling and scrutinized the Rocky Mountains in the framed lithograph on the west wall, in case she was being "surveilled." She had already noticed the missing corner—clean cut—of the ceiling tile in the ladies' bathroom. She had restrained herself from saluting, or mooning, it. She went back through the papers now, pretending to read others again, and finally worked her way through the stack to the question she had skipped. She faced it. Had she been a member of the union? Were they allowed to ask this? For three months, when she worked at Kroger almost thirty years ago, she had been. Not even Deke knew that. She was a teenager. She wasn't married then. Considering how things went, and what she had been through then and since, she couldn't see that there was much to confess or brag about. She never attended a meeting. The only impact she could see it had made was that the steward—he was the chief butcher—had learned her name and phone number. He was the only one. He did not call on union business. She accepted nothing from him. He got nothing out of her except dues. Irene smiled. That was the last job she had before she met Deke and married. She filled in the box beside NO.

Mrs. Champion now returned with a photocopy. She didn't hand it to Irene. She clipped it atop the tax information on the inside cover of the folder. "I just wanted to double-check on something," she explained. She laid her palm on the file and studied Irene. "You've been through all this before; we keep the files forever. We're glad to have you back, but unfortunately it has been too many years; you don't qualify for the 'rehire' prerequisites, so you lose all former seniority dates and benefits. You have to start over just like you have never worked here." Irene knew that. "You have to start—" Mrs. Champion hesitated. "You have to start at almost the same place you started before, $1.05 more than minimum wage." She glanced up, in case Irene had any ideas or regrets. "But minimum's more than it used to be. Everything has risen. You knew that, about the grace period for coming back, at the time of your leaving. You signed forms. I have the forms."

Irene nodded. She had no ideas or regrets. "I signed all the new forms," she said, pushing the stack back. It would be ninety days before insurance would kick in. There were other little details, and the possibility of incentive pay as well as an annual raise, depending on her production performance. Irene jotted these things into her notebook also. Mrs. Champion checked each sheet in her custody before laying it in the file, checked again, front and back. "You're in good shape," she said, and started toward the inner office. It was almost lunchtime. "You will meet with Mr. Al Grayson, your supervisor, at 1:30. After lunch. He shuts his door; nobody knocks during his quiet time. You'll see what I mean. He's on the mezzanine. You know where the midline companionway is, by the old cutting room? Things have gotten moved around. They've even installed three little scary pod bathrooms along the walls on the mezz level. They're not Port-o-lets, and they are permanent, and they are modern; there's just something about that fiberglass skylight. Also, they sort of—well, they're not really, but they seem—" Mrs. Champion whispered, "they seem springy. Spacey.

Who wants to be hunkering down way off up there in the air?" She cleared her throat. "Most of our ladies still come down to ground level."

Irene didn't say anything. She was trained; she thought of it as "factory-broken." She knew all about squatting on schedule, and like most factory workers, especially those on production lines or working for incentive, she preferred not to need a break and drank water sparingly and only for health. It wasn't the stairs; it was the time it took. After you got good at the job, after you made production, there was the hope of incentive to keep you in your chair. You got to know exactly how many seconds a long seam takes, a turn, dropping and picking up something, stopping to answer a question. Time was ticking all the time somewhere in your mind, like a taxi meter, running while standing. Any interruption in the flow, in the progress, in the pace had visceral impact and consequences. "You even sew in your sleep"; that's what Deke had said, anyway. But that was before; that was her first sewing job. But then, when doesn't every stitch, every second, count?

"Mr. Grayson," Mrs. Champion was saying, closing the file. "He's in the office cluster at mid-mezzanine, and you can ask anyone where."

"I'll be fine," Irene said. "Thank you."

When Mrs. Champion had gone, Irene chose a packet of cheese sandwich crackers from the basket on the conference table. She picked up a bottle of water. She had brought a sandwich bag with apple slices in it and a shake of cinnamon. She needed caffeine, and she had decided to splurge fifty cents for coffee. She wouldn't do it every day. But this wasn't every day. She was the last one to be processed through. She was in now. She had the job! She had joined the team.

The hirees had all reported for class at nine. They had watched the film on troops in the field. It was called "Fielding the Team." They were part of the war now, part of the team. After ninety days she would get a Team Frazier lapel pin. Frazier's "product, method, and pride" were making a difference. After the film, they were allowed in the hall of the executive wing to look at the items in the glass case and photos on the wall so they could see what they would be making. When they returned to the conference room, they met the safety instructor. There was a slide show. There were some laughs and many serious warnings. It was a mixed bag. Report every scratch or accident, but don't have any. They knew now not to mess with a lockout tag or an abusive boyfriend. They knew whom to tell if they suspected someone else had problems. Or if a stalker followed them into the parking lot. They learned not to let anyone else in on their card swipe, called "crowding the door." They learned the importance of clocking out on time, within the seven minutes of grace. Failure to do so messed up accounting, who assumed you were sneaking little bites of overtime, and it could hold up your paycheck. It was called "being whistle bit."

They were given their temporary door and ID/time cards, which would be replaced by permanent cards after probation. They must report any lost cards immediately and would be charged fifty dollars for each replacement during probation, that amount deducted from the paycheck of the careless employee. They must work overtime when asked; they must work overtime in increments of half hours and hours exactly, to aid accounting. There were other rules about overtime, but they were told there would be no overtime while on probation, so please not to ask. They were instructed about other "resources." This meant mental health. Irene had put the brochure in her pile of papers to take home and—please, God—never need again. "They're there for you, but let's not tie up the hotline," the safety leader said. "Everybody's sad now and then, but I'm not talking about something chocolate and MIDOL can cure, arright? But if you are feeling dangerous, let somebody know." They knew now to give all wheeled vehicles, even laundry carts and the postal clerk, right of way. They knew to wash their hands before sewing. They knew not to wear lotion on their hands or arms as they sewed the new camo—this was not protocol, just common sense—in case lotion messed up its ability to deflect infrared detection. They knew not to discuss anything about what they were sewing even with family and certainly not strangers. Irene's son was in the field. She wondered what he would make of the new camo. She wondered what *she* would.

Irene's head was brimming with all sorts of first-day information. A bell rang. Someone walked by, headed for the time clock, then others, then the rush began toward the break room and the downstairs lavatories.

Someone was microwaving popcorn. Another was heating up something Italian. The break room and the conference room shared a wall. The relaxing workers sounded like hens. Irene pocketed her change purse and went along. She watched the little bracket-mounted TV offering satellite news of the world while she waited in line. That TV was new, she found out, bought with proceeds from the vending machines, along with a machine that grinds beans and makes fresh-brewed coffee each time you put in the coins. Irene hated the smell of burnt coffee. This was a real treat. She decided to go off the rails of her budget and put in an extra dime and get cappuccino. She carried her cup back to the conference room. She hoped this would not be a preview of her lunchtime every day; the break room was chaos. She shook out another cracker sandwich. Someone going past recognized Irene, faced about, put her head around the door, and then came on in. It was Aldine. "I can't believe it," the woman told Irene. "Look at us!" They hugged. When Irene stood up, Aldine hugged her again. "Girl!" they said simultaneously, patting each other's hands, palm to palm, double high fives, like it was good, all good.

"I'm back." Irene figured that pretty much said it all.

"I thought you were smarter than this!" They had been classmates at school, and for a time while their babies were little, they had attended the same church. Aldine and her family had moved away. Aldine worked in the front office in administrative support. She was a blond now, and she had a Wolff tan. No wedding ring, but a turquoise on her thumb. "Ad sup—that's a typist who knows Word and PowerPoint," she told Irene. "That safety thing y'all sat through a while ago? That was mine." They did some catching up, just like anytime they met. But it had been years. Frazier —and Happy Time—had a way of soaking you up and wringing you out, so there wasn't anything left to spread around. Irene didn't ask about the wedding ring, but Aldine had always been able to read her mind.

"Two years ago," she said, "we found out he likes 'em taller and younger. Where you gonna sit?" Aldine asked her.

"I don't know."

"Don't let 'em put you in that back corner. No way to jump if there's a fire. I'm assuming you're on the mezzanine?"

Irene shrugged. "I report to Mr. uh—"she checked her notes—"Grayson after lunch."

"Mezzanine it is," Aldine said. "You're in the army now. I've heard that's some really voodoo fabric, but you'll get along with Grayson. He's fair." Aldine walked around the conference room. "I can't believe they painted in here again. Remember how they paint? They believe in white paint. And buy it in sixty-gallon drums!"

"Maybe this is some of the same paint from when I was here before," Irene said. "Maybe they won't change colors until they use it all up."

"And then they get halfway around, run out, and have to order another sixty gallons!" The blocks looked velvety and smooth with the latex layers. Aldine was studying new posters, a series of inspirations around the whited walls. She hadn't been in the conference room since last fall, during the annual open insurance options campaign and lecture. Mrs. Champion came back through, trailing popcorn fumes and chatting on her cell. She gave them a look. Aldine was okay; this was her lunch too. She didn't even turn but just waved. Irene was already feeling that nervousness, though, that tension in the stomach, about—about everything: trespasses and debts; territory; loose lips; tale bearers; great, maybe impossible, expectations; humiliations. It is one thing to get a job, another to keep it.

"Ray Silverstein," Aldine read, looking at the poster's tag line. "Does he work around here?"

Mrs. Champion looked troubled, sensitive about the—as she thought of it—Jewish issue. In her tenure they had had Muslim Arabs, a Christian Arab married to a Greek, some Buddhists not always Asian, proud gays with T-shirts to prove it, and they had two workers in wheelchairs and one work-pusher in a leg brace and boot. They had a materials handler with palsy. They had Jacky, who was just Jacky. They had Hispanics. Right now they had three Hmong, a Thai, a Korean, all sewing, and a Chechen data entry clerk. The Kenyan IT tech had written home for his brothers to come on over. He was sending them money. There was a former nun. There was a Philippine newlywed married to a Cuban boxer with a fixer-upper condo and no credit. There was a street preacher, Sister JereAnne. They had a tall, lean, very stylish black Muslim academically suspended all-American college basketball star vegetarian in cotton-and-rubber shoes who had really brought down the mood at last year's Memorial Day lunch hour barbecue cookout but then won friends and the limbo contest. There were Hindu Mauritanian sisters in saris and with bindis. There was a Pakistani intern in audit. The company nurse, Mrs. Giddings, was an Adventist. But Frazier Fabrics did not have a single Jew working there, as far as Mrs. Champion knew. How would you ask? How would you recruit? How would you know? Names didn't always reveal. For a moment all three women looked at Ray Silverstein's poster with "Compensation satisfies; it does not motivate." "No," Mrs. Champion—sighing for deeply felt and unspoken reasons—said, "he doesn't work here."

For very different reasons, Aldine—who thought from her own work experience the poster's verbs were exactly backward—said, "I didn't think so."

3

"What did you do, when you were here before?" Mr. Grayson asked Irene. He was not the first black man she had worked for. She did think he might be the first black man who floor-bossed for Frazier in this plant, and certainly the largest person in the plant. A big man. She was old enough to be his mother. "Wise Ol' Al," his nameplate—held by an owl in a graduation cap and gown—announced. He was an Alabama fan. He'd been a fullback, had photos and honors all around. Framed clippings and headlines, a jersey, crimson and white everywhere, Roll Tide! pennants and banners, pompom fringe hanging out of the closed file drawer, souvenirs and desk toys on sills and every other flat surface. A game ball on the file cabinet. Bear Bryant motivational quips tacked to the corkboard, taped to the door and its window. Had to be honoring the legend; he was too young to have played for Bryant. Last year's Boss's Day mug with a little football-shaped balloon on a stick and containing some untouched sugarless candies. A thriving philodendron snaking its way around the wall, strapped to the ceiling tile frames. In the center of the chaos on his desk was a clearing about the size of a place mat, with a Bible and a can of Diet Coke, both open. The bench by the door was covered with printouts and notebooks and procedures and inventory reports, and there was a folding chair popped open in the space left. He did not ask her to sit, so Irene stood.

"I wasn't fired," Irene told him. "I left to—"

"Pursue other interests. Yeah, I know," Mr. Grayson said. He had already cleared that up with Mrs. Champion. "But while you were here, what did you do?"

Irene replied, "I cross-trained. Bar tack, pocket rivets, zippers. Gents."

"Gents," Mr. Grayson said, tickled, tasting the word. "What else?"

Irene's shoulders and blood pressure rose a little as she thought of the machines. How, day by day, week by week, the fearful and challenging machines had become real, had become partners with her hands on them, so that what had been a strange and nightmarish dreamscape became as familiar as her own kitchen, but the size of two football fields. "Belt loop cutter, pocket welter, pocket hemmer, yoke machine, auto sleeve, Adler bar tacker not Juki." She knew they had a Juki now. "Label sew, zippers, brass and nylon, like I said, gents. Serger, of course. Horizontal finisher, inseamer, seamer." She hesitated. She hated to add the vapor press; it was her worst job, a nightmare in summer with the steam, and frightening. Nobody wanted that job; it was no place for a beginner. She had seen, everyone had seen, what it did to Carly. Of course, it did something *for* Carly too once she signed papers not to sue when the unmaintained steam line broke. After the third set of grafts on her face and arms, and rehab, she came back to work wearing an eye patch and a turban, then later a wig, with a job pushing the mail cart. She had that job for life, it was said. Mr. Grayson was looking at his papers. He glanced up, waiting. She sighed. She was replacing someone who had sewed; maybe the vapor press with its hateful movable bucks wouldn't be an issue. "Seam buster."

"Seam buster?"

"Yessir." She was already thinking how to tell it so Deke would laugh. How Mr. Grayson was an Alabama fan but when he scowled he looked like a bulldog.

"You bowl?" He leaned back in his chair. It creaked. "Bowling team is the Seambusters."

"Men's," she remembered.

"Gents," he said. He loved the word like a new toy; he was going to play. "No. Not anymore. They lost interest. I mean, how many men work here anyway? The ones who do—" He shrugged. "We're not bowlers. So the ladies—you know y'all were Pins and Needles? Yeah, well, the ladies hated it, so they just took over the Seambusters name and the shirts." Irene felt apprehensive, years of factory experience, nothing to do with him at all, anxious about lingering too long or wasting time. Maybe Mr. Grayson had never worked production. It was too soon for her to ask about incentive. If she had been invited to sit, she would have gotten up now.

"I don't bowl," Irene said. Maybe she could. She didn't have babies at home. But she was away from Deke all day; why would she want to be away at night? And a ball and shoes would cost something, plus league dues. She and Deke had bowled together a few times, early in their marriage. She had even sipped a little of his beer, pretended to get happy, but she already was. Another time they had played putt-putt at a state park, when they were camping with the kids.

Mr. Grayson brought his chair back level. Irene blinked. "I've got news for you," he said. He held his hands up, showed her his palms, a train-stopping whoa. "You can't iron this new camo. All sorts of things it'll do for you if you keep in mind not to wash it in phosphate detergent or starch it or iron it. I'm sure they told you downstairs some laundry product does what they call 'enhances the IR signature,' makes it 'inappropriately bright' in night vision goggles. You could get somebody tagged. And even though it's fire retardant, you can't lay an iron on it. In brief, no steam, no vapor, no seam busting on this gig. We're on a new page here." They smiled at each other. It *was* good news.

Betty, the senior on the line, was lurking outside the door, waiting her turn; she was to show Irene around, set her up to be trained. She peeked in, pretended to knock, needing to task on. Irene noticed her flowered cobbler's apron, frizz-permed "Frivolous Fawn" hair, brave claret lipstick matching a professional manicure. Wedding band on her right hand. Widow? She looked older than she probably was. Irene glanced away.

"Is she hired?"

"She's hired, Miss Betty, we're just figuring out for what."

"Don't you Miss Betty me. I may be senior on your line but I ain't a senior citizen! Not yet." Irene could tell this was how they got along, not a quarrel. It was like flirting, sort of. Personable, not sexual. She was a Georgia fan, wearing a Go Dawgs! shirt under her apron. It wasn't Friday, but she had on the red T, black slacks, the bulldog earrings. Nobody in her family had gone to college, but they all went to the home games.

The phone on Mr. Grayson's desk rang, and he ignored it, then hit hold without lifting the receiver. It rang on. He jerked the receiver up and then dropped it like a bomb back on the cradle. That stopped the ringing. His laugh started low in his chest, a rich baritone. He pointed a finger gun at it. They had a new phone system and he was still on the rising side of the learning curve. It appeared he thought discipline, as for a puppy, would help.

"It's respect, Miss Betty," he said. "I 'preciate how long you been young." The phone rang again. "See ya?" he said, waving them out.

"Let me walk her around and through," Betty suggested. As soon as they were outside Grayson's door, Betty told her, "I wasn't here then, but I'll take their word for it: they tell me you can sew. Is there anything you *want* to do, besides go home?" Her reading glasses made her eyes large and soft, but they had a glint.

"Inseams?" Irene answered.

"I'll keep that in mind," Betty said. Meaning, think of something else; inseams are covered.

"You tell me," Irene suggested.

Betty gave her shoulder a little slap of approval and set off down the aisle. They were headed for the empty chair mid-row, just past the cross-aisle break. "You'll train with Coquita on armor carriers."

"Oh," Irene said. It hadn't occurred to her how everything had to have camo, not just the soldiers. She thought an armor carrier was a wheeled weapon.

"We'll whip you into shape in no time," Betty said. "Haven't lost one yet." Then frowned. "Well, except for Vicki. You're getting her chair. But I think she was lost when she got here, if you don't mind me saying. Her mama and I are best friends." She bent to pick up a lost label, pocketing it. "Sometimes all you can do is cry." She finger-flossed a piece of lint from the feed dog and pocketed it. All day long she pocketed things that weren't where they should be, cleaning up messes. Cheering her crew on, never grinding. She was no grinder. She had sewed. She still did. "God knows, she's been there for me." She presented Irene to the women on either side of her and down the row, no formal introductions. "Y'all, this is Irene. This is a good place to work, good people," Betty said. "Say yes." They all hollered YES. So far Irene didn't know which one was Coquita. There were women on each side of her chair. Heads had lifted all down the row and looked Irene's way, and now they ducked back to work. "This is my wild corner," Betty said. "Thank God for penicillin."

As Irene was sitting down, rolling up to her station, Betty leaned over to pick something else off the floor. "Is this a gum wrapper?" she asked. Rules about that too. She took her time, standing up again, feeling bare-handed to see if Vicki—why not? who else?—had stuck Juicy Fruit gum underneath, as though the crime and the clues were all going to be local to this gone worker's stand. Irene noticed the dog tags. Betty was wearing dog tags. "My boy is over there now," Irene remembered. She didn't know if she spoke it aloud. She had tried to make it a habit as often as she thought of Davy, to remind God.

Betty used her toe, made sure the floor plug was in straight, then powered up, flicked on the light, tucked in her dog tags, and handed Irene a grabbed-up bouquet of pieces of interesting fabric. "My boy's home now," was all she said. "Coquita? Show Irene how it's done. Maybe 'bout an hour? then let her go. Y'all play nice. Don't scare her off. We want her back here tomorrow."

That's when Irene found out that Coquita was the light brown jumpy one on her right with Marlboro breath and a shaved head, in a black T-shirt and camo fatigues, who asked, "Your son's in A-stan?"

Surprised, Irene had to think. Should she tell this strange-looking young woman? Not because he was married, but because he was—Davy. He was hers. Also she felt shy because of that "A-stan." Also Irene pronounced it eye-RACK not eee-ROCK. She didn't know how Coquita would pronounce it. And she didn't feel she had the right to call it A-stan. She saved that new word up, though, to tell Deke. "But he's coming home for Christmas," she told Coquita, "and then they're deploying for Afghanistan in February."

"Trained troops," Coquita said, "right here," offering her hard little hand. That hard little hand trembled, seemed to actually vibrate. Coquita pulled it back. "Yeah, I know," was all she said. "Two tours Iraq, one in A-stan," Coquita added. She called it eye-RACK also. "Iraq and Irene, Iraq and I ruin," she said, tapping her own chest, and then laughed so hard she snorted. When she sat up again, she was wiping her eyes.

The platinum blond angel-haired woman on Irene's left was Kit. She made a woohoo gesture with both hands and said, "Can you say PTSD? And all this is what they're fighting for. Plus peeing on schedule and hiking to the boonies to smoke."

"I'm glad I didn't know," Coquita said. She straightened herself up, and then she and Irene got right to work. Coquita believed in hands-on, so they used Irene's machine. Started absolutely from the basics, going down the checklist Betty left, beginning with names of parts, then threading.

"Threading's the beast," Coquita told her. But Irene's steady hands remembered how; she didn't need glasses and she didn't use a threader: she shot it over and under and around and on first try straight through the eye, goosed it a little, gave it the chachacha, looped the threads up, and clipped them. "Damn," Coquita said. "I may be calling on you—"

About twenty minutes later, the first seam Irene sewed through the tough light fabric was true and straight, but she had one piece inside out. She couldn't tell right from wrong.

"That," Kit commented, sewing straight-backed with her chin jutting forward, zooming along, "is the story of my life.

In your first ninety days, you can't be absent or tardy, not once, not even a minute or less late or early. No "time clock irregularities or infractions. One hour docked for any minute thereof. Habitual offenses, summary dismissal." That sort of talk amused Irene a little because she was not someone who was ever tardy; she had worked most of her adult life and did not need to learn good work habits now. But even though she was sure she had planned right and she was tired enough to sleep, she lay in bed that night imagining how terrible it would be to be late. She had set her alarm for 5:00 A.M. but then got up and reset it to 4:30. It was only five miles to the plant, in downtown Ready. She had her clothes laid out. She was ready for Ready. She couldn't do a thing, though, about her jittery nerves. Thank God the cows had mostly quit bawling, and so she lay there, beside Deke, and rested, but she didn't sleep deep enough to dream.

On her day two, Irene was in the Frazier parking lot half an hour early. She could hear roosters crowing, like old men calling *Where's ya wrist watch?* over in the old mill town. Robins singing in the mulberry thicket, and somewhere high, too dark yet to see them, a pair of kildeer. A very fresh sweet April day, with a rind of the Easter moon. Irene had her choice of parking spots. She chose one with an empty space beside her and began to read her "Daily Bread" by dome light. She kept an eye on the clock, and on her rearview. Then it was time to go on in; others were moving toward the building, no stream yet, but handfuls. Irene clicked off the dome light and started gathering things, but before she could get her door open, here came Kit in her little acid green convertible, plunging improperly and boldly down the one-way, shortcutting in from the other lane, facing the wrong way, aimed for the gate. They were drivers' sides door to door, window to window, but Kit never looked around. Irene waited until Kit got out and remote-locked over her shoulder, running like she was late. She was thumbing speed dial as she ran.

By the time Irene had locked her purse in the trunk and got to the door, Kit had ducked in on somebody else's swipe, dashed to the vending area, and was out back sitting on the picnic table with her feet on the bench drinking Mountain Dew. Breakfast. "I don't want him, I've thrown him o-u-t, and I don't care where he lands," she was saying into her phone. "He's a liar. So let him lie. He can lie and maybe on the side of the road or in a gully somewhere 'til the buzzards take him down to the ribs for all I care." She listened and then laughed, "That's it, that's it, start with his lyin' eyes." She brought her feet up onto the table, swung around, and lay flat down, sobbing up at the sky, tears in her ears. Workers looked but went on by; this was Kit. This was private. This was how it was.

The line at the clock stretched back into the building. They weren't allowed to stand in the doorway or queue up outside. Every worker had to swipe in and then stand in line inside the building, being surveilled, waiting for the clock. Someone official checked both records for that, especially in the first ninety days. All of the new hires had been warned. If anyone forgot the rules, there were notices all around, reminding. And, of course, they had signed a paper during orientation, which was on file.

By the time Irene got in line, nineteen back from the clock, she had heard all about what would be listed in Thursday's *Messenger* as "a domestic altercation on Camden Street." Kit's private life was very often public. She came in now, right at the last moment, when the first person had swiped her card and headed upstairs. Kit looked stormy. Grief was under control. Her angel curls were still drying but already crisping with product and indignation. "I hate starting over," she said, but she already had—she always had. She didn't flatten her affect once she came in, figuring right that they'd all heard about it or would. She had no face to save. The one she wore was game. Kit did not even ask first as a courtesy but simply broke in line with just her left arm, leaning way in behind Jacky, the materials pusher, balancing with her right fingers resting on his shoulder. Jacky was listed as white, but he looked a little exotic. There was mystery about

him. Kit, pale as a Kewpie, winked at Miss Anita, the steady black deacon-
ess and drummer at Mt. Moriah and their front-line senior, who proph-
esied, "There be another one, Baby. Save the salta ya tears." Kit swiped her
card through and ran for the ladies' room, leaving aromas of strawberry
and ginger body wash in her wake.

One time Kit had been called out for a dress code infraction; she had
showed up in a pair of inspirational short shorts pulled on over sweats.
Across the butt of the shorts it said TRY HARDER. She had honestly thought
wearing them over the sweats would be okay. She knew not to wear them
without the sweats. Besides, it was winter. They had sent her home.
"Why?" Kit had wanted to know. "Do I get to come back?"

"To change clothes," King and JaNice had told her, "And yes."

"In that case," Kit had replied. Then she had leaned on King for balance and peeled the shorts off.

"No way," JaNice had said, which Kit had taken as encouragement,
not shock and awe. Then Kit had shaken the shorts out, turned them so
King and JaNice could read them, had given them bullfighter's pass, said
"What it says," and gone back to work.

Irene's locker was in the top row next to Sua Nag Vang's. It said so, in
interesting handwriting, on the door. Irene's label holder was still empty,
from Vicki's deletion. While Sua Nag opened her locker and hung her
jacket, set her lunch on the shelf, draped her ID holder around her neck,
tied on her apron, gripped her refilled water bottle under her elbow, and
locked up, Irene waited. "You first next time," Sua Nag said. She didn't
look at Irene. At first Irene did not know the tiny woman was speaking
to her. She didn't know eye contact is bad manners among Hmong. Here
came Kit, who opened a stuffed locker on the bottom tier, kicked things
back in, peeled out of her overshirt, slammed and locked, and loped off
to work. Her hair was banana-clipped up now. Now Irene could see the
ladybug tattoos behind Kit's ears and the Miss Kitty with a red bow tattooed on the nape of her neck.

"Targets," Sua Nag said, not looking.

Day two went fast. They all did. By the time Irene got her first paycheck, she had earned her second paycheck. It began to get easier. Two months to go on probation. She met with Mr. Grayson, for about a minute. All the new hires in miniconferences presented themselves for his remarks, hearing whether or not they were "where they should be at this point." They had been summoned all at once and were beckoned into the office and out quickly, one after another, like chickadees at a feeder. Irene was "where she should be" after the first thirty days and celebrated her first paid holiday, Memorial Day. Then after the second thirty days, she was where she should be, so she sewed on; she was still on track, so she sewed on and on.

4

Frazier prepared for the Fourth of July. There was bunting swagged between great bows of yellow ribbon on the old bell tower. That was Jacky's job. There were red, white, and blue twirly whirligigs along the drive, flags in the whited planters of red and purple petunias by the main gate. Unofficially, Jacky's pickup with a removable billboard in the bed—an election-year sideline he had thought up on his own—readable from both sides of Main Street, rolled slowly through town with PA speakers on the roof playing "God Bless America." He signed up for every parade but thought up something special for the national birthday every year. This year's display was pretty much the cherry on the sundae. He was going to make the national news.

Jacky was the one someone pointed out when someone else had complained at lunch that "no men work at Frazier." There was a pause as they considered him—wiry, broad-backed, shy, helpful, ungrumbling, good as gold, intense, literal, and with a steel plate in his head from something he did not remember and no one knew. He'd been dropped off and abandoned. Some said gypsies left him at the service station when they couldn't sell him. Others said he followed the goat man into town. It was said that

Jacky had been neutered and that "*they* had never descended." Not word one of any of that was the truth; none knew what the truth was. He was fostered, a ward of the state, and he had thrived. He was a man now, and some of them knew it for a fact. In case the new hires didn't know, they heard all that at lunch.

The one who had complained added, "I meant doing what *we* do."

"No man could."

"Ya think? Or are we just pure damn idiots?" That should have been Coquita's line, but she had sprinted out back, to smoke.

"I'm not pure," Kit said, peeling her yogurt foil open, giving it a wide cat lick and then some kitten ones.

Here came Jacky. He had postcard-sized U.S. flags on little poles duct-taped to the sides of his Braves cap. When they hushed as he walked by, he stopped, as though they were waiting for whatever he had not thought until that moment to say. He was wearing his Team Frazier American Pride pin on his work vest, over his heart.

"You prouda me thih time," he said. "I ma' big prans. I hadda grill holes in my cruck." When they weren't kindled by that, he added, "I had hep sperring the wurgs." Last fall he had misspelled a crucial word on his billboards—the candidate's name during the whistlestop: FRAZIER WEL-COMES BARTACK OBAMA. After that he had promised the company never to use the Frazier name without asking and to be sure he had permission to "endorse." He thought endorse meant writing, as on a check. Since then he had signed his signs "Jacky." That was OK? That was OK. He had also promised to seek proofreading help. Someone at the *Messenger* was suggested, but who would ask a newspaper person to help when it was a secret? People who worked there were bound to tell. One of the guys up front downstairs had asked him, "What if it isn't Obama?"—meaning losing or winning the election. Jacky had replied, "Whatever"—meaning Jacky would have made a billboard for anyone who came through, win, lose, or draw. That was hospitality. That was American pride. Nobody knew how he had ever gotten a driver's license, but he kept it renewed, and he had never, so far as anyone knew, gone past the speed or the city limits. Most of the time he rode his bike. Sometimes he pushed it, when he had time to stop and talk along the way.

Irene knew him. He was not much older than she was. She remembered how he had been teased in school. She started to get up and walk away.

Kit was the one who got up. Dusted crumbs. Smoothed her shirt front and eyed herself over her shoulder and shook like a lady duck. "I hate linen," she stated. "Don't wear linen to work." Who but Kit would? She tumbled things around in her purse, spritzed her throat with cologne, rubbed it on her hands, and applied the extra to her hair, then smoothed, smoothed, and clenched the curls. Next she crowned herself with her sunglasses. She was ready. She was "just running out for a minute." She had a phone call to make, but one more bit of table business before she went. "Is it a secret, Jacky?" she asked.

"Yuh."

"A good one?"

"Yuh!" He nodded his head, smiling at the floor. "American pride," he said. He grinned.

"He grins!" Kit said. She scanned the table and pointed her middle and index fingers at her eyes and then at Irene's eyes. "Don't y'all tease him, now. If it's a secret, it's his secret. Wait for the surprise." Irene realized that Kit was warning her off. Irene smiled. She made the same fingers-to-eyes sign right back at her. They all watched Kit's long legs in those low-cut skinny jeans step her way out of there, weaving through the disarrayed chairs. "You're thrilling us, Jacky," Kit called back, looking at him, only at him. Then she put her shades over her eyes and carded out at the door to the executive parking lot to make her call. It was the nearest exit, that was the only reason, but if someone offered her a ride, she'd go. They wouldn't see her till the next day. She'd take off. She took offers. She took risks. She took French leave. She took everything but abuse, and she gave as good as she got, but she kept coming up empty. And she kept coming back to sew.

Kit was the one who finally phoned "the seam buster mystery number." Irene thought she remembered the U.S. Patent number on the seam buster to be 391 3428, how it looked like a phone number, and asked in a lunch lull one day in month two if anybody had ever dialed it. She was just kidding, didn't imagine anyone had or would care— or dare—to find out. Kit dared. "Maybe he's my last and only." On a potty break, she detoured past the machine, which was still in place but shrouded. She used her key-ring laser light, crawled up under the canvas, found the number, and wrote it down on her wrist with a fabric marker. Irene had almost remembered it correctly: 3248 not 3428. Kit was on fire to try it. Why had no one thought of this before? Why had no one tried? "That's the trouble with being married," she told them. "Y'all just give up."

Kit was never going to give up, couldn't wait until the end of the shift. They formed a circle around her on the lawn under the pecan tree as she keyed the area codes 706, 770, 404, 678 before the numbers. She'd disconnect with a scowl or a shiver or a gagging gesture at her mouth, something wrong or "off" with each one—nope, nope, nope, and nope. She took it hard. She was impulsive about random acts, had seen this as a beacon sign of kindness from God, and yet nobody worth falling for. Skunked. Every time it was a home number, not some panting billionaire who answered his own phone. "Maybe it's his limo line," she said. The last one left her furious. "I woke that one up! Who else but losers are home in bed this time of day?" She scrubbed her wrist with hand sanitizer.

"Wait, wait! What about South Carolina? What about South Georgia?" Betty just egged her right on. "How about China? How about Mexico?" No one took it seriously but Kit.

"Hell, Miss Betty, I have to be back on Monday!" Most of the time she was.

Currently they could see Kit pacing back and forth, now in the sun, now in the dapples under the executive dogwoods, making a lazy spiral; she spoke to somebody smoking, looked back at him, waved, laughed, walked on, still talking, walking all the way out to the road. FedEx and a sedan drove in and FedEx drove out, but nobody offered rides. At the table they kept checking the lunchroom clock, anxious, looking sharp to let her back in; everybody had to clock in after lunch. It wasn't forbidden to exit to the front lot, but their cards worked only one way on that door: out. Kit hadn't asked them to. She just assumed someone would let her back in—whatever, whoever. Things usually worked out. Kit generally landed on her feet, and until she did, she was flying.

Jacky was still standing there at the end of the table. They'd forgotten about him.

"Yuh can tease me," he said. But nobody did.

He was loved. He was a fixture. He was somehow grandfathered in. He was a sight. He was forgotten. He surprised them; he was keeping an eye out too. He was the one who jogged over to let Kit back in.

When Jacky finally sprang his Fourth of July surprise, it was a doozy. This was his finest year so far. In giant semipro house-painted letters his truck-bed billboard announced:

MOST FAVORED NATION

NAFTA & TALIBAN

CANT BEAT US

He had stapled up flags all around the sign and screwed flags to his side-view mirror brackets.

Since July Fourth fell on a Saturday, there was no official responder at the plant, but word got around, and one of the news vans drove over from Camden. Small-town story with local interest, but others picked it up. Then some CNN copyreader with an eye for punctuation jumped on it, did some research, and tied the typo to the history of the town, which had started out as Pines's Creek, because the creek rose and ran through Caleb Pines's back pasture. Early maps had it right. Later maps called it Pine's Creek. When the roads got paved and plank-bridged and Pines's Ferry closed and side-road signs went up, it was Pines Creek, because the times and the signs had changed, had caught up with the 1891 geographical protocols: no more apostrophes. The village itself had been known as Pines's—just Pines's—or sometimes in court records Pines's Post Office, which was a pigeon-holed rough-sawn pine cabinet in Pines's general store. When the railroad came in 1892 and the government named the mail drop Pine Creek, Old Caleb Pines took his name back. This wasn't about Georgia pines. This was a family name. This was family pride. He rode to Atlanta and back on the train, gone over a week trying to get it right. He was gone politicking again during the legislative session, and while he was away, folks voted to rename the mail drop. They were sick of the whole controversy and were ready, willing, and able to move on. They did. Mr. Pines didn't think they were able, and kept rounding up signatures and X's of those who owed him money or favors and swore they weren't willing, but the ones who were ready never backed down. They petitioned the secretary of state, and the election records and ballots were sorted through and certified; they won. Maybe they weren't all willing and maybe they weren't ever all going to be able, but by God, they were good and ready. That's what they named the town: Ready.

Cute little story, pure Americana. And then Jacky's truck with the billboard, taken as it was intended. Not an apostrophe issue at all. CNN aired it every hour. Jacky's truck was beamed down from the satellites, and sweet little Ready, Georgia—which hadn't been as ready in the twentieth century for the interstate as it had been in the nineteenth for the train and had gotten passed by: the interstate highway roared on by nine miles away without an exit—ready or not, on July 4, 2009, went international. The twenty-first century finally arrived, not by road at all but from a satellite. There it was. Jacky's surprise! His fresh-scrubbed '69 pickup truck, parked right there in front of the plant, beside the Georgia granite flame-carved monolith reading

FRAZIER FABRICS
Quality Product
Innovative Method
American Pride
S.E.A.M.S. since 1987

Jacky's MOST FAVORED NATION sign in the back of the truck provided angle-parked counterpoint. It was readable from both sides of Main and the railroad line as well.

On Sunday morning, it finally hit Mr. Frazier's fan. He saw it on CNN as he waited in Reagan Airport—he and his family had been to Arlington for a ceremony and the concert on the Mall. The decree went out, and Jacky's truck was towed.

Monday morning could not come soon enough. No one in Mr. Scott Frazier's boardroom—or Gibbs' drugstore or Blaine's barbershop or Jenny and Tom Croft's Hole in One (or Two) Donut Shop, or Mimi's beauty parlor, all with their signs and possessive apostrophes in place—believed Jacky had thought it up completely on his own or, as they put it, "executed" it himself. Jacky admitted that was so, admitted he had help, but his help had made him swear secrecy. Jacky was good at secrets. He knew he was in trouble, but he did not know why. This was a room he had never been in; he was abashed by its sprays of orchids, its fern-filled fireplace with a mantel clock under a glass dome, its rolling ladder along its wall of leather-backed ledgers from almost a century of incorporation, its massed and traditional splendor including a silver coffee service in use right then. Rather than stare rudely, he examined his feet and the carpet beneath them. It surprised him by looking a bit old, a bit faded. Maybe somebody had given it to them, someone they did not want to disappoint. Jacky pulled his mind back to his own troubles. He listened and listened. When he answered, he was brief and—what else?—himself. If he could do better, he would. He did not understand what they meant by "contractions," which he knew only as a birthing term, and he did not comprehend "too political" and just listened, waiting, planning to ask for and hoping to get "another chance."

He was sent back through an adjoining and less intimately grand boardroom and past the assistant's desk, to wait out in the hall. While he was waiting there, Police Chief Lazarus, "strictly as a friend," as he told Jacky, sat beside him on the bench and praised the lettering on the sign and asked him who had given him such good help, but Jacky would not divulge. He himself had done the painting; that was all he would say to the policeman. He had done most of the stencil-cutting also with his neon green utility knife his sweetheart SarahAnn Hurd, Pastor Ben Hurd's daughter, had given him for Christmas.

SarahAnn had palsy but got around great on a pair of canes. And she could swim like a seal. Jacky loved to swim, but he was a kicker and a splasher. SarahAnn was sleek and splashless. The water on her eyelashes, when she blinked open at him after diving in, tore him out of his frame. She had no idea. That was the best of all, after some of the bold women he had dated. Most of them didn't like wearing a bathing suit, or at least didn't like getting it wet. And they never did more than walk around up to their chins; they cared too much for their hair. Jacky and SarahAnn were making slow plans. Their hearts might both be heading for a wreck they couldn't walk away from, but what lovers don't risk that? Pastor Hurd, who had begun to think there might not be any grandchildren in his future, had given his consent for courtship at least and at last to begin. There was an age difference, but not much of one. SarahAnn, who was Pastor Hurd's only arrow in his quiver, had a biological clock ticking loud. But at least it was ticking. Hurd had brought Jacky along through several studies, gathered him into the flock at revival, and baptized him a year ago; Pastor Hurd had himself brought "the new man" up out of the water, well pleased. He had no pastoral or paternal doubts. SarahAnn was no spring chicken, but she was unseasoned, and Jacky was—his pastor knew from frank discussions—well-seasoned, a little salty. "Nuh mo," Jacky swore. SarahAnn was the only one he wanted, now, no matter what the Ready women tried on him.

"Fine," Pastor Hurd said. Only one warning, "Ask," he told him. "If you're sure—"

"I sure," Jacky stated.

"Well, man, when you think you're both ready and before she's an old woman, ask." They shook on it. "Ask," he said again, because he had already talked to his daughter and knew her heart, and because of the way Jacky overlooked the obvious and tended to pass the exits because he missed the signs. Pastor Hurd thought he had handled things well, until he realized he too had overlooked the obvious, when Jacky, at the end of his and SarahAnn's fifth date, stopped at the payphone at BP and called to ask Pastor Hurd if he could kiss her. "I askin'," Jacky said.

The police chief tried several approaches in Frazier's main hall, but Jacky always saw him coming. Chief Lazarus went on in to speak with the others. He told them what he thought. Jacky could not lie and was capable of only literal truth, not half-truths. He told them what he suspected. He told them what they already knew: Jacky didn't even have a clue what NAFTA was. And he sure didn't know a damn thing about apostrophes; the one missing from *cant* was missing in action, not an intentional act. This was Mr. Frazier's opinion also. "He's an idiot, not an idiot savant." Jacky wasn't an idiot, though. Mrs. Champion risked saying so. No matter; that did not rule out sabotage by someone using Jacky as a blunt instrument. That notion caused deep sighs and soul-searching bewilderment. Jacky had kept asking if the sign was spelled wrong or just not true. How could Jacky get a thing from "Not exactly"? He didn't know where to start working on fixing it, which end of the snake to pick up. He had gotten agitated, and that's when they had sent him out in the hall to chill. By the time Lazarus had gotten there, he was calm again.

"We have Department of Defense contracts," they had explained when they called him back in. Which meant what it said, to Jacky, who did not have subtextual skills. He heard it with pride. American pride. They kept saying the sign was embarrassing, and too political, and without that apostrophe almost seditious, none of which concepts Jacky could get a handle on. When Mrs. Champion explained that sedition meant treason, Jacky staggered back, almost knocking over the little table with the ginger jar lamp on it. He landed on his butt, pulled his legs under him, spring-flexed up from the floor as if he had been flung, and resumed his spot on the old rug. He wouldn't look up, just muttered, horrified, seeing all of his dreams going down the drain, "Nuh, nuh." He couldn't think of anything else to say. Exasperated, Mr. Frazier offered to fire him, but Jacky did not know it was a kind of barter. When Jacky heard, "That's all then," he just began packing up his heart and thoughts to go.

"I unna arre't?"

Chief Lazarus looked at Mr. Frazier. Both shrugged. "No," Mr. Frazier answered. "You're not under arrest."

"I fee to go?"

"Just go." Mr. Frazier had swiveled to look out the window until Jacky was out of there. No one else looked at him either. He was cut. Cut to the quick. Only four others were in the room, but they felt like a complete jury.

Convicted, Jacky put his hat back on, the one with the American flags, and walked to the door. Then he turned back and took it off again, and there where he was standing with his hand on the doorknob, in a manly and courteous way—he did not beg—Jacky asked for another chance. Mr. Frazier thought he meant as a materials pusher and said, in his own good time, without looking around, "Dammit, yes!" But that was not what Jacky meant.

He took three tries—he was monitored on security screens—to hang his ID and key card on the coatrack in the lobby and leave. It took him three tries to solve it because he had to figure out how to swipe himself out, turn, dash for the bentwood hook, hang the lanyard, and run out the door before it could click locked again. He finally took off a shoe, blocked the door open, hung the key card, shoved out, grabbed the shoe, and then put it back on once he was on the steps. Mrs. Champion ran after him. He was busy tying laces. He had to retie the other shoe because it felt loose now. Then he had to retie the first one because it was too tight. Jacky liked things forgettably even.

"Where will you go?"

"Use yuh name?" She thought he meant as a reference, and she thought he meant *her* name, and agreed. Who would hire him?

She prayed, "Thy will be done." She meant Father God, not Scott Frazier, not Jacky Lamar Jones. She cried for a little, shook the tears off her hands, then went back inside. "Jacky has left the building," she announced. The keycard and ID wouldn't be noticed for a couple of days; on Wednesday Birdie from Cora's night cleaning crew would turn them in to lost and found.

The meeting had adjourned, and life at Frazier went on without him.

As soon as Jacky got his truck back from impound in the open lot behind the firehouse, he spray-painted the offending sign blank with primer, feeling nauseated with shame and fumes. His friend who had been helping with the signs—it was Vicki Malachy, who could not be said to be impartial—wanted to put something different on Jacky's second-chance billboard: she suggested a double row of stitches all around the sign and something special in the upper corners instead of flags, since the Fourth of July was over. She suggested—in fact sketched on—little footed crosses, painted in tight zigzags so they too looked stitched, sort of buttonhole stitched. Jacky couldn't see it. "Look," Vicki said, "do 'em in black. Bold. Maybe inside a red circle." She looked around for a plate to trace and picked up the lid for the paint. Too large, but she could always redraw them. "Make an impact," she had urged him. "They're bitchin'." But Jacky was in conflict; he didn't want to say so—so he didn't say so—but he thought they looked like swastikas. In fact, they were. Nobody liked swastikas; why would you put anything on the sign that you already knew nobody liked? Golly dog! He didn't want to go through that again. Ever. He held his ground. It might have come to ugly words, though not from his mouth, but Vicki got a phone call. She took a hike way out in the yard to answer it; reception was better near the streetlight. It was Juki, Vicki's mom. The streetlight was buzzing and there were bugs. She kept slapping them away.

"Girl," Juki told her, "Where are you?" Juki was babysitting Vicki's colicky baby, Randal. Not for the first time but maybe for the last. Three hours ago Vicki had dropped him off and supposedly gone to get diapers and some Gatorade.

"My car was making that sound," she said. She made the sound. "I ran by Jacky's to see if he could—"

"Vicki Marie Westmore Malachy," Juki said. "You lyin' layabout Jezebel from Hell, if you ain't back here in fifteen minutes God bless America if I'm not—and I am!—calling Lazarus *at home* and reporting an abandoned child, plus I am telling him I think you're not just a petty criminal, you're uh- uh- a meth whore and dealin' dope and nookie on the side!"

The baby wasn't Jacky's son, but he could have been. And she'd have claimed he was if Malachy hadn't married her. They hadn't lasted six months. He was clean gone, good and gone. Somebody said the Philippines. Somebody else said Alaska. Vicki might be pregnant again, but nobody knew that, not even Vicki; she had gone to get diapers and a pregnancy test, no Gatorade. She was sick to death of diapers. They didn't grow on trees. Life was so not fair. Vicki hadn't even bought the test; she had boosted it. Seemed to be reading the label, then picked up another box to read and seemed to be deciding something, then set the one back on the shelf and the other one dropped right into her big old gold lamé purse. It was beginning to show signs of wear, little bald spots in its glory.

"By the time they get all my lies sorted from yours," Juki was raving over the baby's wailing and writhing in her arms, "and test the Tic Tacs spilled on the floorboard—they're bound to find somethin' to keep ya for if it's only expired car insurance—you'll be in jail long enough they'll jerk you back to Jesus, if anybody can. I know this—I am done trying." She began to sob.

"Doesn't sound like it," Vicki said coolly. But she lost steam after that, finished her cigarette, threw the lipsticked filter out onto the dark pavement beyond the streetlight. It bounced three times, chipping little final sparks off, then went spent. She had come by hoping to borrow money from Jacky. And get him into bed so she could blame him, if the test turned out positive. He just wasn't listening to her very well. She gave him a hard look, but he was working on his project, didn't even notice. Vicki got in her car, tore off, didn't wave good-bye. Typical. Jacky was glad she was gone. She made him nervous. He could not trust her, because she had said—last time—she wasn't coming back. She wanted something that time too, and he had promised God and Pastor Hurd he wasn't giving her any. Now she had left, driven off mean-like, without saying a thing, so maybe she meant it.

Jacky steamed on with his sign. The Fourth of July was over, but he—and Frazier—had American pride every day of the year, and it was his project; he got to say and this time he would. He said it with gold stars. He even stenciled some on the truck's doors and tailgate. The flags on the mirrors waved on. They were nylon. Rain didn't hurt them. He worked on the new sign the whole week after July Fourth. He decided it looked fairly clear, no major wobbles or drips. He rolled it out into daylight from under the tarp-covered shed on Friday and made his round-trip run along Main before parking it at the street curb at Hardee's. There was one traffic light in Ready, and that was the strategic spot. Jacky then walked home sipping on a peach shake.

Frazier Fabrics got a few local calls almost at once. Mr. Frazier took a break and drove by the sign. This time he took it well. Dan Archer from the *Messenger* was already there taking photos. Archer got in the car with Scott Frazier and suggested they use the drive-thru for coffee. They then parked in the lot and sat talking while sipping. Archer finally asked, and not unreasonably, "Scotty, is this the hill you want to die on?" For the mile back to the mill, Mr. Frazier gave that some thought. After he walked back into the plant, he asked Mrs. Deems from HR to gather his captains. They took the sign the way he did and adopted Jacky's sentiments as the motto for their newsletter masthead, ending early a competition among employees for a prize for best company slogan. Since the story on the first billboard had aired, Frazier had been getting a lot of calls; it seemed that the publicity had not damaged the company's corporate image. Nor had Frazier's government contracts been damaged or rescinded.

Jacky didn't know anything about any furor, any calls, or what the captains were thinking now. He didn't have a phone or a TV. He was a radio man, AM not FM. He was hiding out, ashamed. Pastor Hurd had phoned Mrs. Champion to inform her that Jacky hadn't been at church and to ask if he'd been at work. So Mrs. Champion drove out to Pines Creek Park to his little aqua and silver trailer with the used tires on its metal roof to prevent rumble. The steps looked dry-rotted and iffy; one was missing. The railings looked—she could think of no other explanation—wolf-chewed. She glanced around. No chains or pen. Even so, she stood warily in a patch of clover and leaned even more warily, finally ducking her head and shoulders under the rail on his mossy porch and knocking on the bottom of his door, all she could reach. She talked up to him through a crack in the jalousies and then finally talked him out onto the porch. "Oh, Jacky," she kept saying. She had his lost-and-found keycard and ID, which she handed up to him. "People oughta talk to one another. People ought to stay in touch."

Jacky just listened. He heard amazing things. He had his job, they liked his truck, they missed him, all was good again. He knelt on one knee, meeting her at eye level. "Fuh real?" he kept asking. He had always been clean-shaved, something eternally boyish about him. Now he looked clean but grizzled, attenuated, wintry. "Poorly," as her home folks would've put it. When she explained that the others were expecting him back at Frazier, she suggested he might need to go in and get himself together. He didn't. He came right on out.

"Ready." Beaming. She walked to her car, to move things from the front seat for him, but he wanted to follow her back on his bicycle. "Lady furt," he insisted, and gestured toward the road. She drove on. He got to feeling better and better along the way. In fact, he passed her, the flags on his hat fluttering full flat open just before they turned in through the Frazier gate.

That afternoon Jacky was awarded the twenty-five-dollar WalMart gift card that had been offered as the slogan prize for the newsletter, *Focus on Frazier*. The contest had been running for three weeks, and there had been no suggestions except "Sew straight or sew long," offered anonymously. There might have been more, but the suggestion basket was supervised by a spy cam, and since the Vicki incident, those cameras were keeping it real. Jacky's winning motto was

FRAZIER FABRICS
"Seams like old times."

When Mrs. Champion had come to see him the Monday after he left his truck at Hardee's, her visit had landed on him like a rainbow, along with the pot o' gold. He thought he had been rehired until he got the next paycheck, which had credited him vacation pay for the days he had been absent. He went down to payroll and inquired. He didn't want something that wasn't his. He was bringing it back. The clerk made some calls. "You earned it," she told him. "It's paid. Vacation. It's all yours." She explained, tapping on the computer screen. She placed the pay envelope against it, to help him follow the line all the way across. She printed it out and showed him, "Paid vacation."

"They did that fuh me? Fuh me?" he kept asking. Jacky went out to the hall. He squatted, resting his hand over his eyes, his back against the wall. Donny Kilgore came along on afternoon circuit and dust-mopped around him and went on. Someone walking to and then back from the ladies' room to her desk in payroll eyed him, then described him to the clerk as "visibly asleep or sick or praying," all of which were strongly advised against in the employee public conduct protocols, especially when visible from the main doors in what was called "the executive wing" but was really the central tower. The clerk came out, phone in hand, poised for 911.

"You OK?" She shook his shoulder when he didn't respond.

"Juh thinkin'," he told her, rousing after a moment.

"No law against that," she told him.

He looked up but didn't see her walk away. He was more and more aware, though, of everything else around him, behind him, beyond him down the dim hall leading toward the modern lobby under the old iron bell high on its yoke under the peeled cedar loft: the buff-waxed terrazzo with its squeaky sheen; the green sofas and chairs gathered on the edges of the green rug with all the black and white and tan circles; the huge low silver and glass table with its industry publications and its driftwood decoration; the familiar whitewashed brick walls of the old tower; the dainty ficus and the thick bold rubber trees and palms in the brilliant afternoon light; the staghorn ferns on their bark shields; the zebra finches branch-hopping and buzzing in their huge glass cage; the sound of the wall fountain of slate and copper with its shawl of creeping fig; the languorous turn of the three-blade fan like an airplane prop; the fly settling onto one of the slats in the blinds on the middle window; the directory on its stand casting shadows across the lobby floor; the soft and hard of things and the high and low; yellow butterflies in the mounded "Miss Huff" lantana beyond the window; the breakable things and the things that would never break; the shelter of the whole Frazier plant around and over him. He felt himself in the very heart of it. It was so large and strong and real and fine, he would never sufficiently fathom or deserve or honor it. This was America to him. He had never been on vacation before. He was glad to be back. Wait until he told SarahAnn! He got up and went along to work. He wouldn't replace the flags until football season, on his cap or on his truck. And he was already beginning to plan for next year. He could feel the stir, the slow turn, of deep thoughts.

5

Irene's day ninety fell on a payday. JaNice brought the checks around. She dealt Irene's toward her, and for an instant the paper in the envelope was a bridge connecting them, one moment of startling, serious linking. Their eyes met. "Congratulations, Irene." JaNice handed her a little plastic bag with a Frazier pin in it. "You've earned it." She lingered, as though she was listening to something far off. Irene wanted to take the pin home and show Deke; she didn't want to put it on right then, but when JaNice stayed, she wondered if that was what she should do.

JaNice cleared her throat. "You left in—" she began to say. The phone rang, and JaNice answered it. She turned her back, spoke fast, listened fast, then said, "No way. There were twenty-seven this morning, I counted. How many are back there now?" She paused. "Tell King. No, just tell King." Disconnected, JaNice turned back.

Meanwhile, Irene had felt herself tumbling through space. *What* had she left? What had she left *in?* She was not a rebellious breaker or bender of rules. All her infractions, and there had not been many, and none lately, were accidental or ignorant, not defiant, not willfully negligent. She didn't think she had made mistakes sewing. She was upset enough to crumple her paycheck and put it in her apron and then not be able to remember what she had done with it, then find it, keeping it gripped in her pocketed fist. Fear rose up like flame around her. The fear was not lack of courage; it was dread of courage, dread of what it could cost her, that one of these days she would decide none of this stress was worth it and all of it was optional, what Deke kept telling her, and she'd "lose her grip" and lose everything. It wasn't fear of letting go of something bad; it was fear of losing something good she somehow "needed" the bad to get. Not get. Earn.

Irene came from long lines of "earners." Foothills and easier plowing had brought her people down from the mountains. The rich bottomlands had been claimed long before. What was left—thin soil on foothills smallholdings—had kept everyone digging for their lives, cropping corn and beans, garden truck and cut flowers, especially lilies, earning their daily bread. Sometimes that soil washed away, into the creeks and rivers and to the sea. That same erosion washed some of her family downstream into the mills at the shoals. She came from the ones who didn't wash away easily, no matter what. She came from people who in varying degrees believed and practiced how love suffers long and is kind. All her life, from baby bunting on, she had heard blood kin singing like they believed it, believed in the daily setbacks of time on earth as merciful lessons and blessings to understand later. She believed what her grandma had said, pointing to the admonition on the wall at the little cold-water Blue Ridge church—a church that believed in signs—where great-uncle Seaborn, one of the lily farmers, was being buried from, a church they had traveled back in time to find on its ungraded two-track lane, a church with a door for men and a door for women, with spittoons and a hand-scrawled warning: DO NOT SPIT ON THE FLOOR. The sentence PRAYER CHANGES THINGS was what had caught her great-grandmother's eye. Her granny—who ought to know—had pinched, hard, and hissed from behind her paper fan on its stick, "No it don't, Irene. God changes thangs; prayer changes we uns."

Irene came from folks who kept their spoons clean and took what was dished, the sort who tied knots in the ends of their ropes and hung on. Irene pulled herself up, squared up her shoulders. Ready. She was the sort who held out.

"You left in 1990," JaNice said. Not an accusation but a question, or a statement she could refute, if need be.

"Yes," Irene said. "Summer."

"I know exactly when," JaNice told her, with a flash of her eyes. "I got your chair." She inspected the left front side of the plate carrier Irene had just sewed. She was studying perfect seams. JaNice wasn't calibrated for finding "perfect"; she was company-trained for what was wrong. JaNice clipped a thread for Irene and laid it back down.

"Things got better right about then," Irene said, smiling. Relieved. That was blessing enough.

"If you'd just held out," JaNice replied.

Irene groped for something else to say. Her fingertips touched the envelope her check was in. What did JaNice know? What did she need to hear? Irene searched her heart. If there wasn't anything JaNice needed to hear, Irene wasn't obliged, by God, to say word one. Best not.

JaNice lingered. Irene thought of how what seemed to her to be most of her life had happened when she left that chair, and what JaNice thought *her* life was had happened after Irene left and JaNice sat down in it. As though it was the chair that made life happen! There was always going to be another chair. It's not the chair you need to hold on to. But then she thought about how she had had to get down on her hands and knees at Rock City to cross over the little swinging bridge. It was no holiday. How hard it was to let go, one hand at a time, and the other one holding on for all she was able, just to make herself crawl forward, to hold her mind to what was ahead and not look down. Just wanting it to hold still but the others walking along so easily, just laughing and talking to beat the band, making the whole span of rope and planks sway and rock.

Irene was about to say, "Funny how different it can look depending," but before she could, their little moment was over. All she got to say was, "Funny—" The phone was ringing, the Klaxon was sounding downstairs in receiving, JaNice was muttering "No way," and then she was gone.

6

Six pounds of plums or figs will make four or five pints of jelly or jam. That amount was about all Irene cared to fool with at a time, but for a few August weeks she was busy, nightly, measuring sugar, cooking up plums, and dealing with the figs Deke had gathered that day. She'd work after supper right up to bedtime, and sometimes they'd hear the lids popping as they cooled and sealed on the kitchen table after she and Deke were in bed. First thing in the morning, while the coffee dripped, she'd set the little jars away in the cupboard. Sometimes she took the time to make biscuits, and they sat breakfasting together on the porch in their twin rockers, before Deke headed one way and Irene another. Deke would even do tricks, he said, for her fig preserves. "Keep 'em coming." She was gratefully proud of the jam, but especially the batch made from this year's late plums, which glowed in the jars like she'd caught the sunlight with the flavor. She knew the jam tasted good, but she also believed it was good for them. She made sure there were jars for all their children. She was already beginning to gather ideas and items for Davy's Christmas box. She wished she could mail him jam—or sunshine—in a jar, overseas, but she never did. Besides, he had plenty of sun. She'd already sent Sherry, Davy's wife, some of this year's jam, as well as—she couldn't help it, they were so beautiful—fresh plums, a perfect boxful, by overnight. Maybe it was true, like Deke said, that there were actually stores at Fort Campbell and maybe plums in Kentucky too.

"There are now," Irene said.

All winter, on dark mornings, they could spoon that sunlight out. She knew what it was like to be a soldier's wife. Irene's folks had died young. Deke's parents had stood in the gap for her, and sometimes it was their care packages—each with a magazine or three yards of fabric or a pretty kitchen towel or a bag of candy or a packet of seeds or a card with a few perfect crisp bills in it—that got her through more than the winter's dark.

She had put up some of the plum jelly in embossed half-pints with fancy floral seals and white rings. Pocket-size jewels. She liked to take them to work and leave them on the sewing tables of the women who'd stepped away for a moment. She never could catch Sua Nag away. Finally one day she pocketed a jar and headed downstairs to lunch.

Sua Nag Vang did not sit with a group. She usually ate alone, her back to the TV, spooning up lean soup with bits of interesting-looking vegetables. She ate from a plastic bowl with a seal-tight lid, and she brought her own spoon. Her refilled water bottle, its label peeled off, stood by her right hand. Between sips, she screwed the lid back on. When she finished, she placed her spoon and the bowl and bottle in her lunch bag and left them for a minute, went to the ladies' room, then came back, gathered her things, and headed upstairs to sew again, usually the first one at the clock. She was always trying to find more minutes to work, not to rest. She always had a little smile, and her eyes, very bright, were focused on something only she could see. Irene had noticed how she didn't yack at lunch, how she seemed to be listening to something far off. How she never seemed to look at anyone. How she seemed to move in a bubble, silent, through all the racket and chaos—not lost or adrift or isolated, but peaceful.

Irene thought Sua Nag was maybe Thai. She couldn't tell how old she was. Maybe in her forties, about the same as Irene, or maybe in her fifties, maybe even nineties. She was timeless, if not ageless. Irene had seen a cooking program on Thai spices, knew that red pepper was one of the main condiments, and lemon grass. Irene did not know what lemon grass was, but the idea of it pleased her, that somewhere in this world grass that tasted like lemon grew. What would that do to the cows and their milk? She wanted to ask Sua Nag about it. Maybe she had some, grew it in her own garden and could give Irene a "start."

Irene had a gnarled old lemon verbena that had been her great-grandmother's. It had summered on the porch in a lard bucket, then been hauled back down the steps into the root cellar, where it wintered, slowly losing leaf on fragrant leaf, a few holding on until spring's last frost. Her granny used to put a crushed leaf in a glass before she poured in iced tea. But she had also made an herb tea from the green leaves, then poured it cool into a Coke bottle. She had a dime-store cork-bottom sprinkler top for it—didn't everybody?—and that's what she used to plug up the Coke bottle before shaking lemony scent onto clothes on the ironing board, dampening the cotton to relax it so she could iron it flat and smooth. All this was before permanent press and steam irons. Irene had used lemon verbena in pound cakes, lining the pan bottom with leaves. Not too many people got it to last through the winter, though. They'd plant it outside and forget to dig it up. Irene was always rooting cuttings and passing them along. She wondered if Sua Nag had any lemon grass uses like that, or if no grass, maybe she could use some verbena?

It was really hard to find words to talk to Sua Nag, but there had to be some way to communicate without them. She kept trying. She had such respect for the woman. Irene believed herself to be possibly the second-best sewing hand on the mezzanine; she believed the best was Sua Nag. Neither one of them was going to get a prize for it, and something usually got in the way of incentive, but it was how Sua Nag worked with honor. It was her integrity that impressed Irene, not just her "numbers." The way Sua Nag sewed, and did not waste time, it was as though she too, like Irene, was thinking of the men and women who would wear or bear this camo. She sewed as though she worked for the ones in the field as well as for those at home. Sua Nag sewed with passion, and Irene believed she sewed with love. It wasn't easy to care; it was easier to be good at something than glad at it. It was possible to earn incentive and not care at all. Irene had—like Sua Nag Vang—been observing without watching, and she did not judge her coworkers, but she measured them, because she was measuring herself as well. When you try to live up to a mark, one question to ask yourself might be, "how high?" but the other question is, "who drew it?"

Early in what Irene thought of as "the lemon squeeze" initiative, she had decided to sit near Sua Nag at lunch and just sort of mention gardening, grannies, or whatever. Apparently the end seat at the table, to Sua Nag's left two seats away, was way too close for Sua Nag, as she immediately moved down a chair and set up again. Irene asked her, "Does anyone ever call you Sunny?" There was a pause while Sua Nag looked at the far wall.

"No," she answered. They ate the rest of lunch without passing another word.

Somehow it seemed impossible to imagine how to bring up anything about lemon grass or verbena cuttings. "How 'bout that lemon grass!" Irene imagined saying. Nothing in life in general, in Sunday school, or at Happy Time had prepared her for this. She sat there feeling very much in the wrong place. There'd have to be another way to learn about lemon grass.

She waited while the tiny woman tidied up her things and left them on the table for her trip to the washroom. Irene, on a seemingly casual walk by, set a little jar of plum jelly with its label, "for Sua Nag," beside the lunch bag and kept on moving. She hadn't signed her name. Irene didn't stick around; she scooted through the double doors, turned right, and went down the whole length of the cutting floor, where she crossed to the outside wall and stairs, clocked in there, and went up to sew. Her heart raced as if she had committed a crime. It felt good.

A week later when she got back from lunch, right in the middle of her sewing chair was a perfect and anonymous cantaloupe in a grocery bag. She settled it in her tote bag, but she could smell it all afternoon. When she took it home, she told Deke about Sua Nag. "Somebody said she's Hmong," she told him. He knew all about them.

"They're heroes," he said quietly. "All of 'em."

After supper they went to the den and Deke checked e-mail, and then they each sent a message to Davy and also to Sherry and the kids. Deke Googled "Hmong," and they sat together reading. Deke was studying war. What Irene got out of it was about the culture, the embroidery, and about the custom of not looking directly at another person. Also she saw that they preferred things fresh and were not great consumers of processed food or sugar. Now the plum jelly seemed like a terrible idea. Before she went to bed, she checked the calendar—waning moon, just what she needed—and stepped out onto the porch to clip some tender sprigs of new growth from the verbena. She put them in a pint jelly jar of water on the kitchen windowsill to root—this time maybe something the woman could actually use.

During the night Deke had bad dreams. He didn't do that much anymore. Researching what he called the Montagnards had upset him, stirred him up. The Hmong had been heroes. Every last one of them had death sentences on their heads from the Communists. They never fell, unless dead. Being that sort of hero is not something genetic; it is something they choose, something they do, a way of belonging to each other that makes the whole people "one body." Deke couldn't—or wouldn't—tell Irene what that body had done and what had been done to it, but he knew. Those thoughts kept him groaning all night in his sleep, like broken bones.

7

Over Labor Day weekend the newlyweds Link Purdy and his wife K'shaundra moved into the tenant house. They weren't going to work on shares. They were paying rent—had paid a month ahead and signed a contract Deke had printed off the Internet. Link was going to work for wages in town. He already had a job changing oil in trucks. K'shaundra was looking for work. Irene gave her a ride to Frazier on Tuesday. She'd had to wait, wait, wait in the yard, engine running, while K'shaundra got ready. They were almost late. Irene had told her she wouldn't have an interview today, just a chance to fill out the forms and turn them in. K'shaundra was ready for business. She was fully rigged out, looking her best. On the way Irene told her how to find the lobby, how to fill out the forms, and where to turn them in. "But the lobby won't open until 9:00 A.M.," Irene told her, "unless you have an appointment. Which you don't. And you can't come in with me." Since she'd have a couple of hours to kill, K'shaundra had wanted to drive on down to Hardee's and get a sausage biscuit. She surely did think that was a grand solution, but Irene had told her, no, there wasn't time.

K'shaundra decided to wait in the car, maybe sleep a little longer. She needed it. Moving day had just worn her down, she claimed. "Will you call me at fifteen minutes till nine?" she asked. She yawned. Irene had her cell number.

"I can't call. No cell phones in the building, I can't leave the building, and we don't have a phone on the floor."

K'shaundra looked around. She pointed. "Just stand in the door and holler. Just holler my name. I'll get up. I'm used to it," she said.

"I'll have Mr. Grayson call you, if I can get in to see him."

"Who?"

"My boss," Irene told her, "and maybe yours. What if they put you up on the mezzanine where I am, and he's your boss and knows you sleep in the parking lot and need a wake-up call?"

"Don't tell him I'm asleep in the car," she said, laughing. "Maybe he's calling me at work. Maybe this is my workplace. I'll be professional," she said. "I can do professional."

She asked Irene to leave the keys. "So I can work the windows." K'shaundra looked away. She looked sly, like she thought Irene was a fool. Maybe Irene was. Irene needed to think.

"Are you too hot or too cold?" Irene asked.

K'shaundra shrugged. "I just never know."

"It's not too cold now, and it won't be too hot before nine," Irene decided. She had to run to make it to the clock. K'shaundra said good-bye and thanks; she'd find her own way home if she wasn't right here at the car when Irene got off her shift. She had plans to meet a friend for lunch and was going to walk on the sidewalk to town. That's what she said, and it began to seem more real to her as she thought it through. "Don't you worry," she told Irene. Her friends—some friend—would drive her home to the farm "before Link even knows I'm missing." Irene set the electric windows, leaving them halfway. She didn't leave the keys.

In the days to come the Purdys just couldn't get settled in and down at the farm. Their honeymoon was about over. Something was always wrong. Once Link needed Deke to drive over and jump his dead battery. Another time they ran out of dog chow; when Deke ran by in his truck on the way back from the feed store and shoveled a bucket of Purina out to help them with the dog, three pit bull puppies tumbled out of the front door when Link answered Deke's knock. They had signed a "no indoor pet" clause in the renter's contract. "This is not good," Deke said. "You tellin' me," Link said. "They all bitches." That's when Deke noticed that Link had installed a satellite dish on the roof on the far side, just on the roof itself, no tar, no caulk, no flashing—had drilled it in, screwed it on, and there it was. By then it was payday, and their rent was two weeks late; Deke mentioned it. "Gotta get to the bank and get this thing cashed," Link explained. A week later K'shaundra knocked at the kitchen door, shy little taps. Irene was finishing up the supper dishes. Irene could smell beer. K'shaundra didn't step in. "I need to borrow some tampons," she said.

"I hoped you'd come to pay the rent," Irene told her. She invited the woman in, but K'shaundra waited on the porch. Irene pushed the door shut and went to speak to Deke. He was asleep in his chair. She went on down the hall for a moment and then returned and opened the door. K'shaundra was still there. She handed her the supplies. Irene had put a five-dollar bill in with them.

K'shaundra looked at Irene and flashed her wonderful eyes high beam. "Make that twenty and you'll never see me again," she promised. She lurched off the porch and went back across the grove to their house. Irene could hear her desolate laughter as she went.

Link was gone already, but Deke and Irene didn't know. K'shaundra moved out before Halloween, with not a word of notice or a cent of rent. They never saw the dogs again. There were some scuff marks from moving things out, and only one lightbulb was left; even the one in the refrigerator was gone. But the house wasn't trashed.

Irene rented a steamer at the market and cleaned the carpet in the front rooms. She always made things nice for whoever came next. While the carpet dried, she planted spring bulbs along the walk in front and around the cherry tree outside the kitchen window, so there would be daffodils to look at, for the one washing dishes. The autumn leaves were done, and she had raked them away, bagged them for compost. Deke was coming to pick her up in the truck. After she swept the front porch, she unfurled the runner she had brought to keep the carpet fresh. She had bought new mats at the dollar store, and she laid down a bright Welcome on each of the porches, front and back. Energy-saving fluorescent curly lightbulbs had been placed in the sockets and a regular one in the fridge. She had put a roll of paper towels on the holder in the kitchen and placed another on the sink in the bath, and there were new bars of hand soap in the lavatory and by the kitchen sink. She had hung a new plastic liner for the shower curtain. She had bought a wastebasket for the bathroom and a garbage can for the kitchen, with a liner in it and more liners in the kitchen drawer. There were some paper plates, cups, and picnic ware in the cabinet, along with a little set of salt and pepper. She had even provided a small bottle of dish soap.

When Deke came to pick her up, wrestle the carpet machine out to the truck, and walk through, he didn't say anything, not even about the expensive lightbulbs, but when he saw how she had folded the toilet tissue on its new roll into a fancy arrow point of professional hospitality, he stated, "This is not a hotel." A new broom and a mop stood behind the kitchen door with a matching dustpan. On the shelf over the washer and dryer she had placed a small bottle of laundry detergent and some dryer sheets in a sandwich bag. She had written out simple, clear instructions for the machines and taped them at eye level. All the miniblinds had been washed in the bathtub and rehung, adjusted to let light in but maintain privacy. The heat pump had a new filter. On a metal dish on the mantel there were matches next to a beeswax candle. She had lightly sanded the cedar lining in the hall closet, and from time to time as the furnace cycled on, a cedar-spice whiff would waft out. Without a stick of furniture in the house, it seemed cozy, blessed. All the windows and mirrors had been cleaned, and the refrigerator, in the light of its new bulb, looked almost new. The ice maker had a new filter. She had opened a fresh box of baking soda and put it in the freezer. She had put bottles of springwater on the top shelf. Now she dried out the sink so there would be no water marks, tied up the trash, and gathered the cleaning kit she was taking back, her everyday things. "Ready?" he asked, meaning, time to head for the truck, drop off the rug machine at the store in Ready, and then go home for supper.

"I think so," she said. He walked through, smiling. She smiled back. "I could be happy here." She had a little list, budget items or maybe things they had at home. She'd look around. Maybe stop by Fred's. Coat hangers, she thought, and clothespins. She had some of those things. She would have liked to have a flashlight for the kitchen, a basic can opener, some duct tape, a hammer and two kinds of screwdrivers, pliers, picture nails, maybe scissors, a sewing kit, a chain of safety pins, and a little battery-operated travel-size alarm clock. It seemed to her that a house didn't feel "alive" unless time was ticking in it somewhere. Irene imagined a pretty kitchen towel and a fresh new pot holder. But maybe that could be in the welcome basket, with some fresh-baked bread and plum jelly.

She went on out to the yard, set the trash in the truck bed, and began loading the black bags of leaves. She had finished and was in the truck when Deke was done walking through, turning off lights and locking up. Deke had had the place rekeyed. He was swinging a tied-shut Food Lion bag, one of the spares Irene had stashed in the kitchen drawer. He put it gingerly on the floor behind his seat; it landed a little hard and made a telltale kind of clink. Deke grimaced. It surprised her very much what he had done, if she was right about what it sounded like. The thought deleted her growing shopping list and all words right out of her mind, as well as her mouth. They rode along in silence, and he knew she had figured it out: he had waited until she was in the yard, then had gone back through the house removing most of the lightbulbs. The longer their silence went on, the harder it was to break it. "We didn't take 'em to raise," he said, as though tenants were users and takers, so he took first, afraid of softness, of making things easy, and then she knew she was right; the bag was stuffed with confiscated lightbulbs. She never said a word about it. Not one "Do unto others" phrase or shamed sigh escaped her, but he had known her a long time. "I have been done unto," was all he said. He had to bring in the bag. She didn't offer, just slid down out of the truck and went on in and began getting supper ready. She simply couldn't think of anything to say. He set the bag on the shelf in plain sight in the utility room. For a few days she felt that they gave off some sort of bruising energy or odor; it affected her throat.

Irene and her Sunday school class had been praying that God would send them good and reliable tenants. She asked them to pray harder. She and Deke took the advice of folks who had been through it and knew: don't advertise in the *Messenger* or the Camden paper or website; just "ask around." No more total strangers with no references. Nothing noteworthy had happened so far. Not even a nibble.

K'shaundra had been hired at Frazier in shipping, not to sew. Different lunch times, different parts of the building, but sometimes their paths crossed. Irene stood in line behind her at the door one afternoon, clocking out. "Another day, another dollar," Coquita, the next one up to swipe, said and then shoved on out the door.

"You musta got a raise," K'shaundra hollered after her. She seemed happy.

In mid-November, K'shaundra stopped by the mezzanine lockers before first shift. She was way off from her own work station, and she had a request. She drew Irene aside. They stood there with backs turned to the work floor, and K'shaundra asked quietly if Irene would prefer to donate to the no-fault divorce fund by cash or check.

Prefer? Irene wondered, or rather marveled. K'shaundra drew a Planter's peanut jar from her peacoat pocket and shook it. Inside were small bills and coins—quarters, not nickels and dimes. There was a computer-printed label taped on, but Irene did not take time to read it.

"Tell me about it in a hurry," she insisted. "Maybe just skip to the—"

"It's no-fault," K'shaundra said. "I'm not blaming anybody."

"You can't do this," Irene told her.

"I'll tell him," she exclaimed.

"I mean, *here*. Frazier's got no soliciting." Irene shut her locker and turned to go. "I've gotta sew," she said.

"Maybe just five dollars?"

"How can that help?"

"It'll show you care," she replied.

For some reason, Irene burst out laughing. She reached into her apron pocket and felt around. She brought out a quarter and dropped it in the jar. It hit the bottom hard. "Y'all may have to work things out," she said, still amused, and headed for her chair.

Just before Thanksgiving, Sua Nag tried to explain to Irene about Hmong New Year, which fell well before the calendar new year. In fact, it coincided with American Thanksgiving. It had something to do with rice, Irene figured, but the rest was just not getting through. Sua Nag, frustrated from knowing more than she could ever say—and didn't Irene know how that felt!—stared into her own locker on the Monday before turkey day and said, "You work compute?"

"Yes," Irene acknowledged.

"Yes, yes," Sua Nag agreed.

They stared into their lockers, side by side. "You work compute, Google Hmong happy new year!" Sua Nag told her.

Irene did, and that's how she found out about new year customs just in time to wish Sua Nag, "Eat 30!"

"Yes, yes," Sua Nag beamed, looking at her shoes.

Davy sent an e-mail for Thanksgiving and then called. Where he was the dinner for the troops was over, while Irene and Deke and the others were just beginning; they made digital photos to send later—close-ups of the turkey and casseroles and pies and relishes, and the kids at their little table and the rest of them. Every table leaf had been installed to make room and was covered with the ten-foot-long wedding damask Irene had inherited from her great-grandmother, who had created the "entre deux" tatting inserts herself. Davy's wife and children were there too; Sherry had driven down from Kentucky with her parents. Some of the men were going hunting, some weren't. Some of the women were talking about driving over to Dahlonega to the designer outlets just to look and maybe drive up to the Southern Living Designer Show House to see decorations. All the cousins were having breakfast with Santa on Saturday morning.

Irene understood why Davy's wife had come on down from Fort Campbell. It was going to be good to be together, but she knew that what Sherry also was doing was "trading off," so that at Christmas, when Davy flew home, he and his wife and children could truly be "home" for the holidays, Davy and Sherry's home, not riding up and down the highway, spreading him around. If family wanted to see him, they could travel to Kentucky. That was how Deke and Irene were planning it, to drive up and visit. Since Irene had not yet worked a full year at Frazier, she didn't get but five days of paid time off. She was holding on to them for that precious week of the holidays. Deke was driving them up Friday after Irene got off work. They'd drive through, and that would give them Saturday through the next Sunday. She could sleep on the way home, and if he had to drop her off at the plant in her road clothes, not even take her home, she was willing. She'd go through that for a glimpse, let alone a visit. Really, just for a glimpse. What mother wouldn't?

Irene remembered that road crew she had sat watching work last summer. They were machete-clearing brush and tractor bushhogging on the Camden highway. Traffic both ways was stopped by flagmen, while the driver of the tractor power-lifted the mower up to thresh its way along through overgrown ditch shrubs. The elderberries were blooming, and the mower flung the flower heads like bridal bouquets. The young man who had caught Irene's eye had leaped and caught flowers, and several motorists beeped their horns. The crew hollered. The mower was taking a long time. No one knew how long. Drivers who did not want to wait U-turned and headed back toward town, to detour by a different road. As Irene inched closer, she tried not to notice the workers on the crew, many without shirts on, working bare to the waist in the broiling sun, their white prison pants with blue stripes stark against their dark or tanned skin. What if that were Davy, Irene thought. Her heart lurched. *It would never be, never.* She knew that. But what if? Here she sat, looking at someone's son. His family would not get to see him that morning probably. Maybe they did not even know where he was. Some woman gave birth to that boy and had lost sight of him, for whatever reason. He did not seem ashamed or cowed. He seemed interested in his work. He was a young man doing manly things. He took over the flag then and was the one directing traffic. He helped the man on the tractor back out of the thicket and turn and jostle on down the shoulder to the next place he would cut. She could see the sweat on the young man's chest, the bits of green and twigs stuck there. She dreaded looking into his face, but it would be worse if she knew him; she required it of herself to look, brought her eyes up, as though she were looking for the sake of the mother who couldn't be there, or be blessed by the chance to see what she was seeing. She didn't know him. He wasn't looking at her of course. She wanted to report, *He seems happy. He looks well. He is a beautiful young man.* Would she have prayed for him that day, the mother who couldn't be there? Irene could do that much. She could pray for them both. Sometimes, most times, the world was too large for Irene, the list too long. Now all she said, as though she drew them forward by the hands, one on each side of her, "Here's two more."

The young man's voice had broken into her distraction. He was tapping on her window, and when she powered it down to hear, he said, "*Will you just move?*"

She had a chance to speak to him, but all she said was, "Yes," easing carefully into the oncoming lane as he flagged her by, safely past the mower and back into the right lane and on, the other cars following like obedient ducks.

There was a slight change of plans for the holidays, a big surprise for Irene. Deke got a call from Davy at the airport. He had gotten an earlier flight, a whole day earlier, and they cooked up Plan B. Deke would drive to Atlanta, pick up Davy, drive him to Ready, take him by the plant, and just knock Irene's socks off. They'd spend the night at the farm, and in the morning Davy would drive Deke's truck to Kentucky. When Irene and Deke went up for Christmas the next week, they'd go in the car, and coming home Deke would drive his truck back and Irene would drive her car. This was their Christmas gift, this time alone with him. Of course, Deke had already called Jenny and Tonya, and they were bringing supper, barbecue from Sonny's. Davy wouldn't need the truck after Christmas; he and Sherry had a van. Plus, in the new year everybody who could would be gathering in Georgia in February, meeting at the airport in Atlanta, the entire clan mustering to see Davy off as he headed back to his new duty station in Afghanistan. Or they'd all go to Fort Campbell again if he was flying out from there. By then Irene would have earned eight more hours of personal time off.

Plan B was going to work out for Tonya too. She had a special gift in mind for her brother and Sherry. "Don't scream a word," she texted Sherry. "Damn if U tell mom."

"Come on," Sherry replied.

Tonya was up to something. "Gift card. Visa prepaid. On its way today."

"What?" Sherry texted.

"Only good for one thing," Tonya typed. "PROMISE."

"?"

"SWEAR."

"Hint?"

"What JFK Jr and bride did on honeymoon."

"!"

"No," Tonya typed. "Tats."

"Tats? Where?"

"Contstamapole or something."

"Turkey?"

"Turky? No way."

"Way. Cnstnpl iz N Turkey."

"Where tats?"

"Tats where it iz." Tonya could play this game all day.

"CALL ME NOW." Sherry texted, fit to be tied.

The first word Sherry yelled was, "Where?"

"I'm not askin' you to go to Constnattin Friggin Turkey to get tattoos," Tonya said. "They are bound to have a parlor in Kentucky. Or you could come here. That's where we got ours."

Sherry gave it some thought. "You saying that you and Brad got tattooed?"

"It's adorable," Tonya answered. "We match." She sent the photo.

Sherry looked, looked away, looked back. Couldn't read it. Too small. Tonya said. "It's private."

"JFK Jr. and his bride?" Sherry asked again.

"Shamrocks of course."

"Where?" Sherry wondered. "And if you say Turkey one more time I am going to tell your Momma and Daddy what you and Brad have been up to. And I am going to lie."

"Oh," Tonya said. She knew she'd won. They were going to do it! She had known the moment she thought of it. Perfect. "Y'all can do it at Christmas. People are. All over. Roseanne did. And—"

"For the last time," Sherry said, "where? And I don't mean Roseanne. And I don't mean Constantinople."

So Tonya told her.

Deke didn't tell Irene a word about Davy's call. Davy was in Gander, but there was a layover. He could get a flight to Atlanta if he bought his own ticket, and that's what he decided to do. That money was going to be for their present, anyway. His kit would go on through to Fort Campbell; he could claim it there. He'd look kinda rough, he warned his father. "Just as I am," he said, rubbing the fresh beard on his weathered cheek. "Will that do?"

Deke replied, "I owe you some change, buddy." Then he told Irene he had to go to the VA for his annual physical, had a chance to get that done because somebody canceled and he would take that slot and see her at suppertime. He made a few phone calls.

Irene went to work just as if it were any ordinary day of her life. She did wonder about the decorations going up at Frazier; lots of folks on the crew, and they seemed to be in a hurry. Everybody always toured the plant through those doors, good place for the photo op, which is why—besides worker morale—there was always a banner or something to fire them up and on. Plus the flag on the wall. Maybe some bigwigs, she thought when she saw them attaching the yellow bows; she hadn't read Wednesday's *Messenger*. And nothing had been said in last week's "Communication Meeting" on the mezzanine. She'd probably never know; visitors didn't usually come upstairs. She surely couldn't see a thing from where she sat except people sewing.

The bridge and companionway were being decorated with repurposed bell tower bunting from the Fourth of July. Ellen in Front End had the garment steamer smoothing it down; it was being looped up with massive yellow ribbon bows by Ginger in Audit. The matrix-dot banner had been unfastened from the railing—FRAZIER PRIDE SUPPORTS OUR TROOPS— and moved to the wall below the flag, centered—more shouting and arm waving—and taped on. The place was a madhouse; they had to use the other stairs. Irene was sewing again after lunch when somebody hollered. Then there was a commotion downstairs, and Irene thought someone had fallen or dropped something important, but it and more shouting went on, and some part of her harked, because this was a factory, and on the second floor there was always something to be concerned about, especially fire; she paused and listened for the Klaxon to sound, in case they had to make an emergency response. Her mind tracked the escape routes. She could find her way in the dark. Maybe they were testing the alarm system. Sometimes they were repairing it. Maybe the squirrels had chewed the wires on the roll-up doors again. Or there was another skunk; skunk day had been something else: there had been screaming, a stampede. She stopped sewing now—and she never stopped sewing—to ask, "What is going on?" They couldn't smell skunk, or smoke. Kit said, "They never tell us anything up here. I'm going to go see," and she did. Coquita was sure it was a skunk or a snake: "Ah hope ta hell runs the other way. Ah got nothin' to throw."

Betty, walking up, caught Coquita coming back from her locker. She had retrieved a little keychain canister in its holster and was shoving it into the grenade pocket in her fatigues. "Coquita, don't tell me you think pepper-spraying a skunk is a good idea?"

"Might be a snake."

There had been a young copperhead in the corner of Mrs. Champion's office last year. It had been ruled a natural event and not an act of sabotage or disgruntlement. Now what difference would that make to the snake or the person it bit? Betty considered. "First of all, how close do you want to get?" Before Coquita could answer, Betty handed Irene the note she had been sent to deliver from Mr. Grayson. Irene had to read it twice. Irene was being summoned downstairs. Main lobby. Betty didn't know why. She just knew something was going on.

Kit came back, didn't sit, grabbed Coquita, and said, "Come *on*." They headed for the stairs. They walked right by JaNice, who didn't have a chance to say, "No way." She went after them, answering her phone.

"Is it the president?" Irene wondered.

Betty warned, "Don't start a panic!" But she drafted along also. Word about what was going on spread fast. Irene was the only one who didn't have a clue. By the time Irene was on the bridge and heading down the companionway steps, half the sewing floor was heading after her, including Mr. Grayson and Sua Nag.

Irene didn't understand. She thought it must be a general emergency, so she began to walk faster, almost at a trot. She could hear them behind her. All around her, workers were standing, looking at the oncoming crowd, looking at Irene, but she did not notice this. She started to push open the glass door at the end of the long hall, but Jacky opened it for her and bowed her through. The acoustics were different here—a lower ceiling, closer walls, a kind of hush and step-down from the hive in production. Irene almost paused when she saw the crowd in the lobby. She saw Mr. Frazier and Mrs. Champion. She saw all of them looking her way, and someone with a camera. Then she saw Deke. He was not upset; he was holding steady; he was smiling. He stepped forward, toward her, and then she saw Davy. He was in battle dress, rumpled and road tested, jet lagged and caffeine jazzed. He more or less scooped her up, extinguished her against himself. She was beating on his broad back, as far around him as she could reach. Not sobbing, just beating. She couldn't hurt him. It felt like he had on armor. He was strong from carrying a soldier's burdens.

Mr. Frazier told her, "Go on back and show him off, troll him on through, then y'all just go on home, the three of you, and let us get back to work. Irene, I don't want to see you until—" he consulted his watch, enjoying himself—"next year." Then they were stepping through the double doors—"Did he say next year?" she asked Deke—into the factory. Kit got Irene's lanyard and ran upstairs, retrieved her jacket and purse, and helped her shove her rubbery arms into the sleeves. It was like putting socks on a sleeping baby. For Irene, none of it seemed real. She couldn't think what to do. She stood there watching Davy. Her boy was moving through the workers, shaking hands. "You know my mama?" he asked over and over, marveling, as if they were the ones who had come from a far country. Kit finally gave up on Irene, took the lanyard back, ran to the break-room time clock, and swiped her out. "I know that's illegal, so shoot me." She saluted the security camera, handed Irene's lanyard and purse to Deke, and said, "You caint push a string! Drag her out of here." Finally, they went, one time only, first time ever: fire exit, mid-building. Coquita kicked the door open, reared back, and used her boot on the bar; Kit held it, backing it open with her butt and standing there, all the alarms blaring, while Irene and Deke and Davy went home.

"I would vote for him," Coquita said as they hiked upstairs and tried to settle back to work. "And I do not vote easy for any *man*."

It was a glorious Christmas. The family took digital videos with a new camera. They took photos by the hundreds, including of each other taking photos. Irene and Deke were sitting at their own dining table in January, a month before Davy deployed to Afghanistan, sorting pictures and trying to organize them into themes. Right in the center was one of Davy and the baby blowing out the candle on the baby's first birthday cake. Chocolate frosting was everywhere. The cake was almost bald.

Irene got up and went to the kitchen to make some coffee. There was a shy knock at the door, on the glass, one knuckle. Irene remembered that knock. She pulled the curtain back and looked into K'shaundra's face. She switched on the light, opened the door. The hen Mercy shook and flew down like it was morning, and when Irene invited K'shaundra in, Mercy came in too. Walked right in.

"I'm alone," she said when Irene looked past her and around. She wasn't looking for hens.

"How alone?" Irene wanted to know.

"We didn't divorce," K'shaundra told her, "if that's what you're asking."

"Because?" Irene questioned. She gathered Mercy, took her back out, set her in the crate, came back in, and switched off the light. She patted the table.

"You know we never married." K'shaundra sat down.

"Oh." Irene washed her hands and dried them on a blue-checked towel, hung it back on the dishwasher door handle, and touched it to make the pattern even. "And?"

"He had a wife," she said. "Way off somewhere. I couldn't marry with him."

"But you knew that, right? That wasn't a lie on you."

"I did know," K'shaundra admitted. She must also have known this was coming. She handed back the quarter Irene had donated to the divorce jar.

Irene took it, dropping it in a cup on the windowsill. "New project under way," K'shaundra announced. "Plan C?"

"K'shaundra, if you don't need a divorce, what do you need?"

"I want to rent. I want to stay at your place till next summer, maybe. Maybe until next year this time. Maybe just stay here, keep on staying."

"Why?"

"Link's going to jail and he's going to be gone and I know I'll be safe. I like this place." She looked around.

Irene poured coffee, poured each of them a mug. Deke had walked from the other room, had come to stand in the doorway to drink his.

"I think K'shaundra wants to rent our little house," Irene told him.

"It's empty," Deke agreed. "How can you afford it?"

"I'm steady workin'," she answered. "I'm through my ninety days."

"If someone *exactly like you* came to your door and asked you what you are asking us, what would you tell her?" Deke sipped coffee but kept his eyes on her over the rim. Finally she looked away.

"I'd tell her what I tol' Link: 'Some things just don't cut it after while.'"

"What if the girl at your door told you she was sorry?" Deke asked. "Said she was going to pay the back rent?" Irene turned away to the sink, watching their reflections in the window. She tapped the grounds from the filter cup and rinsed it and put it back in place. She got the cookie jar and handed each one of them a tea cake and a napkin. She was thinking, *This is what it is to be grown-up. We're grown-up now. We're all adults here.* It seemed to her that Deke was more grown-up than she was. She pulled out a chair and sat at the table and hoped Deke would sit down with them too, but he didn't.

Finally K'shaundra said, "I'm strongly sorry."

"What if he comes back?" Irene asked.

"He will," Deke stated.

"I'll practice," K'shaundra said. "I *been* practicing."

"What about some night he stops by and he's been walking in the rain because his car's broken down and he's soaked through and just wants to talk to you, rest a little, just get warm. Maybe he's got a bad cough and a fever."

"He's got a motorcycle now."

"That a fact?" Deke commented, then waited.

"He's going on trial. He's going up. He can't win; they've got witnesses." The whites of her eyes were very white. "Not me," she clarified.

"When is the trial?"

"Next week. Atlanta. It's federal. There's a lot bad wrong ain't gonna be fixed."

"You have to testify?"

"It was before my time." She considered. Then she explained, "I'm not implicated."

"Rent's the same," Deke said, "but you'll have to pay something more each time, till the back rent is paid up."

K'shaundra answered, "Will I?" She rubbed her forehead, figuring.

"Well, that's the question, isn't it?"

Irene asked, "Do you have any furniture?"

"We haven't signed any papers here," Deke warned her. He set his mug on the table. It was empty.

"How much do I owe you?" K'shaundra asked, as though it were the first time the thought had crossed her mind.

Despite every warning flag, they agreed. Friends helped her move in. One pickup truck load was it. K'shaundra wanted the contract changed to allow her—to require her—to pay rent every two weeks, payday to payday. She signed the contract "K'shaundra Purdy." She explained, "He was using my name. I won't be using his."

"We must be out of our minds," Deke said. A week had passed. "I never see a light over there," he realized. K'shaundra always parked around back, out of sight from the road. The front porch light stayed off, and there was nothing on the front porch or in the yard—no ornament, no chair. It was bleak. The blinds always looked the same. It appeared as though no one was living there. At first they thought it might have been from caution until Link's trial was over. They had no way to know how that was going. But if it was a budget thing, was she keeping the furnace off too, to shave a bit more off expenses to keep on paying them the back rent? Had she even paid to have the power turned on?

They thought about that, talked about that some during supper, and later Irene gathered up a quilt, a tote with cans of soup, some cookies, packets of cocoa mix, a handful of tangerines, a jar of her bread-and-butter pickles, some peanut butter, a sprinkling of candies, a box of crackers, and some cheddar cheese. Deke went to the utility room and got that Food Lion bag of lightbulbs, in case that was why she was in the dark. Deke had his key. If she wasn't home, they were just going to set the things inside the door.

They drove down the grove lane and eased over the berm onto the long barn access, then back around by the little house and to the front again and parked, headed out. Her car was in back. She didn't respond when Irene called her name. Deke knocked, knocked again louder, and then announced he was going to use his key, which he did. They couldn't see her at first, dark against the dark paneling in a dark room. She was sitting on the carpet, her legs scissored straight out, her back flat against the wall. She was facing the door. They heard her breathing, snuffling through a bloodied nose. They must have just missed him. Maybe he fled when he saw their lights coming as they circled through the grove. If Link left heading back toward the bypass, he had not gotten far. Deke flipped on the lights, and K'shaundra begged him to turn them off again. He didn't. He switched on the floods front and back on the porches and went out to the truck and got his pistol. While he was out there, he called 911. When he came back in, he slid the burglar chain into its channel. He walked through the house putting bulbs in where they were missing, leaving them burning. No windows were broken. "How'd he get in?" The knob lock had been pushed in. She'd have had to open it from the inside. Deke wondered if she had given him a copy of the new key.

K'shaundra was down but hadn't fallen. She seemed to have slid, like she was still standing where he had thrown her against the wall before he left and just let herself go. True. She knew if she fell he'd finish her, kicking. Link was a kicker. He had killed with his boots. Or let her believe it, stopping just short. Part of his art. Something broke in her this time besides ribs. Something like chains. Irene was kneeling beside her, offering her a wet cloth, talking, listening.

taking advice."

"He won't do it again," Irene stated.

"Did he get anything?" Deke looked around the empty rooms.

"Me," she said. "Next time I'll kill him," she vowed.

Irene said, "No!"

"Don't worry," K'shaundra assured them. "I'll get him out in the yard," as though it was a matter of blood on the carpet.

They raised her to her feet. She could stand.

"I thought he was going to prison," Irene said.

"Next week," K'shaundra replied. "Judge has the flu."

8

By the end of March, their "strike soldier" was in Afghanistan, K'shaundra's rent was almost caught up, the wild plums along the creek were already setting fruit, and the martin scouts had come and inspected the nest sites and flown to fetch the others. Deke and Brad had the poles back up, the gourds ready since February. There were bluebirds in the houses along the line fence trail on Dutton Road. That had been Davy's Eagle Scout project. A wren had built a nest in the grapevine wreath on the door at church. Barn swallows were mudding up their nest walls on the back porch light, and Deke was already saying he couldn't see why they'd put up with that again—just what he always said. The early jonquils had started the season along the pasture fence almost a month ago, and now the paperwhites were blooming on the sunny banks. The heavy part of calving season had begun. The pastures would be green by the time the calves could eat it.

The water in the pond was still deep cold when Irene took a printout of some of her computer research to work. She had found pictures of carp, bream, bass, and catfish. She had some photographs of the farm and a map. She had already given Sua Nag cuttings of lemon verbena and had shown her the photograph of her great-grandmother in the oval frame, the one where she was a baby in that wicker carriage and Irene's great-great grandfather and great-great grandmother were standing so still and stiff, their eyes fixed on a far view, holding steady for the long exposure. There was a date on the photograph: 1907. One by one Irene had dealt the other photos down, generation by generation, showing that little baby's life and finally showing Irene in the picture when she had arrived on the family tree. In one she and her granny were holding hands. Irene showed Sua Nag one with the family lined up on the porch of the unpainted house, with the various buckets and containers of "pretties"—pass-along plants her great-granny had collected through friendship and visits and gifts and ditch rescues. One showed the very bucket of verbena Sua Nag's cutting had come from. Irene had taken a photo of it on her own porch last fall, and then a view of the house from across the road. Even at that distance, you could tell that verbena was really something. It was on wheels; it had to be. Somehow Irene had been able to get all that across—or thought she had—without looking anybody in the eye or waving her hands or speaking loud or otherwise making a fool of herself or unwittingly insulting Sua Nag in particular or the Hmong in general.

Sua Nag, in return, had brought Irene the only photograph she had of ancestors: a modern snapshot of her husband's grandfather and their whole family bank fishing at Pines Creek the first summer they came to the United States. The old man was wearing a suit, as though he was on his way to church, or thought fishing was holy. He had on a straw hat and sunglasses, and Irene could not really see his face. He was looking away from the camera and had a good-looking right ear. Sua Nag and Mr. Vang and their children? Yes, yes, Sua Nag nodded, three children, all grown now. Irene had already shown her a photograph of Deke and their three children, all grown now.

Irene had given this relationship some thought. She hoped one day she could learn some Hmong words. And she hoped that Sua Nag could learn more English ones. But until then she trusted that Sua Nag could understand more than she could speak back. After all, she was a naturalized citizen. Sua Nag had a driver's license and could read directions for all sorts of things and newspapers; Irene had seen her looking at newspapers—not just the pictures or sale ads—left on the table in the break room. They sat together at lunch, and in the space between them at the long table, their backs to the TV, Irene spread out her and Deke's latest idea, pages in order, a list to go down to be sure she made her points and that Sua Nag could read later and mark the ones she did not understand. She walked Sua Nag through the idea. What it all boiled down to, really, was maybe. Maybe the Vangs would like to come to the pond and fish? "No charge," Irene said. "We won't bother you. Welcome anytime." She showed the printouts of the fish and made hand measurements of their usual sizes. She didn't think the carp were good to eat; she wasn't sure. But they weren't dangerous to humans who didn't scare easily. She didn't think Sua Nag did. She thought they would like the way the hossy carp snorted and guzzled, their little eyes staring up sleepy and full of their own possibilities, like a baby at the breast.

The map Deke had drawn for the Vangs had the access lane off their back drive highlighted in green. He had drawn a little car on the map, to show where to park. There were some trees and shade.

There was one gate with a padlock. Deke had the key copied. He had drawn that pipe gate on the map, and the little padlock was circled in blue. He had chosen a blue blank for the copy of the key. He wanted to put it on a ring, but Irene had explained to him about the keys on Sua Nag's lanyard. Irene wasn't sure how to convey this part, but she pointed to the key, held up her own lanyard, and then pointed to the outline of the key on the map with the arrow to the blue circled padlock. "For you. Anytime."

Sua Nag kept on looking at the photographs. She touched the one of the long shot of the farm and pond. The cattle were off in a far field that day, and of course the lane was between fences. The fences were to protect the wheat, not the cows. "Wheat, not pasture," Irene explained. Sua Nag said, "Yes, yes."

"The cattle don't come to the pond," Irene told her. "They drink from the creek down there." The dam was fenced off. The chicken house was on the other side of the road, beyond the hill, nowhere near the creek. Sometimes it smelled pretty funky, but generally, even on days when the trucks came to clear out the broilers and haul them away and clean the house and lay down the new sawdust, the smell didn't oppress. Deke had planted pines and other evergreen windbreaks, and they had exhaust fans drawing the air the other way, into the cedars.

"No bull?" Sua Nag asked, looking at the photo of the cows way off. They rented one. He arrived in a trailer, created a sensation among the cows, did his work, and was gathered back up again into the trailer and driven away like a sultan to his next harem. This made sense, in bloodline ways, was safer, and kept it really easy to schedule calving.

"No bull," Irene agreed.

Sua Nag offered her hand and Irene laid the key in it.

"This big deal," she stated.

"Baby steps," Irene replied.

Sua Nag liked that. "Baby steps," she repeated.

Coquita breezed by, headed for the clock. She rapped a nicotined fist on the table as she passed. "Time to sew, ladies," she said. "Tea party's over."

The first time the Vangs came to fish, it was April. Sua Nag came to the house and knocked at the door. Irene was at the grocery store. Deke had been practicing. "*Nyob zoo,*" he said. He had about given up on *nyob,* but his *zoo* sounded a lot more like *zyhawn* than it used to. Sua Nag held out her right hand, palm flat, like half an applause, and wavered it for "so-so." Deke didn't scare her; they had met in town, but she had not come to visit. She showed him his own map like a ticket. She wouldn't come in. The others were in the car waiting, vigilant but not looking. Sua Nag held up the blue key. "OK?"

"Yes, yes," Deke said.

"Baby steps," she told him, heading for the car.

When Irene came home, Deke walked her to the stairs; she followed him up. The attic door wasn't locked. There was enough room to walk through the stacked cartons and bins. From there they could see the pond.

There they all were, two in folding lawn chairs and one on a turned-over drywall bucket, and no fishing going on at all. Just old Mr. Vang in his straw hat and sunglasses, his grandson, and Sua Nag. Sitting there, backs to the world, looking at the water, avoiding the world's eye, catching some rays.

Strangely, mysteriously, but not for the first time, Deke astonished Irene, left her speechless. They stood side by side, his arm around her shoulders, hers around his waist, watching the Vangs through their attic window. Deke sniffed. No noise, just tears. "This was a good idea," was all he said.

At their lockers the next morning Sua Nag said, "Nice, but you need get duck."

Irene thought about it. There were wood ducks in winter, but they flew on. There was a Canada goose once. There were coyotes, but someone had told them to put a donkey in the pasture and the coyotes would stay away. They did, and they hadn't lost a calf since.

"Maybe ducks," Irene said. She'd ask Deke what he thought.

"Papa Vang bring give duck," Sua Nag said.

So that's how all that got started. No one knew where the gray geese came from. Irene could tell these were not the kind of ducks you name. Papa Vang liked duck soup.

Irene was down along the creek, thinking about what they might do with the tax refund while she was picking plums from the sunny side. She had walked the creek, harvesting the easy ones, and had not yet reached the turn-back point. She was saving room in her bucket for the ones she saw on the way back. It was a clear evening, warm, with a blue sky. The wheat had about another month till harvest; the field was strong and green. The breeze would move across it like a hand; she loved to watch it. From time to time cars or a truck went by. She heard them, but the road wasn't visible; it ran atop the hill. As the evening came on, the sun cast shadows of the unseen vehicles on the trees she stood among. That or something else caught her attention, as though she had heard her name. When she looked up, she saw two trucks and a car. The trucks had driven across the center line and across the oncoming lane to park at angles on the margin. They were headed the wrong way, so that was odd. The sun was low enough that she couldn't tell the color of the vehicles; they were in silhouette. Then a sedan came into view, parked like the trucks. Doors opened, and men got out. She recognized Deke and realized that the other truck must be Brad's. They didn't shut the doors; just came to the edge of the hill, stepped through the barbed wire fence, and started down through the wheat toward her. There were two people in the car, and they came on also. She set her plum bucket down.

Were they crazy, wading through the wheat like that? Four abreast, not in a row to minimize the damage? Sometimes when there is a hawk near, the hens hush, vanish, or hunker down as if they know what's good for them. It is instinct. Everything goes still while the shadow passes over. Irene had such an instinct; the sound left the film of her life, and in that warning silence a moment when she could have run. Something in her wanted to run. There was a fire in her chest, in her throat, challenging her to run and keep on running. If she kept on running, whatever the threat was it couldn't gain on her or bring her to the ground.

They were closer now; they had walked down the hill far enough that they were not silhouetted against that perfect sky. They came on, stirring life up, grasshoppers lifting into the light, settling back into the dark, with each step.

He already knows. Whatever it is, he already knows. At least he already knows, Irene thought. *Deke knows. I don't have to tell him.*

It couldn't be held against her, her wanting to run; the struggle against it was tremendous, was wearing her out. How suddenly tired she was. How she longed to lie down, as a woman in labor lies down to give birth. What a wonderful thought, "to give birth." To give. Birth. She had given. She had given birth. And now she was going to have to take. She was going to have to take death. She dropped to the earth, lay vanished in the wheat. She rested, between the pangs of taking death. But Irene couldn't take death lying down. She rolled over, face to the ground, and gripped handfuls of wheat, right at the roots, holding on as though some tearing wind was about to blow her away. She got up, first to a squat, still holding on to the wheat. Then she balanced on one hand and rose. She was standing it. She could see their faces now, recognizing Brad and Deke and memorizing the two strangers; she could see the glint of metal and medals on their dress uniforms. The cloth looked black in shadow. Her face was in sunlight from the nose up to the crown of her head. Like a mask of light. Like someone drowning in darkness.

Old Mr. Vang, his grandson, and Sua Nag heard it, that one piercing shrill cry against death, like an eagle's scream.

They had been arrayed along the bank of the pond, watching the ducks. From where they were, they could see the road, could see the trucks and then the car careen across and park crazy on the shoulder. One by one they had turned to watch, then got up and stood. They stood watch. They were a long way off, and it was almost sundown. They could see the four men coming across the field. They watched Irene vanish, like a magician's assistant, into the green as the men came on. They saw her rise again. They heard that shrill cry. They had heard that cry before, in another country. It wasn't an eagle then either.

9

May 3, 2011
Soldier's Remains Return Home
Journal-Constitution Staff

ATLANTA—In remembrance and honor of Staff Sergeant David G. Morgan, Governor Sonny Perdue has directed that the United States flag and the State of Georgia flag be flown at half-staff from sunrise to sunset on Monday, May 3.

Morgan, 29, of Ready, was killed by enemy fire April 21 while leading his rifle squad in fighting near Kunar in Afghanistan. He was a strike soldier with the 2nd Battalion, 502nd Infantry Regiment, 2nd Brigade

("Strike") Combat Team, 101st Airborne Division (Air Assault) of Fort Campbell, Kentucky.

A funeral and burial service for Morgan are planned for Monday at 3:00 P.M. at Pines Chapel Baptist Church on Dutton Road in Ready.

Morgan's remains were returned to Fort Campbell, Kentucky, on April 29 from Dover, Delaware. The remains will be flown back to Georgia today, arriving at the Camden Tri-State Airport at 10:15 A.M. The Georgia National Guard, law enforcement, and fire department personnel will participate in the arrival ceremony.

An hour before Davy's plane was scheduled to land in Camden, law enforcement and fire personnel in Ready were on task. Ready's motorcycle unit—which consisted in fact of one man and one bike—was stationed at the city limits, to thread the hearse safely through the three-way intersection. There were blue lights already flashing at the bypass, slowing folks down, officers ready to halt oncoming traffic and direct the cortege down Main. Every side street, every driveway would be blocked. Another patrol car waited at the Hardee's light to stop traffic and guide the procession onto Old Pines Road. The Forest Service fire truck waited where Old Pines vee'd into Dutton. Then three miles unpoliced until the driveway to Pines Chapel, where National Guard and the Legion created a living gateway, but for those three miles, every mailbox had a yellow ribbon and a flag. Cell phones kept everyone in touch. The air was filled with flying messages. Some of the Legion were at Tri-County, in Camden, watching for the plane. So were some of the Guard. Pines Chapel didn't have a large parking lot; blue gravel smoothed down with crusher run could hold maybe the first seventy cars. From what the Legion had heard on the phone, they would be needing more room. They voted on the west field beyond the church. It had been mowed that morning by volunteers from the Men's Class—Deke's pals—and with landscaper's paint they began marking off a traffic lane and boundaries.

The Women's Class had the church open and aired, and would close the windows and turn on the air-conditioning at 11:00. Food had already been delivered to the kitchen and more was coming, enough for an army. Coffee makers were set up and ready to be switched on. Someone was back there now halving lemons and making lemonade. Sweet tea and unsweetened were ready in ranks of gallon jugs. The portable freezer borrowed from Hardee's was full of ice.

Why were they doing all this? Because it was all they could do, and it kept them busy, and together. One of the younger women, Debby Bridge, stood in a hall door watching Beatrice Haney straighten a candle on the table in the sanctuary. The table had been moved to the side, at an angle, to leave room for the casket when it arrived. The Bible was open, and there was a cross but no flowers on the table. Later there would be plenty of flowers. Bea changed out the bookmark from purple to white with gold silk fringe. When she entered the hall, Macia Gordon said, "A lot of folks going to be standing outside, I've just got a feeling. Have to leave the doors open." They didn't have a PA system or any need, before, for overflow seating or parking.

"This is for the front row," Bea said. "Their turn. They have to hear it. They need every word. The rest of us, we're here for them."

In Camden, Davy's plane was late and was going to be later, perhaps an hour, perhaps two or more. The message passed along the roads, cell by cell. People had begun parking where they could and waiting, all along the eighteen miles between Camden and Ready at every little settlement, church lot, turn lane, and store. Sooner or later they got word about the delay. Some had to go home; some had to pick up kids from preschool. Most came back. More arrived. When the school buses ran and Davy's plane had not landed yet, parents brought the children and stood along the route. The sidewalks in Ready began to fill. The crowds grew. Frazier Fabrics had closed in Davy's honor for the day, all day shifts. When afternoon began to wane and Davy's plane was still delayed, Frazier canceled the second shift also. Some people had brought chairs. Others sat in their cars or on tailgates. Still others sat on jackets on the grass. Infants napped in adult arms. Toddlers sat on their daddies' shoes. Pigeons on the roofs flew up, circled, and settled again. There were hundreds of flags. As the wait grew longer, it also grew shorter; no one was going home. People in houses along the route opened their kitchens, their bathrooms, their porches. The librarian brought out chairs, even the little ones for children, and set them on the lawn. Outside the nursing home, wheelchairs were lined up. From time to time an attendant backed a chair up, wheeled it inside, then brought it back again. Some citizens had begun to climb the fire escapes and perch along the rooftops. The newspaper staff already had a rooftop tripod set up, wind-braced, aimed south. Another photographer walked at ground level, making candid shots. No one could see as far as they wanted, and everyone kept looking, even though they knew, from the cell phones and word of mouth, that the plane hadn't even landed yet. Mimi's customers kept their eyes on the windows. Mimi had canceled all permanent waves because the ladies just couldn't let direct sun hit that lotion, and she knew they would jump up and run out. It was all just cut and dry for Mimi. This was her fifth war, the last one, she hoped. But she watched the mirror; Sergeant David Morgan wasn't going to get past her.

Every person along that route had a story. Everyone was part of the story. Everyone knew only part of the story. Everyone had a different perspective and motives. There was no explanation, really, for what was going on, for what was coming to pass. The editor of the *Messenger*—when it began to look as though nobody was forsaking the vigil—made some phone calls, and after that there was a helicopter from the Toccoa station bringing that perspective also. News at eleven. If then. If not, then whenever. "For the duration" began to take on new meaning for the pilot of the news 'copter. Before he would get the video he had been sent to record, he would have to return to home base and refuel. What he reported then, before he even began his story, brought more people to Ready, to line the way.

No one knew how late the flight bringing home Davy's body was going to be, so they stayed. Through speculation and rumor, cell phone to cell phone, various versions of how and why passed along the groups lining the roads—it might be past afternoon, might even be "on toward dark." When the afternoon train came along, no faster than a man's easy walk, gently hooting at the open Norfolk Southern grade crossings, the pedestrians caught up children and held fast. Little fists waved their flags now that something was happening. But that was all that was happening. "Do you think the plane has even taken off?" someone asked, and that question made its way along the ranks. Faces scowled up at the clouds.

In Camden, Irene had more time than usual to watch her family interact. Tonya and Brad and their kids, Jeff and Penny, were sitting in an L of leatherette using the coffee table in the first-class lounge as their work surface for crayons, games, and one of those puzzles with pieces shaped like the states, cut out of wood. Tonya was playing UNO with Jenny and Kev's crew; they were a bit older, past the coloring book stage. Jeff had already turned the map puzzle over so the names and colors were hidden and had worked it upside down and backward. Then he too played UNO. Irene didn't see a thing to fret about, but she kept looking over. They were not making a lot of noise, and this whole room had been closed off, just for them. When Penny held up a square piece of the map, Brad said, "Mmm, could be Colorado. But it could be Wyoming too." Irene glanced again. Jenny and Kev were still sitting back-to-back like bookends, facing different directions. Kev had pulled his chair out of line and made a little gap between him and the others, working on his laptop. He had a paper due in one of his classes.

Irene stood, stretched, and took a little walk around the waiting room. She gathered empty snack wrappers and remnants of cold coffee in paper cups, and put the trash in one of the bins. It seemed natural, not planned, when she cut back to the group in front of Kev's screen. He was typing, fast but intermittently, as though he was thinking something up. He didn't even look up until Irene said, "Just read me one sentence. One. I promise to be fascinated no matter what." Kev's topic—by now they all knew it—was "Beyond Kriedler: Lesson Plans for Peace-building in the Middle Schools." Kev didn't like the topic anymore, or middle schools much; if he had his druthers he'd be done with the classroom. He was still teaching two classes a day plus serving as assistant principal. Kev had sights on full principal or, better yet, a life in the quiet golden light of the pigeon-haunted old courthouse at the county office, administering from behind—as he imagined it—a vintage dark oak partners desk, with an assistant to screen his calls, maintain his calendar, and—if he could get that job before his Ph.D.—help him format his dissertation. He rubbed his face with both hands and focused on Irene. He looked tired. Nobody had had much sleep. She thought about telling Kev what the eye doctor had told her when she had gone to see if bifocals would help when she was working at the clock factory, close-focusing all day. "Every hour, lift your eyes and look off, look as far off as you can see." But she could tell that Kev already was focused on something far off. Kev's beard had already grown out enough to audibly scratch his hand as he rubbed his chin. He did not seem to understand what Irene was saying, as though she were speaking in a foreign tongue. She patted his shoulder, walked on back to Deke, and sat again. He flipped his cell phone shut and shook his head. No news.

"I couldn't wait," Jenny was saying. Not about Davy. About summer. "Now it feels like time has stopped." She faltered. "It's been—" She paused, counting the years since she had had a whole summer off, no classes or tutoring.

"Too long," Tonya said. "Your bathing suit is older than Penny."

Jenny was going to be done with her master's by December. Kev had almost another whole year to go.

"I'm not making any plans," Jenny said. Summer was all she had. How long was that? Then she would keep right on teaching eighth grade social studies, same room, same morning sun, same Thermos and philodendron.

Irene hadn't told Deke that Jenny and Kev were having problems. Jenny had asked her not to, had begged her not to. "Not until it's for sure; maybe it won't be for sure." But when Irene had suggested that maybe their situation was due to stress, Jenny had replied carefully, "There are many people who live as we do and still love each other."

"If it's stress, that can change," Irene had said again. Thinking about Jenny's sweet long summer at home now that she was finishing up her master's, she thought, *Things are already changing.*

Jenny hadn't wanted a big wedding, hadn't even wanted a chapel wedding. "We're going to elope," Jenny had told them. "Only we're telling you."

"Save your money," Kev had added.

Deke had looked at Irene and said, "Well, that works too. Catch ya later," and pulled his hat down and walked on out to the barn, got on his tractor, and drove out across the field, down the swale, leaving the discussion to Irene. It was either that, he told Irene later, or "knock the jerk flat on his ass, and that wouldn't do anything but get the ground dirty." In many ways it had been like that all along with Kev—no captions, just turnings and mostly away, and silence. Irene didn't believe it was possible to squander love, and Jenny was in love. So.

Last Christmas, on a drive home from a mother-daughter shopping trip, Jenny had confided that all was not well in her marriage. When Irene had talked to Jenny about stress and how things were not going to stay the same and that nothing ever did, Jenny, looking hard-eyed and older, had said, "All that's changing is the locks." Then she told Irene how over the past summer Kev had been leaving before seven in the morning to commute to his early class. An eight o'clock again!" Jenny had wailed when he told her. But Jenny had found out there was no eight o'clock class. Kev was simply leaving early, finding a quiet place in the library, and reading magazines and newspapers—newspapers, it turned out, with an eye toward the classifieds. "Mom," Jenny had continued, clearing her throat, "if he takes a job way off—" Here she had swung her hand out, as though pointing across the continent, imagining it all out there, everything she had heard from him in his feverish confession, an arrayed arc of choices: Seattle, Denver, St. Louis, Graceland. Then, sounding very much as she had as a child, she announced, "I'm not going."

Irene had driven five miles before asking, "Will he be back?"

"I'm not leavin' the light on," Jenny had retorted.

Then they had arrived at Jenny's, gotten out of the car, sorted through bags and packages. Irene had taken hen eggs from Mercy and her little bronze and black flock out of the trunk and slipped the basket over Jenny's wrist. Nothing in her lifetime had prepared Jenny for what her mother had to say: "Your daddy will help you with the locks."

They had stood still, just that one more moment, looking at each other, burdened and unburdened.

"You been prayin'?" Irene had looked away. Somebody was coming along the road; they both looked. Silver pickup, king cab. Nobody they knew. They waved anyway.

"Is 'Oh God Oh God Oh God' a prayer?"

"He's heard it before," Irene had said. "Now and then, throw in an Amen."

"You pray too," Jenny had told her, "for that dissertation paper. He's gotta finish by next July." She had turned at the door, glanced back, "Or he'll think it's all been a waste."

All? Irene had wondered.

There were many reasons the flight had been delayed. Sherry and the children and her parents wanted to fly with Davy's casket, and the military plane they could all fly on together was too large to land at Tri-State. Smaller corporate and private jets could hold the passengers but not the casket. The governor himself had been consulted. A solution had been found. Then other difficulties arose in logistics, and then rough weather. By the time the aircraft approached Camden Tri-County, it was coming in through twilight, the sun already below the horizon. Flags were still at half-staff. No one was worried about the governor's sunrise-to-sunset decree at this point. The crowds and the welcomers had not wavered or diminished. This day was far from over.

Davy's family had had a day lived privately, as much as it could be in such a public moment. That isolation—or consideration—had blessed them; they were in a between place, where ticking time had stopped. When the word finally came, Deke nodded, yes, on their way, and Irene—not knowing if any of the others knew about the tattoo, how Sherry had insisted on seeing it if at all possible—stepped close and whispered, "Did she see it?" Deke told her the undertaker had been the one, had borrowed Sherry's phone and taken a picture, close up, nothing else, "Just that, only that," Deke said. "Well," Irene whispered. It was odd how she felt, as though some part of her had hoped. Doubt and hope were alike in some way, and they had gone. They were missed.

Irene stood watching the jet taxi toward them. Deke stood behind her, his right arm around her, his broken hand in a fresh cast pressing against her heart, knowing exactly where she hurt. She could feel his heartbeat against her back. It was one pain between them, connecting them. She laid her right hand on the cast; he had broken his fist punching a hole in the wall when the chaplain and the colonel had come to the door with the news. Now, as their son returned under a U.S. flag, they were wrapped together in a pledge pose. The plane rolled to a stop.

The rest of the journey would be stored in fragments. For days, months, years memories of moments would rise up, swirl, sweep over all of them. Irene would always be gathering them into the one story, twenty-one miles of road from the airport to the churchyard, twenty-nine years long. It was quite dark by the time members of the motorcade left Camden. Escorted, they had no delays and moved at a steady but dignified pace. Cars stopped or moved to the side of the road and parked while they passed. All along the route, past the city limits, there were people waiting, as they had been all day. Candles, flashlights, lanterns: each person offered some light. In the towns there were more people, and their faces were clearer by street-light, but they were holding candles also. There was at least one person along the road by every mailbox. When the motorcade came to the turn onto Main, the throngs began. A mile down Main they passed Frazier Fabrics, its 24/7 floodlight-lit flag at half-staff. The factory was closed, no night shift. All the workers had been given the afternoon and until noon the next day before they'd have to report for work. On both sides of the street young and old, strangers and friends, neighbors, coworkers, fellow citizens stood in vigil, their faces uplit by the candles.

A mile more and the procession turned at a stoplight. They were almost at the city limits, end of the streetlights and sidewalks. There was Jacky's sign, his truck with headlights on, home-rigged flashers blinking. Jacky, now holding a lantern, had painted GOD BLESS THE WAR. THANK YOU SGT DAVY, along with a heart.

Irene wondered if there had ever before been a funeral at night.

Now the turn at the fire truck and the last three miles to the chapel. The motorcade rolled a little faster past the mailboxes with their flags and yellow ribbons and the candlelit groups standing in the driveways.

An hour was spent in the church, with every possible comfort and hope celebrated. The overflow crowd stood on the porch and steps and continued down into the churchyard and out as far as the road, honoring with silence and attention as they had all day. Whip-poor-wills—the ones crying, "Chuck! Wills! Widow!"—called, heedless of the voices and music from the church. When that part was done, the silvery casket was brought back out again, slow-stepped across the uneven grass and to the grave. The family again took the front seats, and all the rest of the seats except one were filled. Had someone miscounted? Were they all there? Who was missing? It began again with familiar words both true and new, and then came to an end. When this part was done, the folding of the flag began. Those hands—hands of mortal men—worked like machines but driven by passion for honor and perfection so that each tribute of the thirteen folds was perfect, each crease and tuck, tuck, tuck an everlasting triumph over death. The eighth fold had honored the fallen soldier and his mother; the tenth had honored his father. They were all folded into it—everyone there, watching, now folded with Davy into that flag. The flag—its journey from the war zone through this day above the casket, honored glove to glove, perfected, completed—reached the presenter, who slowly turned, knelt before Sherry, and passed the perfect triangle with its field of stars from his hands into hers, on behalf of a grateful nation.

The Guard and the Legion had had all day, and they had figured it out. Vehicles had been parked just so. Headlights washed the dark stripes down the trousers and were reflected in the insignia and brass of the riflemen who fired the three volleys. Fire breathed out from the gun barrels. Davy's baby cried, just a moment, and Sherry turned the child so those great staring eyes could take in everything. The whip-poor-wills hushed. The smoke drifted away.

A one-armed bugler, on the hill in an angle of tiki torches, his shadow wavering into the dark pines, offered "Taps" to the stars. The last note faded away, the final salute ended. As the Honor Guard half-stepped out of their lives, moving down the line of family and then away, the last two who stopped to speak to Irene were the men who had strode through the wheat that evening bringing the news. They had come a long way to this long day. It was almost midnight. Irene didn't know what was next. No one did. People were moving away from the grave and toward the church again so that the workers could seal the vault and backfill. Deke wanted to help despite advice and a broken hand. Irene was walking all around in the crowd, recognizing people, listening, wishing them well.

In the shadows, on the edge of things, a form with windswept angel white hair, unpegged, untamed, and wearing a slim white sundress with a little black jacket that was hardly more than a sketch had caught Irene's eye. It was the oddest thing, how they worked side by side every day and now they were shaking hands.

Kit's hands were shaking. "He was two years ahead of me. I never caught up. You know I had a crush on him forever."

Irene side-stepped on the rough ground and roots. "No." Something dropped inside her so hard she glanced down. Dug in her heels. Made herself look up. Never expecting or knowing what to expect next, but not this. She looked around for Deke. Where was Deke?

"Kid stuff," Kit said. "He didn't know me. Never even noticed me." Her voice broke. Kit stamped her right foot, like a doe about to bolt, wobbled on those tall shoes. Irene put out a hand to steady her.

For the life of her Irene couldn't think of a kind thing to say but the truth. "I bet he noticed."

"Nope," Kit explained. "You never heard of me before that first day at work." Irene waited. "You would've. Yes?"

Irene considered.

Kit added, "He didn't even recognize me that day at the plant. Nah." She slowly drew in a deep breath and more slowly exhaled. A silence ensued. Two trucks and a car drove off into the night. A brief spatter of laughter came from across the churchyard, and heads turned. So did theirs. Suddenly Kit awkwardly embraced and released Irene back into the moil and flow. "He's the best, that's all. But you already know that." She turned, to move on.

"There's—" Irene began.

"Why I keep lookin'."

In the church Vicki Malachy gave up the search for the lighter, and with the last cigarette from the pack between her blackened lips she headed up the aisle to the candle flames on the altar. Vicki had gone pierced and Goth over the summer. Everything about her bore the glint and scorch of hell. Ask around; ask her mother, who'd done everything but put a warning in the personals in the paper: to whom it may concern, as of this date I am no longer responsible for debts public and private and so on and on and on. Vicki had a new way to push her mother's buttons. "Say something!" Juki would yell. Vicki would reply, "Dot dot dot," with smoke rings.

She leaned flat-palmed on the open Bible, her body already beginning to show the new anonymous pregnancy. She had on what she thought of as her lucky black leather miniskirt, black ankle boots, and a studded black vest over a sleeveless tee. When she couldn't get the skirt zipped anymore, she had bored a hole to either side of the placket and installed a chain and padlock. A brilliant solution as she saw it, for she could adjust it out, link by link, for as long as she could drag the skirt over her belly. Oh and she would. Some instinct caused her to turn, her jaw still jutted from lighting the cigarette, to look toward the back of the church. Juki was there, silent as a mouse. She had slipped in and seated herself by the baby carrier, beaming out disappointment.

"I never was exactly the Bride o' Christ," Vicki exhaled around the cigarette. "Get over it." Last month's purple highlights in her spiky dark hair were now red. She felt one of the pages, stuck to her palm by sweat, tear or give along the spine. She turned back to it, pushed the wide satin bookmark aside, gathered a chunk of pages, and heaved them over deeper into the good news. She put the bookmark back, but the torn-away page showed, so she opened to it and then folded it over itself. This time nothing showed. Except Vicki's rounding belly. After last summer's scare, after a lull, Vicki had found another lone wolf in the dark.

"Say something I want to hear," Vicki dared.

"You took the words right out of my mouth," Juki returned. She would have said more, but one of the church ladies came in, stepped behind the pulpit, and rummaged around on the shelf. "I've got one!" she called to someone in the kitchen. They were about to light the chafing dishes. She glanced at Vicki, at Juki. Old story. "Don't mind me," she said, and trotted out holding a lighter in her fist. They weren't making much noise back there, no chatter, just the necessary sounds of work: directions, last-minute rearrangements, chair scrapes, and adjustments.

Vicki headed back toward her mother after checking behind the pulpit also, in case there was another lighter. She'd have been glad to have it, one less thing to buy.

Juki was holding up the baby's bottle, sniffing it. The baby had been asleep, was still asleep. Juki thought she knew now what had cured its colic.

"No, it's not apple juice," Vicki said before her mother could.

Now Juki wasleaned over, sniffing the baby.

"Beer?" she asked. "You mixed beer with the juice?"

Vicki blessed her with a radiant smile. "Why waste the juice?"

From the hall doorway, one of the kitchen crew beckoned, "Ladies? Come in for the blessing."

Juki stood. She had brought food, enough for her family and more. She moved forward, taking the baby carrier and, after a moment's thought, the bottle bag and the rest of the kit with her. As she eased past, Vicki took the bottle, tipped it up, finished it off, and slid it into the mesh pocket on the tote. They were both relieved when Vicki, with plans already made, exited the side door and landed with a clump to the ground rather than face the people coming up the steps headed in to supper.

Irene and Deke and their family were at the front tables being waited on. The rest of the people would serve themselves, buffet style, from the lined and laden tables. Juki set the baby and the kit beside her chair. She detoured toward Irene to lean down and speak a moment. Her one hand gripped the edge of the paper tablecloth while the other balanced the food she'd brought, and she whispered, "It wasn't supposed to be like this," before moving on.

Irene wouldn't leave until the grave was filled and smoothed, the flowers carpeted it, and the fake green turf carpet and folding chairs were loaded into the van—going, going, gone. Even then she and Deke remained. Family and friends had children to care for, stock to see to even at that hour, and work the next day. This tremendous and staggering time-out between before and after was almost over. When the church ladies had finished clearing things inside, they wrung and hung the towels on the wooden rack, then made sure lights were off and windows and doors locked. The lot and field emptied. Irene and Deke walked out one more time across the trampled grass to the undertaker's canopy, the only shelter from all those stars, to thank the men who had used shovels, no backhoe, to fill the grave by hand. It didn't matter how many times she said it; she would offer it to each and all. It was no trouble; it was for Davy. "Thank you" was her theme, and her mantra—the mother's prayer—was "Safe home."

When they arrived home, the dusk-to-dawns were on out at the chicken houses and by the barn. They were automatic. The surprise was the porch light. "Oh," Irene said, heartsick. "I wonder where Mercy is." She had not thought of her little free-range Sebright once all day. While Deke headed to the barn, Irene turned and surveyed the lot, the fence lines, the fields. No frog song now, and she could almost count the cricket sounds between the lulls. The pond looked black and was so still the stars twinkled in it.

Deke returned with the news, "Somebody did up the chores." He had his gloves with him, had forgotten to put them on the shelf. He tapped his leg with them up the grassy slope to the house. There was going to be dew, and neither one of them had on farm shoes. The stepping-stones were single-file. Deke let Irene have them and walked by her side, vigilant. Even after the short nights and long day, he was on patrol. He had learned the hard way what he would never forget: there was something out there, always something out there. For a moment he stopped, turned, and looked back, doing a slow reconnaissance of the dark lines and corners. Irene paused beside him. She was used to it. They didn't speak, but when he shook his head, she moved on in step with him. As they came around the thicket of hydrangeas taller than Irene, they could see the porch. They had company. Sua Nag was asleep in a chair, tucked into herself tidy and small, and K'shaundra had fallen back and settled atilt in the swing with one long leg on the floor. Both waked instantly and fully when Irene exclaimed, "Mercy!" There she was in her little crate on the wall. The light glinted from her eye, but she didn't fly down.

It was harder on Deke because he couldn't think of anything at all to say. And he couldn't leave. And he wouldn't cry. Irene knew what to do: open up; let everyone in; listen. For a little while it was all K'shaundra, not hiding her battered face now that they'd seen it. Link had busted away from custody, the best she could explain it, shoving guards, stealing a gun, and then stealing the transport van, shooting, wrecking, and taking to the woods. He had found her. But this time she had a cell phone and managed to connect before he broke in. He was out of bullets, so he beat her with the stolen gun. That's why she'd missed work, missed hearing the news about Davy, and why she'd stayed away from the church. Link was gone. He'd already been taken away. There'd be no trial; he'd messed all that up this time and was in a federal prison somewhere. She'd waited till dark to walk over from the farmhouse and started the chores first, so if there was someone at the house, church ladies or friends doing things around, she could slip back home without being seen at all. "Then I recalled that little chicken needed her step-up stick," she told them.

Then it was Sua Nag's turn. She drew the story in the air with her hands, acting it out, and when it got to the good part, everybody went out on the porch and K'shaundra and Sua Nag performed the ballet together. Sua Nag imitated Mercy, stepping in place on the porch floor to show how the hen had fidgeted on the railing, looking up at the crate on the wall with her left eye, then her right eye, then her left eye again. They had figured out about the little ladder Deke had made and had been about to put it in place. Mercy had seen it and hopped down from the railing, ready to climb, when—

"Boom!" K'shaundra hollered. "Boom!" And then together, "Boom!"

Irene and Deke jumped and grabbed hold of each other. Mercy eased up into a crouch in her crate, craning down. K'shaundra and Sua Nag were trying to convey their shock, surprise, and terror when noise from the concerted gunfire volleys during the funeral salute had rolled across the valley and crashed into the farm buildings and their ears. Sua Nag had from long and old instinct dropped to the floor on one side of the hen, and K'shaundra had done the same on the other side. Instinct in each had said, "It's back" or "He's back," and both had dived to cover the most vulnerable of all, but they had missed. Before they could save her, Mercy had flown straight up—never mind the ladder—a sudden rattling whuff of a launch across the porch, right up into her crate on the wall. Then she had shaken herself, turned, and curtsied into place. K'shaundra and Sua Nag ended the story right there, with a similar curtsy. Everybody laughed.

"Then we waited to see if the light bothered her awake, but she stayed put," K'shaundra explained.

"We stay put," Sua Nag added with that way she had of not looking.

There was a pause then, and Irene asked them to come back inside so Mercy could get her beauty sleep. But they gave quick good-byes and didn't linger. Just like that, then, K'shaundra vanished around the side of the house, and Sua Nag found her way to her little car, turned it around, probed her way out to the county road, and was gone.

Deke and Irene moved quietly through their house turning lights on, turning lights off, finding comfort. Later in bed they lay side by side, his right foot and her left foot touching. Nothing had changed that mustn't. It was still night, still dark, but the dark wasn't empty. It teemed with dreamers and vigils. When daylight came, there would be something to do with love.

ABOUT THE AUTHOR

MARY HOOD is the author of the novel *Familiar Heat* and two short story collections, *How Far She Went* (winner of the Flannery O'Connor Award for Short Fiction and the *Southern Review*/LSU Short Fiction Award) and *And Venus Is Blue* (winner of the Lillian Smith Award, the Townsend Prize for Fiction, and the Dixie Council of Authors and Journalists Author of the Year Award). Hood's work has also been honored with the Whiting Writers' Award, the Robert Penn Warren Award, and a Pushcart Prize. A 2014 inductee into the Georgia Writers Hall of Fame, Hood lives and writes in Commerce, Georgia.